Hard Passage North

by
Martin Hicks

AuthorHouse™ UK Ltd.
500 Avebury Boulevard
Central Milton Keynes, MK9 2BE
www.authorhouse.co.uk
Phone: 08001974150

This book is a work of fiction. People, places, events, and situations are the product of the author's imagination. Any resemblance to actual persons, living or dead, or historical events, is purely coincidental.

First published by AuthorHouse 11/9/2009

ISBN: 978-1-4490-3284-5 (sc)

Printed in the United States of America
Bloomington, Indiana

This book is printed on acid-free paper.

Contents

Prologue

The August morning was growing towards noon and the already high temperature was climbing steadily as the Ogeechee Volunteer Rifles, in company with the rest of Brigadier General Robert Toombs' brigade of Georgia infantry, converged on the Virginia Central Railroad depot in Richmond's Shockoe Bottom. The long column of sweating men came tramping up Seventeenth Street to the big Seabrook Warehouse, to wheel off the left onto Grace Street where the depot lay, only to come, almost at once, to an untidy halt with their further progress blocked by a multitude of already arrived soldiers. File after file of idle men extended along the street, almost from the intersection itself towards the depot building, where a tangle of halted wagons had also stalled. The arriving men craned their necks, gazing over the heads of those waiting in front of them on Grace Street, only to see still further columns of troops stretching away from the depot building in other directions. From their other side still more soldiers were approaching along Grace Street itself, threatening to completely choke the approaches, which were already steadily turning into a confusion of men, activity and noise. Toombs' regiments were rested at ease on the shouts of their officers and sergeants, to gaze around some more as it became increasingly apparent to them that if there had been such a thing as a timetable for getting General James Longstreet's command away from the city and up the Virginia Central track to Gordonsville then it seemed already to have run into problems.

The new arrivals could readily see that this was no small matter of a brigade or two of men reaching the railroad simultaneously to wait around briefly for the arrival of the trains to carry them north. Rather, from the numbers already visible, this situation had all the makings of a pretty major foul up. Not only the depot and its adjacent streets were clogged by troops and vehicles, but still more groups of men had been dismissed from their ranks to occupy the vacant ground that lay along past the depot between the railroad and Shockoe creek, spreading the congestion still further, and, as more and more units of infantry arrived, the depot and its environs seemed to have become an impromptu marshalling point for a substantial portion of General Robert E. Lee's army.

Many of the waiting soldiers lounged or sat, their attitudes and poses indicating that they had been there for some time. A few more fortunate ones had found precious patches of shade, while others had simply stretched out to drowse in whatever space they had been able to settle themselves in, but the huge majority of them stood, sweltering in the prickly heat of the still ascending sun. A scattering of the more active or inquisitive among them had retained sufficient energy to continue pacing around their formations and groups, seeking whatever enlightenment they could find about this latest chaos of a troop movement that the staffers and the railroad officials had jointly managed to cook up.

But whether the waiting men stood, lounged, sat, lay, or prowled, they also scratched, persistently and vainly, particularly at armpits and crutches, which were the principal gathering places of the almost universal army affliction of body lice. From enlisted men to colonels and generals, almost everyone in the Army of Northern Virginia had their crop of "greybacks," and all along those lines, and among the other waiting groups, fingers clawed at clothing, many men doing it almost subconsciously, to gain what momentary relief was possible from the exasperating itch. Although most of them recognised that scratching simply antagonised the creatures, they still tended to do it, maybe on the premise that since the lice gave men little peace, the men would give them none either.

The air all around the creek bottom was filled with a hubbub of noises from the steadily growing crowds of soldiers. Above all else there came a buzz, the collective talk of many hundreds of men, filling the air with complaints, wisecracks and general chatter, with the overall sound being reminiscent of the humming of a gigantic nest of bees. Intermingled with this rang the shouts of officers or train masters and the exasperated bellows of sergeants. Horses stamped and snorted or occasionally whinnied while mules brayed. The harness of their arriving or departing vehicles creaked, and wheels and axles rumbled or squeaked and all of this mixed with the less obtrusive sounds, like the persistent tinkling clink of bayonet frogs or tin cups on canteens as more men arrived or those already here fidgeted and moved around. From the depot itself came a chorus of further noises, the screech of train whistles, the harsh hiss of escaping steam, the slamming of doors and the clanking and jolting of wagons and cars as trains arrived and left.

Hanging also in the heat was a collection of familiar odours. There was the inevitable pungent smell of sweat, together with the more pervasive, ammonia like smell of long unwashed bodies, and a lingering stink of faesces, not only from arriving, departing or waiting animals, but from the many boys who nursed the second of the army's prevailing trials, after body lice, that of camp diarrhoea, or "the flux" as many termed it. These mingled with the smell of tobacco smoke from the pipes used by many of the men, and with the stagnant stenches from the margins of Shockoe Creek itself. The rail depot too reeked of further things, train smoke and engine oil, spicing the overall mix, and completing an unholy combination that was near to overpowering in its potency. Thus the great troop redeployment lay stalled among its noises and stinks, with the delays made still more of a trial by the fact that it was all taking place on one of the most miserable days of sticky heat and humidity that the summer in this tidewater region of Virginia had so far come up with.

The "Blues," as the men of the Ogeechee Volunteers were more inclined to title themselves, in memory of their long discarded original uniforms, had marched up from their camps, away to the southeast of the city, that morning. They had begun at sunrise, enduring the familiar ritual of starting, stopping and waiting all the way in along the Osborne Turnpike, as the converging brigades of the departing army vied for the road space, not only with each other, but with all of the more mundane traffic, both military and civilian, which routinely made its way in and out of the congested city by that route.

But while the journey, in the rising heat, had been fraught with its familiar host of delays and exasperations, the final leg of the march had, in some measure, compensated for that. For it had then been back along Main Street for the boys, skirting the side of Church Hill to descend to Shockoe Bottom, while the residents of Richmond, or considerable numbers of them at least, had turned out along the sidewalks to see the soldiers pass. Whether word had previously gotten around that this further part of General Lee's army would be coming into town on its way back to northern Virginia, for rumours of the coming movement had been circulating in the camps for well over a week, or that the crowd had simply begun to gather once the soldiers started arriving, it was impossible to say, but out many of the city's inhabitants had willingly come, to clap and cheer the arriving boys. Women and children predominated in the crowds to be sure, but there had been a smattering of men also, some of them, as their uniforms and dressings indicated, soldiers still nursing wounds sustained in the heavy fighting around the city at the end of June. But today, as before, the city had made an occasion of it, cheering and waving, with some of the girls even stepping into the street to cascade handfuls of gathered summer flowers over the troops as they passed by. Perhaps this time it was the town's way of saying its own big thank you to these dirty and shabby soldiers, the "heroes" who had saved the city from the huge union army that had threatened its gates back in the spring, but whatever the reasons, the presence of the crowds was a filip to the troops. They readily joined in the mood of the occasion, waving and whistling to the girls and exchanging hurried passing remarks with the men in the crowd as to what they were going to do with Johnny Pope and his Yankees, when they got up to the north. It had been enjoyable. It was always uplifting and inspiring to hear the applause and the cheers of the citizens of Richmond, which had today been sustained all the way along the eastern part of Main Street, to continue even after the turn up Seventeenth towards the depot and, as a result, the men were in high spirits, by the time they arrived at the railroad.

But the substantial crowds on the sidewalks were now well surpassed, by the numbers of idle troops at the depot. The straining southern railroad system, with its ill-maintained tracks, locomotives, rolling stock and equipment, was clearly being tested to the very limit of its capacity in attempting to transport such large numbers of men, together with their weapons and equipment. This was demonstrated amply by the fact that, for all that additional units were steadily arriving along Seventeenth and Grace Streets, so far, hardly any of those already here seemed to be continuing on up the line on trains, so, now that the cheers of the crowds were past, this was starting to look like a long and tedious day.

Daniel Ryan waited in his place among those of his mess in the Company B files barely around the corner on Grace Street. These men around him were his friends, sharing their soldiering experiences as a group, trusting and relying upon each other. In the file in front stood Isaac Kane, their sandy-haired, thin-faced, mess cook and a gifted man at that art, even if a shade too inclined towards complaint about the army's many shortcomings. Beside him was Saul Philips, brown haired and short bearded, one of the foremost rumour spreaders of the company, but, like Kane, a friend since before their group had enlisted, the previous year back in Eden Station in eastern Georgia. There too was Joseph Thompson, one of their section corporals, tall, black-bearded, firm and capable, while occupying the final place in the file, beside Thompson, was Tom Gibben, black-bearded also, but swarthy and small, as befitted a boy with Creole blood in him, on his mother's side. He was quick-witted and clever and another of the pre-war Eden Station group.

On Ryan's left side was Otis Ballard, a stocky, powerfully built, Bulloch County man, with short, darker brown beard and hair and the look of a rogue about him. Ballard had a sarcastic remark for every army custom, rule or drill, but, being a few years older than most of the boys in their Company B mess, there was a strong element of practical common sense in his approach to life and soldiering that could sometimes be separated from the sarcasm. To Daniel's immediate right was John Fitzpatrick, Irish, like Ryan himself, but smaller and of slighter build, with light brown hair and closely-trimmed beard. Fitzpatrick was idealistic and considerate, to a greater measure than most soldiers, standing out for it in this assembly of free-spirited volunteers. Beyond him stood Mick Daley, another Irish immigrant, but almost the antithesis of Fitzpatrick in both appearance and temperament. Daley was, like Ballard, stocky and muscular, with an almost black head of hair and straggling beard. His character was antagonistic and, even among his friends, he had a gift for argument, always seeming to find the remark or comment to anger those around him. Mick was no thinker, following his first instinct in his judgements and actions, but what made him a friend was his loyalty, for running alongside the irritating belligerence was a deeper vein of kinship with his comrades. It had been said, in only mild overstatement, that Mick would take the shirt from his back for his friend, if he thought he needed it, but then start an argument about the way that the friend wore it.

Missing was the final member of their group. Edwin Jones, still another Eden Station volunteer was currently in the Winder hospital here in town, recovering from a bout of dysentery. Its severity had been confirmed by the fact that while many men negotiated their way through such an experience in camp, Jones, on Surgeon Thomas Sterling's insistence, had been evacuated, though word had recently filtered back of his recovery being well under way. His comrades had been relieved by that news since their group had already lost two of its number to battle and disease and it was a well-acknowledged fact that all too many of those who got ill and headed into town on ambulance wagons found that their next wagon journey was to the cemetery.

For, in truth, in spite of serving and fighting only a handful of miles from their capital city and all of its stores and depots, these ragged, dishevelled, sickly and infested men, in common with the huge majority of the Confederate Army of Northern Virginia, were walking proof of a host of equipment and supply shortages. It could be readily seen in their dress. The colourful and flamboyant original uniforms, that had adorned the host of privately recruited units, formed all over the southern states in the early days of 1861, when most of these boys had enlisted, had long since disappeared. Even the drab, replacement uniforms provided that spring, on their own units' adoption into Confederate

States service, were now little more than ragged remnants. Uniform jackets and trousers, if not totally worn out and replaced by anything else which was available, were dirty, sweat-stained, repaired in most seams and patched in elbows, knees, seats and crutches. Corduroy or denim cloth trousers were common now as were captured Yankee trousers of light blue wool, but these latter were not popular as summer garb since, being woollen, they were cruelly uncomfortable in the heat and humidity. Garments made of homespun cotton cloth, of almost any shade, were now worn by many men in the ranks. Cotton was better in the heat and homespun was more available, through being turned out on a host of domestic looms all over the south. As for tunics, though a variety of shades of grey or brown, most in various stages of raggedness, still predominated, these garments varied widely in fabric, shade, style and cut. Clearly the most important thing for the men regarding jackets and pants was to have a set, however they were come by and whatever style or manufacture they might be, this being borne out by the presence in the ranks of a considerable number of jackets of any civilian style or colour.

Hats among the enlisted men had become equally varied. The small "kepi" forage caps, modelled on a French army style, adopted at the start of the war as official military headgear had now been largely superseded by brimmed hats of almost any style or colour. These, with better sun and rain protection, were more comfortable on the head and, most important of all, they were more readily available. They might be made of felt, leather, cloth or even straw, but if they shaded and sheltered then that was the main requirement.

Equipment shortages were also widespread. Backpacks, with their straps, that constricted a man's chest and dug into his shoulders on the march, were by now largely absent. Many had been discarded early on, in favour of carrying the most basic of personal possessions, and whatever carried rations of food that were available, at the left hip in a twelve inches square haversack, made from dark waterproofed canvas, or off-white, greased cotton. Thus equipped, the men rolled any spare items of clothing, into a blanket which was slung over the shoulder in a horseshoe loop, with its ends secured at the hip by a tied cord. Belts and webbing, ammunition pouches, even those haversacks for carrying possessions and food rations, were all in short supply and various improvisations had been made by those lacking some or all of them, with those gleaned from dead or captured Yankees often being the principal source of replacements.

The worst scarcity of all was in footwear and all through the previous months a proportion of the army's soldiers had been marching and fighting without proper shoes. The south lacked the manufacturing capacity to reliably equip the thousands of soldiers who now served in its armies, a situation made more acute by those armies' habit of persistently marching their men all over the countryside, and wearing out shoes at a prodigious rate by doing so. The best of shoes might last for months, though they inevitably wore out more quickly during the campaigning seasons, but footwear made of poorer materials and of more slipshod manufacture could easily wear out in weeks. Boys thus deprived took to wrapping their feet in anything that was available, to afford them some protection, which could range from crude moccasins made of rawhide, sacking or canvas, to the most meagre strips of carpet, cloth or whatever material could be procured, until replacement shoes became available. With chronic shortages at the quartermaster's department, the men's wants were now most likely to be supplied from home, or plundered after a brawl with the enemy, when shoes, like everything else, could be gleaned from dead Yankees. The upshot of all of this was that as the men of Company B gazed around at the crowded, noisy depot, there were hardly any two of the now thousands of milling soldiers there, including themselves, who were dressed, equipped and shod the same.

Daniel Ryan still wore the short tunic of light, "butternut," brown which had been issued in the spring, though it was now seriously ragged, in spite of much patching and repairing. His pants were of brown cotton homespun, similarly patched and repaired and his felt hat too was shapeless and worn from hard service. The "brogan" shoes on his feet, with little in the way of distinction between left and right, were worn and getting more so, with their final disintegration likely sometime in the nearer rather than more distant future. In addition to the cartridge box, for ready ammunition, on its black leather shoulder strap, his blanket roll, water canteen and the "captured" haversack, that he customarily carried, today was also his shift at lugging the heavier iron cooking pan that the boys of the mess, no longer naïve enough to trust the company skillet wagon to keep up on a journey of any length, had decided should be brought along.

The boys around Daniel Ryan were dressed and equipped similarly to him, though each had his own variations of garb, depending how he had made good his own shortages. The worst clad by some margin was Mick Daley, for in addition to the shortages that affected everyone, Mick was reluctant to carry any spare items of clothing that might have been available to him. Nor was he willing, in spite of those around him quickly becoming adept with needle and thread, to do much in the way of repair to such clothing as he possessed. Dishevelment therefore reached new levels with Mick and that in a regiment and an army where it had become an almost universal state of being.

Even its weapons reflected the army's shortages and make do approach to provision. The arms carried by the infantrymen were of many different types and performances. All carried long muskets, and virtually all of these were by now percussion weapons, using a small explosive copper or brass cap to ignite their black powder charges, but there were widely differing varieties of these. The best of them had rifled barrels and fired a conical bullet, of around .58" calibre, nicknamed a "minie ball," after the Frenchman who had designed it. These were modern, accurate weapons, with most being American made "Springfields" or imported "Enfields," of British manufacture with a shade smaller bore, though some Austrian "Lorenz" muskets, of smaller calibre again, were also in evidence. A few men even carried a Belgian variant though these were unpopular due to their additional weight and their brutal recoil. Present also, in considerable quantities, were a variety of smooth bore muskets, which were of larger calibre, .69" for the most part. These weapons fired a round ball, usually with a few buckshot added to the load for good measure. "Buck and ball" smoothbores were pretty effective at close range, but lacked the accuracy of the adjustable-sighted rifled muskets over greater distances.

The Southern Confederacy had quickly discovered limitations and shortcomings across all of its manufacture and transportation system when it was faced with the demands of war. From the start of hostilities good intentions had been plentiful, but these had proved insufficient to supply and distribute what the new country's soldiers needed. Shortages quickly emerged across the whole range of what the army used and required. Clothing, footwear and weapons were visible and obvious examples of this, but, in addition to these, even more grievous examples of inadequacy, and more dismayingly of waste, had, from the beginning, occurred in the provision of food, for the south's soldiers.

Already the new Confederate currency was declining chronically in value and many farmers were increasingly reluctant to trade their produce for suspect paper notes, especially when the prices paid by government agents for their produce were barely more than half of what they could command on the open market. Prices steadily increased to compensate for the currency inflation intensifying the problem, but even when sufficient food supplies could be obtained by commissary officers and agents, the transportation means, to take those supplies to where they were required, was too often lacking. As a result, food rotted at rail depots and in warehouses through a shortage of locomotives, rolling stock, space on railroad timetables, or even wagons or animals, to haul it to where it was required, and the soldiers at the front went short as a result.

Each day, every soldier was due, by regulation, eighteen or twenty ounces of flour, depending on whether it was corn or wheat, a meat ration of twelve ounces of salt pork or twenty ounces of beef, as well as potatoes, vegetables, molasses and coffee, but what the men were routinely issued was seldom anything like these amounts or this variety. It quickly became standard practice for units about to embark on marches or campaigns to prepare three days of cooked rations, on the day before starting out, for each man to carry with him, but those rations depended on what could be supplied by their sorely harassed commissary. On any day, meat might arrive with no flour, or flour might arrive with no vegetables, or vegetables might arrive with no meat, not counting the days when nothing at all arrived, whereupon it was up to the men to make of it what they could in terms of meals by foraging or procuring from local sources through purchase or charity. In addition, the food that survived as far as distribution in the camps was often what was best preserved or cured and thus the diet of the troops leaned heavily towards salted meat, or cured bacon, with flour, often in the form of unparched ears of wheat or corn. Coffee to drink was chronically scarce, due to the Yankee sea blockade of southern ports preventing its importation, and inferior tasting substitutes, made from various fruit concoctions, peanuts or other questionable ingredients had progressively appeared in its place.

All of this meant that southern soldiers ate irregularly and were often forced to subsist on foods of very doubtful quality. It was far from surprising that they had steadily become subject to such a range of illnesses and infections, some directly caused by their inadequate or sub-standard diet and helped along by often contaminated water supplies and poor sanitation. There were few men who had not recently had, or were not presently suffering from the besetting diarrhoea, with considerable numbers also laid low by dysentery or even typhoid. Further infections like malaria, measles and influenza also ravaged the camps and the lice and other parasitic infestations were clear evidence of the lack of opportunities to launder clothing, bathe, or even simply wash, these being dependant on water and soap supply, though not all of the men, by any means, took up such opportunities even when they were available. Among some of the boys in the army ran a culture of neglect of hygiene and the widespread illness and infestation gained further impetus from this. Thus at the rail depot, where this great multitude of high-spirited, filthy and infested men gathered on this steaming mid-August day, the air stank of their intimidating mix of odours.

Today was heavy and hot, and large sweat patches stained the armpits, chests and lower backs of the waiting soldiers' tunics. Sweat dripped also from Daniel Ryan's nose and chin as he continued to gaze on the details of the chaotic scene that surrounded him. He balanced his grounded Enfield musket by its barrel and changed hands with the heavy cooking pan, feeling a slight twinge of pain in his right shoulder as he did so, a legacy of the wound he had sustained in the fighting some six weeks previously. It had been a "spent ball," or so the surgeon had said, which had struck him on his right side, where his neck joined his shoulder. He had been lucky, they had told him, the ball had missed the neighbouring blood vessels and bones and his recovery had been straightforward, to the extent that all that now remained of the injury was a slightly uneven, greyish-purple scar on his skin. Certain movements of his right arm still gave that small dart of discomfort, but, he reflected, many men had paid a much higher price in the course of those battles and a man who had made a virtually complete recovery from such a wound had no real cause for complaint.

"Some re-union," Ballard said to the group as a whole, jerking Daniel from his thoughts, as he eyed the congestion and the lack of evidence that any travelling would be happening for them anytime soon.

"Must be a helluva delay with the trains," Phillips said.

"Every day we ever had with the trains was helluva," Kane said. "This here looks like there ain't hardly no trains at all."

"A nice wait in the damn heat for us all," was Daley's forecast, but Daniel was again only half-listening, having caught sight of a collection of women, moving along the lines of waiting soldiers, with jugs of some kind of refreshments and trays of what looked like food. The hospitality committees were at least making themselves busy down here, he thought gratefully as he watched them approach.

The refreshments turned out to be lemonade and, when their turn came, the men unfastened their tin cups, which customarily hung from the straps of their ubiquitous haversacks, and held them out for filling. Next came the trays, of little corn-flour cookies, and the men received their share of each with elaborate thanks and gallantry, these pleasantries being directed especially towards those ladies who were anything much short of outright old age. The novelty of receiving and acknowledging concluded, the women moved on and the men, manipulating mugs, cookies and weapons, adjourned to their idle observation of, and comment upon, what was taking place all around them.

In the depot itself, plumes of smoke, puffing of steam and the screech of whistles indicated that some trains at least were continuing to come and go, but there was no sign of their own departure. The boys settled down to finish their tepid and sour-tasting, concoction of lemonade and their cookies, in the course of which the customary relays of the afflicted began leaving the ranks again, heading over to the ground towards the creek, to relieve the needs of their ailing bowels. The welter of noises and smells increased, if anything, as still more units arrived to extend the lines and form still more of them around the depot, with the most recent arrivals now halted in columns that stretched back across and around the intersection on along Grace Street and well down Seventeenth Street.

But this army, in spite of all of its shortages, privations and ailments, still marched with something of a spring in its collective step. In spite of everything that remained short, defective or mismanaged, it sustained a spirit of optimism, this, in large part, through a notion of its own superiority, for it was, so it believed, simply better, man for man and unit for unit, than its adversary and it had also found itself a general. Robert E. Lee had been appointed as its commander at the start of June and he it was who had planned and led the great onslaught on George McClellan's Yankee Army of the Potomac over the last week of that month. Already the men had taken to awarding their new general a succession of nicknames that were clear evidence of the growing regard for him. "The Old Man," "Uncle," or "Marse, Robert," or "Uncle Bob," all were signs of an affection that most in the army now felt for the man. Lee had demonstrated sufficient of the hallmarks of a skilful, fighting general to gain the approval of his troops, in spite of the grievous casualties sustained in driving the mighty union host from the suburbs of Richmond. Now it seemed he had developed an appetite for taking the war up north, to free the still occupied part of the state of Virginia and thereby menace the Yankee capital city of Washington with attack. In this army, the general's wishes now approached the force of divine edict, or more simply, if, "Marse Robert," wanted to take them up north to whip more Yankees, then that was fine with his men, especially since a run at the enemy was the acknowledged best way of relieving their own supply and equipment shortages. So they waited, standing, sitting, slouching or sprawled, while the great transfer of fighting men on the worn down railroads, from the environs of Richmond on the James River up to the Virginia piedmont east of the Blue Ridge, slowly proceeded. There were indeed more Yankees up there who needed attending to and, though it may appear to be a faltering and ill-organised episode, this confused event at the rail depot was the start of that process.

Chapter 1
The Recruits

It was into the afternoon when their own sergeants were finally dispatched by the officers to the companies and sections, calling the men of the Ogeechee Volunteers to assemble, with the orders being quickly echoed by the section corporals. The men came from their sitting or lounging places, to gather their equipment, laid aside for comfort's sake and form into their files once more. Having been called to attention, they began in due course to shuffle, past the other still waiting troops, towards the depot and the sidings, only to halt again along the side of the building. The wait there was brief. The ranks were soon moving once more, dispatched towards the other side of the depot, by the shouts of a flushed, sweating and profane train master, who carried a sheaf of crumpled and much scrawled upon papers under his arm. They moved on, making their way through the still teeming crowds to the rail lines, where successive trains noisily continued to arrive and depart. There were no coaches on the one that had arrived for them. Instead it consisted of a variety of flatcars and the men were steered across to these in sections, slinging their muskets over their shoulders on their leather or fabric straps in order to free their hands for clambering aboard. Blanket rolls were set down on the worn and splintered wooden planks for sitting or lounging upon and this settling and shuffling around continued as still more men were crowded onto the cars by their labouring NCOs.

The sun blistered down in its scorching climax of heat and glare, until at last, its cars laden with a jumble of shouting or cheering men, the locomotive up ahead screeched its whistle and the train jolted heavily into movement. After some further jerking and bumping together of trucks, the motion gradually settled into a steady departure from the depot. Up in front, the engine puffed and laboured noisily with the men now being showered, in the largely windless afternoon, with hot fragments of cinders from its smokestack, which sparked a further noisy upsurge of dodging and jostling on the cars. But at least they were off, with wheels grinding and juddering on sections of the worn and neglected rails, as they toiled mightily out from the depot for the boys to take their departing views of Richmond. The buildings of Valley Street went slipping past to the right, with Butchertown to the left of the tracks across the sluggish waters of the Creek, which stretched on to the north past its basin, roughly parallel to the initial route of the railroad, until each went its separate way round the respective sides of the bulk of Mansfield Hill.

They were away on their journey to Gordonsville, where the advance portion of the army had been for almost a month, dispatched there by General Lee, with General Thomas "Stonewall" Jackson in command, to prevent Johnny Pope's Yankees from spreading on south and cutting this very railroad. Those advanced divisions were up there now, marking down that man Pope and his men for a good licking and, if the newspapers were to be believed, they had even been dealing out some early chastisement to some of the Yankee army last week, in a stern little fight fought near a place called Slaughter Mountain, to the north of Gordonsville, in the stretch of land between Orange Courthouse and Culpeper. That fight had sent the advanced enemy force scuttling back northwards. So now, with the dispatch of the bulk of the army's remaining troops to the area, and the straining of the Virginia Central Railroad to near breaking point in so doing, it was only a matter of time, the boys repeatedly told each other, before further chastisement took place.

The movement of the train, once the labouring locomotive managed to get up any kind of a reasonable speed, provided something of a welcome draught of air for the men on the train, subduing, at least to a degree, the overpowering heat and humidity of the day. The cars were a babble of excited talk, for even although most of these men had travelled by train to Richmond from Georgia, the previous spring, there was an air of excitement and anticipation about striking off to the north on this new campaign. Not surprisingly, the main focus of that talk among the train passengers was on where they were headed and the man they were going to confront.

Many of these boys were farmers or farmers' sons, but, included in their number was a fair mixture of storekeepers, mechanics, craftsmen of various trades, teamsters, some lawyers, teachers and even a proportion of the land-owning planter families of the south. The great majority of these citizen-soldiers were therefore literate, with many of them being pretty well-educated by any standard. They were well able to negotiate their way through, and comment upon, the contents of the Richmond papers in particular, and the southern press in general, which had, all summer, been collectively trumpeting their denunciation of Major General John Pope, the new commander of Union forces in northern Virginia. Even General Lee, a man reputedly not given to indulging himself in personal criticism of his adversaries, had, it seemed, let his dislike of this newly arrived Union officer be known. To, "Marse Robert," Pope was not an opponent to be confronted, outmanoeuvred and defeated, like any other Union general, but a "miscreant," more of a common law breaker, who was to be "suppressed."

It was not just that the Yankees under Pope were intruding into a pretty sensitive area of Virginia, although that was certainly true. The Virginia Central Railroad stretched north and west from Richmond, up through Gordonsville and then on to Charlottesville and eventually to Staunton, connecting the capital city with the Shenandoah Valley, that rich agricultural region, which was a prime supply source for the army and for much of the city as a whole. Gordonsville, around which the army was to concentrate, was on the Virginia Central, but it was also on the Orange and Alexandria line, which ran northeast to the Potomac River. When Pope and his Yankees had begun to assemble around Culpeper last month, further up that Orange and Alexandria Railroad, pushing patrols down towards Gordonsville, then, rather than see vital rail links cut, southern commanders had to do something about it.

General Lee was at Richmond with his army, watching George McClellan's main Union Army of the Potomac which was, since the fighting of the final week of June, still sprawled around its base at the Berkeley Plantation on the James River. Powerful and menacing, it could not, in spite of being forced away from the city at the beginning of July, be ignored. But what could be done about Pope and his army? McClellan and his men were still down there on the James, too near Richmond for comfort and certainly too much of a threat for the southern army to simply leave and head off some place else. After considering and consulting, General Lee had sent Stonewall Jackson, with two infantry divisions, off to Gordonsville in the middle of July, reinforcing them with a third division when this move prompted no response from McClellan's force. Although, after some manoeuvring around, Jackson's troops had knocked Pope's advance back on its heels last week in that fight to the south of Culpeper, the southern force wasn't anything like strong enough to take on Pope's whole army. So now Lee was taking the chance of reinforcing the troops at Gordonsville with much of the remainder of the army from Richmond, but, in taking this step, he was gambling that McClellan, whom he knew regarded Pope as a threat to his command prospects, would be in no great hurry to help him. In addition, there were indications which suggested that McClellan's army was about to be withdrawn by water from the James River region anyway and moved back to the area around Washington. Thus Longstreet's men were set on their way and Pope's army would, for the immediately foreseeable future, get the undivided attention, as far as that was possible, of Robert E. Lee and the bulk of his re-assembled Army of Northern Virginia.

Yes, Pope was a threat, the men knew, to the region and to the railroad, but there was more to it than that. He had been transferred to the east, coming from the campaign on the Mississippi River, full of bluster and boast, but even that would not have marked him out as a figure of particular hate in the south. There were, after all, plenty of blustering, boastful Yankees reported on in the southern press. No, the real, stick in the throat, hate for Johnny Pope came from the orders that he had issued to his troops, after his arrival in the east, which marked a deliberate departure from what had been regarded as the civilised treatment of civilians when conducting a war, a degree of which had survived, at least this far, in Virginia.

Pope had published orders which sanctioned the mistreatment of civilians in the areas occupied by his army. He now required all males living in those areas to take an oath of allegiance to the United States. If they refused to take that oath, they would be driven from their homes and their property would be confiscated. If, having sworn, they thereafter supported, supplied or aided the southern forces, they would be hanged. Pope had also decreed that his army should live off the local area, requisitioning supplies, but with payment or compensation only being offered to those loyal to the Union. To many of his troops, such an order was all the encouragement they had needed to indulge in widespread looting and theft, and this was currently happening all over Culpeper County, and various adjacent parts, where Pope's army was spread.

It was unthinkable that conduct like that of these particular Yankees against civilians should be not only tolerated, but sanctioned and encouraged by the enemy generals. In the south however there was a growing suspicion that this was how Abe Lincoln, and the black republicans in Washington, wanted it. Pope himself was a republican and he was acquainted with Lincoln, having been a member of his military escort to Washington when he had gone there last year to be inaugurated as president. What Pope was doing in Virginia now would undoubtedly have the sanction of the Yankee government, if indeed it had not been its idea in the first place. There was a strong hint of, "taking the gloves off and getting tough," in dealing with the seceded southern states in these orders, with their people being made to suffer materially for supporting their states instead of the administration in Washington. All of this was in stark contrast to the behaviour of General McClellan, who, while down on the peninsula all through the summer, had posted guards on private homes of note, and had punished those of his soldiers convicted of violating the property of civilians. Pope and his men were clearly of a different mould to that, and the railroad passengers, currently heading north, voiced grim pleasure at the chance to get to grips with them. If ever a man had asked for a good licking, the southern troops told each other, as they converged on Gordonsville on their wheezing, decrepit trains, it was Johnny Pope and this move to the piedmont whetted their appetite to be at this "miscreant" and his band of brigands, especially since, by doing so they might get the chance for some plundering of their own, at the expense of the Yankees.

Those trains wheezed and clattered on their way following the great northwest curve of the Virginia Central line through

Ashland and Atlee's and Hanover Junction, beginning its route then to the west. The progress however was far from continuous. In addition to their own halts for wood or water, more delays resulted from bridges or stretches of line which, while vainly awaiting repair, required all trains to slow to almost walking pace in negotiating their way past. As though all of this was not enough, further halts had to be made every few miles to provide toilet breaks for the afflicted bowels of many of their passengers. Each time the locomotive screeched and hissed to a halt, a scattering of boys would detrain, with varying degrees of urgency, to drop their pants and attend to the needful, before sheepishly returning, fastening buttons as they came, to clamber aboard again to endure the sarcasm of their comrades.

It was seventy odd miles by rail from Richmond to Gordonsville and the previously near to four hour peace time journey was, over the sorely straining railroad with its added variety of delays and interruptions, an impossibility. The now much extended trip offered ample time for a man to think, especially once the first wave of high spirits on commencing the journey had slowly subsided into a more measured pattern of talk among the various groups on the cars. It was easy to simply drift out of the chatter and wisecracking to allow thoughts to run, if that was what some of the more reflective travellers were inclined to do. For, in spite of all of the bravado that had heralded their departure from Richmond, some men did not altogether buy into the idea that this trip to the north would be some kind of adventure, with the enemy duly whipped and all equipment shortages then made good from the great abundance of Yankee supply. Almost all of those on the trains had seen enough of fighting over the summer to know that even if a whipping for the enemy was the ultimate result of the coming campaign, that result would inevitably have to be purchased with blood. The Ogeechee Volunteers had been involved in three full scale fights and other lesser encounters during what was now being referred to as the "Seven Days," fighting around Richmond at the end of June. They had, as the currently fashionable term put it, "seen the elephant," and it was not all valour and glory. Valour there was in plenty, Daniel Ryan reflected to himself, but valour gave no protection at all against the storm of iron and lead that swept the battlefields of this war. Too many of the valorous now lay in their graves or languished in the overcrowded hospitals and it would be naïve to think that the coming campaign would be any different. The Yankees were still in Virginia and the unfinished job of expelling them was there to be done, but beneath the boys' bombastic talk of chastising Johnny Pope and his thieving brigands lay a starker reality. Daniel recalled only too well, on top of all the abominable sights, sounds and smells of battle itself, the other trials of contact with the enemy. There was the numbing fear that had gripped him and many other boys as they waited for battle. There was that crushing ordeal of living on one's nerves when a fight was in prospect, the trembling limbs, the almost jumping out of one's skin upon nearly any kind of gunfire, the short-temperedness with comrades, the knotting of the stomach, for hours or almost days on end, the inability to relax or sleep properly. He recalled it all only too well, indeed, since that last, horrible episode of bloodshed at Malvern Hill near the James River, the six weeks or so of comparative respite, when these things could be pushed to the back of the mind, now seemed all too brief as every clattering wheel turn of this train lurched them all on towards the next episode of destruction. Daniel could feel the beginnings of that tension rising within him, even now with the journey north only just begun and, above all, he knew that one incontrovertible fact ruled over the next few days and weeks. He looked around the flatcar, knowing with absolute certainty that not all of these ragged boys who lounged there, hiding their uncertainties by joking and skylarking, would be alive when this coming campaign, victorious or not, was done.

8

There would be more cripples, many more, and there would be more fresh graves, marking the abrupt extinguishing of still more young lives and there was no sign yet that it would soon end, or that it was even drawing near to an end.

The journey north to Gordonsville stretched on and on, through the afternoon and evening, until it had taken more than double the pre-war time. Eventually, the train carrying most of the Ogeechee Volunteer Rifles, puffed slowly into the junction town in almost complete darkness, to find the place crowded with troops and lit by flickering lanterns and torches, though the air here seemed noticeably less humid than that down on the James River at Richmond. The men were disembarked and pushed their way through more crowds to assemble near the depot. They waited there in the flickering torchlight until the officers got themselves organised and rejoined their men. Finally, shouldering their arms, they marched away from the town, on a road lit only by moonlight, for a mile or more before being dismissed into a dark tree surrounded meadow to set up their camps. The boys improvised torches, by the flames of which fence rails were collected and fires were built. The mess cooking pans, which Daniel Ryan and Saul Philips had brought along, were put to use in warming a portion of the flour and meat hash that they had cooked the evening before into a spitting, sizzling mess for quick devouring by the hungry men. That done, they set to turning in for the night in the still warm, but less oppressive, air.

The Thursday dawned warm again and the temperature began to climb as the sun rose higher in the clear sky. There was, predictably, no sign of the regimental or company wagons, so, after parading for roll call and orders of the day, still more of the prepared and carried rations were assembled by Isaac Kane for breakfast. The mess dined on bacon with corn meal flapjacks heated in the same large pans, with Daniel himself relieved by the fact that it would be more than a week before he had to carry that particular brute again. The off-duty men spent portions of the day drilling in their camps and those camps were steadily more awash with rumours, most of which involved an imminent offensive against the braggart Pope. As the day passed, further brigades of infantry arrived and the fields and woods around the town grew more and more crowded as the men made camp, the army gathered its strength and the generals prepared their next moves. In the evening more of the carried rations were warmed and eaten, but already the food supply up here was taking a turn for the better.

The most striking thing that the men of the Ogeechee Volunteers ever recalled about that brief stay they enjoyed around Gordonsville was the transformation in their food supplies. Notwithstanding the absence of their own wagons, Jackson's commissariat had, for a month now, been provisioning his men from the local farms and that Thursday evening, the first delivery of what became a brief but plentiful supply of corn flour, bacon and vegetables was made around the newly set up camps. Better still, by the following morning, fresh meat, beef and pork, was coming in, mostly on the hoof, delivered by the commissary for slaughter and butchering in camps and, from that Friday, and on through the succeeding few days, the men dined on cuts of meat long since unheard of in the military ration.

With the beef and pork came best wheat flour, which baked up into mouth watering bread, or dumplings, or pancakes, or anything a competent cook like Kane could devise. Meals became large, regular and varied and the men quickly deduced that up here, things were different. For the contrast, between an area like the peninsula, around Richmond, campaigned over and picked clean by the troops of both armies and this, where the farms and stores had, at least till now, been spared the presence of large numbers of ravenous soldiers could not have been more marked. Sure Pope had tried earlier in the summer to advance down here, sending cavalry as an introduction to Yankee occupation, but that had been halted a month ago with the arrival of Jackson's men, before even his swarm of locusts had much more than sampled the region's produce. There was still plenty to go around meantime. It was bliss and it was savoured by the men, although, all too soon, it was ended.

All that Friday the trains kept coming in with still more of Longstreet's brigades. It was not that the men of the, "Blues," could see any of this from their camps, but they knew what a train whistle at the now distant depot sounded like and throughout the day, as for the preceding ones, a whole succession of these indicated that, piece by piece, "Old Pete's," force was gathering. The roads too were busy with the arriving columns of infantry from the rail depot, heading for camp grounds selected by Longstreet's officers, and, throughout that Friday, more and more guns, caissons and wagons, which had come up from Richmond by road, were to be seen, all spreading out into further camps around the area. The impression gained by the men was of a mighty assembling force, gathering itself for the coming blow against Pope and, by the evening this was pretty well confirmed by the arrival of marching orders for their own brigade. It was breaking camp in the morning, and the customary chores of ration cooking were the orders for their final hours in this bountiful place. Camp news and stories had it all spelled out. Just to the northeast of Gordonsville was Orange Courthouse and beyond that was the Rapidan River. On the north side of this water obstacle, the Yankees were said to be positioned, gathering in their formations, and apparently willing to make a stand there on the river line. Tomorrow's advance would be to confront them and, in the busy camps, amid the smell of cooking food there was an almost palpable atmosphere of tension and anticipation.

The spectacle that unfolded in camp later that Friday evening began almost unnoticed. A mutter of talk, that made men turn and look as they sat around their fires, burned low, after ration cooking was done, in deference to the heat of the evening. But, even as this mutter spread, men were getting to their feet to look and within seconds some had begun to move, in ones and twos or small groups towards where Rodger's tent was pitched. Daniel Ryan stood up in company with the others of the mess and in due course joined those who made their way to swell the crowd in front of the captain's tent, shuffling around to see between the heads of those already there and take in the scene that met them.

Standing there, escorted by corporal of the guard Henry Bayfield and two of his pickets, were three black men. They were young, Daniel Ryan thought as he scrutinised them, maybe late teens or early twenties. Two were of average height, but the third was substantially taller. He looked down on Bayfield who was no midget himself, then nervously flitted his eyes past him at the body of men now gathered in an almost complete circle, hemming himself and his companions, together with their guards, onto the space at the front of the captain's tent. The three arrivals were poorly clad, being dressed in patched and ragged jackets and pants and Daniel got a glimpse of worn brogans on their feet, though, in truth, he thought, they were no worse off than most of the men who now gazed at them. Rodger was there, with Boyce and Fenwick on either side, and the sergeants, Jeffers, Bradlee, Sangster and Bailey too, were in close attendance.

"So where did these here boys come from," Rodger began, silencing the murmur of talk that had persisted among the watching men?

"Post number three saw 'em, out in front, cap'n," was the answer from Bayfield.

"And how did your men run 'em to ground, corporal?"

"We didn't run 'em down sah," Bayfield replied. "They come on in themselves, reckoned they wanted to see the general." Daniel heard a ripple of amusement pass around the watching men and saw Rodger's expression also change at the words. The captain looked around at each of his lieutenants in turn, before restoring his gaze to Bayfield and his charges.

"Came on in?" The words were quietly spoken, as he paced the couple of steps to stand in front of the three black men.

"You won't be seein' any generals," he told them. "I'm only a captain," he spoke with heavy irony, "but likely as high as you go tonight, so what do you want here?" There was a nervous shuffling among the three before one of the shorter ones spoke at last.

"We had to make our way through the Yankee army to get here." Daniel found the boy's manner and tone surprising. He looked straight at Rodger and his voice was measured, maybe not confident or uppity, but certainly not obsequious or subservient either.

"Oh!" Rodger observed, "and why, might I ask, would you do that?"

"We want to join the army and fight." The surprise on Rodger's face was matched all around the crowd of watching men.

"Join the army!" Rodger almost spluttered the words, but the reply was firm.

"I am a free man and I have papers to show it," the negro said firmly before turning to the others.

"These men left their owner's service when the Yankees came. Their men looted the place and burned them all out because their master wouldn't take the oath. They ran off rather than join the Yankees and work for them. We are southerners. This is our home and we want to fight them." A further murmur, this time of something akin to shock, ran around the circle of watching men. Daniel heard it and looked around at the faces. Every eye was on the three blacks and there was a feeling, was it hostility, no, maybe not, something else, but what?

"Fight them" Rodger's tone still could not conceal his incredulity. "These two at least should be goin' back to their owner."

"You'll have to take them through the whole Yankee army to do that captain," the man responded, "and even when you do, you won't find nobody on their place. The Yankees burned it and ran everybody off."

Rodger looked at the young man for several seconds after he finished speaking, then he turned and paced away as though he wanted time to think. He got as far as Boyce and Fenwick and paused to exchange more muted whispers with them. After a few moments of this Fenwick made off, heading, Daniel Ryan reckoned, for the major's tent to land the problem on him. That done, the captain turned again to the three "recruits."

"What are your names," he demanded, upon which a further ripple of movement and muttering went around the watching circle of men.

"I am Eli Winder," the first man said. "This is Josh," he gestured to his companions in turn, "and this is Matthew. They worked on Mister John Hale's property up in Loudon County - till the Yankees came," he added.

"And you," Rodger addressed him again, "what was your occupation up there in Loudon County?"

"I worked for an undertaker up in Berryville in Clark County sir." The man's answers were clear and, Daniel Ryan found himself thinking, he sounded like he had an education, a pretty uncommon thing for black people.

"Damn sure I wouldn't be runnin' off if I was no undertaker," he heard Ballard mutter beside him. "They're doin' better business than anybody these days."

The captain went on questioning the three newcomers, getting answers mainly from Winder and mostly nods or "Yassuhs," from the other two. He was still engaged in this when footsteps heralded the approach of Preston, together with Fenwick and the new adjutant Walter Cole, who, Daniel

Ryan reckoned, had something of the look of a studious owl about him. Rodger stepped across to meet the major and, with formalities and a few further whispers exchanged and the men called to attention by Jeffers, the two of them, along with everyone else in the company, faced the three negroes.

"Stand the men at ease, First Sergeant," Preston rapped as he eyed the three black men. On Jeffers shout, the watching circle of spectators relaxed.

"Join the Confederate army," the major growled at the three in front of him?

"Yes sir," Winder began, with the same composure in his voice as before. "Virginia is our home. We are southerners too and we have the same reason to want to fight invaders as you have."

"You have, have you," Preston barked? He looked closely into their faces before he, like Rodger before him, resorted to pacing away, with the captain at his heels. They took a further turn at conversing in murmurs, before the major turned again to the three black men.

"So you want to fight the Yankees," he growled. "How come you want to fight when plenty o' your kin are runnin' off to join 'em?" The man did not flinch, but looked straight at Preston as he answered.

"What we saw the Yankees doin' up in Clark County and Loudon County was just plain thievin', burnin' and ill-treatin', 'specially of black people. They weren't askin' no questions before they did it. No sir, men that rob my neighbours, burn out their places and insult our womenfolk, they ain't no friends o' mine, no matter what they say about it after." The major heard him out, and when Winder had done he looked the three men up and down for a further spell, but when he spoke again his tone had changed somewhat.

"Hear this," he told them, "Anybody that gets signed on here is in for the war and the punishment for runnin' off from the Confederate army is death. Do you understand that?" The three heads nodded disjointedly.

"Captain Rodger has questioned you already," Preston went on, "but I have just one more question for each of you." He paused and drew breath.

"Will you fight?" He looked Eli Winder squarely in the face as the black man looked steadily back at him.

"Yes sir," he said clearly, "I will." Preston moved to the next man, whom as Daniel recollected had been introduced as Matthew.

"And you," he said.

"Yassah," was the reply.

"Yassah what, boy," Preston growled.

"I'll fight," the boy said. The major moved on to confront the taller man, Josh.

"I will fight," the voice was steady and firm even before the question had been put. Preston turned around to the watching group of officers.

"Sign these men on, Mr Clegg," he called. "If they fight, like they say, then that's three more for the damn Yankees to worry about." He strode away as the watching men dissolved in talk. It was Bradlee's voice that the men heard next as he addressed Rodger.

"Beg pardon cap'n, do they git muskets 'n' rations?" The talk ceased as the men all around awaited the reply. Rodger's response was prompt and firm.

"Once these boys are signed on sergeant, they get the same as everybody else around here."

The three "recruits" were escorted away with the adjutant, while, behind them, the discussion redoubled as the men of Company B, seeing that the episode was over, turned away towards the remains of their fires. In common with others all around them, those of Daniel Ryan's mess erupted in talk as soon they reached their fire.

"Don't know about no black soldiers," Daley began.

"Plenty o' black soldiers in this army already," John Fitzpatrick asserted.

"But most o' the rest're ditch diggers and cooks and teamsters and servants, like Levi, the major's boy," Kane put in.

"Jackson's got them under arms in his outfits," Phillips observed.

"Can't give 'em a gun," Isaac Kane asserted. "Once ya make soldiers of 'em yo're makin' 'em the same as us. 'Sides, I sure wouldn't trust 'em with a gun around me." There was a mutter of responses to that and it was clear from them that not everyone felt that way, with Ballard being among those who took a different view.

"It ain't that simple," he said. "When the Yankees come through anybody's state or county, ev'body's places whether they're farms, stores, workshops 'r plantations or whatever else are goin' t' git robbed or burned. They ain't goin' t' leave 'em be jest cuz there's blacks on 'em. So have we got to do all the steppin' up and stoppin' the bluebellies while them black boys jest stay home and don't take no risks 'tall? Way I see it, they got the same duty to pitch in and defend the place like anybody else has."

"So why don't we jest set 'em to diggin' trenches and drivin' wagons or cookin' chow then," Daley resumed, "instead of makin' 'em real soldiers?"

"I'd rather go on riskin' Isaac's cookin'," Daniel Ryan told him.

"That means we can stop a bullet and they get the safe jobs and don't take any risks," Fitzpatrick observed. Thompson listened to it all before putting in his customarily brief observation.

"If we kin fight then they kin fight, and, if they'll fight and take their share of it all, then they're doin' a damn sight more than some o' the skulkers we got around here a'ready, them who went missin' down at Richmond when the fightin got goin'."

"Hold on Joe," Kane interrupted, "ain't no call to bring none o' that up."

"Why in the hell not," Gibben said testily? He lowered his voice marginally. "We all saw who ducked off into the trees back in the summer when our turn came to fight. Even if there's none o' them at this fire, they're still around here, leastways they're here till the next fight comes along."

"Who'd ya rather have beside you Isaac," Ballard put in, "one o' these boys, who disappears when the time to fight comes, or a black boy who stays there and does his share?" There was a chorus of shouts at that and Kane shook his head.

"Ain't that simple," he snapped. "We don't know what they'll do when the fightin' starts."

"Damn sure we don't," Thompson said. "Nobody knows what he'll do till the time comes, but, if they say they'll serve and fight then I say give 'em a damn musket and the chance to do it."

The three newcomers returned some time later in company with Bailey, but, as they found themselves a space to settle and sleep, a succession of comments passed around the camp from a number of the Company B men which gave clear notice that Thompson's view of things was certainly not shared by everybody.

The drum roll roused the men into the earliest of daylight to assemble for roll call and orders. As Daniel Ryan took his place he saw the three blacks being placed in the ranks by Henry Bayfield. The corporal pushed and prodded them into positions of ease and attention in turn, as the start of their military training, while Jeffers looked on and although a few men sniggered, most of those in the ranks contented themselves with observing. The roll was called, with Josh and Matthew being given the surname of "Hale," for their previously departed

18

owner, Rodger then stepped up with a businesslike air. It was marching orders as announced the previous night and, since he had been brief, men began to speculate whether a quick breakfast might just manage to precede the departure. So it transpired and, having hurriedly eaten and with baggage and equipment gathered, the regiment formed on the road with the rest of the brigade, in the van of Longstreet's now assembled units, ready to begin their march, heading for their much anticipated business with these Yankees up ahead. The step off came within minutes as the heat gathered and the men quickly renewed their acquaintance with the tribulations of summer marching, well-remembered from the peninsula.

Above the dried up dirt roads hung the now familiar cloud of light brown dust, where the baked hard surface of the dirt road had been broken up by thousands of hooves, feet and wheels and pounded into fine powder. It plastered sweating skin and dampened uniforms in a layer, clogging in nostrils and throats and collecting under collars and cuffs and inside ears. It had been the biggest trial of dry weather campaigning down on the peninsula, worse even than the heat, and it looked like being just as potent here in upland Virginia. The three black men marched in the ranks, but without arms, haversacks, cartridge boxes, blankets or more seriously water canteens. They said little to those around them, as though apprehensive as to what the enlisted men would make of them. Even though the major had given formal approval to their presence, there was a suggestion in their behaviour that they realised that it was the response of the men around them that would really decide what kind of a future they would have, in Company B in particular and the regiment in general.

The talk and wisecracking in the files around them soon got going, with a number of comments, a few of them pointed and critical, coming their way, but they seemed to prefer a sheepish grin or a nod to any kind of verbal response and the banter gradually died as the boys got tired of it and settled down to making the best they could of the dust and heat, using water canteens regularly to rinse their mouths and throats. The clouds around the column grew steadily, becoming so dense in places, that they obscured all but the nearest comrades and files around them from the marchers as they struggled along in its choking gloom. Some took to wearing cloths over their mouths, against breathing in too much of the dust, but others held that it made little difference with the dust and instead made a man's face and neck hotter and sweatier still. What was needed, they told each other, was a good fall of rain to bind the roads once more, at least for a time, until the whole sequence of drying out and crushing down took place again. In the meantime, there was little to do but set one's teeth and push on to the river up ahead.

Different men, including those in Daniel's mess had given water to the three newcomers, this being acknowledged by careful politeness and in due course, at one of the morning hour halts, Bradlee had approached them.

"We got two other men with no arms, same as you boys, in this company," he told them. "Ya'll all have weapons as soon as we got 'em to give ya. Meantime," he went on, "ya'll find a canteen, or a water bottle, to be a better thing to have than a musket on a lot o' days around here." Daniel saw the three heads nod in response just as Jeffers' call came along for the column of march to reform and the musket stacks began to disappear as the men moved back to their files, some taking a last swallow of their remaining water, readying themselves for the next episode of the ordeal on the road.

"Even if ya can't git no canteen right away," Ballard called over to the newcomers, "git somethin' to carry water in. If ya don't, ya'll suffer for it." Daniel Ryan saw the words invoking another bout of furious nodding from the three recruits as they scurried back to the column.

"Look at 'em," Daley growled as he watched their response. "Them, do a man's work? They'll be down the nearest rabbit

hole as soon as the first bloody Yankee spits in their direction."
Daniel Ryan looked at him but said nothing. Mick certainly
didn't look like joining the "give them a chance" group either,
he thought, not by a long shot.

Chapter 2
A Face Off on the Rivers

In company with the others of Company B, Daniel Ryan found that the ordeals associated with marching up here in the Virginia piedmont were offset, at least initially, by one thing. The improvement in provisions, noted around Gordonsville, was sustained as the tramp to the river line proceeded through the Saturday. On that day Daniel took his turn at carrying the other mess pan, the smaller, older one, but it had a hooked handle, which made it possible to simply hitch it over the belt, leaving the hands free. But carrying pans seemed a shade less tedious when there was every prospect of a full portion of good food to cook in them at the end of the day. Therein lay the consolation for around here there seemed to be no shortage of good rations, which left the heat and dust, and the familiar thirst at different times of the day when the water bottles ran dry, as the main drawbacks.

Having thus endured, and finally halted at the end of those blistering hot hours near the village of Verdiersville, the men had the compensation of being found by their newly arrived wagons. Cal Jeffreys of the commissary seemed in a better humour than most could remember, as he oversaw the issue. They subsequently feasted on fresh beef and vegetables with wheat flour bread, while the rations prepared at Gordonsville stayed in the haversacks. This was the way to campaign the boys told each other again, for a march in the heat, provided good water was sufficiently available, was made somewhat more bearable by a good meal at the end of it. What was more, around the camp, the word was that the enemy were still there, spread along the river line just up ahead. Tomorrow should see them in contact with these thieving Yankees and then there should be the chance for plunder to make good the many shortages in the company.

Most of the army was now concentrated up here, with Jackson's men said to be advancing on parallel roads to the west and Johnny Pope about to be taught a lesson he wouldn't soon forget. So the talk went as light faded and the night insects began to twitter and sing. The next day or two would likely bring on the fight. Daniel heard the talk and nodded with the others, but after the camp had settled, he saw in that period before sleep came a collection of dim forms around the camp, turning and fidgeting in their places. Clearly others also, in spite of the camp talk, were finding that rest, in spite of their exhausting day on the dusty roads, did not come readily, now that the enemy was near.

Dawn brought the familiar drum roll, which roused the men at their customary early hour. They were paraded, for roll call and orders of the day, and then breakfasted, on flapjacks and sliced up beef, before collecting belongings to resume the march. Daniel noticed that all three of the negroes had acquired water containers of some description, bottles of glass or clay and these hung across their shoulders on lengths of string or rawhide as they took their places in the ranks. The long column formed and set off, with the morning clear and pleasantly warm, though, men knew well that the newly risen sun would soon change that. They passed through Verdiersville itself, taking the road to the northwest at the crossroads where the cluster of buildings stood. The march was steady, though not forced and the Rapidan River, where the road crossed over at Raccoon Ford, was reached in the middle of the morning. The brigade deployed off the road to be pointed towards the river by a small cavalry picket, sent ahead by the general to reconnoiter up to the river bank and probe the enemy dispositions on the far side.

Having secured the southern bank, a skirmish line was pushed out by Major Preston along the stretch of waterside, to the west, or upstream, from the ford. The balance of the men went into camp a short way back from the river, in time to avoid the worst of the day's heat by setting themselves up in a stand of woods, where they spent time erecting blanket or brush shelters among the bushes and trees. Rations were produced and still more local beef was heated and consumed, with the off-duty men then stretching out to rest for the remainder of the afternoon. As they waited, stories began to circulate of a coming attack, but that wouldn't be today, Kane said. The day was passing, with the sun sinking lower and the light would soon be gone, besides everyone knew that old Jackson had a religious thing about fighting battles on the Sabbath, and anyway their own brigadier was supposed to be away for the day visiting old congressional friends, and that would likely mean the broaching of a bottle or two. Colonel Henry Benning of the Seventeenth Georgia was in temporary charge, and all of this would surely not be happening if there was a fight planned. No, they would have the rest of the day and tonight at least to rest. The troops were perfectly happy to go along with that idea, even if Kane was no general, but events seemed to bear out his words, until orders arrived from Benning for the regiment to go, with two others of the brigade, and guard the road down to the river and the area around the ford. As the men got ready to move out, still more orders arrived, this time to prepare three days rations ready for a march at daylight. This, though most men still had a portion at least of their Gordonsville rations, put a different complexion on the night duty, since men on river picket couldn't cook at the same time. It was therefore a dissatisfied detail that moved out towards the ford in the evening, fully aware that if they wanted rations for the coming march there would be little in the way of rest when they came off duty.

It was late, probably after midnight when the rider came trotting up the road from behind them towards the positions around the ford. Daniel Ryan was on the road with his section, on their way from the picket camp to relieve the sentinels at the river, and the men stiffened at the sound of the horse's hooves, with several of them unslinging their weapons as the horseman approached, visible in the shafts of moonlight shining through the trees and by the inevitable dust kicked up by his trotting horse. As he drew closer, he could be made out through the trees, a smartly uniformed, staffer, Daniel Ryan concluded. His hat was pulled well down, yet he looked familiar as he reined in on reaching where they stood.

"What regiment are you men," the voice was loud and peremptory.

"Ogeechee Volunteer Rifles, sah," Sam Bradlee, the sergeant, snapped in reply, as the others shuffled into a line beside the road.

"Where are your officers, and the rest of the men? General Toombs desires to know why half of his brigade is here around the ford when he gave no such orders. The ford is to be picketed by others and there are now fresh orders for the brigade."

"The detail to guard the ford is down at the river, sah," Bradlee told him. "Ev'body else is along the river or camped over thar, Colonel Benning's orders," he added, pointing off down the track towards where the overnight camp had been set up.

"New orders now," the man snapped, "the brigade has marching orders and this detail is ordered back to the brigade camps to cook rations and prepare. Get your detail back and rejoin the other pickets sergeant," he added. "Then its back to the brigade for you." He wheeled his horse and moved off where Bradlee had indicated in the direction of the picket camp while behind him, as his dust swirled around them, the enlisted men relaxed as they reformed on the road and moved off after him.

"Sounds like somebody could be goin' to get had fer supper, when the ole congressman gits a hold o' him, fer movin' his little soldiers around without him knowin'," Ballard muttered.

"We'll jest keep ourselves clear o' that there conversation," Bradlee told him.

By the time they reached the river side and the picket positions, those revised orders had already circulated. It was pack up and move out, back to the camps as the officer had told them. Fenwick, the new lieutenant, met them on the road at the picket post, a chastised man, by his manner, who, having only recently joined the officer corps of the Army of Northern Virginia, had seemingly gained an understanding of which rank exceeded which, but not, as yet, how to pass on blame when one of higher rank came looking to apportion it, especially when the censure was on behalf of the brigadier himself.

"Stand where you are with those men Sergeant Bradlee," he rapped irritably. "Everybody else on this picket, it seems, will be joining you directly." He moved off and the men waited, with little to do but watch the activity around them as those from the outposts were gathered from where they had been stationed along the river around the ford. Preston arrived and demanded to know on whose authority his men were leaving their positions and hastening to form on the road, chivvied by their NCOs. The staff captain was more than willing to tell him.

"Reckon we should be stayin' on duty here until we get relieved," Bradlee grated to those in the rank beside him.

"Reckon we know who's in command o' this here brigade," Kane said, "'an' if he wants us back at the camps to cook, that's where we'll be headin'." Around him the others pulled faces at his words as the major called his assembling men to order, still under the eye of the captain, who, having seen the orders he had brought being carried out, edged his horse back along the track, past where the bulk of the picket now stood, making his way back to the river road, where further activity showed that the other regiments were similarly assembling.

The regiments at the river were marched back to the main camp and dismissed to their cooking with no further word of explanation, and with only a brief hour of rest once that was done, but it was after assembly and breakfast, as the Monday morning came in bright, and the heat began to grow, that new stories began to circulate. Yankee cavalry had gotten across the river during the night to rampage around this morning on the Confederate side and now the orders were changed. The pickets had at first light been restored to their posts along the river at Raccoon Ford, and Daniel Ryan's reprieved section from the previous night had gotten the second morning duty. Even while they were on watch, more stories followed as the time passed, these later rumours actually suggesting that those Yankees had come pretty close to capturing "Jeb" Stuart, the army's flambuoyant cavalry commander. Relieved and back in camp, they learned that still more details were circulating. The near capture of Stuart was confirmed, but, what was worse, these latest rumours were suggesting that the Yankees had gotten across the river, to get started on their trouble making, at none other than Raccoon Ford, which, after their own pickets had withdrawn last night, had seemingly lain unguarded for the rest of the hours of darkness, and that against orders which, it emerged, had come from Longstreet himself. The boys in the "Blues" were astounded at this latest news.

"Reckon there'll be hog shit flyin' now," Joe Thompson told the others of the section. "We surely ain't heard the last o' this."

Thompson's words were indeed prophetic. By evening still more rumours were flying hard on one another's heels. Longstreet himself was investigating the incident. Toombs had been placed under arrest, but worse, as the evening approached, further editions of the camp talk were circulating, namely that Toombs had ignored the arrest order and had declined to be relieved of his command. The camps were alive with excitement and talk as the men digested this latest news and discussed its further implications. It was becoming a day like no other in their military lives, at least not since the one, back in the spring, when their own colonel, and a proportion of their officers and men, had refused to leave Savannah, to come to Virginia, but this day was not over yet.

It was evening, after the long hours of story and counter-story, ever more dramatic versions of which had mingled with the duties and drills of the day. No mention was made of it all at the evening roll call but it was as many of the men attended to their supper, that the regiment received orders to parade again, and, on assembling and being marched beyond the camps to a pasture field, found that the whole brigade was gathering there. The men waited briefly, the ranks alive with murmured talk, which the officers and NCOs made little attempt to silence. Before long the general appeared, riding at the head of his staff. The ranks were called to order and silence fell like a curtain. Toombs was clad in his full dress, brigadier's uniform, with his gilt-wreathed hat pulled firmly onto his head and his sword buckled to his waist. A flamboyant scarf, of the type for which he was known, this one a rich, blue silk, creation, adorned his neck over his tunic collar. His face was flushed as he dismounted and paced to the middle of the brigade square, tossing his head as he was prone to do, to look around the long ranks of men before raising his voice to speak, commencing then on a denunciation of generals and West Point trained generals in particular who were making scapegoats of those in the army who were there to fight.

The boys in the ranks stood through his impassioned words, Daniel Ryan watched and listened, impressed, almost in spite of himself, by the speechifying politician's skills that the man clearly had at his fingertips. But, as he listened, and glanced occasionally along the rank at the reaction of those around him, Daniel was becoming more and more puzzled. What was the meaning of this show? It was a matter for the high command to decide who was to blame for whatever had taken place at the river. Why was the general involving the enlisted men of his brigade in it all? He might be a longstanding politician, but this was not an election and the men would have neither say nor vote in the outcome of it all so what, if anything, they were expected to do was beyond him, unless it was an attempt by Toombs to somehow make a distinction between being a Georgian and being a Confederate soldier. The general reckoned he was submitting to neither removal nor arrest, but the army was not a democracy and what Jones, or Longstreet, or Lee himself would make of that, when they heard about it, would no doubt be seen. Was Toombs inciting them to join him in defying orders? If so, then the consequences would be grave, not just for him, but for any others who involved themselves in such a thing also. Armies liked to have their chains of command respected, and their orders obeyed, even the most naïve country boy in the ranks had figured that out by now, through punishment, if not through instinct and observation. But Toombs seemed to be directly challenging this most sacred military convention. This whole thing had now gone from serious to near comical and was now reaching the stage of being downright ridiculous.

But, in spite of all of that, Toombs was a popular commander and cheers echoed down the ranks as he got to the end of his talk. Having seemingly gotten the edge off his temper, with his tirade about the iniquities of Virginia, West Pointers in the army command, he stalked away, with the shouts of his men ringing in his ears, to remount and depart with the officers of his staff jingling away at his heels. Sure, they liked Bob Toombs. He always had a good word for his men and he had a genuine concern for their welfare and if a good cheer was what he wanted he had certainly gotten it here, but, at the end of it all, it changed nothing of the situation that existed and the predicament that he had gotten himself into. A few minutes after the brigadier's departure, the men were dismissed, back to their laid aside meals and other duties. Now the camps erupted into further talk, bubbling with all that they had heard and seen, with the negro recruits forgotten meantime, while the talk focussed on Toombs, and, though the drumbeat of lights out came, and the off duty men took to their blankets, the whispered conversations and speculations as to what might come next were far from done.

Morning came, with its rituals of assembly and breakfast, and with it the news that Longstreet's reaction had indeed been swift. The brigadier had been forcibly removed from command and ordered from the army's camps. He was now on the way to Gordonsville under guard and Benning was in command of the brigade again. The camps hummed with renewed gossip, especially when it was rumoured that one of the trophies that the Yankee cavalry, whom Toombs' removal of the guard at the ford had allowed across the river, had secured in the course of their raid was a copy of General Lee's plans. These called for an attack across the river to be launched on Wednesday morning. Maybe, some of the boys reckoned, on hearing all of this, Longstreet's anger, and that of the other generals, was pretty understandable, but emerging also in the talk was something that Toombs had referred to the previous evening when he had addressed the brigade and that was the distinction between being Georgians and Confederates.

This army was named for Virginia and although Longstreet was a Georgian, whose family were South Carolinian, Lee, Jackson, Stuart of the cavalry also, and many others of the army's senior officers were Virginians. Some men were taking issue with this, saying that states that sent thousands of men to serve as ordinary soldiers in Virginia had a right to have their men commanded by their own officers. But other men reckoned they should be commanded by the best officers in the army, men who would win victories and if these best men, like Lee and others were Virginians so be it. Success was more important than states rights in matters of life and death like this. The talk and the arguments went on around the camps through the day as men voiced their views. Philipps' was emphatic.

"Too much o' state's rights in this here army could get us all in a fine mess," he said. Ballard took a similar view.

"Better a Virginian who knows his soldierin' business than a horse's ass from some place else, who don't," he said. Most of the mess, including Daniel Ryan seemed to go along with that.

As for Benning, "Old Rock," as he was known to his men, was Georgia through and through. He had been a judge, back home, but as a soldier he was reckoned to be a shrewd judge also, of men and situations, and liked by the rank and file. If he was in charge now then that was fair enough for most of the brigade, but though the whole thing might be settled, at least for the meantime, many men speculated that they had not heard the last of Brigadier General Robert Toombs.

"Looks like the ole congressman's got to l'arn the same lesson as Fletcher an' a few others did last spring," Thompson told the mess. The others looked at him.

"And what lesson would that be," Gibben inquired?

"Why that this here war's gotten a mite bigger than any one o' these, "quality folks'" reputations," was the big corporal's reply.

The news of the impending advance was what, as Ballard put it, "got the ole congressman off the front page o' the paper." Delayed for one day already by the confusion around the ford and an apparent absence of the cavalry, the next day also passed with no word as to when their departure would be, but other rumours now spoke of the Yankees being gone with their positions along the river now deserted. All day the men had been ready with rations cooked and gear packed, as the stories persisted, but with little to do but continue to gossip or ruminate while they waited. It was not until evening assembly came that the orders were issued for the men to turn in at nightfall to allow them to rest until the appointed time, around midnight, came for the march to begin at last.

By the light of the moon the camp was roused, without drums or other noises, to assemble in the still warm air, arranging equipment belts and straps about their persons until the word came to step off. They moved out onto the road, with the dust already billowing around the files in its choking cloud, making an almost surreal sight as it drifted among the men in the shafts of eerie light. The road took the column through the trees down to the ill-fated ford, for the successive files of men to see there, as they arrived at the river, the imposing figure of William Benning. He was a strongly built man and he waited there now, letting his horse cool its legs in the shallows, while he sat, silently watching the men cross and letting them see him do it. It was said that Benning was part Indian and even in the pale light of the moon, as the men looked at his dark face, further obscured by the pulled down brim of his hat, they reckoned they could believe it. He had the look of a bushwhacker about him, Daley said, especially in the middle of the night.

No time was given to remove shoes or socks and the companies simply ploughed on into the river when their turn came. The water came almost to the men's waists in mid-river and the progress was hurried along by the officers calling to those, who paused to dip canteens into the water to top them up, to close up, making it clear that they too were in no doubt that "Old Rock" was sitting back there for a purpose and that would be to look for a well-ordered march on his first full day in formal command. On the far side, the files were briefly re-formed before the squelching men were pushed on, with the road turning steadily northeast and the way marked by that hanging pillar of dust kicked up by those who marched below it.

The most frequent consequence of crossing a river or a creek without keeping footwear dry was blisters and these could be expected to form and fill as the march left behind whatever watercourse had been negotiated. When the shoes, particularly those brogans, made of less well-seasoned leather, got soaked, they often softened and stretched, flapping cumbersomely on the feet. But as it dried, the shoe leather contracted and hardened, punishing the feet in turn as a consequence. Understandably then, the men preferred to halt at a river or creek crossing and remove shoes, socks also, if they had them, and pants as well, bundling everything up to tie things by their laces around necks or onto ramrods and, by keeping the footwear dry as a result, to avoid the subsequent blisters. But, to officers, this caused delays, with piled up jams of their men at the fording places, removing or replacing pants or lacing and unlacing shoes, and rebukes therefore came down from the colonels and the generals. So, reading such situations, many tried to dispense with the practice of halting at fords, and thus it was today, especially with Benning sitting there, watching, like a damned vulture, for something to fasten onto, in order to show, by reprimanding some victim or other, who was in command. Today, as a consequence of all of this, the blistered feet got second priority and the quick and orderly crossing got first. So, with a chorus of complaints about all of this running along the files, the column pushed on. Already, in the dusty gloom, the water canteens were in regular use.

Dawn came and the wearying troops were allowed a further hour to eat and rest before resuming their march as the sunrise approached in the eastern sky. Some men treated their feet, with a few of the minority who had a spare pair of socks, substituting them for those soaked in the river as a way of heading off the worst of the blisters, but the river crossing was well behind them now and the damage was largely done. Of the Yankees there had been little sign. A few abandoned camp sites, and a littering of discarded rubbish, poked through by a few of the arriving Confederates in the hope of finding something of use. But clearly Johnny Pope and his men had skedaddled, taking themselves off to the north to seek the protection of the next water obstacle, the Rappahannock River some miles further up ahead.

There was a mixture of feigned disappointment and grim satisfaction among the men at the Yankee retreat, but Daniel Ryan, having seen the signs repeatedly since Richmond, knew that in their deepest hearts, few of those around him, in spite of what they said at times like now, really looked forward to a fight. Battle was such an experience that, once boys had seen the blood and death of it, they would regard it differently in future. After the first time, men nerved themselves for it, as the only way of ultimately ending the struggle through victory, and as a source of often much-needed plunder, but, save for a minority of the incurably pugnacious like Mick Daley, they would never again be enthusiastic about it. But now, with the Yankees and the prospect of an immediate fight gone, talk was cheap and numbers of the boys voiced their "disappointment" that the enemy had not tarried long enough for them to come to grips, but, Daniel Ryan knew, that when the time came again, things would be different.

With breakfast eaten, they were called into column again to march, now almost parallel to the Rappahannock River, towards Kelly's Ford the stories said. The hours began to pass with heat and humidity again an ordeal. The dust was ever-present, getting into eyes, ears and mouths, which regular swills of tepid water only temporarily relieved. It silted its way under tunic and shirt collars and cuffs and proceeded to rub and chafe into the skin below, raising rashes or weals on the necks or arms where it did so. Hour halts gave some respite from the conditions, giving the men a chance to re-organise themselves, and rest briefly, but, in this kind of heat, the halts were all too short and were often spent trying to replenish empty water canteens, with this made difficult through streams or wells being reduced to trickles or discoloured remnants by those further up the column having gotten to them first.

Near to noon they passed through the little crossroads hamlet of Lignum, pushing steadily on to the northeast. Along the roadside lay belongings, thrown away by fatigued or struggling men up ahead, with blanket rolls, in particular, littering the verges. Some in the company, Daley among them, began to loosen their own blanket rolls to do likewise, till they heard Jeffers' shout from behind.

"Ya throw 'em away now, but whad'll ya all do the first cold night?" A few more went flying into the brush, but most, including Daniel Ryan's, stayed on the men's shoulders, waterproofs, for those who had them, included. In the heat, these now burned bare skin, but, rather than ditching them, some now rolled them inside their woollen blankets.

In the late afternoon they reached another creek. This, the talk went, was Mountain Run. Here, likely since Benning was nowhere to be seen, the column was halted for the men to remove shoes and socks before splashing across, gratefully savouring the reviving coolness of the stream and refilling water canteens as they went. After a further brief halt on the far bank to replace their footwear the march resumed. Then it was on in the heat again, with only the hour halts to afford occasional relief from the dust cloud, though with the sun now sinking, the worst torment of the day was thankfully past.

The ordeal ended near sunset as the column wheeled off the road and along a track into an overgrown pasture field to settle there. The Rappahannock was just up ahead they were told, and Kelly's Ford was just downstream, but water details would be confined to the brackish streams and creeks that fed the nearby river, at least until dark. The Yankees were picketing the river line and there were to be no indications to them that the Confederates had arrived in strength. Camp was set up and the men began collecting wood and water, until more orders came around through the sergeants, forbidding the lighting of cooking fires that would reveal their presence to the enemy. Water collectors set about their business at dusk, heading away towards the river, to eventually straggle back in ones and twos, while others readied what rations they had for eating cold.

"Boy!" The men nearby paused in their own chores and turned on hearing Tom Powell's shout.

"You boy!" Again the voice came, peremptory and a shade angrier in tone than before. A finger waggled in the direction of the three negroes, where they sat under a tree, the taller boy, Josh having just returned from the river with their three water bottles. Powell held out his canteen towards them.

"Go fill that up boy." There was a long pause while everyone looked and no-one spoke. Powell shook the canteen gently and called again.

"Get a move on now boy," he called, in a gentler tone this time. Across the camp, Eli Winder got slowly to his feet.

"You talkin' to me…., Mister Powell," he said quietly. Daniel Ryan was certain that he could hear a tone of, perhaps not outright fear, but certainly unease in his voice.

"Any one o' you niggers'll do," came the response. Winder looked across at the canteen, but he did not move.

"You an uppity nigger," Powell growled, "cuz I ain't waitin' here all night?" Still Winder did nothing and, seeing those around him watching, Powell sighed and also got to his feet. Around the camp, others too had risen to watch.

"Maybe you need a good whuppin' to teach ya yore place around here boy," he growled. "When a white man says jump then black boys jump.., nigger." Daniel saw the anger rise in Winder. His shoulders stiffened and his face tensed as he spoke.

"I'm a free man," he declared in a firm voice. "I'm here to fight the Yankees, not run errands for men like you...., massah," he ground the last word out between his teeth. At that, Powell snorted and he started towards him.

"Uppity black shits is one thing I can't abide," he growled as he advanced. His hand still held the canteen, but as he reached Winder, he suddenly dropped the wooden container and swung it hard on its strap. Winder moved to dodge, but the edge caught him a glancing blow on the side of his head. He looked around the camp as he moved away a step. Powell swung again, but this time he missed completely as Winder ducked below the swing. The canteen continued around on its arc until it came to a sudden halt, having caught the arm of Thompson, who had promptly stepped over towards the incident.

Powell swore at Winder but then he suddenly lurched to one side, pulled off balance as Thompson caught the canteen strap and hauled on it. His other hand grabbed at Powell's tunic and he pulled him close so that his face was pushed into Powell's.

"Take another swing with yore canteen and I'll push it down yore damn throat," the big corporal growled.

"I was swingin' at the goddam nigger, not you," Powell shouted, but, to Daniel Ryan, it was his voice that now showed a tone of uncertainty and apprehension. Thompson pulled him an inch or two closer before he answered.

"If you got all this spit to spare, maybe you should go git yore own water." Around the camp there now came shouts from others.

"Let him go Joe!"

"Leave him be!" Elmer Bentley, of Powell's mess, moved across clutching an iron pan in his right hand, but, before he could reach Thompson and Powell, he found his way blocked by Ballard.

"Reckon you won't be needin' that there pan if we ain't havin' no fires," Ballard told him.

"Outa my damn way, Ballard," he rasped. Ballard caught his wrist, as others from the two messes began to square up to each other. Daniel found himself facing Charlie Thorne.

"Don't have to be this way Ryan," Thorne rasped.

"Step away then," Daniel told him. Behind him there was another shout, this time it was the voice of Jeffers, and, shifting his eyes from Thorne, Daniel saw the First Sergeant striding in among the embattled group as Ballard and Thompson each released their grip on their adversaries.

"You lucky boys," Jeffers called as he took a long look about him. "I got pickets to post and guess what? All o' you energetic boys who're on your feet can take the first duty. Get yore soldierin' things and fall yoreselves in." For a brief moment or two, nobody moved. Then habit seemed to take over and the groups dispersed towards their respective musket stacks. As he moved across for his own canteen, Daniel's eyes fell on Mick Daley, who, for all of his loyalty and pugnacity, had not moved through the whole commotion.

"Good to see you stickin' with your friends Mick," he growled.

"Ain't my business helpin' no black boys," Daley returned, "Tom Powell's a friend o' mine too."

"Stay there on your miserable arse then," Daniel retorted.

Daniel crouched on a little rise of ground overlooking the river, with John Fitzpatrick again as his partner and while Fitzpatrick rested, he occupied himself by watching the water as it coursed slowly past their position. It was calm and cooler down here near the water and there was not a sign of activity or life on the other side. The moonlight shone on the river from downstream and whippoorwills called to each other, their noises mingling with the insect sounds and the occasional cries of other night creatures whose routines seemed undisturbed by this intrusion of man and his war into their habitats. Daniel pondered for the umpteenth time on the events in camp, reflecting particularly on the actions of Thompson, for in his view, the big corporal's involvement had been no accident. He had contrived the confrontation with Powell by stepping into the line of the swinging canteen. In a crude and unconvincing way, he had disguised it, but his actions were on behalf of the three negroes and Daniel found this, above all else, surprising.

When it came to it, Daniel felt no particular prejudice either way about the three newcomers. As various men had said, if they carried their share then there was no real objection to them joining Company B, and if they stopped a bullet, then that was their lookout like everybody else. But it was clear that some of the men were not so prepared to let the matter stand like that. Tonight may have been the most pointed example of hostility that the three had received, but the warning signs had been there since their arrival. The comments and remarks of some men had given clear notice of how they felt and now, but for Jeffers appearance, the thing could have sparked a large scale company brawl. Daniel cast his mind over the confrontation between those of the two messes, trying to recall who had involved themselves and who, like Daley, had stayed back. How divided was the company over this he wondered? Was it something that would be forgotten in a day or two, or was it deeper than that? Maybe, especially with the three black men constantly around the camp and the column, the rift between their own mess and Powell's would persist and that was something that would do the whole of Company B, whose men had to depend on each other, no good whatsoever. A problem like this could spread like a rot, eating away at unity and togetherness by causing men to take sides, and, resulting in a divided and hostile group, regardless of anything the three black boys themselves did. Casting his mind over the events, Daniel Ryan found himself wishing that the three of them had come into the lines at some other camp or had pursued their enlistment somewhere else, anywhere else other than Company B.

He tried to push the problem from his mind by letting let his eyes wander upstream and then, catching sight of a floating fragment of driftwood, he followed its progress downstream, letting his gaze slowly turn eastward again. That branch and that river, Daniel mused, would eventually reach the bay and then the great ocean, the same one whose waters, far to the south, also received the flow of the Savannah River and, half a world away, that same ocean washed on the shores of County Kerry and the rest of the coast of Ireland. In Daniel's thoughts tonight, it somehow made them both seem closer, or at least signified a connection, however faint, of all three places to each other, joined by the events of his own life and, in some tenuous way, by the rivers and the sea.

He thought of his home of the previous three years at Eden Station, all those miles to the south. It seemed almost unreal to think of such a distance, though the hundreds of miles and days of travel to Bryan County was small, compared to the size of the wide ocean that now lay between him and the place of his birth. Yet this same moon also shone on Kerry, in Ireland, and on Tralee near his home. What would those at home make of all of this if they heard? What would they say of his becoming a soldier after all? The custom had always been for the Connaught Rangers to recruit for the British army in the west of Ireland, carrying the boys off to the far ends of God's earth, all around their empire. Yet here he was, having avoided all of that, finishing up in an army anyway, over here in America, to fight for the state of Georgia, his new home, against what? The Yankees, black Republicans and abolitionists? Those who threatened the rights and institutions of Georgia and of the south as a whole were the enemy, but Daniel cared little about the political details. He knew that the south now fought for its independence and to simply be left alone. It was a region based on agriculture, be it the plantations of the richer, the farms of the many or the harsh bottomland subsistence of the poorer whites.

And then there were the black people, and so his mind came back to the three newcomers. They were principally the labourers of the wealthy, though some of the more prosperous farmers also owned single or small numbers of blacks to help work their farms beside their owners. Some were bonded out or free blacks, but the great majority of them were slaves. There was something distasteful about the trappings of slavery to someone not native to the south. Daniel had seen no black people whatsoever during his formative years in Ireland, whereas over here, he had seen many of them, in their subservient place in southern society. He had also seen them auctioned in Savannah, a sordid thing, to his own way of thinking, yet something common enough in the day to day working of southern life. But also in that day to day southern life there lay a paradox. Many owners treated their slaves kindly enough, caring for their welfare in a paternal sort of way, the way that some of the lords who owned the great estates back at home did, if not out of totally generous instincts, at least out of a desire to preserve their investment and the social order that gave them their lifestyle. Cruelty was present also, among other owners, and some slaves were badly ill-treated. But tenants and labourers were cheated, ill-treated and starved all over Ireland by that other brand of landlords and their factors and he had heard that things were no better in the mills and factories over the water in England. White or black, for poorer men, it was not a fair world. America was supposed to be a land of opportunity, cast in a different way from places like Ireland, but this opportunity did not extend to these black people, nor did it for many of the poorest white immigrants. But, in spite of it all, the idea of the chance to better one's self persisted, and this was maybe what made the difference between here and back home. Perhaps it was what made this place worth being in, and more important worth fighting for.

As for the war itself and his recruitment into the army of the south, that had been less to do with these things. It had been simpler than that. Georgia had become his home and it was the threat of invasion last year by Lincoln's call for troops to invade and occupy the south, that had prompted his own and most of the boys of the regiment's enlistment. But did defending Georgia really mean coming all the way here, to fight in Virginia, hundreds of miles from his home? Some men had refused to leave their own state, but, to Daniel, it was largely as Jacob Thornton, the second colonel of the regiment, who had died in the fighting around Richmond, in the summer, had stated. The fight for Georgia began here, where the Yankees invaded first, since, if Georgians simply sat idle while Virginia struggled alone and fell, then the Carolinas would be next and then the Yankees would be at Georgia's door and the whole south could fall like a succession of skittles, toppled one at a time by the invader. No, the southern states must stick together and fight as one, wherever the invader appeared, and if that was up here, then so be it.

Daniel's thoughts circulated as he sat and watched the river idling past in the moonlight. The decision to resist was an easy enough one to come to, but the fighting itself, when he had been confronted with it those weeks ago, had been a shocking ordeal of bloodshed and death. It had not been gallantry and triumph like the orators had promised and the Yankees had not buckled and fled, nor had they asked for terms. They had eventually been driven away from the southern capital, but at a huge cost in death and injury, and now the fighting was moving north with the Confederate army under the new leaders it had found, advancing to re-possess the portion of the state that the Yankees had taken in the spring. Perhaps one big battle and the war could indeed be ended with independence won. Daniel hoped so, he earnestly hoped so. At the final measurement, he was a volunteer, in the army until the war ended and victory was won and then he would be back to life in Eden Station, perhaps back to his store job with Hal and Martha Bennett.

But then there was Constance Warner, Constance...... , Daniel half-smiled as he thought of her and their walks together which had signified a kind of slow-moving courtship, until the war had come. She was lonely and bored now in Eden Station, so she had repeatedly told him in her letters, with almost all of the boys away and nobody left to flirt or gossip with. It was as though she thought that the war had been thought up as a means of inconveniencing her rather than being resorted to in deciding any greater issue. But she still wrote to him, as he did to her, though their letters were fewer now. Maybe, if this campaign was successful, it would not be too long before the fighting ended and home life could be resumed and Constance's loneliness and boredom could be ended.

But would it be Eden Station for him, or that other option, maybe more ambitious than any return to Georgia, of moving west and getting land of his own to farm, that he and his friend Fitzpatrick had talked of and tacitly agreed on? A dream, dependent as it was, for the time being at least, upon them both surviving this war, but closer to the substance of his reasons for leaving Ireland in the first place. The idea of such freedom and his own property could never be realised in Georgia. It would require the bolder step of casting loose and heading away from their adopted home, hazarding everything on the prospect of a better life somewhere else. Daniel was roused from his thoughts by a movement and he glanced over to where Fitzpatrick had stirred from his doze against the tree and looked around him, before pausing to listen to the sounds of the night. He glanced across at Daniel who held out a hand palm upwards to indicate that all was quiet. Fitzpatrick nodded but did not resume his doze as, over the trees behind them, the moon sank lower in the sky.

The Yankees, it seemed, had not deployed their men all along the river bank. Instead they had covered all of the bridges and the fords on this stretch of the river, placing strong forces of infantry and artillery at each, to command the crossings, while holding the remainder of their forces back from the Rappahannock. The following day, the army had established this when it had prodded and poked at some of these places with its own troops and guns without finding a weakness. Up and down the riverside, artillery duels had broken out with the guns thundering across at each other, sending their lethal discharges whistling through the thickets and ploughing up portions of the river banks. While this went on, the adjacent infantry crouched or lay under cover and waited for these exchanges to run their course and fade eventually into uneasy calms. But what all of this revealed was that the fords and crossings could not be used to transfer the army across the Rappahannock meantime and therefore things had reached a comparative stand off.

The men discussed this development. If the river could not be crossed in strength then the Yankees were secure over on the far bank, and they could sit there, supplied by the railroad and so the whole campaign would have reached an impasse. What was worse, camp rumour had it that McClellan had begun evacuating his huge union army, away from the James River near Richmond, up to northern Virginia by ship and, if they too came to the river line here, then the Army of Northern Virginia would be hopelessly outnumbered. There was clearly a pressing need to break this deadlock at the river and everyone was pretty sure of that. But, if they could not force a way across the Rappahannock and quickly get to grips with Pope's men, more and more of those other Yankees were on the way and the job of whipping them would steadily move away out of their reach. What was to be done? The men could talk all that they had a mind to around their fires, but the generals were the ones under real pressure. They it was who needed to come up with some kind of answer to the problem of the river and the sooner they did so the better.

Late in the day, orders came for those brigades of Longstreet's command to extend northwest along the river. It was known that Stonewall Jackson's men were over to their left and that other bridges and fords stretched on up the Rappahannock towards its junction with the Hazel River. Perhaps, the talk said, the general was extending his army's left, moving Jackson's men along the river to test each place in turn for a crossing, with Longstreet's divisions from downriver, taking over the picketing of the successive bridges and fords from Jackson's men as they headed away northwest. The camp of the previous night was hurriedly broken up and the long column of men headed off along the south western riverbank, while, at different points along the way the artillery duels continued. Maybe there would be a weak spot, or so some of the talk on the march went. Maybe old Stonewall was onto it and a lodgement could be made and the campaign resumed. It was better, Daniel Ryan concluded, as he lugged the heavier pan again, mollified, thanks to the later start, by the hope of a shorter march, to think this way. It was better to seek that vital weak spot, rather than to dwell on that other possibility, that their army would be held in check, here on the line of the upper

Rappahannock River, until the Yankees had gathered so many troops and guns that the whole thing would be hopeless.

They made camp at dusk near Norman's Ford, as the cannon fire died down, posting pickets down to the riverside and eating the last of the three days rations with no word of when the next issue might be. This was the southern part of the region which had been picked clean and pillaged by the Yankees. Things, the boys told each other, would be different from now on unless somehow the commissary could get the railroads organised and the destroyed bridges over the Rapidan River repaired so that they could do what they had not managed to do all spring and summer, supply the army adequately from the depots around Richmond. There was rumour also of a forward depot being set up at Orange Courthouse, but only time would tell whether the commissary had learned the lessons about supplying the troops from the disjointed earlier experiences down on the peninsula. The night was humid, even near the water, and to the left there was an outbreak of picket firing, that died away as full darkness fell. Maybe tomorrow they told each other as they settled to sleep. If there was a way, then tomorrow they would find it.

The Friday dawned, humid and hot again, with the march being resumed as the leading elements of other units came up to take their place near the ford. They moved off, heading upstream again as before, with their progress marked by the billowing clouds of dust. The morning stayed hot, with the only relief being the trees which shaded parts of the road and brought some relief from the glare of the sun, if not coolness to the sweat-soaked men. But as the day progressed, the weather began to change. The sky steadily clouded, with sultry yellow overcast gathering and by the middle of the afternoon it was dark and threatening with black thunderheads above. Seeing the signs, some of the men who had discarded their own blankets now left the ranks to forage for any that were still to be found at the roadside, but these were few and numbers of the marchers who were now lacking in these items took to eyeing the sky with some unease.

The storm broke in the late afternoon as the regiment neared Rappahannock Bridge where the Orange and Alexandria railroad crossed the river. Large drops of rain began to spatter the dust on the men's tunics and pants, bringing an initial feeling of cooling relief from the rain. But the downpour grew quickly heavier becoming so intense that, within minutes, the men were soaked and the roads were flooding, with mud quickly taking the place of dust as the marching trial. In the overcast of the storm, as the rain teemed down, the column was dismissed to bivouac in an already sodden field. Daniel, as was his custom, paired with Fitzpatrick to make a shelter from their two waterproof blankets, supported by their stoppered muskets, settling underneath on their elbows on the already wet ground. Daniel recalled Jeffers' words as he saw Daley, and others without blankets, huddling under the dripping trees at the edge of the field. Daley could be a damned fool, like he was doing over the three negroes, but he was in their mess and a friend for all of that, so Fitzpatrick waved him over.

"Are ye sure ye want to do it John," Daniel Ryan cautioned his friend, "when you think of the damned stink of him?" But it was too late, Mick was already on his way. He reached the shelter and pushed his way underneath between the two of them.

"This is fine of you boys," he told them, "I was getting' soaked sittin' over there with that crowd."

"Gods teeth Mick," Daniel Ryan told him, "stop shakin' your wet all over me or you'll be back over there with that crowd."

"If you take up all o' the space you'll be back out too," Fitzpatrick growled at him.

"Yeah," Daley protested, "I get the idea, this may be kind, but it's grudged." Daniel looked at him.

"If it was grudged, Mick, you'd still be over in the trees with the others."

"I'm glad I got out o' there," Daley told him. "Them three niggers are over there." Ryan and Fitzpatrick exchanged further glances at that.

"Why're you down on them three so much," Fitzpatrick asked him. "You've given them little peace since they got here."

"Sure if they'll fight, they're just as good around here as anybody else," Ryan added." Daley's sour expression, showed his disagreement.

"Ain't the way I see it," he growled. "Strikes me that them boys have notions way above their station comin' here. In this life, white men are number one and blacks are number two. That's the way it is and that's one o' the reasons for bein' here in the first place."

"What's wrong with them offerin' to fight," Ryan went on. "They might stop the bullet that you could've got." At that, Daley gave a deep and profound sigh.

"You two may have got some sort o' an education from the monks or whoever else back home," he said, "but you just don't get this do ye? Over here niggers are at the bottom of the pile in life, but see comin' a close second to that," he looked at them as though half-expecting an answer, "it's ourselves, the damned Irish. If the niggers weren't around then we'd get all o' the shit in this here free country instead o' just some of it, well us and the Dutch and the Italians and anybody else that ain't long arrived here. How often have ye heard people back in Georgia, and up here as well, blamin' whatever goes wrong, or whatever thievin' or law breakin' they hear about on us. You've heard them say it, the both o' ye. If there's a riot, or a brawl, or anythin' else, it's sure to be no account niggers or ignorant bog Irish that get the blame for it. It's no better than back in Ireland. Well, as far as I'm concerned, things are tough enough for the Irish over here, without uppity blacks startin' to muscle past us in the peckin' order o' life." They heard him out and there was a pause before any reply was made. When it came, it was from John Fitzpatrick.

"I know the things that happened in Ireland," he said, "and I came here because this was supposed to be a place where a man could improve himself by his own efforts. In spite of what you say, and I know that a lot of it is true, I still think that and look for that. I'm not fightin' here to keep blacks below us in life's peckin' order, as you put it. I'm fightin' because governments here get elected by people and when people in a state say we won't be governed by you any more, they've got a perfect right to do that without havin' their homes invaded and their property stolen or destroyed. By fightin' I earn the right to have a say and make my own way, without people pickin' on me because I'm Irish." He looked at his two companions. "Maybe those three blacks get to earn the same right by fightin'," he said, "and maybe that's what worries some o' the ignorant cusses around here who won't let them be."

"Ah John," Daley said. "The trouble with you is you're one o' those idealists." Daley said the word as though it was some sort of disease. "You don't live in the real world like the rest of us."

"I'll take my world over the one you were talkin' about any time Mick," Fitzpatrick retorted. At that, it was Ryan's turn to sigh,

"Typical Irish you two," he said. "You'd rather fight each other than anybody else." Silence ensued at that as, a few inches above their heads, the downpour hammered on the makeshift tent without let up.

In the darkness the storm intensified again, with the rain thundering down on the men's shelters and overwhelming any weak fires that had been coaxed into life under the trees. Rivulets, that quickly became torrents, ran across the meadow, flooding the lower parts of the ground until more and more of the men were under the trees. Overhead, lightning flashed, throwing the surroundings of the camp into vivid white relief, while the succeeding claps of thunder rolled in deafening peals. Among the huddling men, the talk went around of how all of this would inevitably make the river rise making it harder, rather than easier to cross, but to Daniel Ryan's mind the storm presented a much more immediate problem of flooded camps and soaked possessions.

Morning came and, though the intensity had slackened, still it rained. There were no rations and the men, few of whom had managed more than fleeting dozes in the storm, awaited orders, huddling in their saturated clothes under their tree or gum blanket shelters until, with the arrival of full daylight, the drum rolls roused the regiments to assemble. Around the camps they stirred themselves, helped by the shouts of the sergeants, gathering belongings into sodden blankets or glistening waterproofs and donning webbing belts. The ranks were quickly formed, a hurried roll call held and the orders of the day briefly read, before the column, without benefit of breakfast, was formed and moved off, heading northwest towards the railroad, on the quagmire roads, with the rain fading and at last ceasing.

By mid-morning the brigade had reached the railroad line, inland from the river. Towards the crossing, artillery fire had resumed, steadily increasing as noon approached. The men looked on as they approached in their soaked and steaming clothes, seeing little but the cannon smoke rising into the air in clouds above the trees nearer to the river. Was it the same old stalemate or could this be the crossing at last?

"Action today," Bradlee shouted as he came up. "Yore pieces better be dry in time."

"Some chance o' that," Daley told him. "Even if the muskets are dried, the damned ready cartridges in me pouch are stuck together."

The column was halted to await orders while, towards the river, the cannon fire intensified. Word passed along that others of their own division had already been deployed at the river and their own turn would come next. Still they waited until, in the now brightening afternoon, their own column was directed towards the Rappahannock by a flustered courier on a lathered, mud-spattered horse. They moved on, guiding on the railroad and hearing the cannon ever louder as they closed on the river. Finally, in the middle afternoon, they were deployed into line at the edge of a wood looking out across open fields towards the railroad crossing. Ahead of them, just visible among the trees, were other ranks of grey infantry, men pulling back from the bridge, while shot and shell swept over them.

From the crossing itself, smoke was rising, not the dirty off-white smoke of gunfire but the darker smoke of something burning. It was the bridge, the boys told each other. It had to be the bridge. One only had to let one's eye follow the railroad tracks towards the river to see that they headed straight towards the rising cloud. Even as the men watched and waited to be sent forward, that rising column of smoke grew, with traces of flame becoming visible from where the structure itself must be. The ranks were halted and the brigade stood and watched as the distant bridge burned in its shroud of smoke and crackling flames with the noise of collapsing trestles and supports occasionally audible through the continuing surges of gunfire.

There was nothing to be done about the bridge. It continued to burn under its cloud of smoke and rising steam. There would be no crossing here unless they were all to wade. The men waited, while the generals had some further thoughts, until the long ranks were eventually pulled back and stood down, as the lingering pall of smoke from the wrecked bridge still rose and drifted in the sky. Shortly after, the column was reformed and headed away, again northwest, on still muddy roads, as the evening approached, making their way towards the next crossing this one at a place named Beverley's Ford. In the dusk they were halted, short of the ford, and with fires being permitted for the first time since reaching the river line, a small ration of beef, gleaned, it was said, from abandoned Yankee camps on this side of the river, was issued, which the men quickly cooked and greedily devoured. Blankets were set out to air and dry and the boys relaxed briefly before turning in. The initial talk in camp largely reflected a growing sense of exasperation. Getting at these particular Yankees was proving to be a complicated and tedious business and this subject was aired for a while, until, almost predictably, the baiting of the three black recruits resumed, though, as it had since Thompson's intervention, it stayed at the level of comment and jibe rather than anything more direct.

As the camp began to settle, Eli Winder detached himself from his two companions and made for the bushes. As he returned, John Fitzpatrick accosted him.

"Don't pay too much heed to all o' that camp talk," he told him. Winder stopped and looked at him.

"No," he said simply?

"Most o' them are good boys," Fitzpatrick went on. "Once you boys have shown them what you're made of, like when we get in a fight, they'll come around, you'll see." Winder listened.

"Yeah," he drawled. "Reckon I will."

"Just give 'em some time," Fitzpatrick finished and Winder nodded and moved away. Likely he wasn't too convinced, Daniel Ryan thought as he watched him go, but then neither was he either. He shook his head gently. Sure most men would be accepted if they proved their courage and dependability, but this might be very different from that, and Fitzpatrick should see that as well as anybody else. Even if most men were prepared to accept these newcomers, if they made good enough soldiers, there were others, whose dislike of them went down a lot deeper, into the darker regions of men's souls, and Fitzpatrick should have known that too. Daniel sighed, maybe Mick Daley was right about some things. Maybe the idealistic

John Fitzpatrick did, at least in some ways, live in a different world from the rest of them.

The Sunday was distinguished by a brief service, officiated over by a local preacher that took place, after the men had paraded for roll call and orders. They were to march again, northwest once more, this time towards the village of Jeffersonton, to relieve Jackson's men who would sidle further on, to try still more of the upstream fords. A ration of flour and beef had arrived and, following the brief sermon and prayer, this was distributed though with no time allowed to cook and eat, it was packed into haversacks as the column of march was called. The weather had settled again and the marching column formed in the light of an ascending sun. Then the setting off was delayed by congested roads, but the flour and beef stayed in haversacks and the men were kept in their files as they waited to march. Many grumbled as they stood around about how, without the preacher, there would have been time for breakfast, reckoning that, to soldiers, breakfast came first and divine worship second. Others disputed this, but as Daniel Ryan listened to these wrangles, he reflected that at least the three black boys were getting a break.

At last they moved off, with the dust mercifully absent from the still wet roads, but delays continued to bedevil progress, with flurries of activity followed by periods of bewildering waiting. Still the guns rumbled along the river, but Benning's men remained obstinately on the roads, always seeming to be just upstream or just downstream of where the action was taking place. The day passed in this way until, late in the afternoon, they were directed to camp, short of Jeffersonton but with ample time to build fires and cook. The rations re-appeared, and, with wood gathered and water canteens replenished from streams and creeks, fires were quickly kindled. Soon the smell of cooking beef filled the air. Kane chopped their pooled mess ration and added flour and water dumplings seasoned from his herb bag. The boys of the mess gathered to eat, hungrily devouring the mix, before a spell on the picket line occupied Daniel's section into the night. But at least, he ruminated, there had been no further confrontations between the messes, nor had there been any further baiting of the three negroes, beyond a few sarcastic remarks or jokes at their expense. It was as though there was something resembling a truce in operation in the company, for the meantime at least, and, as far as it went, Daniel Ryan was glad of it.

Monday dawned clear and bright and the company duly paraded for orders, which were read to them by Rodger. It was northwest again, the mixture as before, to Jeffersonton initially and then the good lord would know where. In the growing heat, canteens were filled, but no further rations were issued, nor was there time to cook any that might remain. Out onto the road they formed their files, Daniel, with the smaller pan hanging from his belt on its hooked handle. Many men chewed on whatever chunks of cold meat or bread that they had left, thankfully still spared the cloud of dust on the drying, hardening surfaces. But hardly had they moved off when there came the sound of galloping hooves behind them. The faces squinted around to see a single rider, coming up the column, visible only as an obscure shape above the marching men and the forest of shouldered, moving muskets, for the order to march at ease had not yet been given. The horseman came quickly up, coming into clearer view round the curve of the column on the road, waving and calling as he came.

"Make way, boys," he yelled. "Move over and make way." The call was quickly taken up by their own officers and sergeants as the rider passed on along the column. The men behind him shuffled across to the side of the road, as a heavier thunder of hooves and the sounds of cheering grew from down that road behind them, heralding the approach of more riders. The heads turned again, squinting into the low sun as the group came on, vague shapes also above the swaying, gleaming forest of musket barrels, near enough now for the figure in front to gain shape and form as he came into full view.

"That's old Pete," Gibben shouted and the shout was taken up all along the column. Longstreet was a burly man who sat a big brown horse and he swung into view, with his grey coat buttoned up, in spite of the heat, and his wide-brimmed hat pulled down firmly on his head. His beard was long and it spread down over his collar towards the chest of his coat as he approached at a steady canter. The shouts and cheers moved with him as he passed the waiting infantrymen and the ground now thundered and trembled with the pounding of horses' hooves. He was close now, his big horse seeming to tower over them as they watched him come and now he was here, only yards away and the cheering was loud and tumultuous. Daniel Ryan watched the fragments of the drying dirt of the road being kicked into the air by the horses, to spatter over the nearby men. Then the general raised a gauntleted hand in acknowledgement of the cheering, and his teeth showed in his beard as he shouted to the men.

"Save your breath boys," he called as he drew level with where Company B were still arranging themselves and their weapons along the roadside. "You got a long day ahead and you'll need it." But the men ignored his words, raising hats from their heads and waving them in the air, as the big man thundered past, followed, at a few yards distance, by his staff, with the general's headquarters flag, carried by a sergeant, fluttering along behind. The ground below the waiting men's feet still shook, as the cavalcade cantered away with harness jingling and creaking and the occasional snort from one of the horses. Daniel looked on after the general had passed, getting a glimpse of the determined set of his broad shoulders before the riders of his staff following behind him, obstructed the view and the continuing curve of the road ahead began to swallow them all up again, their progress now indicated only by the cheers of the unseen men up ahead and the fading thunder of the hooves.

"That man surely looks like he means business," Kane called, as the sergeants began waving their men back onto the dirt road where the tracks of the horses lay fresh. They moved back into files and waited for the column up ahead to move off. There was something about what they had just seen, Daniel Ryan thought. Longstreet's manner was always business. There was no show and posturing about him, for he was decidedly not like other officers, like Jeb Stuart of the cavalry, who enjoyed the acclaim of the men and seemed to seek out that sort of thing. It was as though, having seen "Old Pete" pass, and having heard his words, the boys in the plodding infantry could sense that something was afoot, and all of this marching up along the river bank was not just a matter of chance. As though to confirm his thoughts, as the column shuffled into movement again, from the direction of the river, cannon fire began again, with smoke soon rising above the trees closer to the waterside to indicate the place.

Longstreet had been right. It was another trying day of marching in the sticky heat with clothes growing quickly damp and sweat patches spreading under armpits, around necks and down the backs of tunics. Water soon ran out and replenishment was inadequate from poor streams and worked out wells. The day's march took them on to the north west, past Sulphur Springs, where Jackson was reputed to have gotten a part of his outfit stranded on the far side of the river by Saturday's floods, almost getting it overwhelmed by the Yankees. Their own men did not pause there, heading still further upstream, till by late afternoon, they were coming up towards another crossing place which some men were calling Waterloo Bridge. At every ford and crossing, the cannon still exchanged salvoes of fire and these duels periodically swelled up into sizeable and mean little fights before fading again into more measured exchanges.

At Waterloo Bridge, they took over the camp site of some of Jackson's men. They had gone again, heading on along the riverside, ever further upstream. The men of the Ogeechee Volunteers made camp, with men immediately out to look for water and wood. Today it had been noticeable that still more worn out shoes lay discarded by the roadside, lying in fragments in their ones and twos along the way, indicating that, for the units up ahead also, the familiar problem of barefooted soldiers was again getting worse. It could be seen in their own column. Barefooted men, or those who marched with their feet wrapped in makeshift protection, were slowly but steadily increasing in number. Daniel had seen numbers of shoeless men down on the peninsula in the summer, but this was the closest to home that the problem had yet come. Somehow this army could not seem to supply its soldiers with shoes of even the most rudimentary kind. Whatever footwear men could obtain, did not seem to last in this hard, campaigning season, with leather wearing through all too quickly, and, even more often, the stitching, which joined soles to uppers, giving way. Some boys tried to repair shoes, fitting or stuffing insoles of leather, or whatever else came to hand, inside them or attempting to re-stitch seams. But threads and twines, and the leather edges themselves, rotted steadily with the wettings from creeks and the continuous damp of sweating feet. So the sad truth for shoes, was that unless and until they could be replaced, one had pretty well to do without, wrapping the feet in whatever could be procured and adapted, or in the case of some of the farm boys, to whom shoes had been an unfamiliar departure from home practice, simply get on with their soldiering with toes sticking out.

Clothing, ragged from the start of the campaign, was wearing out too and rotted belts and other straps, on haversacks or water bottles, were being replaced by rawhide thongs or pieces of rope or even string. The camps were now home to increasingly ragged and unkempt men, with companies more and more resembling collections of tramps. There was little sign of the sorely inadequate quartermasters being able to do anything much with the job of trying to supply the many items in chronic shortage in an army which now marched further and further away from its depots and supply sources. Everyone knew that in the army, wagon priority went to ammunition first, ambulances next, commissary next and quartermaster last so there was least chance of all of replacement clothing arriving in their camps while on campaign, since what the army had failed to achieve around Richmond in the spring and earlier summer, it would be unlikely to manage over the greater distances to be covered now. Thus, the men foraged, stripped the dead or adopted makeshift remedies, while waiting for the next "brawl" with the Yankees as the best chance of re-supplying themselves.

That evening, in the absence of any of the wagon train keeping pace on the congested and still drying roads, there was again no rations issue. The men foraged around the fields and farms in the locality, Gibben getting a little pork belly from a sympathetic farmer to put with the corn flour parched from cobs taken from his requisitioned field on their way back. It was little enough, though Kane turned it into passable quality, if not quantity, with his usual competence. Close by, the three blacks contented themselves with roasted ears at their own fire, conversing in low mutters as they consumed them. As full darkness came, Bradlee arrived and took them off for their first session of picket duty, eliminating, at a stroke, the jibes and jokes at their expense. Down on the river, the grumbling artillery duels having died down with the coming of night, the off-duty men stretched out, on the grass, or on blankets if they had them, and slept.

Chapter 3
Breaking the Deadlock

The Tuesday brought no further marching orders. Instead the regiments of the brigade waited in their camps, performing their periods of duty along the river, their attention mostly directed downriver towards the crossing where, with the sunrise, the artillery fire had begun again. It was a welcome break in the marching pattern of recent days, especially since it was once again showing every sign of being a steaming hot day. With time off duty to spend, some men tried to wash, either themselves, their clothing or even both, using side creeks or the quieter portions of the river, away from the contentious crossing places, but mindful of the lurking menace of sharpshooters along other sections of the bank. In the camps, while some men slept others got down to some darning and repairing as the latest rumours began to circulate, first and foremost about General Thomas "Stonewall" Jackson.

For days the army had been shifting to its left, upstream, seeking a place, be it a ford or a bridge, where it could get enough men across to mount a serious attack on the Yankees. So far, this tactic had been unsuccessful, with the enemy defending every crossing place strongly with guns and infantry. The only time Jackson had found an unguarded crossing place at the weekend the rising waters from that storm had isolated, and almost brought disaster to the men sent across. But now the talk in camp was different for although they had again relieved Jackson's men the previous afternoon, at Waterloo Bridge, assuming that they would head upstream for the next crossing place, they were mistaken. Jackson had indeed gone, but not a few miles upriver this time, instead he was off altogether, heading, with three divisions of infantry, away up the river, well beyond the enemy flank, up into the mountains towards Amissville, aiming to get far enough past the enemy outposts for an unopposed crossing, where the river wasn't much of a barrier anyway. This was not, so the stories said, just to get to grips with the Yankees, but to march right around their right flank, get into their rear and cut the Orange and Alexandria railroad which supplied them. Doing this would force the whole of John Pope's army out of their river positions, compelling them to retreat towards Washington, to restore their fractured supply line, and maybe just opening them up for a real whipping on the way.

But would there still be time for this? McClellan's huge Yankee army, returning by stages from the banks of the James River, would reinforce Pope's men most likely. If all of them came here to the Virginian piedmont then the southern army would be outnumbered by more than two to one and any advance northwards would be hopeless. No, the opportunity for success depended on being able to strike at Pope's army while McClellan's host was still in transit and out of the fight. This would be a week or two at most, maybe less than that. But being stymied here on the rivers had already spent some of that time and nobody knew how much was left before the Army of the Potomac units began arriving, to gradually change the whole complexion of the campaign here. By reading the newspapers of both sides, it could be deduced that Pope and Lee, at the outset, had commanded similar numbers of troops, but what was Lee playing at if these latest stories about Jackson were true? He had in effect divided his army into two halves in order to send Jackson off around the Yankee flank. If this was true, the general was taking an incredible risk. He was giving Pope the chance to hold part of the Army of Northern Virginia off with part of his force, while he destroyed the other part with most of his troops.

The camps and positions were alive with the stories and with everybody's views about them. The whole thing got a good going over in Daniel Ryan's mess of Company B. Some scoffed that the rumours and stories must be wrong, while others reckoned that, if they were true, the "old man," must have lost his mind. He had taken risks in June by concentrating most of the army on the north side of the Chickahominy River near Richmond in preparation for his attack. He had just about gotten away with it back then, but surely nobody, not even this Yankee blowhard Pope, would be so dumb as to fall for such a strategy again. It must fail, at least the pessimists said that it must. The Yankee generals would see through it and they could not be fooled a second time. The men argued about it all, but growing in the talk was an increasing respect for this man Lee. Why, if he had done this he must have a stronger nerve than any saloon gambler. Thompson, who did not always join in such gossip, spoke up for the general.

"I reckon he's done it the only way he could if'n he wants to win," he told them.

"Win?" Daley was scathing. "He'll get nothin' better than a lickin' for us all and if old Jack don't come out o' the hole he went in, we could be back down in the steamin' heat at Richmond with our backs to the damn town again."

"I reckon, that if we'd jest gone on sittin' on the river here, that would ha' happened anyways once McClellan's boys showed up," Thompson retorted, "this way we maybe get the chance to lick Pope's army afore the rest o' them Yankees git here."

"At least we'd a' had the whole army here to face 'em," was Daley's response. Daniel Ryan said little, leaving others to side with Thompson or Daley as they saw fit. But his mind was agog with what was apparently happening. That calm and dignified old man, whom they had seen down in Georgia at the start of the year and again in Richmond in the summer, seemed, in reality to be a preposterous gambler, taking such colossal chances with his men's lives, "to win," as Joe had said. If it was all true, it was risky to an extent that hardly bore thinking about.

Down on the river the guns continued to thunder around the crossings, but, in the late afternoon, these duels were forgotten as the commissary wagons came creaking around to halt and prepare for a rations issue. The men assembled, with Jeffers overseeing, as a supply of salt pork and flour was issued. The issue of food had gotten the boys attention back to their bellies and less concerned about the general's state of mind. With fires mercifully allowed, work began immediately in each mess on cooking and eating, with plate licking concluding the exercise. Thereafter, in Daniel Ryan's mess, it was business as before and back to grand strategy, with each having his say. Admiration for the old man's backbone was widespread, even if grudgingly so among those who doubted the wisdom of this latest move. Night came, with a spell of picket duty just before first light, but, so far at least, no word of a further move.

The commissary wagons, who had managed to come around less than one day in two since arriving on the Rappahannock line, staggered everyone by appearing again the following day. The rumours were now of a march, but there was nothing about it in the orders of the day after dawn and the morning was drifting on with only the renewed cannon exchanges on the river to speak of. But near noon, the wagons arrived and what passed for a three day ration was distributed, to be cooked and packed away, with the men ordered to be ready to march at four that afternoon. This, for most of those in the camps, was good news. If men had to march in this kind of summer heat, then starting late in the afternoon, thereby avoiding the worst of the day's warmth, was just about the best arrangement one could have for it. The camps reeked of frying bacon, with many of the men consuming a good portion of it immediately, saving on what would have to be carried and satisfying one's appetite also. Canteens were filled and equipment gathered and arranged and pretty well on time the files were formed and moved off. The sun, although descending, was still hot and setting out late in the day also did nothing to help the dust, which was rising again from the now dried roads and soon the column of shuffling, sweating men was obscured in its tormenting gloom.

They made first for Amissville and from there turned north to cross the upper Rappahannock by the ford at Hinson's Mill. This time again, the men were allowed to break ranks, remove shoes and socks and even their pants before making the crossing. The water was refreshing and boys splashed handfuls of it into their faces, wetting cloths or handkerchiefs to rub round their necks and then topping up canteens before they reached the steeper far bank, where pants and footwear were replaced. Past the sodden approach they slithered on a steep incline away from the river before reaching a more level stretch of the road as the sun sank.

On the column pushed, with any cooling benefit from the river quickly spent on the laboured climb. Into the evening, with sunset approaching, and still the march continued. The pace was steady, but not forced and hour halts were observed and while the needy headed for the bushes, others took the chance to relax and stretch out for a few minutes, take a drink or maybe use a further draught of precious water to rinse the cloying dust from the face and neck. They moved on as the sun sank, passing through a little village named Orleans, so the locals, who came to the roadside to clap and cheer, told them. There was more water and, for some of Company B, sweet cornbread scones, given out by a beaming little woman at the far end of the sequence of houses.

"Ain't it great," she told her companion, who helped her with the distributing? "Ain't it fine to have our own southern boys back around here?"

"A good wash and some better clothes would surely benefit the poor dirty darlin's," was the other woman's reply. The boys grinned and agreed, keeping their eyes on the scones.

The heat had eased and the evening air was soft as the great red orb of the sun finally disappeared behind the wooded hills on the horizon to the west. With the dust excepted, the march had not been too trying, especially since up here, the locals, as they had at Orleans, made a point of coming to the roadside to see the troops go by. They cheered and clapped in their little groups, and, better still, brought more buckets of fresh water or even some additional morsels of food for the passing men. Further on, as the afterglow began to fade, the column crossed the headwaters of the Hedgeman River to push on still further as the light faded and the horizon slowly merged into the twilight.

With the late start and the less trying marching conditions, more talk went up and down the ranks. The customary jokes and wisecracks that enlivened all but the most gruelling tramps along with the whistles and compliments to any member of the female gender at the roadside below sixty, moved up and down the files, but now too there were the beginnings of hints as to where they were heading.

"It's Salem," so the talk went along the column though the name meant little to Daniel Ryan. "Up on the Manassas Gap Railroad, that'll be the way old Jack's boys went, then east, so we'll be headin fer Gainesville and maybe Manassas." The name perked the men up. The scene of the war's first major battle, and a celebrated southern victory, seemed a good place to be going. They were coming full circle, after all the events

64

of the spring and summer. Maybe, some said, there really was something symbolic or ordained about it all..

"It's fate, I tell ya," Saul Philipps said again and again. "No better place to give 'em their last lickin'."

The march took them on for almost a further half hour through the growing darkness, before they were directed off the road to bivouac anywhere they could find space among the already settled crowds of men.

Their column was shepherded on beyond the camps to be dismissed in a ploughed field farther from the road.

"No fires," Bradlee told them, "the scouts reckon thar's Yankee cavalry around over thar t' the east."

There was discontented muttering about that, but this got rather worse when it emerged that the field they had arrived in had been recently manured. The angry boys picked around, trying to clear spaces for blankets to be laid and, soiled and smelly, thereby attracting every kind of marauding insect, they laid themselves down. Most of the boys settled for making the best of the predicament, passing a collection of jokes around about how the manure got there and eating a cold portion of their carried ration before turning in.

The sun had risen when the camps were roused, but there seemed to be no great element of haste in the preparations to move out. After parading for orders of the day, fires were lit, breakfast was warmed and eaten and only after this was done were belongings gathered and marching files formed. The column got going, still heading north, but with many more halts and delays today since the road was choked with wagon traffic. They moved on in the growing heat and dust, reaching Salem, where local people once more lined the road to clap and wave handkerchiefs, passing out water or even buttermilk to the grateful troops. At Salem, the stories and rumours were confirmed, with the column turning to the east, leaving no doubt that the plains of Manassas and the rear of John Pope's

Yankee army was the destination. Up ahead, as they emerged from the stretches of forest, which flanked the road, now rose the successive bulks of Pig Nut Mountain, with further away, the Bull Run range, vast and forested, filling up the landscape towards the horizon over to the right of the road. Here too was a railroad, the Manassas Gap line, derelict and overgrown with weeds, running parallel with the road, west to the Shenandoah Valley and east up into the Bull Run range, stretching on beyond to where the flatter land of Northern Virginia opened out towards the Potomac River.

Just east of the village curiosity was aroused by the sound of cheering from up ahead, being taken up by successive passing formations. On hearing the sounds draw closer, the men were alerted, craning their necks, as they approached, to see the cause.

"It's Marse Bob," the shouts went up among a sudden forest of waving hats that obstructed much of the view forward. Grubby fingers pointed to where the general sat, with his staff behind him, in a meadow, over to the left of the road, just far enough away to avoid the worst of the dust cloud. The men roared, joining in the acclaim of those in front, as their own files closed on the place where the Lee sat his horse, occasionally doffing his own hat to the passing men. Company B hats were snatched from their owners' heads and waved furiously in their turn, getting the same acknowledgement from the general, who raised his own felt hat as they drew level. He was greying still more, Daniel Ryan thought, on catching a glimpse of the general's head as he passed on, replacing his own hat, but still straining his eyes back towards where the cluster of officers sat on their little hillock of grass.

Shortly after this encounter with the general, the column was called to a halt as, over to the southeast, there came the sound of firing. It was fairly distant, with a suggestion of smoke rising into the air above the mixture of trees and meadows that stretched towards the lower slopes of the distant mountains. The clutter of men, wagons and guns waited on the road. Horses and mules near enough to the verges, moved and stretched to crop at any remains of greener grass there, while the men looked for shade, breaking ranks to rest in any sheltered places they could find by the side of the road. Some even sidled quietly off to seek water or beg food at any nearby farms, while their less enterprising comrades lounged in the long grass under the trees. Presently word began to filter, from group to group, back along the road.

It was cavalry, the message reached them, and the old man wanted them cleared out of the way before going on. The troops, not involved stayed where they were beside the road, content enough to rest and relax in the rising heat and humidity of the coming middle of the day. Daley and Gibben went to seek water, returning about twenty minutes later with canteens full. Daniel took a large mouthful from his returned canteen, finding that there was an earthy taste to it but it was comparatively cool and that was welcome to boys who reckoned that the biggest trials of the day's heat would still be to come.

Near noon they were moving again, heading southeast, making for the hamlet of White Plains to camp just short of the village, surprisingly early, in the middle part of the afternoon. It had been an uncommonly short marching day, easier than expected, in spite of the starting and stopping and the inevitable dust. There was plenty of time to look for water and firewood, before breaking out what remained of the three days rations from Waterloo Bridge. Daniel Ryan promptly set out on a further foraging expedition with Otis Ballard, trusting that their early camp from a place near the head of the column could get them to a source of food before the volume of men from the following brigades arrived to swamp every option. They followed a track that wound into the trees, encouraged to continue by the smell of wood smoke in their nostrils and on reaching the far edge of the wood, they found themselves looking out across a wide meadow to where a small farm stood about half a mile further away along the track. They made their way along the trail, until, on reaching the top of a small dip down to the yard, they saw a group of female figures, in straw hats, skirts and aprons, working down there on the lane that led up to the house. They exchanged glances before resuming their approach, to enter the lane and head up towards the house and the group, who had ceased working to watch them come up. They moved up the lane warily, squinting, as they approached at the watching women, one more mature and two younger ones, one of the latter with a small child fussing at her heels. Ballard raised an arm and waved to them, but there was nothing in return. They had been working on the paddock fence down in the dip in front of the house and the older woman stood upright, as they drew near, removing her straw hat to wipe her brow.

"We wouldn't have to fix it so much lately if your boys would leave a few o' the rails," she told them. Ballard removed his own hat and nodded gravely to her.

"That'll be Jackson's boys," he assured her, shaking his head slowly to show his disapproval. "Why ma'am, it's a known fact that all o' the light-fingered bummers and fence rail stealers in the army was collected together into Jackson's outfit, so's that he, good, god fearin' Christian that he is, could spend his time convertin' 'em all into better habits." On reaching where the women stood, he gestured to Daniel and then towards where a few boughs of timber lay together with an axe, mallet and pegs for splitting them.

"And what outfit are you boys from," the woman asked, staring straight into his face?

"Why we're "Old Pete's" boys," Ballard answered, bowing towards her. "The mannerly, good-livin' part o' the Army o' Northern Virginia wuz all put under "Old Pete," Longstreet."

"You sure don't talk like no folks from around here," one of the younger women said, getting a scowl of reproach from the older woman for her pains.

"No ma'am," Daniel Ryan said, "we're from down in Georgia." Ballard gave them all another expansive smile.

"Bulloch 'n' Bryan Counties," he said. "That's jest a short step from the fine ol' city o' Savannah."

Their looks did not change with this announcement, maybe suggesting, Daniel thought, that the news of Savannah's charms and graces had likely not reached this far into rural Virginia, but, for all that, the old woman was perfectly willing to continue the discussion.

"I'm supposin' that you boys, all the way from Georgia, are here fer the same reason as all o' them others that come by," she said, re-establishing her previous dominance of the conversation.

"Why ma'am," Ballard said in his exaggerated drawl, "we Georgia boys only come by fer a sip o' fresh water outa yore well, but we'd be happy to help you folks fix yore fence and we'd sure appreciate a bite o' vittles if ya could spare any." He stepped over and lifted the axe before nodding to Daniel, who arranged one of the boughs over the wooden block, steadying the lower end with his foot for Ballard to start the split. He swung the axe and unerringly centred his blow on the bough. As the blade struck, Daniel felt his brogan move with a jolt. They lifted the other tools and began to hammer, using the pegs to steadily split the bough down its length for use. The job done in minutes, they repeated the process on a further bough, then another while the women watched and the child sucked its hand, half-hiding behind its mother's skirt, as it eyed the two newcomers.

The splitting done the rails were slipped into place and they turned back to the three women to find that, not too surprisingly, the older one was not the least bit taken in.

"We're obliged to ya both," she said. Ballard opened his mouth to speak, but she raised her hand to silence him.

"I suppose you Georgia boys ain't had nothin' wholesome t' eat fer weeks, like all the rest o' them Dixie boys that's come through here," she said. Ballard grinned at her, and Daniel Ryan noticed the hint of a kindly expression cross her features.

"Our menfolk's in Powell Hill's division," she said, "Charlie Field's brigade, that's Stonewall Jackson's boys," she added proudly, pointing an accusing finger into Ballard's face and then, after her moment of challenge, she relented and gestured them both towards the kitchen window.

"They was through here Tuesday and they're hale, a mite thin, like you boys are, but healthy. They didn't do no light fingered bummin' or fence rail stealin' but they're in one piece and the good lord's t' be thanked fer that." She started towards the house, pausing briefly to allow herself one more admonition.

"Y'ain't bringin' none o' yore critters in the house," she snapped. "They didn't, so you surely ain't."

The younger women, save for the one observation about accents, had stayed quiet, contenting themselves with exchanging whispers and sniggers as the performance was carried forward, principally by Ballard and the older woman who continued their exchanges as the whole party moved towards the house.

The rail splitting yielded the legs and wings of a chicken, thick with their grease, some hoe cakes, which they wrapped in a cloth, some beans, and, for good measure, an egg for each of them. Daniel's eyes widened as the old woman pushed it into his hand before turning to Ballard. They thanked them all elaborately, especially for the eggs. The older woman now seemed almost embarrassed.

"You boys can help yoreselves to what's left in the orchard yonder," she called as they took their leave. Daniel Ryan said nothing, having, on their way in, noticed that the trees had been stripped of all but their damaged fruit, presumably by more of Jackson's men.

They ate a chicken wing each on the way back to the bivouac, licking greedily at the grease on their fingers when the meat was gone, but even so, the provisions from the farm turned the evening meal into a comparative feast in their mess, with all eight of them getting a goodly portion of the stew that Isaac Kane concocted from it all, while they exchanged the latest rumours. Daniel, noticed that Ballard had kept his egg in his haversack, and he did likewise. It would be a fine treat for breakfast, he thought. Feeding done, the camp turned in early, wearied enough by the march and the energy-sapping heat of the day. Tomorrow, if the camp stories were true, would bring them to the mountains and the gap, which they would need to use, and maybe fight for, if they were to reach the plain beyond and link up with Jackson's men there.

It was after licking his plate clean that Daniel pulled off his right brogan. Since Ballard's blow on the log with the axe, it had felt different and, sure enough, when he examined it, the stitched edge had begun to pull away from the sole, part of the way along the side. All those wettings and dryings, as well as the relentless day to day wear on the leather had taken its course. With his thick woollen socks on his feet, the problem was not yet pressing, but, with the leather itself pulling apart, there was little that could be done in the way of repair, so the situation with the shoe would only get worse and where the right shoe led, he mused, the left would likely soon follow.

The men were roused in daylight the following day, Thursday, if Daniel Ryan's recollection was correct, to parade for a brief inspection, roll call and orders. It was on to the southeast again, through the mountains to join up with

Jackson's men as the rumours had already told them. Today their division would lead the march. This was better news, as, up at the front of the column, there would be less dust and hardly any horse and mule mess to trample through and with such thoughts in their minds, and on their lips, the men dismissed to breakfast and preparation.

There was only a reduced portion of leftover food to serve as breakfast, but as Kane dished what there was from the pans onto the plates, Ballard and Daniel produced their eggs, breaking them into the remaining grease in one of the just emptied hot pans to see them sizzle and form. The others gathered to look on in envy, as the eggs began to cook and spit.

"I ain't had eggs in months," Daley, said ruefully, "likely even longer'n that."

"Ya ain't gittin' that one neither," Ballard snapped at him. The others said nothing, instead contenting themselves with standing or squatting there around the fire, looking at the pan and the bright yellow yolks that stood out prominently in their white surrounds, as they continued to spit and sizzle. Then Thompson broke the silence.

"Nossir, ain't hardly heard o' no eggs in a long time." Daniel Ryan looked across at Otis Ballard, who at first did not seem to see him, concentrating as he was on flicking some of the remaining pan fat over the eggs with his spoon. Daniel kept his gaze on his friend as the others still waited.

"When's the last time you had egg," Thompson asked Kane?

"I can't hardly remember as far back as that," Kane replied, as he went on eyeing the pan. "It sure was a long time ago, a real long time."

"I never had any eggs this year," Gibben said, "ain't had eggs since last Christmas, maybe even afore that." Ballard at last lifted his eyes.

"Well ya kin all take yore goddam greedy eyes off a my egg," he snapped, "and quit tryin' ta talk yore way onto my plate."

"Boys that mess together share things," Fitzpatrick said, and got a withering glower in return for this observation. At that the onlookers restricted themselves to hunching around the fire to continue contemplating the pan where the two sizzling eggs completed their cooking.

Ballard persisted in his sourness for the few seconds more that saw the two eggs chased around the pan a little by knife and spoon before they were captured and, in due course, dished onto Daniel's and his own respective plates. Daniel watched him, knowing, by his mannerisms, that he was relenting.

"Four of us sittin' around eatin' one damned egg," Ballard rapped, "ain't worth takin' time over, ain't hardly enough for a taste." He started to cut at his own egg, dividing it into rough quarters.

"I must be gettin' soft in the head," he muttered, upon which Daniel Ryan elbowed him in the ribs.

"Hold right there," he growled. "Who said anybody's gettin' a share of my egg?" Ballard dropped his plate and made a grab for Daniel's, but was a fraction late as it swung out of his reach, while the others guffawed with laughter.

It was a taste, but little more than that and it disappeared quickly, gobbled down along with the amount of leftovers that each of them got, but somehow the tiny portion of yolk and white that they were able to savour made the breakfast a little more memorable than usual. The plates were licked with extra thoroughness just as the call came from Jeffers to assemble.

"That's the way," Daley said, "startin' the day with eggs."

"What you had wouldn't start no mouse's day," Gibben told him as they moved to gather their belongings.

Out on the road, the files formed into column and the men stepped off, reverting within minutes to marching at ease. The road now wound upwards, but not steadily, undulating instead into the lower slopes of the Bull Run Mountains. Longer stretches of the way were lined with swathes of forest, creating welcome shade for the labouring men in the ranks, but seeming to confine the dust in even denser clouds around them. Through the morning there were further signs of Yankees. Faint rattles of gunfire occasionally rang out, over towards the mountains which now stretched away up ahead, with glimpses visible when the screen of trees thinned or broke. Details of infantry had been dispatched to ward these intruders off, but this time on the road, the column of toiling men and lumbering vehicles made their way southeast without further pause.

As noon approached, more sporadic outbreaks of gunfire, closer at hand this time, brought the progress briefly to a halt and companies of Anderson's lead brigade were dispatched to push these latest horsemen away before the march was resumed.

"It's all Lee's fault," said the rumours, "all o' our cavalry's bin sent to join Jackson," though this was already common knowledge. There had been no sign of horsemen along the column so their customary job of screening the march now had to be done by the sweating, swearing infantry, a tedious thankless job since men with horses could simply mount up and ride off before the approaching boys on foot could ever come to grips with them.

"Ain't nobody gets everythin' right," the boys told each other, "not even Marse Robert." Others nodded at all of this talk, but it was clear that if anybody in the Yankee army was at all interested, they now had exact information as to the whereabouts of Longstreet's men with all that this could mean.

"They could stop us cold," so the talk went. "A damn division could block the pass up thar fer days, its so goddam narrow. Thar ain't hardly room fer the road, let alone the railroad, and the creek that go through the place. It could all be a goddam trap fer the first boys goin' through." All along the files, men heard the dark predictions, but most of them said nothing.

Once again, the day was clear and hot with only the tiniest of fleecy clouds in the sky. Up ahead now the road was still rising, not steeply, but winding gradually upwards into the mountains, with the horizon line and its undulations extending in a continuing barrier from the south to the east, and on northwards, squarely across the path of the toiling column of shuffling men and creaking vehicles. The way grew steeper as they advanced, with the line of the mountains now a higher horizon in front of them, but, by the early afternoon hour halt, when the dust thinned and subsided, there was a definite pass to be seen, a dip in the face of the mountains towards which the road extended. This, so the talk said, was the pass, the gateway to the plain beyond; that flatter land that stretched away towards the Potomac River. If the Yankees wanted to stop them reaching that plain, and linking up with Jackson, then this, so it was being said, was not only the best place, it was the only realistic place to try it. A strong force here could delay the column for hours or even days, if Johnny Pope was alert to the chance, and they would pretty soon find that out. For these men who made up this dusty sweaty column, now drawing up to the pass in the mountains knew that they were about to learn, by their own progress through that pass, just how much, those annoying cavalry vedettes, who had tracked their march and progress for the last two days, had been able to pass on to their high command. Just how much had they seen and reported and how much had that information been heeded among those generals at Union headquarters?

Chapter 4
The Gap

As middle afternoon passed to late afternoon, the dusty column closed up to the western end of the mountain pass. There was a tension in the ranks now, especially when, up ahead, there began a crackle of musketry as the advance pickets tangled with whatever Yankees were up there, but as the boys kept telling each other, it all depended how many there were and how long the march was delayed as a result. Down the column behind them cheers were audible, faint at first but growing, giving advance notice of the approach of somebody important. On the shouts of their sergeants they were halted and cleared the road, seeing almost at once, a body of horsemen approaching, who, on emerging from the dust cloud, turned out to be not only Longstreet and his staff, but Lee also. The cheers and hat waving seemed a shade less fervent this time, as the dust shrouded cavalcade trotted forward, to turn off the road, before ascending something of a hill a little further on. Perhaps, Daniel Ryan thought, that spatter of gunfire up ahead, indicating the possibility of a fight, had sobered the minds of the waiting men.

Across from the group of officers, the troops waited, as word passed back that the leading regiments had been pushed forward to move whatever Yankees were up there out of the way. A renewed ripple of expectation ran down the files with the news, since this pointed to a fight and who knew how sizeable it might turn out to be, or how much of a delay this would all impose upon the general's plans. Within minutes that fight seemed to come a little closer when Jones' other brigades were called to reform on the road, while, up ahead, the generals conferred and pointed, with old "Neighbour," Jones of their own division over there now also, clearly involved in the conferring and the pointing. The talk went on and the distant gesturing also, but there was no immediate resumption of the general march.

The main column, stretching on down the road from where their own brigade had been reformed, still stood and simply waited, as the sun lowered in the sky, while the hum of questions and conversation along the files of curious men, mingled with the grunts and snorts of animals and the creaking movements of their harness. Time went by, and there was nothing much to see or hear. Word began to filter back. It was cavalry up there, you could hear it by the sound of their lighter calibre carbines, sharper and higher pitched than the heavier bark of infantry weapons, but they were going, pushed back by Anderson's men towards the far end of the pass, so the way would soon be clear.

Sure enough, the scattered firing in the pass grew more scattered and fainter as time passed, so the talk must be true men told each other. Their own boys must still be advancing on towards the farther end. Meantime, the sound of thousands of voices engaged in endless speculation at this end, from the waiting generals on down to the waiting enlisted men, hummed in its giant, insect swarm buzz. Daniel craned his neck again to see up ahead, noticing immediately that a courier had arrived at where Benning sat his horse at the front of the column. The rider wheeled his horse and galloped away, upon which shouts of command started to relay down as the men were called to order and the advance resumed. Along the road they pushed, stirring the dust again, and moving among the stalled wagons of Anderson's brigade, to gain the front of the column as the mountains began to rise on either side.

But then, from the pass ahead, the scatterings of picket fire suddenly grew into a much larger volume of shooting and at this, the marching men on the road were jerked into full attentiveness, craning their necks to look up towards the front, though it was impossible to see past the various obstructions in the way. But above the tree and brush covered hillsides up ahead, a drifting cloud of gun smoke began to rise, showing that those advance regiments of Anderson's had certainly run into something, and, from the shooting now going on, that something was rather more than a cavalry picket. Heavier volleys began to roll suggesting that the Yankees had indeed sent troops and not just cavalry to block the gap.

More couriers came galloping over from the gaggle of generals on the hillock, and now their own officers were yelling orders which were quickly taken up by the sergeants. The brigade, shouldered arms and lurched into double time, following into the gap, while Jones rode his horse with his staff from the hill to reach the road and turn into the pass at the head of the men. Lee and Longstreet's groups were also on the move, but they rode a little further back, as though to observe the developing advance.

Still there was nothing to be seen up ahead but drifting smoke as the tree-lined sides of the pass steadily reared above them. To their left flowed the creek, now moving among larger boulders and beyond it stretched the rusting lines of the disused railroad, all now crammed into a space which was in places less than a hundred yards wide. To the left, or north, the pass sides were steeper, with near precipitous slopes rising beyond the railroad, broken only with trees and vegetation. To the south, the hillside was maybe a shade less forbidding, though almost equally high, with rocky outcrops visible among a variety of trees. But on either side those mountains stretched steeply upwards for close to two hundred feet. It was the perfect place for an ambush, or for a blocking force to deploy, yet their ranks were still advancing into the pass, so whoever was delaying them must be at the far end rather than in the pass itself.

The column moved on, with men shuffling and panting heavily at the faster pace, their muskets bouncing on their shoulders, steadied by the forearm with the sweat-soaked fingers of the hand wrapped round the butt. Other companies, had gotten to the far side of the creek and were using the rail bed to make their way forward. From up ahead there came still heavier gunfire with those familiar, rolling, regular volleys of musketry growing, indicating the presence of considerable numbers. More shouts came from the officers and the column came to a ragged halt, with men bumping and pushing into each other in the process. Eyes went immediately to the mounted officers, to Jones, and then back to where Longstreet, had appeared, spurring ahead, riding up to Jones to confer further. The men watched, seeing him point and knowing by his gestures that they were next to be committed to whatever fight was going on up ahead.

A courier rode across from where the generals sat, to rein in next to Benning. The words were inaudible from where Daniel Ryan stood, especially with the continuing tide of musketry up ahead, but it was not long before their purpose was clear. The brigade was called to deploy and their own men were directed, with others of the regiment, into the brush beyond the road to the right. As they did so, Daniel Ryan stole a glance at where the three black recruits jogged forward with the others. One now brandished an old flintlock pistol in his right hand as he clutched a cloth rations bag in the other, while the others grasped large knives. Daniel's inspection of them was disturbed by Major Preston's call as they moved off into line, his voice just audible with all of the other noises.

"It's up the hill for us boys, and there's a bottle of drinkin' whiskey for the first man at the top."

There was a hint of a laugh along the line, especially at his added words, "specially if he's ahead o' the Second and Twentieth regiments there." The men gave a brief cheer as they shook out into a rough line and started towards the lower slope. Daniel heard a shout from Bradlee, presumably aimed at the three negroes.

"Git back off a' that battle line afore ya hurt somebody with them damned things. Stay the hell outa that front rank till ya git some damned weapons worth havin'."

They pushed into the trees and scrub, closing on the slope with almost all of them slinging their muskets over their shoulders by their straps as they went, freeing their hands for the climb, before starting to scramble over the rough ascending ground, aware that not just Benning, or Jones or even Longstreet, but Lee himself would likely be watching their performance. Daniel glanced behind as he climbed, to see down in the pass, Anderson's remaining regiments, in a loose line, advancing to the east, followed by the balance of their own brigade. There too were the rusting weed strewn lines of the Manassas Gap railroad and the path of the creek. Farther on still, just beyond the creek, was a large stone building, shrouded in gun smoke. The sight of it all was quickly lost as the trees and the shoulder of the hill, blotted out any continued view of the pass or of the fight going on to the east.

Up on the slope, the climbers struggled forward, as the hill became steeper and the ascent got tougher. The men, rather than moving in a continuous line, tended already to collect into groups, where the going looked easiest, to get the advantage, ignoring the shouts of officers and sergeants, who repeatedly fussed at them to deploy as this happened. They stuck to their task, sometimes having to scramble over rocks, and pause then to push and pull each other on over these steeper parts. In places there were what could have been paths, of a sort, perhaps worn by animals, for there was little damn reason that Daniel Ryan could think of why anyone else should want to make this climb. But the tracks were more often hardly worth the name, for no sooner had a group of the sweating, panting men collected onto one of them when it ended in some further obstacle causing them to disperse to either side to seek a less difficult way of continuing.

Those of their own mess stayed in a rough group, as they laboured their way upwards, ignoring the thorns and branches which pulled and snagged at their already ragged clothing and scratched and tore at the skin beneath. The afternoon heat was still strong as they struggled on, and, on either side, there were only occasional signs of the others of the company, let alone the others along the line. At times, in the brush and the contours of the hill, they lost sight of everyone, beyond those in the most immediate vicinity and Daniel Ryan, as his breath came in gasps and his heart pounded at his ribs, still found the thought flitting through his mind that those in their little band might even be on their own. An image came of the eight of them arriving at the top to find that everyone else had halted or turned back. He could hear others around him gasping and panting for breath while Daley, and others, cursed as the bumps, scratches and grazes of the climb continued to come.

Still they went on, with the sweat now running down their faces to drip from noses and sting into eyes, Daniel could feel it on his body also, trickling down the inside of his shirt to collect and soak again the fabric around his waist and his arms. But, even now, panting and pausing to wipe this perspiration from his eyes, he found the time to glance back again. He found himself looking into the face of John Fitzpatrick, as he climbed beside him, and, catching his friend's gaze for an instant, he grinned at him and saw Fitzpatrick grin in return, almost stumbling then, as, almost too late, he switched his eyes back to where he was going, hearing John giggle as a result. Ryan laughed too, feeling in the humour, an air of boyish prank about the whole thing even though, as both of them well knew, it was plenty serious enough. Several times, they found themselves drawing close to, or joining and crossing the paths of other groups and here the men were sometimes forced to pause, to take turns at negotiating these parts till their routes diverged again.

On they went, wheezing and panting, while the weapons bounced and jumped awkwardly on their shoulders, but this gave them that important extra hand to help them climb. They were nearing the top now. Daniel could feel it by the angle, the heat and the more consistent glare of the sun on his back and the slight, but perceptible change in the slope of the ground under his feet. To either side they could begin to see other men stretching away through the trees and brush in irregular bunches, with, as the summit approached, the officers feverishly shouting and gesturing to their men to form, till.....
all of a sudden they were there. Their group came stumbling up to find William Boyce, their own Lieutenant, just ahead of them, sweat-soaked like the rest of them, but directing them into some sort of line with the flat of his drawn sword.

"Form boys, form," he gasped. "Let's get a line now, form!"

"How come a damned, soft-livin' officer's gotten up here ahead of us," he heard Daley, who had little time for Boyce, since back on the peninsula, mutter between wheezes of breath, "when we jest about bust our guts gittin' here?" There was no reply, just the frantic thudding of heartbeats against ribs and the gasping pants for breath of those around him as they formed into a rank of sorts. The group jerked into motion again, as Boyce gestured them forward, moving across the flattening summit towards the edge to see, as the reverse slope opened up in front of them, just yards below, an astonishing sight.

There, below the rim, in some places less than forty yards away was a toiling line of Yankees, heading for the top in an almost exact copy of what they themselves had just done. They could see them clearly, dodging in and out of the boulders, trees and scrub. Their little blue caps, their hair and beards, the metal badges on the front of each man's cartridge box belt and the sun gleaming on the barrels and bayonets of the weapons they carried as they passed over unshaded parts of the hillside. Eli Winder came up beside Daniel, his face shining with sweat and the old pistol gripped in both of his hands.

"For God's sake will you point that damn thing out there," Daniel blurted out between laboured breaths, as he fumbled a cartridge from his pouch, "down there would be good," he added, "at them blue fellas. That Eli is the Yankees, jest in case you never saw any before." Winder nodded and almost managed a grin.

"Thanks fer that," he gasped, "'em white folks all look the same to me," and Daniel, in his turn, could not suppress a chuckle at the quip.

"Get primed boys," it was Boyce again, but he was screaming the words, "and pour it into them." The rush to load began, even as more and more men arrived at the top, stretching and thickening their own line along the summit. Ramrods clattered in musket barrels, as they heard shouts of alarm from below. Then the first shots rang out, scattered and dispersed to start with, but quickly growing in frequency and intensity into ragged volleys of fire. Below, as the gun smoke eddied, the blue line wriggled as men sought cover. Daniel Ryan sighted on a sergeant, who stood waving the men nearest him into shelter in the rocks around them. He squeezed the trigger, feeling the Enfield lunge into his shoulder, seeing the thick cloud of smoke erupt around him and smelling the acrid stink of it in his nostrils. The cloud eddied away, and the man was nowhere to be seen, as Daniel fumbled in his pouch for another cartridge. He could hear the buzz now as occasional minie balls droned past from the muskets of the men below, but he ignored them as he inserted and rammed his next shot. The firing grew around him and the summit was smothered in off-white smoke from the discharging muskets. Here and there, a man in their own line at the top of the hill lurched backwards, as a bullet from further down caught him. But even as he registered this, Daniel felt, rather than saw, a slackening in the musketry from below them. As though acknowledging this, their own officers began to shout along the line, bellowing to their men to cease firing. Daniel heard the captain's voice, cracking as he shouted. He came along the line yelling the order, striking at the musket barrels with his sword as he went, and gradually the shooting died away and the smoke, around them and ahead of them, began to disperse.

There was little sign of the Yankees as the last eddies of smoke cleared. An occasional glimpse of a drab blue uniform jacket further down the slope, which vanished into the trees and scrub as quickly as it appeared. They stood there momentarily, at the top, panting still from their exertions in the climb, or from the nervous tension of the brief fight, or maybe from a bit of both. Boys looked at their companions on either side and grinned at them, enjoying their little triumph even as they began to wonder what to do next. They were not left in doubt for long. Jeffers came along, pushing and pulling boys into motion as he reached them.

"Are ya stayin' up here all week," he yelled? "Move yore asses down that there slope after 'em."

"Didn't reckon he'd be happy," Fitzpatrick said as the firing faded, but as it did so there were other sounds that caused men to pause and look at each other. All along the line there was a hesitation as they strained their ears, trying to distinguish what they now heard, above the sporadic shots from the Yankees on the slope below, and the noise of the fighting down in the pass. For there was more, cannon fire now, that must come from down at the pass, and those guns must be Yankee guns for no artillery had come forward through the pass with their own infantry. They looked and then the moment was past as the sergeants and officers yelled and they began to move off again, starting to slip and stumble almost immediately on the down slope and finding that going down was very little, if any, easier than coming up had been. Daniel heard Ballard's voice as the line moved, shouting to the three negroes just beyond and behind him.

"Down thar's yore guns 'n' whatever other stuff takes yore fancy Josh," he yelled. "Jest git on and pick 'em up, 'n' don't forgit the damn cartridge boxes." The men moved on in a rough line, stumbling across an occasional fallen enemy, around whom some of the nearest men quickly grouped to relieve them of their shoes, belts and other items of clothing or equipment. Daniel passed one and glanced down. The man had been shot in the head, but he only had a fleeting image of blood and staring eyes, before he was past, his eyes searching for the hidden traps and pitfalls on the broken slope ahead.

It was evening as they descended steadily down the reverse slope, pushing the Yankees on ahead of them, moving through occasional exchanges of shots, then trying to reload, while still straining to keep pace with the rest of the line. Through the bushes and trees they went, scrambling around the rocks, and occasionally using muskets to help themselves and each other in the descent, still exchanging fire with the retreating enemy, though seeing hardly anything of them now in the steep, wooded terrain. The light faded as they descended, the low sun having disappeared behind the summit behind them plunging most of this side of the hill into deep shadow.

As they neared the bottom of the slope they heard more and more sounds of the fighting at the pass, from where a dense cloud of dirty, white, drifting gun smoke rose above the trees and, where the rocks and scrubby woods permitted, they caught glimpses of movement through the smoke clouds over to the north as dark figures flitted among the trees and brush, where the light of the sinking sun still shone through the pass and out to the wooded ridges beyond.

"They've a fine little brawl down there," Fitzpatrick muttered, between gasps of breath, and Daniel grunted. Behind him Ballard joined the conversation.

"Reckon, once we git down off'n this hill, we'll be set on their flank," he gasped. Daniel nodded, half to himself, as his mind began to dwell on this thought. So, for their own men at least, the fight was likely not yet over. If the Yankees were still blocking the way, then their breathless scramble up and down this mountain would get them to the bottom squarely on the enemy side of the pass. Perhaps Anderson's men would be pushing a way through to link up with them, along with the rest of the brigade and whoever else was needed for the job, but down here on the wooded ridges beyond the pass, it would be hard to manoeuvre and hard also to see the approach of others, be they friend or foe. Surely the rest of the brigade and Anderson's men had pushed on through? It all depended on how many Yankees there were, but as the tension and excitement of the brief fight at the summit faded from him, even though his heart still raced with the exertion of the descent, Daniel Ryan found his mind casting ahead with further unease. Success at the summit might have gotten them into a stiffer fight on this side of the pass.

The going near the foot of the mountain was easier and the arriving men collected into something resembling companies as they reached the bottom, with a scattering of them being immediately pushed out ahead as a rough skirmish line by their officers. Daniel and his companions moved into their ranks, jostling with others as they formed. Around them there were a few shouts of laughter and they turned to look. Coming up to take their places in the line were the three black men. One had a black felt officer's hat on his head, but all of them were now festooned with cartridge boxes on black leather belts, Yankee haversacks and metal water canteens, with each of them clutching a Yankee Springfield musket.

The assembling men looked them over, with some grins appearing, while a few even left their places to go over and prod or dig at them, especially at Josh with the hat.

"Be a goddam general in no time," a voice said.

"Maybe reckons he is already," retorted another.

"I'd pull that cord off o' the hat, Josh," Gibben told him, "else the captain'll git all jealous like." Others however showed no reaction, contenting themselves with looking coldly on. Jeffers however had no patience for the novelty.

"Will ya goddam form up," he yelled, pushing at a succession of the boys as he moved along. William Boyce had appeared once again and, he eyed the three briefly.

"Looks like the best equipped men in the company," he said. He too moved off, while the sergeants got to finishing the job of pushing and cajoling the men into line.

Out ahead there was no sign of the Yankees they had pursued down the hill, but up ahead the ground was forested and undulating in a succession of ridges that they had seen from the hill. Down here, it was all trees and brush with a hundred places for an ambusher to wait. To the left towards the road and the pass, there were steady rolls of musketry, with glimpses of the telltale cloud of dirty smoke still drifting through the trees. From farther east away from the pass itself, where the first wooded ridge crossed the road and rail line, there was the continuing crash of artillery, indicating that the Yankees at least still had guns up to support their infantry. Was this a large force after all? The questions swept through Daniel Ryan's mind. Would they all be stalled here? Had the Yankees caught onto the whole plan, and resolved to keep Longstreet's and Jackson's men separated, while they concentrated their strength against each in turn? Finding the enemy here had been an unwelcome surprise, suggesting that the Yankee generals were reacting to the southern tactics and maybe moving their forces around to the places where they would do most good. If this was what was happening, who knew what lay ahead, for if the Yankees were aware of the approach of the rest of the Confederate army, then they would surely strain every resource to try and keep the separate halves of their enemy from re-uniting.

The lines assembled and, with skirmishers out ahead, they moved forward, drawing as they went the beginnings of fire from a largely unseen enemy line. On they pushed to come to a halt, as the men from their own skirmish line loped back to join the main line with dark shapes appearing among the trees in front and the clouds of musket smoke indicating that the enemy was prepared to meet them. The line halted and, primed their weapons again before opening fire by ranks on the shouted commands. They poured several volleys of musketry into the smoke, as it rose among the trees, before resuming their press forward, but the return fire was already slackening. The enemy had once more faded away, their presence becoming more of a succession of flurries of shots from a retreating skirmish line, than the sustained heavy volleys of a standing line of battle. Only the cannon redoubled their fire, as the infantry faded away from the front, the discharges tearing through the trees, till this too began to slacken.

It was dusk and the volume of gunfire declined steadily, now being increasingly marked by the flashes of those weapons that still fired in the gathering gloom, with even this slowly fading away as the enemy departed. As they went, the fight at the pass moved to its end, falling gradually quiet as light receded, but as the fight around them ceased, and the shouts of officers and sergeants began their attempts to reform their sections and companies, some men began to signal and then around them others stopped to listen also. There was still some intermittent shooting going on along the line towards the pass, presumably as the skirmish lines gradually eased out of contact, but gradually more and more men were still, straining their ears to hear.

It was a more distant sound, a rumbling away to the east, like thunder, but it was not thunder so it could only be gunfire, distant gunfire, a faint but steady roll of small arms, mixed with some heavier thumps of cannon, coming again to them through the gathering gloom of the approaching night. Men stood still to listen and, as the full darkness descended and the crescent of the new moon rose, there were sights too. Away to the east, visible through gaps in the trees, the darkening sky was illuminated by faint yellow flashes. At that men began to look at each other, seeing in the expressions on the faces of companions in the almost faded light, that each of them was fully aware of what that distant fighting must mean and needing to know, as they exchanged those looks, that they did though few enough words were said. For those flashes of distant yellow light and that pervasive, persisting rumble could mean only one thing. Out there to the east, somewhere on that distant Manassas plateau, the Yankees had at last caught up with Jackson and his men and these things, that they were seeing and hearing at this moment, might well be the sight and sound of their own comrades, brought to bay by the enemy and perhaps fighting for their lives.

The gathering night saw most of the remaining troops in the column pushing through the gap, to arrive at the eastern end. Their own bivouacs had been quickly set up there on the wooded slopes beyond the eastern entrance, where the exhausted men of Anderson's and Benning's brigades had already sunk to rest in their own makeshift camps. But from over on the road they could hear the, rumbling of passing vehicles and the tramp of many feet with the clinking tinkle of metal equipment.

Jeffers came by, collecting men for a duty, no doubt, Daniel Ryan thought, as he caught the sergeant's eye. Sure enough, the familiar words came to him.

"You'll do, you lucky boys. On yore feet." He took them along, while he gathered still more men, finally turning to issue his instructions when he had about a dozen men grouped around him.

"Git yore asses out among them Yankee dead and wounded," he told them. "Go through their cartridge boxes. Don't bring the ammunition, they got Springfields and their stuff ain't no use fer our Enfields.

Find the blue-wrapped cartridges and bring 'em back here. Only the ones wrapped in blue paper," he repeated. "Now git goin', afore its too dark to see blue from anythin' else." He waved them away in both directions and they shuffled off, to seek out the enemy fallen.

Within about twenty minutes the light had faded as he said to the point where colours were unrecognisable and Daniel and John Fitzpatrick were ready to leave it at that. Each of them had collected a number of the distinctively wrapped cartridges in a pocket, but virtually all of the dead had already been relieved of their shoes and they made their way back to the bivouac, meeting others of the section on the way, to report to Jeffers. The sergeant had a cloth bag and the arriving men emptied their pockets of the blue cartridges into it, but the First Sergeant offered no explanation of why he wanted them, simply dismissing them to gather again in their group and think at last of rest. Many sank immediately into sleep where they had slumped down disregarding blankets, while off to the east, the rumbles of battle declined only slowly, drowned out by the closer movement sounds, but leaving any who remained awake, now that full darkness had fallen, to ponder over what had taken place down there and what had been the outcome.

But, in spite of all of the coming and going through the gap, there were neither additional orders nor any word of a rations issue. The invisible convoys of wagons and columns of moving soldiers went on into the night, but there was not a sign of their own brigade wagons. So at that, for all spared the duty of the picket line, there was time for rest, a supremely welcome prospect to men who had hiked through the just ended day in the summer heat, to scale a mountain, and fight a battle, at the end of it.

First light had not yet started to illuminate the snatches of sky, which were visible through the tree canopy when bugles blared, and the drums rolled their grim tattoo. The sleepy men were thus gathering before anything resembling daylight had come. This time, after the briefest of parades for roll call and orders of the day, it was straight onto the road, where one of John Hood's brigades, of Texas soldiers, was already moving to form the head of the gathering column. Daniel Ryan toted the heavier pan once again, as they struck away down the dusty road. The sun was still below the horizon as other brigades moved out onto the road behind them. Along that first half mile, on either side of the road, lay stripped and plundered corpses of more Yankees, victims of last night's fighting, whom those Texans up in front had clearly gotten to first. A succession of half-clad bodies lay there, their skin pale and white meantime, but some were already beginning to discolour, darkening in the growing heat, and showing the now familiar signs of starting to swell and bloat.

A few miles down the road was Haymarket and beyond that was Gainesville. Both turned out to be sleepy little hamlets of few buildings, largely bereft of people, with only a few children and a couple of dogs, turning out to watch as the dust-plastered column passed through. At Gainesville, the files turned a left oblique, to join a different road, which stretched away to the east, but this road was different, for it was, men said, a turnpike. There were few such roads in southern Virginia, with such a surface, bound and compressed together with stones and gravel to give a hard, but stony consistency. It was different on the feet, giving a sure push off, but it was unyielding also and, even through shoes, the surface felt hot and its top layer of sharp stones would inevitably be severe and unforgiving on the many barefooted men.

As always the dust, though somewhat less on the turnpike, was enough to make life difficult, and while the men had replenished canteens from the creeks around the pass, there was still no word of rations, with any commissary vehicles seemingly marooned far down the column of men, ammunition wagons, ambulances and guns. Notwithstanding their hunger, the marching files were full of life, with their customary succession of complaints about shortages, and no rations, and the usual crops of jokes, wisecracks and songs. Then the rumours began to sweep up and down the files once more and slowly the mood began to change.

Up ahead, seemingly lurking on the edge of the old Manassas battlefield, but still in being, and waiting for the arrival of their approaching column, was Stonewall Jackson's command. So the Old Man's plans were working after all men said, but, as last night's distant fight had shown, the Yankees were up there too, likely gathering their strength also for a large scale fight. Hearing all of this, some men brandished their muskets and set up a yell, but others stayed silent, and, as on the previous day, a mood of expectancy and slowly growing tension began to permeat through the column.

But there was a notion here also, as Philipps had said, of something like destiny, Daniel Ryan thought, even as he felt his own failing brogan shift on his foot with each step. Up ahead here was where the first great victory of the war had been won last year over the Yankees. It had caused such celebration in the south when the news had come in. Daniel Ryan let his mind go back to the day when their own company had heard it announced at their drilling session in Eden Station that eternity ago and the mixture of jubilation and trepidation it had caused, with boys worrying that the war would be over before they could strike a blow. Now, he thought, they were here in person and it was looking like the next great clash of the armies could be on this same northern Virginian ground as before, with the chance to finish the job, but at what cost? Around him some of these thoughts were echoed by Daley's words.

"Maybe we'll get to do the job right on the damn Yankees up here this time." He was answered by a few hoarse yells as the shuffling tramp of feet on the hard road surface went inexorably on.

The column moved eastwards, with the undulating road passing through a mixture of fields and woodlots, while gunfire erupted and grew once more over there to the east, but now the cloud of rising smoke was just up ahead and those sounds of battle were close. The men gripped their weapons and almost instinctively the pace of the files increased. If Jackson's men were being assailed again up that road, then help was just about here and they would soon see what the damned Yankees made of that.

And then, seemingly, they were there. The files ahead were wheeling off the road, to the right, turning away from the smoke cloud, and leaving the continuing undulations of the turnpike up ahead empty. Those smoke billows still rose into the air to the northeast and the crackle of musketry continued unabated as they drew steadily up to an intersection with yet another side road, where a small detail of soldiers and a mounted officer waved the column off to the right. Then their own files reached the junction and they wheeled off, following onto a dirt road even as the fight, up on slightly higher ground to the north, continued, marked by its smoke pall. It was getting towards noon and the army was at last re-united. Johnny Pope and his Yankees were out there in front though nobody could see a damn thing of it all through the heavy woods, behind which they were being directed, which obscured everything to the east.

Their march went on, south, more or less, from the position of the midday sun. They passed a farmhouse and moved on a further distance, till, on relayed shouts of command, the column shuffled to a halt. More shouted orders and they were faced left to the east and moved off the road. In front were fields with more woods beyond and the men halted and waited, with no further orders arriving to move in any sort of advance or manoeuvre. No word of any kind, while up there across the turnpike the smoke cloud rose and the gunfire persisted, while down here, as the sun beat down, the men stood and sweltered and the last of their canteens' contents were drained. Presently, with a skirmish line out in front, they were stood down and some immediately settled themselves to rest in whatever shade they could find. Away to the left, the sounds of heavier fighting were now subsiding, though skirmishing fire continued, but, over here, the men simply settled themselves or headed off to look for water or for something to eat. The day was once again stiflingly hot and the buzz of talk rose above the groups of lounging men, but for all of the smoke, sound and excitement on the far side of the turnpike, as far as actual fighting was concerned, down around here, there was, so far, not a sign in the world.

Chapter 5
The Plain of Manassas

Above all else, the boys of Company B would remember that afternoon, and indeed the day that followed for the heat. It was prickly, energy-sapping high summer heat, made all the more oppressive by high humidity. Men dripped with perspiration when they did nothing and movement or effort of any kind in the conditions left them soaked in sweat and utterly fatigued. Notwithstanding the hot, sultry weather, there was much coming and going throughout that Friday afternoon as Longstreet's divisions and trains arrived and arranged themselves in the woods and fields south of the turnpike, but through it all there was not a sign of the brigade commissary wagons. These remained stubbornly absent, compelling those whose hunger was growing ever more acute, to resort anew to foraging around the farms and orchards of the local area. Daniel Ryan's mess dispersed quickly to procure what food and water they could, before the simple volume of arriving men on the scrounge cornered every morsel that might be available. Ryan and Tom Gibben headed out with the mess canteens making for the nearest creek. On arriving, they clambered down to find a sergeant there, hurrying the men along and shooing them away when they had collected their water. Ryan looked at him inquiringly.

"Cavalry boys reckon thar's Yankees down thar t' the south beyond our flank" he said, "and not no patrol neither. They say there's thousands of 'em, a division, or maybe more'n that, just settin' down thar on the other side o' the railroad. So if'n they move up this way, then it'll be hell to pay fer sure. So fill up quick and git on back to yore outfits." Some men questioned the news, but Ryan just shrugged and set to the canteen filling, moving along the bank of the little creek to get the best access place. The current was slow flowing and the water brown in appearance, but it was water and on a day like today it would have to do. He knelt down beside Gibben and began flattening the canteens into the water in turn to watch them bubble towards full, as more men arrived to get their share and the sergeant's warnings became more urgent in tone. Having drunk themselves, and topped the canteens up once more, they each splashed some water over their faces and necks and got up to go, while still more men gathered at the creek.

Back at the halting place, Daley and Philipps still lingered, retrieving their canteens to drink deeply before departing on their quest for food. The others had not yet returned and there was little in the way of shade that was unoccupied. Ryan and Gibben moved a few yards nearer to the road and began stretching out their blankets, using a rail fence as support, to create shade beneath, placing the canteens in the shaded patch to prevent the water from getting too hot.

Daniel Ryan had supplied himself with a Yankee water canteen down on the peninsula. Other men had gotten them also, but opinions were divided about them. The Yankee canteens were factory produced and made of identical, lightweight metal halves, soldered together and provided with a cloth cover to insulate them. But their main fault was that, being metal, they were prone to heating up on a hot day and so therefore did the water inside. Some men, including a couple of their own mess had tried them and discarded them to return to the miniature barrel wooden canteens, workshop made in the south, which were rather heavier, and bulkier to carry, but better for keeping the water inside somewhat cooler. Daniel was meantime undecided, but those Yankee canteens were not the things to leave out in the sun on a hot summer's day.

Having set up, they lounged beneath their shelter, while a fitful breeze occasionally flapped the blankets, but on this side of the turnpike there was little else, but the renewed and growing hum of thousands of conversations around the fields, to disturb them. It was over on the far side to the north of the road, presumably where Jackson's men were positioned, that the activity was. Since their arrival, that sector had never been completely quiet. At the very least there had been picket firing or maybe somewhat more, together with artillery exchanges, but now these sounds were growing again, swelling into a volume that suggested another full scale attack. The telltale smoke billowed into the air, maybe a mile or more away to the northeast. Daniel could feel the tension rise in his chest as he watched the smoke rise and listened to the crackle and rumble of battle. Around him, other men in the bivouac stopped what they were doing to look, before resuming their talk, while some made comments meant for others to hear, as though to hide their own apprehensions.

"Looks like Ol' Jack's boys are getting' it again."

"Yankees ain't fer takin' no siesta time."

"Maybe we should head over and join that there party."

"Go yore damned self if yo're keen like."

Daniel looked around the bivouac, with his eyes coming to rest on the three black men, who stood in a group while Dellings demonstrated musket loading and priming, smiling to himself at the earnestness of their expressions as they attended the sergeant's words and movements. He watched for a few more moments until the sound of approaching footsteps took his attention and he turned to see Powell and Petersen approaching with their own collection of water bottles. At least

Powell had gotten the idea of going for his own water, Daniel thought, then he squinted upwards, aware that the two men had stopped close by and that their shadow cast over where he sat.

"Ya reckon they'll fight?" It was Petersen's voice. Daniel stayed where he was, looking around at the musket drilling once more before responding.

"They said they would," he replied.

"Yeah, but will they?"

"Give 'em the chance and likely they will, but there's other boys around here that didn't last time and maybe won't this time either, only they're white."

"Reckon blacks ain't up to real fightin'," Powell muttered.

"Anybody'll fight, if they got reason enough that is," Gibben said. Petersen looked around at the drilling.

"Well if they do fight and make real soldiers, then some o' the things about this whole war ain't right," he said.

"Reckon we'll know about that afore too long," Gibben told him, as they turned to go. Daniel Ryan looked at his friend.

"Is that a truce or somethin'?" Tom Gibben picked at his teeth with a strand of dry grass.

"Maybe," he said, "but it don't matter overmuch to me. I'm here to fight Yankees, though I'd be happier if I didn't have to go up against boys on our own side." He jerked a thumb at the drilling. "Right or wrong, the major gave them three the chance to fight, so now it's up to them."

The mess foraging obtained apples, some corn cobs and the carcasses of two rabbits, but only the apples could be immediately consumed, since with, "no fires," ordered, the meat and flour could only be prepared and stored in haversacks. The remainder of the afternoon was spent in the shade of the pegged out blankets as the sun slowly lowered in the sky. The attention of the resting men was periodically drawn to the north where further surges of musketry and artillery fire, and billowing, further clouds of gun smoke, spoke of further fighting on Stonewall Jackson's front. Each time these episodes seemed to run their course, before subsiding into irritable exchanges of picket firing and in this way the hours passed and evening drew on.

The last of these outbreaks commenced after sunset, but this one was not away beyond the turnpike. It was on this side, much closer than the others, no more than half a mile away to the northeast, and therefore close enough for their own units to be called to arms when it began. The firing lasted a while, flaring into spectacular explosions of musketry and artillery, which lit the darkening sky and illuminated the trees and fields, flaring into further violent surges as it moved steadily east, suggesting that the Yankees were being pushed back along the line of the turnpike. The men watched, aware that the brigades to the immediate left of their own division had been drawn away towards this latest clash. They waited, resting at ease in their ranks, until virtual darkness had fallen over the fields and woods.

In the last of the dusk, their own division was moved slightly forward, advancing by its right in a great arc, crossing the creek where they had earlier gotten the water, until the line faced almost due east, with its left flank in the woods. Only then were their own brigades stood down and pickets, including Daniel Ryan's section, detailed while the remainder of the men settled to rest just as the company wagon arrived.

Saturday dawned, still sultry and close. Over towards the turnpike, as the men stirred, the coming of morning was marked by a brief flurry of cannon fire, but this soon subsided. The early sky remained cloudless, but there was a haze today that gave the sun an orange tinge as it rose over the hills and woods which marked the Yankee positions. Having paraded for roll call and orders, the hungry men were stood down, but, with fires still forbidden, there was nothing to be done with such food as was in the haversacks. Today's word was spreading through, namely that the old man would strike the Yankees and, while some in the company outwardly whooped and welcomed this, others, acknowledging the approach of battle, by silence.

The morning drew on and the sun ascended, with the oppressive heat again increasing steadily, but still there was no news of an attack, although limited flurries of musketry and more artillery fire broke out from time to time. Noon came and went and the sun beat down, increasingly hazily on the sweltering men who lay or lounged, in the shade if they were fortunate enough to be bivouacked in the woods, or near enough to take shelter there, while those in the fields again improvised shelters from their blankets as best they could. Daniel noticed that everywhere he walked now in the fields, the grass strands caught in his shoe, emphasising that the rent in the stitching was getting steadily wider. Surely a brawl would give an answer to that he thought, but there were still no orders, so the men waited, happy enough to do nothing after marching for much of the previous week, but with the knowledge that, with the enemy this close, it would be too much to expect to stay out of the fight for much longer.

The afternoon had come in its haze of sultry heat when suddenly it began. Musketry and then cannon fire welled up, on Jackson's front across the turnpike again, by the sound, and the direction of the renewed smoke cloud, but this time, unlike the short-lived outbreaks of the morning, it had the makings of a bigger affair. Once again, it was far enough away not to concern them directly, but still men got to their feet to gaze across at the rolling smoke, their eyes intent and some of their jaws working nervously as they watched. The firing continued to grow, with massed volleys of musketry and the duller, deeper thunder of cannon, until it had all the thunderous noise of a full scale battle. More of the men were standing now, fixing their eyes on the great cloud of smoke, which drifted very slowly to the east while below it the fighting raged. As they watched and listened, Jeffers came around carrying the cloth bag that he had collected blue-wrapped cartridges in, on Thursday night, after the fight at the gap. He called the men of the nearby messes to gather, and when they had done so, he poured the cylinders out onto a blanket telling each of them to keep four. The boys waited for some kind of explanation.

"They're cleaners," he told them. "Yankees make 'em and issue 'em to their men. Ya load and fire 'em like any other cartridge, but they don't fly as true, cuz they ain't rifled. Feel 'em." They did as he said and Daniel Ryan could feel a shorter stubbier shape than a normal minie ball with a wider skirt around the bullet base. Jeffers looked around at them.

"Feel it," he said? "It'll scour the musket bore, some at least, but don't waste 'em. There ain't no more till we shoot some more Yankees, use one every ten or fifteen shots maybe." He got to his feet and moved away with his cloth bag while the boys looked around at each other.

"Better'n nothin'," Gibben muttered, "might save yore shoulder some." They dispersed, some pushing the cartridges into pockets, while others peered at them or felt them some more, as though unconvinced of what they had just been told, or maybe taking Jeffers' errand as confirmation that their own turn was almost here.

Sure enough, within minutes, the assembly call came and the men scrambled, with heartbeats quickening and uneasy stomachs, to gather belts and roll blankets before taking their muskets from the stacks. They formed their lines in column of brigades, with their own out in front, followed by Anderson's, while, across the turnpike to the north, the battle still thundered, showing few signs of declining in intensity. Their own orders were now here. You could always tell by the couriers, those pink-faced boys that ran the generals' messages, rode along, some of them were full of their own self-importance anyway, but when the word was to advance or attack there was something about the manner of them, an extra urgency or a drama, Daniel could not think of a word to describe it. The men ribbed them, especially the younger ones, mercilessly and today was no different.

"You lost boy," and this often came from boys who were little or no older than the couriers were?

"That's a mighty big hat fer yore little ol' head."

"Does the Gineral know you've gone a wanderin' off now?"

"My god, thar's a child in them thar boots and coat."

"Don't you go droppin' that there letter to yore gal."

"Come outa that thar hat and talk to us sonny."

So it was now. The chorus of comments and wisecracks, some of them, Daniel Ryan reckoned, likely forced to conceal men's fear, followed the couriers along the lines as they sought out commanding officers with their orders, while the plumes of dust kicked up by their hurrying horses, drifted away towards the east. Phillips took in the direction of the latest messenger.

"Our invite to the ball," he muttered.

"Reckon so," said Daley, but, by Daniel Ryan's reckoning, Mick still seemed pleased at the prospect of a fight.

Now Colonels appeared along the lines, summoning their company commanders into little clusters of activity, where a deal of gesturing, pointing and animated talk went on, before the captains moved away to summon their lieutenants in turn and explain to them, with some more gesturing and pointing, what the generals required of them. Then the orders passed on from company officers to sergeants, whose bellows alerted the men and sent them off on the preparations for an advance. First blanket rolls and haversacks were stacked and left with a small guard detail, the latter precaution having been taken since the time, down on the peninsula, when the boys had left their things unguarded and had come back later to find them ransacked and pilfered. They would not be caught like that again, so those with the worst bowels or other disabilities were left behind with the company belongings. In deference to the heat, canteens would go, but the rest, except for weapons, would be left behind. Possessions piled and left, the ranks re-formed, and, as more orders rang out, the long, fluted bayonets were fixed, with a rolling chorus of metallic clicks and scrapes. This done, the muskets were shouldered and the ranks waited that further eternity of seconds till the order came relaying along and the Ogeechee Volunteer Rifles, guiding by the centre, moved off, making for the woods up ahead, where their picket had been placed the previous night.

In his place in the front rank, Daniel could see pretty well everything of where they were going, but to either side there was, for much of the time, little to be seen, bar the sweating men closest to him. But, just occasionally, on these undulating fields, there was the chance to glimpse along the line, seeing the colour, its pole pointing slightly forward, at the centre of their long rank, and even one or two rare sights of the other regiments, to the left or right of their own, with their own waving forests of gleaming musket barrels and bayonets, and their blood-red flags, hanging nearly limp also on this almost windless sultry day, all of it giving an impression of strength and power. Beyond the brigade the smoke continued to rise in banks from the trees to the north, while the roar of cannon and the crackle of musketry went on without interruption, but now the battle sounds were from their own side of the turnpike. Daniel could feel his heart pounding in his chest, its beat growing ever faster as the battle drew nearer and it was close now, seeming to gather around them ready to engulf them in another wild episode of blood and death. The right shoe continued to move around on his foot, however, needing just that extra degree of concentration to stay in time with the rest of the company without tripping or snagging the now partly detached sole on some obstruction, so glances to either side, while impressive and imposing, were also fleeting, due to his other preoccupations.

They were drawing up to a belt of trees and orders were ringing along the lines. The muskets were lowered, to the, "carry arms," position, to avoid the weapons' muzzles and their long bayonets fouling the lower tree branches, then on through the trees, growled at repeatedly, by the file closing sergeants behind them, each time that ranks were broken to negotiate tree trunks and bushes. It was humid in the woods, though the sweating men were spared the glaring sun there. But now came tell-tale signs from along the ranks, louder, more bitter, shouts and curses from the sergeants, who marched those several paces behind the main line to keep the men in place and order as, here and there, a man left his place to run their gauntlet. As the curses rang out, men turned to look. Daniel's eye caught the figure of Hobbs as he ducked away from his place, just as he had the last time, to a succession of curses from those around him. Then he recognised Bradlee's angry shout, followed by Hendrick's voice. It was all happening again and with the same ones as before.

"Git back in there, ya skulkin' b...d."

"I gotta go back Sam, I'm sick, honest."

"Git back, damn ya!"

"It's my guts. Goddam it, I can't hardly walk."

It had happened down on the peninsula, only there most of them had simply made quietly off to hide in the woods, and here it was again. In camp, where thoughts and reactions could be more measured, it might be understood. Some men simply did not have what it took to make these journeys into the gunfire and the blood, but here, when it was all taking place, and everyone was struggling to keep control, there was much less tolerance of it. Along the line the shouts and mutters went. They were damned skulkers and cowards, and they needed a bullet for deserting their comrades.

The ranks pushed on through the trees, amid a whole mixture of sounds, the footsteps of the men in the undergrowth and on the dead grass, leaves and twigs, the snapping of branches from tree trunks and limbs by men pushing past, when magnified by the trees, sounded like the thrashing of some monstrous creature picking its way through the gloom. Then, off in front, narrow shafts of bright, dazzling, afternoon light came glaring through the tree branches, growing steadily brighter, until it was out from the shelter into the sunshine once more, but only briefly, as they crossed a dirt road and plunged into further woods which flanked its other side. More pulling, tearing branches and thorns, with shouts and curses and thrashing until finally the dazzling shafts of light again told of the trees ending and open ground beyond.

Clear of the woods, the ranks were halted briefly, to close the gaps left by the faint-hearted and straighten and dress the irregular lines, before moving on again over the undulating ground. Already, away to their left, the battle had drawn closer again, spreading across the turnpike into the woods and farm lots on this side, still to the north of their own position and route but definitely drawing nearer. They would see now, some men told each other, as their sergeants snapped at them, to hush and listen for orders, but still the mutters went on up and down. They would see, and that Yankee braggart Johnny Pope would see too.

The long lines trampled steadily east, pushing through a succession of undulating fields, crossing another small creek and scrambling across fences before negotiating a further side road. Few of the fields had standing grain, Daniel Ryan noticed, being mostly pasture, much of it overgrown, with one or two bearing the stubble of an already harvested crop.

More orders rang out, this time for a left wheel and the men, guided by the shouts of their NCOs, shortened their stride, while the outer right flank of the brigade straggled around its wider arc to restore the alignment, before the next command resumed the advance, but this time it was towards that column of smoke and the thunder of cannon and musketry that grimly hinted at what was shrouded within it. Ahead lay more woods and a dip of lower ground that ran between two ridges or hills. Up there was the fight and Daniel Ryan tensed himself, as his heart now thumped hard against his chest seeing that moment of gut-wrenching violence come ever closer. Around him the familiar sounds came, bellowed orders and shouts of encouragement mingled with the sounds of feet swishing in the dried summer grass. Mixing with these were the familiar rhythmic sounds of bayonet scabbards clinking against water canteens, but, these latter sounds now had to be listened for, obscured as they were by the thunder of the battle, which had rolled eastward in successive surges over towards the turnpike to their left.

It was passing from afternoon towards early evening and all around them the shadows lengthened, pointing their extending fingers east, in the line of the brigade's advance. Twice more they crossed rail fences and a further country lane, rutted and dusty, to reform ranks on the far side and resume the tramp. Daniel's right shoe flapped awkwardly on his foot, with the stitching of sole to upper having parted down most of the outside, still he kept pace with those around him, though with some difficulty, on the broken ground.

That ground now rose gradually towards a ridge over there, to their front, flanked on either side by woods, where heavy fighting, under the customary shroud of gun smoke, was already in full progress, bringing the deeper rumble of artillery, mixed with the higher-pitched crackling blasts of mass musketry, thundering across the fields. They came upon the line of a creek, and began to follow its course, stretching out on either side of the water, with sergeants yelling at men who disturbed the formation by stooping to splash water on their faces. Several times, the brigade divided, with part on either bank of the creek and each portion trying to keep pace with those on the far side. Most of their own regiment were just to the right of the water as, coming up towards the smoke shrouded ridge in front, they could see that their route would lead them into the next section of woods, which lined the creek's right hand bank, while, in an arc which stretched across to their left front, the battle still raged, drawing ever closer as they tramped up towards those trees.

Daniel's mouth was dry now as he watched battle arrive again. His mind went back to the summer, where their first ordeals of combat had taken place on those blasted fields around Richmond. The faces of boys who had fallen in those fights came flashing persistently back into his mind, in spite of his attempts to keep them at bay. It did not do to allow ones self to think this way. It could sap the will and eat away at the resolve needed to do one's duty. Another order rang out, relayed along the line as they reached the trees, and the men again lowered their muskets to the, "carry", each of them with his fingers now gripping the trigger guard, with their musket barrels resting down the channel between right side and right arm, as the lines entered the shadows and congestion of the wood. He could feel his heart thundering in his chest, thudding so hard that it seemed to threaten to obstruct his throat and prevent him breathing. Behind him, he heard the continuing shouts of the file closers rise as, here and there along the ranks, another figure left the line to make for the rear. He heard Lake's voice, pleading with the unrelenting NCOs.

"I'm sick, goddam it Sarge, my guts are cuttin' me in half. I can't go on."

"Ya skulkin' shit, git yore ass back there inta….." Bailey's subsequent words were lost to Daniel Ryan, drowned out by the crash of approaching battle, as the long ranks pushed through the trees, still moving slightly uphill, pushing branches away from their faces and feeling the familiar tearing and dragging of twigs and thorns. Here lay dead and wounded men, dark-coated Yankees, some still and quiet, but others squirming and writing in their pain. Many men ignored them, though others seemed to exult in what they came across.

"Catch a bullet did ya Yank?"

"Ain't no, "on to Richmond," now, huh?"

Up ahead, the light of the evening was growing again, but a yellower light, less dazzling than earlier, as though the sun had gone down or haze had obscured its light. They were closing on the edge of the wood, and now, with more bellowed orders, the ranks were halted just inside where the trees rejoined the fields. Out there, to their left, the smoke clouds drifted as battle raged, deafening the ears with its noise but now the shouts came along, relayed by officers and sergeants who bawled to make themselves heard, to load to shoulder. Ahead, beyond the trees, looming occasionally from the drifting smoke, was a formed rank of troops, stretching diagonally away, and that rank was dressed in blue. Along the grey/brown line in the trees cartridges were bitten and poured and ramrods clanged as the charges were pushed home.

"Pour it dammit!" Daniel heard the shout and glanced around to see Adam Bailey standing with the three black men. He saw the sweat shining on Matthew's face and the furrowing of his brows as he struggled through the steps of loading his musket. This was a hell of a way to have to learn but at least they were still here, he reflected as he readied his Enfield. Around him the weapons were going back to the shoulder arms and again the lines lurched forward, having to strain, in the din of ever closer battle, to hear and recognise the shouts of command. On they went, covering the few steps that took them from the trees to the edge of the meadow and then came the order to halt and prime. The metal percussion caps were fingered from pouches and pockets and thumbed into place on the nipples below the musket hammers. The order came for firing by ranks and the long muskets of the front rank went up to the present at that fleeting, smudgy blue line as the fingers pulled the curved hammers back through that solid clicking movement to fully cock the weapons.

"Aim low boys," came Jeffers shout from behind them, followed immediately by the order to fire. The blast was deafening, in spite of all the welter of sounds around them. The muskets kicked back into the men's shoulders with their recoil as the evil acrid smoke engulfed them all, irritating eyes and noses as the musket butts thumped down onto the hard ground and the process of loading began feverishly again. The front rank men instinctively turned to allow the muskets of those behind them to bear on the smoke cloud which now hid the enemy line. Cartridge, bite the flap, tear the paper, pour the charge, even as the shattering roar of the rear rank volley, crashing out almost into the ears of the front rank men, assailed the senses. The smoke billowed around them all again, even as their reloading was continued. Push the bullet and the paper after it, draw the ramrod and ram it all home, replace the ramrod before fumbling for a fresh cap. In the middle of this the muskets of the rear rank men withdrew just as the front rank weapons were readying for the next volley. Up the heavy weapons came and the bellowed orders again brought the crash of the volley, making the ears ring anew from the concussion of the noise while the smoke swirled around them again. Then back to reloading, as, with a movement detected in the corner of the eye, the muskets of the rear rank men appeared again through the smoke. Around Daniel, some boys still muttered or called the steps of loading, even as the blast of the rear rank weapons seared the senses again, adding their smoke to the still lingering remains of the previous volleys. Daniel Ryan pulled his mind back to the present, as his own rank aimed again, but there was only smoke to be seen out in front as the next volley blasted out. Then it was back to the reloading process yet again while ears rang, noses ran, throats rasped and eyes watered and smarted in the swirling smoke.

They volleyed five times, seeing almost nothing of their targets through the smoke cloud, before the command came, along the lines, to cease firing, upon which the muskets were loaded once more and ported as they moved forward. The smoke ahead thinned and eddied as the ranks stepped out onto the open meadow and moved steadily on to the place at the far edge of this flatter ground where the dead and wounded of the enemy lay thickly. Here was blood and prostrate broken bodies, some of the fallen men reaching for or clutching at their hurts, while others twitched or writhed on the ground, while still more lay inert and seemingly lifeless. Through the continuing gunfire, from all around them, rose a garbled chorus of screams, wails and cries, competing with the deafening thunder of battle, as that carpet of injured men nursed their agony and beseeched those nearest them for help.

The long ranks of Benning's brigade traversed this frightful place, trying, not always successfully, to avoid stepping on injured, dying or dead men, with the sergeants yelling savagely at any men who made to leave their place for shoes or other plunder. On they marched through the drifting smoke till they came to the edge of this latest ridge crest, sensing the slight falling away with their feet rather than seeing anything much of it in the still swirling smoke. They began to descend, emerging from the smelling clouds, to see in front of them glimpses of the now closer turnpike and even of the rolling woods and ridges beyond. Other struggles, each smothered in its own cloud of dirty smoke, and heralded by its own combination of crackling musketry and crashing cannon, carried on the now relentless killing of the day. Shells were whizzing overhead, to burst in the air and send showers of their deadly fragments cascading downwards, but, for the moment, Daniel Ryan ignored them. He ignored his thumping chest also as he looked out instead towards the sparkling stones of that macadamised road at the glimpses of this panorama of destruction that now, through some quirk of clearing smoke and eddying breeze, stretched out beyond from the northwest across to the northeast. It was surely the largest view of a battle he had ever seen, but hardly had his mind registered the thought when the scene began to change and obscure again. Still more clouds of drifting, billowing gun smoke swept over the road and, even as his mind acknowledged the grandeur and the utterly breathtaking nature of its horrid destruction, his attention was forced back into the more local and immediate struggle of life and death that was continuing all around him..

The brigade line still advanced, moving diagonally downhill, approaching a dirt road, wreathed in smoke and littered in debris. Daniel let his eye follow the road down towards where a smoke obscured crossroads marked its junction of the turnpike. There too was that creek, marked by its margin of growth and brush, likely the one they had followed for the last part of their way here, now to their left in its swale of sheltered ground. Above them the shells still burst, coming, by their smoky trails from across the turnpike and now there were shouts from their right as emerging from the smoke beyond a bank that fringed the far side of the dirt road, loomed another formation of blue-clad Yankees. But as their own ranks marched towards the crossroads, these men were on their flank and the farther they marched towards that turnpike, the more these men would flank them and have advantage over them in the inevitably coming fight. Benning rode past, his hat pulled down towards his eyes as he gazed intently at the smoke shrouded ridge to the east. He rapped out an order to an aide, even as he trotted his horse on followed by two more of his staff, still gazing balefully at that hill to their oblique right. Around Daniel Ryan came the shouts of further orders to wheel to the right and face this new threat on the hill beyond the dirt road, now vanished in a cloud of gun smoke, as that blue rank, having halted, opened fire. The bullets came whizzing through, some droning on past, while others gave those wet, squelching thuds as they struck flesh, while still more an intimidating, crunching impact as they splintered bone. The line around Daniel Ryan writhed, as men lurched and fell, pushing into others as they went down, while around them the line slowly straightened, till at last the Ogeechee Volunteers faced directly across the dirt road towards this new enemy. It was as their own muskets came up, that the second Yankee volley came. It was a shade ragged, less precisely delivered than the first, and it flew slightly high, having been delivered through the bank of smoke, so that the men could hear the minie bullets whining past their heads, but it was deadly enough and more men went down as those wet, sickly, whizzing thumps resounded along their line. Numbers of men were on the ground now, some grasping at their comrades as they lay, but at last the regimental line stood with their own weapons up to take up the fight. The commands came along and the reply was delivered in its choking smoke and thumping recoil. Then the race was on to reload even as they anticipated the next Yankee reply.

Up and down the line behind the ranks the officers paced, waving their swords and yelling encouragement to their men, but those same swords were ready to be used also for keeping in place any whose instincts for survival encouraged them to leave their place in the firing line.

"Serve it up to them boys," Fenwick shouted as he stood behind his section. Boyce tended to call on them to "pour it into them," and it was only seconds till they heard him bellow those very words. Daniel, absorbed with his loading and firing, still allowed himself a half-smirk as he heard his mental prediction come true. Rodger too paced up and down calling out to the slowly diminishing line of men that marked his company.

"Press them here boys, press them here." The double line of men stood there, soaked in their sweat and blackened by the powder, as the battle continued, trading volley for volley with the scarcely seen enemy across that road as steadily more men crumpled and fell, or lurched backwards from their place, with the force of the heavy bullet they had taken. Conrad Bell was one of these, toppling down from where he had stood, three or four places along the line from Daniel Ryan. He clutched at his stomach and screamed, the sound of his voice piercing and loud, even above the deafening musketry. His screaming continued as he lay and writhed among the grass, his voice, audible to those around him, grating on those who stood nearby still loading and firing. Beside Daniel, Tom Gibben lowered his musket and made to loosen his canteen, but was shouted away by Boyce.

"Get back to your firing," the lieutenant shouted, gesturing with his sword. "You can't do him any good."

All around them fragments of cartridge paper, a few of them blue-coloured, flapped and drifted through the smoke on the hot air, and in truth, the whole field felt as hot as a furnace to Daniel Ryan. He was drenched in sweat, and was repeatedly having to wipe his wet tunic sleeve across his face as the perspiration ran into his eyes. Occasionally the smoke cloud around them eddied or thinned, to show to any who had the time to look, that behind them the sun was now down behind banks of clouds that rose to the west and the evening afterglow now guided the day to its end. But here, as the acrid cloud engulfed them again, it remained a grim test of resolve. Where they were deployed there was hardly a shred of cover and their two ranks endured there, among their dead and wounded, on the gentle slope that flanked that dirt road, loading and firing their increasingly fouled muskets as quickly as they could.

The Confederate line, urged on by their officers, inched ever forward, trying to close up to the road itself, and dislodge those Yankees to make them pull back up that slope on the far side. Every twenty or so seconds, the next exchange of volleys would take place and more men would collapse from their places in the line down into the jumble of blood and prostrate wriggling shapes at their feet. The line extended on up the hill to their right and there, visible in glimpses through the drifting smoke, the colours of the Fifteenth Regiment had reached the road, waving in the air above the smoke, pushing the Yankees on the far side away from the bank and part of the way up the slope beyond. Further to the right there was only smoke and fire and noise, with nothing visible through the stinking cloud. Survival had come down to the few yards to either side that could be made out in the slowly drifting billows and the few men who stood beside and around in that space. They loaded and fired with relentless unflinching persistence, awaiting the shot that would bring them too down into the mess of dead and dying at their feet. Still the screams came from Conrad Bell, now lying just behind where the diminishing double rank had edged forward towards the road, his shouts grinding on the nerves, never easing, let alone ceasing. In the straggling line, those who remained stuck grimly to their work, sometimes shouting to each other, their own words mixing with that of the officers.

"Just hold on boys," they yelled to each other.

"Not a step back, boys. Not a goddam step."

"Keep up your fire." Then Rodger came along behind the line again, minus his hat. He stopped where Boyce stood and yelled to him words that, in the deafening musketry, were impossible to hear. He turned and looked along the line of blackened, sweat-soaked men who still stood, loading and firing, just in front of him.

"Just keep it up. Come on boys, just hold fast a little longer." Those still unwounded stood and blazed away, but now the ammunition was starting to run short and the boys were beginning to rummage through the pockets and pouches of the dead and dying for whatever remained. Overhead, even through the clouds of smoke, they could sense that the sky, was darkening as evening turned towards night and still there were no signs of supports and the bleeding and dying around them went inexorably on. On the far side of the road the smoke briefly thinned and drifted and they could see the enemy line, with its shambles of dead and wounded littering the grass around it, but, even as he used this sighting to aim for his next shot, Daniel Ryan caught a hint of movement further up that rise beyond which the enemy had made their stand. He looked again, disbelieving, as the smoke eddied again, just enough for him to make out a further formation of troops who had crested the hill and halted behind and above the remnants of the original Yankee line. There were shouts of anger and dismay as others saw them, halted there, not advancing to join the men in front, but content to stay to their rear and by shooting over their heads from the higher part of the slope, to add their weight of fire to the struggle, now becoming grievously unequal, for still only Benning's men, standing amidst their fallen comrades and their blood, were on this side of the road. The fire from the far side was now coming in enormous blasts of bullets and they were felling men in still larger numbers. In places now, along the line, the smoke was eddying to reveal more men down than those remaining standing.

The shuffling southern advance had faltered and now, in the face of this searing torrent of fire, and, with no sign of help, the boys began to move again. Recognising the impossibility of prevailing, they now inched back from where they had been halted near the road, moving slowly away from the withering blasts of death. The officers looked around, having seen this movement back, but, for the most part, they said nothing. Back the men went, still in a rough line, loading and firing until, seeing the inevitable, the officers waved them back with their swords. The smoke still swirled around them, but now the ground was descending behind them and, glancing back, Daniel Ryan caught a glimpse of the creek bed at the bottom of its gully, the one he had glimpsed earlier, and now diagonally across the rear of their position. There was cover there, from this withering fire, a depression, along the side of which they could shelter, while still keeping their fire on the Yankees across the road. The gloom around them was deepening as they moved beyond the edge of the dip and a few more steps took them below the top, to where a measure of safety lay from the volleys of musketry that still swept across the field, buzzing like angry insects over their heads. They knelt down to load and some stood up to fire, unable in the gloom and the smoke to see anything at all now of the Yankee line and firing only at the orange-yellow muzzle flashes of the more distant enemy muskets.

So the battle was continued as long as the ammunition lasted. Stretching out on the hillside ahead of them almost all the way to the road lay a carpet of broken bodies gradually fading from sight as the darkness aided the dirty banks of smoke in covering these blasted fields of northern Virginia, hiding the abominable things that littered the withered yellow grass from sight, at least until the coming of a new day. Across the road the firing at last slackened and began to fade and the smoke began to drift and thin, until finally, save for a scattering of individual shots, it died away. At last, well after total darkness had fallen, the field, at least the part of it where Benning's Georgia brigade had poured out its blood and its stubborn endurance, save for the shrieks and wails of the wounded men all around them, quietened.

A drizzling rain had begun to fall as their skirmish line inched forward across the dirt road, where so many injured had crawled to escape the fire that had swept either way just above where they now lay. The advancing line reached the far side to cross an earth bank and the remains of a broken down fence, where whole sections of the posts and rails had been splintered and demolished by the gunfire, feeling their way in the darkness. Up on the slope the enemy dead and dying lay thickly and many of the advancing men, Daniel Ryan among them, now paused to furnish themselves with the things they lacked. Shoes, belts socks, haversacks and even pants were pulled from the dead. But, though Daniel Ryan tried several fallen Yankees as he tried to keep pace, none of them wore shoes that were as large as his own. Chivvied by Bradlee, their sparse line pushed on towards the top of the slope, still wading through a carpet of fallen wailing men, but Daniel knew that, whatever the circumstances, short of renewed battle, shoes had to be gotten at the first opportunity, or other hands would be on them.

The darkness was deep and near complete, with no moon penetrating the cloud cover, and only the glow of flickering fires scattered around the fields to give any light at all. The fighting, save for the isolated shots exchanged by prowling pickets like themselves seemed over. But, sure enough, the far side of the summit on their own front sparked into life as the withdrawing enemy cautioned them to keep their distance. Daniel crouched in the grass beside John Fitzpatrick and Otis Ballard, as the bullets buzzed past. He heard Daley muttering to Philipps a little to their left and being growled at in turn by Bradlee. In his pouch he had two shots left in addition to the one in his musket, all gleaned from a fallen soldier. His limbs felt leaden and heavy, and his mind was fuzzed and weary, as though, in a way, he really wasn't here in this desperate place of death and misery.

He moved away along the line just in front of his comrades, inspecting the fallen Yankees, by feel more than by sight, and moving more and more urgently, until at last he came upon a soldier who seemed somewhat bigger in build. He rummaged for the laces of the boy's shoes and pulled them from his feet, only to hear him groan and feel a spasm of movement run through his frame. Daniel jumped back, still grasping the shoes, feeling a surge of mortification at having robbed a man who was not yet dead, even though he would have no further use for shoes for some considerable time if at all. He looked at the dim shape of the fallen Yankee for another number of seconds, but, seeing no further sign of life, he turned and, stuffing the shoes into his tunic, retraced his steps back to where those of his own section still crouched.

The Yankees had skedaddled to the east, likely away towards Centreville, where the fortifications from last year still stood, and so the braggart, Johnny Pope had been attended to. Even the enemy rearguard, which had stayed up here on this hill till well into the night, was now withdrawing, and it was the muted signs of this in the darkness that had prompted the advance of the southern pickets. So the army had done what it had been set to do, but at another monstrous cost in blood and suffering. Daniel allowed his mind to range over these thoughts, thankful that he had again escaped death and injury, though the skin of his shoulder was raw and the limb itself ached from the recoiling of the powder-fouled Enfield, in spite of Jeffers' blue-wrapped "cleaners." Looking around that field, in the dusk, at some of those who had not escaped, had brought him forcefully into contact again with the frightful destructiveness of this war. It was like Malvern Hill, back in the summer, all over again. Yet it was victory, but if this was what a victory looked like, what kind of a thing was defeat?

All around where they crouched were the noises of battle's aftermath. The screams of disabled men, and of mangled horses too, still rent the air, mixing with the less strident but maybe more unsettling cries and mutters, for these were words that a man could hear and understand, even if there was nothing he could do about them. All around there were men who begged for help, or a bullet to end their suffering, or most of all for water. Some yelled, some mumbled and others cried, but the words, the entreaties, the cries and groans went on and on and they could not be closed out.

"Water, fer Chrissake get me a drink of water."

"Help me, oh God, help me!"

"Please, just a little water."

"Shoot me, please, anybody, just shoot me."

"Water..... Waaater."

"Oh Jesus, oh God, the pain."

"Gimme some water, my throat's so goddamn dry,"

All around them the noise went on, while in the distance behind them and over across the turnpike, a few lanterns flickered and moved. Some were out to look to the wounded, but not, so far, over on this side where the Yankees had not yet gone completely from the field. Daniel Ryan's near to torpid mind registered all of these things, the sights, sounds and smells. The smells, the sickly reek of blood, and that horrid smell of flesh persisted, mixing with traces of smoke and faesces and urine and death. They registered for a time at least, until utter exhaustion won and, crouched against a fence post and leaning his head on the barrel of his musket, in the midst of all of the bleeding, dying and the bedlam of shouts and cries, with the spattering rain gradually soaking through his clothes, he dozed.

Daniel awoke, stiff and cold into a grey first light. The rain had gone and a fresher breeze blew across the hillside, wafting strands of smoke and blowing the litter of cartridge paper scraps around the hunched forms of the sleeping and the fallen men. Around him a few of the others had already stirred, though many still slept. He struggled up on stiff, sore legs and stretched, wincing as his raw and strained shoulder reminded him of its plight and feeling his still wet clothes cling to his limbs, restricting the movement. Ahead of him Bradlee, Thompson and Ballard had gathered into a small group talking quietly as he approached. Bradlee turned as Daniel reached them.

"Brigadier's back," he said. "He got here in the middle o' the fight yesterday, 'n' he's back in command." Daniel looked out across the littered fields and across to the north beyond the turnpike, not more than marginally interested in what the sergeant was saying, while around them others of the section stirred to stretch in turn before slowly assembling into a loose group. As they gathered, Daniel Ryan pulled the Yankee shoes from his belt and inspected them. In the light of day, they looked somewhat disappointing, being well worn down, an improvement, certainly, on those he still wore, but not too much better. He unlaced his old shoes and tossed them away, replacing them with the newly acquired pair which seemed at least a size larger, though the soles were worn and the uppers scratched and scuffed. Having stamped around in them a little, he rejoined the group. Saul Philipps was missing, gone, so Ballard said, to the hospital to have a wound in his arm treated.

"But he'll be back," he went on. "Didn't look too much and he won't want to wait around that place down there."

They had no blankets or haversacks, but around them lay dozens of dead and wounded Yankees, many of whom still carried theirs. It meant having to deal up close with the horrors of the field, but hunger was a mighty good convincer and the boys spread out to forage the dead and the dying for the things that they would no longer need, many rifling pockets for money or valuables in addition to their more obvious wants. Daniel and John Fitzpatrick moved together across the slope, where the Yankees had stood the evening before, among others already at work on these men. All the way up the now muddy side road a scattering of southern soldiers pulled at any shoes that remained, as well as haversacks, blankets and anything else to be gained from the corpses of the enemy dead. Daniel did likewise, equipping himself with a replacement waterproof and a woollen blanket, draping them over his shoulders, but by now, since the Yankee dead were almost all barefooted, the chance of better shoes was likely gone. The two of them prowled and rummaged through a collection of haversacks, and pockets too, finding enough in the way of rations, mainly hardtacks and some salted pork, for a decent breakfast.

The sights were unspeakable. Shattered limbs showed graphically the damage a minie bullet did to the body of a boy, not to mention artillery fire. Here lay the decapitated and the disembowelled, with their blood sluiced into the mud by the rain, and there lay other boys, who had been killed by a single neat hole in the chest or the head. There were many more, men who had not been killed outright but had bled to death, some, lying with their dead hands clenched where they had clutched or pulled or scrabbled at their wounds trying to staunch the flow of blood. Such sights stretched away, from any place where a man now stood, across these trampled, littered fields, into the distance in whatever direction he chose to look.

Some now worked among the wounded, but Daniel and his companions, beyond giving an occasional draught of water to a few who were still conscious, stuck to their quest for food. Some of the Yankees still carried coffee rations and they steadily gathered these into a small, cloth coffee bag, gleaned from a dead soldier's haversack. Up on the crest of the hill, fires still smouldered, many from last night's battle, while others, with their drifting wisps and wavers of smoke marked where men laboured to set them, keep them alight and build them up into appreciable blazes with wood still wet after the rain. Having collected enough for a meal and maybe something spare, they headed back towards where the others were gathering.

There were no pans, but Thompson and Ballard, had built a fire, and were engaged in heating a Yankee canteen above its flames, softening the solder till the two metal halves could be prized apart for use as cooking pans. As they worked, more of the mess returned with their collections of plunder. Kane had gone back across to the creek and filled a collection of canteens with water, while Daley and Gibben, brought word of a column of abandoned Yankee wagons run off the turnpike at the bottom of the hill, full of army rations, beef, crackers and more real coffee. They had brought back all they could manage and it was split up into portions for everyone to carry in their newly acquired haversacks.

A breakfast of some briefly soaked salt pork was set to spitting and sizzling in the two makeshift pans, casting cooking smells around the hillside, to mingle with those from other fires. Hardtacks were then cooked in the grease and when it was ready, the boys produced plates, foraged, like the food, from the fallen Yankees, and Kane dished up the meal, before rinsing one of the pans to boil water for the captured coffee. Everyone ate ravenously in a group around their fire, with the dead and the dying within yards of where they sat or squatted. Food eaten, and plates and cutlery licked and stowed away in their foraged haversacks, they waited around their fire, boiling more water and drinking successive cups of coffee, till Jeffers arrived with Bradlee and Bailey.

"You lucky boys," Jeffers called, "you lucky, lucky boys. It's doctorin' and grave diggin' now fer them that the good lord has decided to spare, and that's you, you lucky boys." Bradlee paused at their fire as the other two moved on.

"We'll start with our own on that slope over the road yonder and ya kin be thankful fer the rain, cuz if it wuz still hot like yesterday they'd be stinkin' and swellin' worse by now, so shift yore asses afore the sun comes out agin." There was a discontented mutter at his words from some, but others just shrugged. Who knew what further clothing and equipment needs might be made good or whatever else might be gleaned from the dead in the way of rations or valuables? That at least would be some compensation for getting the job of burying them.

As the day advanced the weather improved and with the rain having passed, the clouds broke up and steadily cleared while the breeze continued to dry the fields. The section had laboured for much of the time on removing wounded to an improvised hospital at a large house, down on the turnpike, while others had begun work on pits for the dead. The former were carried in blankets or on blood soaked litters to the yard of the house and turned over there to harassed orderlies, who pointed out where they were to be laid, before dismissing those who had brought them. Inside the house, and under awnings round the back away from the road, surgeons worked and Daniel, with his experiences of field hospitals on the peninsula still fresh enough in his mind, stayed clear of that as far as he could, wanting no sights or reminders of what was going on there.

During the afternoon word spread that Jackson and his troops were pulling out, heading away to the north east, across Bull Run Creek by a ford up there along the dirt road at Sudley. They were off on Lee's orders, the stories said, to flank the Yankees out of their forts and rifle pits at Centreville and maybe they would push Johnny Pope into still more trouble. But there were other rumours too, that McClellan's Potomac Army was up there too, so how many Yankees would they all have to tangle with, between here and the Potomac River? Nobody had much of an idea. That was the job of the generals and they would leave it to "Marse Robert."

Their own waning hours of daylight were spent retracing their steps of yesterday over the still-littered fields, back to the brigade stepping off point, to collect equipment and belongings left there, with some boys stepping away to forage among the remaining corpses, now swelling and discolouring as Bradlee had warned. There was little to be had from these men indicating they had already been looted by earlier details of the needy. On reaching their own camp ground, the men were dismissed to recover their own gear, some taking only what they chose from their piles, if they had gotten better that morning from the Yankee dead. Their own mess resolved almost unanimously that they would dispatch the heavier pan to the company skillet wagon, relying instead upon the lighter one and the two improvised canteen halves for the meantime.

Philipps belongings were divided to be taken on meantime, in case he did return and, having collected what they wanted, the column almost immediately re-assembled. Old Pete wanted his boys ready to march at first light, Bailey said, so it was back to the east, at least as far as the Sudley Road, to be ready for the coming march.

As the files reformed, Daniel Ryan looked along the remaining piles of belongings that no-one would now be returning to claim. A few of the departing boys picked through these for anything of use, but Daniel Ryan could not bring himself to join them. Each of these bundles represented a man, one of their own, who, along with his comrades, had stacked his gear yesterday, believing that he would survive and return to claim it, and now? Daniel looked at the forlorn piles and, in his mind, attached faces to some of them. There were Bell's things and Canby's, and Jim Dellings', John Sangster's and Charlie Thorne's. He knew that Thorne and Dellings had been taken off the field alive this morning, so maybe they would survive, but the others? Their remaining belongings would lie here until gleaned by a further battlefield detail or by some local foragers and then the footprint of these men would be gone. Daniel felt a surge of sadness rise through him as he looked at these pathetic bundles, while others concluded their brief prowl through them before returning to their places.

Eventually they had left the place, moving north onto the turnpike to head east again, having to shorten their files to two abreast in the jumble of traffic on the road. Eventually, with the sun down, the column was steered off the road to make camp. The role was called and, orders having arrived, they were read out by Boyce. They would march in the morning, early. Following Jackson's route, the men reckoned, to get around the right flank of the enemy positions at Centreville and maybe force another battle. Dismissed to eat and sleep, they set up fence rail fires and cooked more of the food they had gathered through the day, feasting on Yankee beef, fried rabbit pieces and hardtacks, and boiling up more coffee, as they had in the morning. As the mess ate, Philipps returned with his arm bandaged and, a plate of food was dished up for him also. While much of what they had gathered earlier was eaten by the end of the evening, a portion still remained to be packed in the haversacks of each man of the mess for the coming march.

The Monday was the first day of September and the regiment was paraded early on a clear morning, with a breeze blowing through the camps and trees, flapping canvas and waterproof blanket shelters, swaying branches and detaching occasional leaves that fluttered around on the gusts. After assembly and breakfast, the brigade moved off, taking the road that crossed the turnpike and following it to the north to cross Catharpin Creek at Sudley Springs Ford, and Bull Run itself a little further on, without the benefit of removing shoes or pants for either. The road had a surface of drying mud and although this eliminated the problem of dust, progress was of the frustrating start and stop nature, saddled once again with the artillery and wagon train, as they made their way north. Toombs had indeed returned, being seen along the marching column at the head of his staff, responding with a wave to the cheers of the men.

The column stayed on that road for most of the morning, before turning southeast, passing a succession of hamlets along the way as the day wore on and cloud began to gather from the mountains to the west. Up ahead, as the afternoon ebbed, there was gunfire and the march pace was increased as darker and more ominous clouds built up across the sky. The column wound on, now with large spots of rain beginning to splash down as they were turned off to the south, on a side road, towards where the musketry had again swelled to battle proportions, with the telltale smoke cloud marking where this latest collision was. The sky was now dark and overcast, with the rain growing rapidly worse, quickly flooding the crowded road as flashes of lightning and peals of thunder followed the onset of the downpour. The men laboured through what was fast becoming a blinding deluge. Visibility steadily reduced in the teeming downpour till it was impossible to see more than a few yards. Up ahead the gunfire was slackening, not too surprisingly since the boys down there must be having trouble seeing any enemy let alone keeping handled cartridges dry enough to discharge their muskets at them.

The men were halted in the road, upon which they made for the trees which lined one side to take their chances with the dripping branches, before being assembled again, as the storm still raged, to retrace their steps to the northwest, finally falling out to bivouac in gathering darkness in the dripping woods near one of the hamlets they had passed through earlier. As the rain slackened, they laboured over a fire, which, with its sodden tree boughs and fence rails that they had managed to gather, stubbornly resisted attempts to build it to a suitably drying size. So they sat around their smoky result in the darkness, warming more of the foraged Yankee rations. Around them the woods still dripped and a dank mist now hung under the trees. The fire was the best chance for any sort of comfort that night, so, with the rain now past, they gathered still more wood and, having tried to dry it around the fire they had managed to build, fed it steadily, finally succeeding in building it up into a sizeable blaze as slowly, their saturated clothes and blankets steamed and warmed and a measure of comfort came. On top of it all, Daniel Ryan had begun making successive visits to the dripping bushes, concluding from this, that his bowels were once again succumbing to a further bout of the army's commonest ailment.

Chapter 6
Invasion

The weather had settled again by the morning of the Tuesday, with the rising sun drying the grass and slowly diminishing the puddles and sloughs on the muddy roads and trails. Assembly included no marching orders, but the columns were formed to await them and the men stood in their files for near to an hour before being stood down, to rest along the roadside for a further hour until word eventually came along that the army would remain in camp today. Finally dismissed, the boys boiled and drank what remained of the real coffee and ate the remaining rations before setting to organising equipment, foraging for further food and, above all, resting. Many, especially those who wore plundered Yankee shoes, unfamiliar to their feet, treated blisters, some at least gotten yesterday after those fords at Sudley.

As the day went on some men collected water and, although without soap, made a stab at washing themselves, and even some of their clothing. Others left things as they were, deeming that in mid-campaign it was pretty well a waste of time. Washing tended to disturb one's lice anyway and there was no point whatever in prompting the intensified itching torment that would result from that. Considerable numbers from the company, including Daniel Ryan, were now fully afflicted with the flux and toilet excursions were a regular feature of the day, persistently interrupting the chores around the camp. The commissary remained absent, so the supper for most depended on whatever they had foraged that day, this being corn and apples for Daniel Ryan's mess. The temperature fell during the evening and, for the first time that Daniel could remember, since coming to Virginia months before in the spring, the night air, as well as dry, was cold, bringing the newly acquired blankets into use.

The chill lingered in the grass underfoot and a white film of hoar covered the leaves and branches around the camp as the sleepers awakened to the drum roll next morning. The men as they assembled, trailed clouds of smoky breath, all of it giving a hint of coming autumn, contrasting with the humid heat of recent days. The sun was just below the horizon as, roll call and assembly done, the Ogeechee Volunteers formed their column of march. It was off again, Rodger had told them, heading north west into Loudon County where the armies had not yet campaigned or foraged to any extent, making for the town of Leesburg which lay near one of the bends in the Potomac River. The march began, towards the river initially, but then turned more to the west with the roads still muddy from Monday's downpour, which meant ploughing through the remaining puddles and morasses. Many of the boys, after their day of rest, were in good spirits and talk was much on the licking they had given Pope's boys, as well as the usual speculation as to where they were headed.

Loudon County, where supplies should be more readily available, was a welcome enough place to make for, but already there were other rumours. Some reckoned that the army was bound for the Shenandoah Valley to provision there and threaten a crossing of the Potomac. Others declared that the march was for the river, without crossing the mountains, straight into Maryland instead, to advance on Washington from the north or west, or maybe head for Baltimore. Maybe, men speculated, the old man simply wanted to force the Yankees to battle again, somewhere across the river, while they were weakened and disorganised from their licking on Saturday. The day passed and by late afternoon they were halted, to camp around a hamlet called Frankville on the road to Leesburg. Beyond, as the men now knew, lay the fords over the Potomac. There was no rations issue and the boys were left to content themselves with corn and unripe apples foraged from the nearby fields and orchards and, cooked into a hash in the improvised pans and the one remaining one from Richmond.

As the evening gathered, a further detail of returning men, who had made the journey from Richmond, arrived in camp. Some were recovered from wounds or sickness with others returning from detached duty of one kind or another. Edwin Jones was among them and he arrived at the fire looking thin and pale, but alive and recovered. His hand was pumped and his back slapped by various members of the mess, relieved at seeing him. They sat till lights out, listening to Jones' account of his hospital stay and his tedious journey north to rejoin, over destroyed railroads and choked roads, turning in to their blankets in a better frame of mind as a result of his return.

The following day saw the march resume, still to the west, on a clear and sunny day, with the morning cool, but gradually warming as the sun ascended. The road had improved, with the remains of the largest puddles drying, and a firm surface now on most of its length, though with sufficient dampness remaining to keep that surface hard for the time being. But the talk on the march was changing. Gone was the wisecracking and banter, for persisting rumours of an imminent crossing of the river, was doing something in those ranks introducing harder discussions among the men, during the hour halts mostly, but also as the column tramped those rain compacted roads, following the sun as it edged west.

Somehow, with the news and speculation about Lee's plans, attitudes were changing. To many, these rumours meant nothing at all. There were rumours every day in the army and while sometimes they were true, other times they were not, and this was no different. Every day brought its own confirmation of how accurate the latest gossip was. But, to other men these stories were different. Rumours about fording the river were different. Defending the south, they said, did not mean invading the north, and once they crossed that river, they would be doing the very thing that they had enlisted and spent all summer fighting the Yankees for doing.

The discussion now ranged up and down, sometimes even flaring into outright argument, as to what this war was all about and why everyone was here fighting in it, and, as the march drew them closer to the river up ahead, it became clear that many of these men had come to Virginia to confront an invader and for nothing more than that. Crossing over the river was aggression and some were now openly saying that they wanted none of it. As the day passed, they drew steadily closer to Leesburg, halting to camp, in the early evening, at Newton Hall just short of the town. In the camps, again with no rations issued, the talk continued, with every sign that there were sharply divided views on what the general, and the army, should be doing next.

Friday arrived with the drum roll rousing the slumberers from their blankets to another clear and cloudless dawn. The march would be short today, Rodger told the assembled men. They were to pass through Leesburg and camp beyond the town between it and the Potomac River. The roads were now dry, but, with the surface beginning to break and crush into dust with the passage of feet, hooves and wheels, the men soon marched in the beginnings of a familiar, light brown cloud. A short march, the boys told each other, would be welcome today.

Here, if indeed they were headed north to cross the river, was the last town of any size in Virginia and its citizens might be the last in Virginia to see the troops and their leaders. They would not see much of Lee, for there were other stories around the camps, borne out by what was to be seen on the roads, that the general was riding in an ambulance, disabled by some kind of an accident with his horse back there on Monday when that fight and march in the thunderstorm had been taking place. Reports of him said that he was now splinted and bandaged on both hands, one of them supported by a sling, and was travelling north, at the pace of the wagon train.

They came in along Market Street to find that, in spite of the previous passage of Jackson's divisions and other units of the army, they still got the full treatment from the locals, who had turned out in numbers for them. The streets were lined with townspeople, out to cheer and applaud the arriving troops and, what was even better, to give them what food they could prepare. It seemed that every local woman had baked and brought her wares to the roadside in relays for the famished men to pause and help themselves to at least a few delicacies. There were cakes and flatbreads and scones, sweet corn bread and buns of every description. The troops took enthusiastic advantage of this generosity, with elaborate gallantry and gratitude on both sides, and on seeing their unkempt state, the locals even made some offers of soap to help.

The crowds lining the streets were most numerous through the middle of town. There people cheered, waving handkerchiefs and flags and offering their cakes and scones and drinks of lemonade and buttermilk to the passing men, bringing pitchers and buckets of water to the roadside for the soldiers to drink or fill canteens. With all of this going on, the passage through town was slowed, and the boys made the most of it, waving and calling comments in return, particularly to the girls, before passing on out to the north of town, to cover only another three miles before making camp on the fields of a farm. The place had just about the biggest watering hole that Daniel Ryan had ever seen. It was a limestone spring which fed a huge pool, still full of fresh, cold water in spite of the fact that hosts of Jackson's men had apparently helped themselves to its contents the previous night.

Daniel Ryan had now, as the previous days had threatened, contracted what was turning into his worst case yet of camp diarrhoea to take with him, wherever the army ultimately decided to go, but so too had three others of the mess, namely Philipps, Daley and Gibben. Daniel attributed it to the overripe rabbit meat that had lain too long in their haversacks, but he knew that it could equally be the result of any other bad food or indeed bad water. It made life harder, with unannounced darts to the bushes, at any time of the day or night, and it was getting painful to walk with one's hindquarters growing red raw, to say nothing of the sickly, nauseous, weakness in the stomach and bowels themselves. He had this evening dispensed with his soiled drawers, rinsing them in water before rolling them in his blanket roll. Such things, delayed the toileting for those critical further seconds, and too easily became casualties of an active dose of the flux, so they were better kept clear of the engagements, at least until the condition had settled somewhat.

He continued to eat with the others of the mess, though deriving much diminished pleasure, even from the better food available around Leesburg, but knowing from previous bouts of the flux, both in himself and others, that, if he did not eat, then he would just grow weaker and still more serious ailments might follow. As though to compound his woes, on inspecting the shoes he had gotten only days before, he found that there was already a small rent along the outside of the upper near the sole, similar to what had happened with his previous discarded shoes, but this time the poor quality of the leather rather than the stitching was apparently the problem. These brogans too were now onto borrowed time and he would have to be on the lookout for replacements once again.

The camps on the farm had filled up with visitors from the town that evening, as the commissary wagons came creaking up the road. There were enthusiastic shouts from the men as news of their arrival spread and issues of flour and meat were the result of their visit. Many of the townsfolk too had brought gifts of food and with these supplementing the issued rations, an air of festivity spread through the camps as the evening drew on, with the event increasingly turning into a giant levee. The groups of local people, continued to arrive, coming out by various modes of transportation, bringing still more samples of food and drink, to fete the men and be serenaded in their turn by regimental bands. The time passed in pleasant dalliances, for all who were so inclined, but as the evening and the festivities waned and the visitors departed, the boys gathered again around their fires and the discussions resumed.

Even in their own company, not everyone saw crossing the river to invade the north as being the way to defend the south and this brand of talk, coming close at times to outright argument, flickered like a flame through the camps. Now that the army had driven its enemies out of Virginia, the generals were proposing, so the stories said, to go straight ahead and cross the Potomac River into Maryland or maybe even head north into Pennsylvania. Disapproval for this remained widespread, with some of the talk verging on mutinous, at the prospect. The close proximity of the river seemed to animate the discussion and argument, extending it into that warm and humid night. It was as though being this close to the river, and to enemy territory, emphasised for men a need to speak their piece and make a decision that was now more pressing and imminent. The debate in their own mess had been instigated by the newly returned Edwin Jones, but others soon joined in.

Their fires burned steadily down and, even after taps, still the muted talk went on.

"It ain't like defendin' our homes, or Georgia, or Virginia, or the south when we cross that river,"

Jones told them. "As soon as we cross over, we're no better than the Yankees. We are invadin' other folk's homes and we are wrong in the eyes of justice," he added.

"But the papers reckon that a lot o' them folks over across there in Maryland are southerners too and they'd join us except that the Yankees won't let 'em" Gibben told him. "If we cross over then we're liberatin' them folks and lettin' them choose, which way they want to go, north or south."

"Southern papers would say that," Isaac Kane said. "North or south the papers'll say what suits 'em best and sometimes that means telling the rest of us any damn lies they want. Edwin's right, crossin' over there puts us in the wrong and I got a bad feelin' about it." Daniel listened to the talk as it ranged around the bivouac. He could see a point in what men like Jones and Kane were saying, but, to him, there was another argument also, a simpler one and that was to do with winning. As a lull came in the talk, he resolved to speak. But in the meantime, Bradlee had arrived and quickly had the attention of the group.

"If you boys're so full o' spunk that ya don't need no sleep, then I'll remember that in the mornin' if there's work to get done," he rasped. He stood there for a few moments more, listening to the murmured talk from different parts of the camp.

"Ain't hardly nobody wantin' their rest tonight," he said, "and all cuz we're near at the river and the soldier boys can't see why they got to cross over when they git the order."

"Don't strike me as right invadin' folks' homes," Jones grunted.

"Don't rightly know if right and wrong are still a big part of what we're all tryin' to do in this war," Bradlee said turning towards where Jones lay supporting himself on one elbow.

"Them Yankees we all talked to and traded with down on the Chickahominy River," the sergeant went on, "they reckoned they were in the right, even with all the invadin' they were doin', they reckoned that their United States was more important than any of the states that were a part of it. So they think they're right. We think our own state is more important so we think we're right. Standin' over here on this side o' the river thinkin' that yo're right ain't gonna make them go home. They'll be back over here as soon as they get reinforced, refitted and rested and re-organised and by stayin' over here and not crossin', we'll be givin' them all the time they need to git their next invasion ready. Abe Lincoln's a'ready called for more men to go on with the war, so, to my way o' thinkin', we got little…." His words ground to an abrupt silence and the others turned to see that Boyce had come by, as duty officer, on his own round of the camps and had clearly overheard the last of Bradlee's words. He eyed them as they looked his way.

"At ease," he said amiably. "It surely ain't a restful camp anywhere tonight." He took a little more time to look around them.

"I'm gatherin' that some of you boys, like others around here, would rather decline the hospitality of the great state of Maryland." There was silence initially around the fire as some men, reluctant to speak to an officer of such things, went on looking at each other, while others looked down at their feet or into the fire. Boyce saw the reaction and sat himself down near the dying flames.

"Speak freely boys if you have views on it. Ain't no point in thinkin' it and not sayin' it. I won't be rushin' off to put any man on report for just speakin' his mind." The silence continued for a few more seconds before Jones finally cleared his throat.

"Some of us reckon we enlisted to defend the south and not to invade the north, lieutenant."

"Well that's surely a sensible enough point of view," Boyce answered, "but, as for the general, from what I've been told by the colonel, he's got bigger problems to worry about than that one."

"I don't know what you mean," Jones told him.

"No matter what else happens," Boyce went on, "General Lee can't keep the army here. This county may have supplies, but most others up here, have been picked clean of everything by the Yankees. You could see that back over around Manassas and Centreville, when you went lookin' for food at the farms. They gave us what they had left but what was left wasn't much, and there's no supply line up from Richmond any more, even if they had enough supplies to send, since we, or the Yankees, burned all the road and railroad bridges back there over the Rapidan and Rappahannock, and every other river and creek, over the past couple of weeks. No, we can't stay up here, unless we want to get even thinner than we are now. We can't go east. We'd butt straight into the Washington defences and the land between here and Washington's picked even cleaner than Manassas and Warrenton. We could go all the way back south, but that would be handing the whole northern half of the state back to the Yankees when we just spent a lot of blood and effort turning them out of it. We could head west to the Shenandoah Valley, and, from here on west, there's supplies for sure, but if we do that we leave the road open, all the way back to Richmond for the Yankees to use once they're ready to try again" He paused and looked around the group, "or we can move north like the general thinks. That way the Yankees have to follow us and try to protect their own cities, like Baltimore and Philadelphia as well as Washington. They can't just let us march over their back yard and do nothin' about it. Up north in Maryland and in Pennsylvania there's plenty of supplies, because they haven't had any armies of hungry boys marchin' about up there like the folks down here have. So we don't have a lot of good choices, if you look at it the way the general has to. If we want to eat, and keep the Yankees out of Virginia, then north is where we've got to go." He looked around the group and shrugged his shoulders.

"You men go right ahead and talk over what you think about it all," he said. "You surely ain't the only ones to think that crossing over's the wrong thing to do. But to end up with half of the army crossin' over and the other half stayin' on this side would be just about the worst thing that could happen. Even with the last of our reinforcements arrivin' from Richmond, the Yankees still outnumber us by thousands and it would be crazy to divide our force so that they could outnumber us by even more." He stood up, nodded to them, and paced slowly away, leaving them to their own talk.

To Daniel Ryan, what Boyce had told them made sense, but there was more to it than what he had said, so, while the others seemed to take pause to consider or digest the officer's words, he seized the moment and spoke up.

"I don't care much about invadin' or not invadin'," he said. "Since they passed that conscription law in the spring, I'm in this war till it's won, like everybody else around here, and once that's done, I want to get back down to Georgia to my real life. To me that means gettin' stuck in and whipping those Yankees till they're ready to give it up and a river doesn't make a tinker's curse of difference to that. They're back over there cuz we licked them and chased them off and now we've got them on their knees. We need to finish them off, not wait till they recover and come back, cuz when they do, as we all know, they'll still outnumber us and still have all their guns and wagons and train loads of supplies better than us. I say we should keep after them and do whatever it takes to win. If we aren't in this to win then we should never have started it at all." Thompson looked across the fire at him as he finished speaking.

"Them's sensible thoughts Daniel," he said, "and I go along with 'em." There was silence for a few seconds more, before Otis Ballard spoke.

"When ya hit yore enemy hard, you got to go on and hit him good again, and don't go lettin' up jest cuz he wants ya to." There was a ripple of grunts around the fire and he let these subside before he went on.

"That's jest my way of sayin' that I go along with what Daniel said too."

But, in spite of all the talking and discussing that had gone on, there were clearly some in the camp who would simply never be convinced. Certainly the majority seemed to reckon that the only way to beat the Yankees was to keep after them, especially when they had licked them this far, but others still demurred. It was wrong, they reckoned, and they would have none of it. The argument and discussion did not end that night in the camp outside Leesburg. It was still there simmering away the next morning when, after roll call and a cold breakfast of bacon and corn flour fritters, they were formed up to head on to the fords. The mess put in one more discussion on the whole matter, but it was becoming rancorous now, even among boys whose friendship went back well beyond their enlistment. They knew that Jones and Kane might well balk when the time came, but Daniel found it somewhat disturbing that he had not heard John Fitzpatrick speak on the matter. He had been conspicuously quiet through all of the talk, and now, as the time for crossing drew close, Daniel wondered if his friend's comparative silence on the matter meant something more than what it superficially seemed.

This time, as before, the mess divided on the same lines, with Kane and Jones roundly against the move north, while Ryan, Ballard, Thompson, Phillips and Gibben were, if not in outright favour, at least going along with the idea. Fitzpatrick and, surprisingly to Daniel, Mick Daley also, had not yet declared their views or intentions, but, if they were reluctant to cross the river, they were running pretty short of time to do anything about it. This final talk among their own group was also coloured by the common knowledge that many other companies and regiments were similarly affected and there were already numbers of men, from Jackson's divisions, who, rather than head on across with their regiments, had stayed on this side of the Potomac. It was known that many of these men were disabled, by the dysentery and diarrhoea outbreaks that were sweeping the poorly supplied army. More of them, it was said, with blistered or bleeding feet, were simply unable to continue without shoes or other items of clothing, but a further number of them had simply refused to go.

The generals, while exhorting officers to discipline their men and suppress any sedition in their units, knew that they simply could not start taking more severe measures against large numbers of their soldiers. Hanging one or two for breaches of army law, Ballard said, was a different matter to hanging a lot, besides the army likely didn't have near enough rope for that many boys. Furthermore, the newspapers, received from various parts of the south, confirmed that the whole invasion idea was far from unanimously supported down home by the people or by their leaders, so the generals knew that they had to go carefully or they could finish up with very little of an army to do anything at all with.

The talk went on about the whole thing as the sun rose in the sky but still no word came to march.

"Some o' the North Carolina boys had meetin's in their regiments 'n' took votes on what to do," Gibben told the mess as the discussion went on.

"Don't reckon that's the best way o' doin' things," Jones came back. "Holdin' votes would mean that boys gotta go along with invadin', even if they don't want to, jest cuz others voted to do it."

"A vote seems fair enough t' me," Saul Philipps said.

"Leastways abidin' by a vote would mean boys stuck together," Ballard added, "and not finish up with ev'body goin' their own way." Jones was not impressed.

"I don't intend takin' part in no vote," he said. "I'm fer makin' up my own mind on this."

"I reckon your mind's made up already, Edwin," Daniel Ryan said.

"Ain't you done the same," Jones retorted? "Seems to me that's what everybody around here's doin'."

"Could finish up with no regiment that way," Philipps said, "or jest a part o' one." Daniel listened and watched. Most of all he watched Fitzpatrick and Daley and, at length, in response to the latest exchanges he got his answer. Mick was for going along, as Daniel had been reasonably certain that he would.

"The only way to win this is by fightin'," he said, "and if finishing the fight means crossing that river onto Yankee ground then that's just how it'll have to be." But, Fitzpatrick, to Daniel's dismay, challenged this.

"Lord knows I've thought on this," he said. "I heard what you boys have said about keepin' after the Yankees till we finally lick them, but, in my heart I'm against this step. The last thing I enlisted in this regiment to do...."

"You didn't enlist John," Daniel snapped, immediately irritated by the view his friend was revealing at last, "we all enlisted and we did it together." Fitzpatrick glared back at him.

"I still get the right to have a point of view, and make up my own mind and I sure as hell didn't come all this way up here to go plunderin' the homes and towns of anybody up north. I reckon that to do that would be a crime and would, like Edwin says, make us no better than the Yankees. I've thought about it all, but I want no part of invadin' the north." There was a further chorus of shouts and responses to his words, some to agree and more to argue and it was clear by these shouts and comments that their group was utterly divided, and not just divided, but with the two points of view now beginning to confront each other in increasing anger. Bailey stepped in to call a halt to this trouble before it led to worse than words, dispersing them and standing to watch them go before stalking off to other matters. Everyone knew that the sergeants had been gauging the mood of their men, especially since the mutterings had begun at the start of the week and it was clear that they had been reporting back to the officers on what those men were saying. This too, with the rising level of anger and discord in the camps might be a further source of trouble.

Back at Savannah, when a minority had balked at the idea of travelling to Virginia to fight, the whole regiment had been paraded and addressed by officers and ultimately the men had been given their choice to stay or to go. But, while some anticipated that this might be done again, before the regiment was ordered across the river, it did not happen that way. It was done on a much smaller scale, company by company, with captains addressing their men and exhorting them to obey orders and stay with the flag. Their own turn came now with the company finally paraded for morning assembly and orders of the day. Rodger paced for a few moments before giving them the news.

"The regiment will break up camp here and march to White's Ford where it will cross the Potomac River with the others of the brigade. Once across we are to head for the Monocacy River and the railroad and will set up camp there till further orders are received." There was a mutter in the ranks at his words and a ripple of movement along the lines of men.

"Stand still on parade," it was Jeffers' voice, bellowing the words. Rodger looked around the faces and cleared his throat.

"I would urge you all to do your duty and stay with the flag," he said, "but I am instructed that any men unfit to continue the campaign, for medical reasons, should report to the surgeon," he continued. "Those men so reporting will fall out now." There was a shuffle as a few left the ranks. Out of the corner of his eye, Daniel saw Edwin Jones go. Sure Jones was only days back from hospital, but he was not the only one with troubles. Right at this moment, standing here at assembly, his own backside felt like it was on fire with its raw, chapped skin. Jones, as far as he knew, had no such affliction, but he was using the excuse of illness and was going. Others were going also, with Rufus Fenton, Ollie Cartwright and Nathan Morris among them. Daniel, as he saw them move away out of the corner of his eye, began to wonder if this excuse of unfitness was going to be the ploy by which the regiment, or indeed the army divested itself of the men who would not join in this coming invasion of the north, without giving itself the awkward job of having to discipline large numbers of them once they refused to go.

The army's commanders had clearly shown on previous occasions, that if they thought it warranted, their men would be hanged or shot for any of a number of what they regarded as more serious misdeeds. Desertion was certainly serious, especially in the eyes of the generals, but would they feel able to punish men in this way if their numbers were considerable, especially if some of their families, communities and state politicians back down south felt the same way they did about the idea of invading the northern states? Perhaps a camouflaging excuse like the sickness or lameness of those remaining south of the river would be their chance to side-step the problem. But, even as he pondered on this, around Daniel Ryan, the trickle of men leaving the ranks was soon done and the remainder were dismissed to break camp. On the way back, they found themselves rubbing shoulders with the three negroes. They eyed each other briefly.

"You boys comin' along," Gibben drawled? They gazed back evenly at him.

"Ain't done till it gits done," Eli replied.

"Good enough fer me," Gibben told him.

As the others of the mess gathered their gear Jones returned and started to collect his. They looked at him as he stood there and, for all of his stubborn opposition to crossing the river, his manner was now somewhat sheepish as he assembled his own belongings. He lifted his musket from its stack and turned to where they stood watching him.

"I'll be seein' you boys," he said quietly.

"Where'ya goin' Edwin," Kane asked him?

"Sterling says all of us who don't go across are bein' sent on west, t'ard the Shenandoah Valley," he said, "Old man don't want a whole crowd of us stayin' round here, foragin' the place clean, so we're gettin' rations when we reach Winchester and any who're fit and'll go back are to rejoin from there." Daley stepped up and faced him square on.

"So you're hardly back here and now you're off, and leavin' your friends and that's it," he growled. Jones looked back at him.

"We've been through all o' that more'n once," he said.

"Well I ain't goin' to say you're a coward Edwin," Daley told him. "I've known you long enough fer that, but what you're doin' is still plain skulkin' by god......" There was a chorus of shouts as Jones made for him and Daniel jumped towards them with the others, feeling his backside rasp with pain as he did so. Gibben and Ballard were quicker and Daley was hauled back and then restrained by them, while Thompson got hold of Jones, so he wasn't going anywhere the big corporal didn't want him to. Bailey arrived and glared at them all.

"Edwin git outa here," he hissed. "Go join them others that reckon they ain't comin' along. Take him off outa here, Joe,"

"Yeah, git him outa here," Ballard rasped. "It wuz him that started this whole thing off around here. There weren't a damned soul spoke of it till he did." Thompson shuffled the still struggling Jones away as Kane, his face red with anger, turned and yelled at Daley.

"Ya bog Irish shit," he shouted. "That's my goddam friend and he ain't no skulker." He turned and started to throw his own belongings together into his blanket roll and pull his equipment belts over his shoulders.

"Well if he's skulkin'," he muttered, "so am I." He turned, grabbed his musket and paced away after Jones and Thompson.

"What yo're all doin' is wrong," he shouted over his shoulder. Daniel watched them go, then turned back to see Fitzpatrick move back to where his own belongings lay. He called to him.

"You too John?" His friend stopped his packing up and met his gaze.

"Isaac's right," Fitzpatrick told him. "They're only bein' honest and if I go along on this thing up north then I'm not bein' honest with myself either." He pushed away from Daniel and moved to take his musket from its place as Ballard spoke to him.

"We've gotten this far by stickin' together John," he said, "not by splittin' up." Fitzpatrick wheeled and looked at him in turn.

"Maybe so," he said, "but this whole thing is wrong, and I'm takin no part in it, and neither should you. You're the ones who're doin' wrong by goin' ahead with it, so this time, I'm stickin' together," he nodded towards the departing figures of Kane and Jones, "with them." Having looked at the two who were departing, he seemed to falter, looking around then at the others, and perhaps realising, as he did so, that by choosing some he was turning his back on more. He took a breath before he spoke again in a quieter voice.

"I count you boys as my friends still and I hope none of you end up spendin' your lives on a thing as unworthy as this is." He strode off to join Jones and Kane, where they stood a small distance away, while Thompson stepped back to where the others stood. For a moment they all faced each other across the camp, before the three who were going turned and moved off. Bailey had come back over and had seen the last of the argument and scuffle. Now he saw Jones, Kane and Fitzpatrick go, moving away and joining with the others of the company who were, "declining the hospitality," as Boyce had put it, "of the great southern state of Maryland."

The sergeant turned towards those who remained with a scornful look on his face.

"Better off without the likes o' them," he muttered. At that, Ryan whirled, feeling his buttocks cringe as he did so, and glared at him.

"What in the hell would you know about that," he snarled?

The ascended sun glistened on the water in shining dapples of dancing light and the whole scene on the river was a combination of beauty, mixed with power. The beauty lay principally in the natural surroundings here at White's Ford, bathed, as it was, in dazzling sunlight, while the power lay in the procession of men and weapons that bespoke the passing of the army. The banks on both sides of the river were clustered with trees, on almost all of whose branches and boughs the mantle of leaves survived. In their last flush of summer fullness, they clothed the scene in a rich setting of every green shade, with only a very few beginning to turn towards the yellows of the coming Autumn.

Out in the middle of the river on the downstream side was an island, lined with more trees, from which a detached spit of stony gravel stretched upstream in the middle of the water. The columns crossing over were taking advantage of this, fording in a zig from the Virginia side to the gravel, followed by a zag, back from there to the Maryland bank. The Potomac River was maybe something around three hundred yards wide here, but the ford was bringing the water up no further than the tops of the thighs of the wading men already out there. Daniel Ryan shaded his eyes against the sparkling surface as he looked down and along the column presently negotiating the river. There were wagons furthest upstream and down from them the infantrymen waded, with their pants around their necks and shoes, tied by the laces around their swaying, shouldered muskets, which caught the sun also and criss-crossed the flashes of light from their polished barrels as the men moved. On the downstream side was a further formation, of cavalrymen this time, who had halted their horses in the water to let them cool their legs and drink.

Out on the river many of the men were fumbling at canteens, filling them with the river water, while still more were using their free hand to splash water up into their faces, beards and hair, while the irrepressible souls splashed still more water around at each other. From the far bank came snatches of music as a band played the men and animals across, with a selection of the airs and marches that were popular among the troops, among which "Maryland My Maryland" seemed to be getting the best reception.

Their own column halted on the southern bank to remove shoes and pants, waiting there while those in front entered the water and started across. The ground was muddy and the bank had been dug down into a more gradual slope to make the passage of wheeled vehicles easier. The sun was warm overhead and the atmosphere was one of carnival and celebration as the great procession of wagons, guns, animals and men made their way over this strip of water that separated Confederate Virginia from Union Maryland, in effect wading across a border to enter what was now another country. The boys hooted and laughed and called wisecracks and comments to each other and to anyone passing by or within earshot.

Daniel Ryan fastened his shoes around the tip of his ramrod by their laces, tying his haversack and cartridge pouch to his musket barrel by their straps and wrapping his ragged pants, like the others, around his neck. In front, the ranks were pulling away across and their own officers were calling them back to their files to begin their own crossing. They moved on down the trampled bank and stepped into the water. Even here, close to the shore, it seemed icy cold and the men shouted and exclaimed as it splashed over their feet and up their legs. On they pushed, out towards the middle of the stream, with more exclamations as the water rose steadily towards the tops of their thighs culminating in a chorus of screeches and calls as the icy current finally came to the more intimate places.

"That'll give the damn grey backs somethin' to think on," Ballard shouted, and a succession of yells and laughter answered him. Daniel Ryan said less, having endured the agony of the water reaching his raw backside with gritted teeth, he now found that the chill of the current was actually having an almost soothing effect on his affliction and he was thankful for that at least.

Now and again, along the column, a man would lose his footing to stumble and splash away on the tide before struggling to his feet in a welter of spluttering, to guffaws of laughter from his friends. One or two floundered further down to be picked up by one of the cavalrymen, recovering their balance by steadying themselves against the flank of the man's horse. Daniel had joined in the shouting and laughter as, up in front of them, Steve Gifford disappeared in a cloud of spray, when he felt someone cannon into him from behind almost sending him headlong also. He turned when he had recovered his balance to see Tom Gibben stumbling back to his feet, minus his musket, shoes, trousers and haversack. Bradlee was on hand to bellow at him while the others chortled.

"Ya clumsy, useless good fer nothin' dirt grubber," the sergeant shouted. "Yo're stayin' out here till ya find that gun and gear and when we camp yo're gonna be diggin' sinks fer the goddam whole army." Daniel and Mick Daley stayed out there with Gibben to help him find his gear and laugh some more at his predicament. The musket and the cartridge box, with its now spoiled ammunition, were soon recovered, the former with the pants still tangled around it, by Gibben successively submerging to scramble around for them on the river bed. Several more dips below the current recovered the shoes but of the haversack there was no sign, though Tom was less than worried at this.

"Weren't no vittles worth a damn in it anyhow," he said, "and even if there had a' been they'd be spoiled in the damn river." Still prodding him, they made for the mid-stream spit of gravel, pausing there for Tom to re-secure his gear to the musket barrel, before they all ploughed into the final stretch of the river. Here the water turned out to be marginally less deep and they finally emerged, streaming and dripping, onto the far bank, this one trampled and dug down also, but additionally more slippery with mud.

They found a space, where some other men were starting to move off, to don their pants before sitting to replace socks and shoes. Daniel checked the fault in his right shoe, finding that the rent in the leather had encroached further along the outside of the upper and was now about three inches long. The need for replacements was growing, but when and how he would come by another pair he had not the slightest idea. As for his more pressing affliction, he had found some relief in the extent to which the icy water of the Potomac River had numbed his livid backside, but he now felt it steadily renew its burning throb.

Beyond the river a short way was another waterway that had been bridged by capsizing a long canal boat across what remained of the water and the men waited their turn to cross, using this more precarious method. This was the Chesapeake and Ohio Canal, boys were saying, and it flowed, like the river, all the way back down to Washington itself. Some of those boys looked carefully to their right, downstream, on hearing this, almost as though they expected to see something that might corroborate it, before continuing on their way over the makeshift crossing.

The initial route in Maryland, for Longstreet's men, followed on a road that ran parallel to and just east of the river as it curved back to the north. With the carnival of the crossing over, the long columns followed on in a dense cloud of light brown dust. Daniel Ryan was increasingly afflicted and preoccupied, not only by the dust but also by the degeneration of his shoes, and even more by the state of his backside, now extremely inflamed and raw from the continuing bouts of diarrhoea. He hobbled on with the others of the company, seeking to avoid the ignominy of asking for a pass to leave the files for such a condition. In the army right now, it was easier to count the boys who had stayed regular than those with diarrhoea. Philipps, Daley, almost everybody in their mess, had the flux to some extent, but none, it seemed, had buttocks as badly affected as his own.

They had passed the great aqueduct, which carried the canal across the Monocacy River, where it flowed to join the Potomac as it turned to the west again and, pressed on to the north. During the first hour halt of the afternoon, as the column paused on its way along the undulating land farther from the river, Daniel had gone, after another visit to the undergrowth, to take his turn at refilling the mess canteens in one of the swifter flowing creeks that swept down near the road and on to the river beyond. The stream bank was busy, with many men similarly engaged and Daniel and Ed Hill had moved upstream a stretch to get to the water, reaching a patch of rocks where they stopped to do their re-filling. Daniel had crouched down with his canteens, clenching his buttocks to spare his raw backside, when the shots rang out. There were two of them, high pitched cracks, more like smaller calibre cavalry carbines than the heavier report of infantry muskets. Hill dropped the canteens he was holding with a shout of surprise and then swore as he flattened himself beside Daniel on the stream bank. Daniel looked across at him to see blood streaming from his sleeve, down his hand to drip onto the rock and into the water. The shouts of warning went up and down the creek bank as other men scattered for weapons and fanned out into what cover they could find. Daniel grabbed at Hill's tunic and pulled him over onto his side. The sleeve was now soaked in blood and Hill's teeth were gritted as he watched Daniel lift the tunic sleeve gently and peer at the injury. Daley and Ballard arrived at a run, crouching as they came, together with Peters and Vallance of Hill's mess. They squatted among the stones which led down to the creek, biting cartridges and jamming them into the muzzles of the weapons as they settled. Loading complete and caps in place, they looked at Hill and then at Daniel, as they crouched just downstream, near to the water's edge. Hill was cursing, a continuous sequence of oaths, interspersed with grunts at the pain of his wound, while, from nearer the road came Bradlee's shout.

"Stay down boys! Stay low, till we git a line on where they are."

"Goddam, blue belly sons o' bitches," Hill grated through his teeth.

"Could be broken," Daniel said to him, scrutinising the injury, while the others scanned the brush, across the creek, beyond another expanse of stony ground, where tussocks of straggly grass grew in between the rocks on that far side of the water.

"Gotta be in that brush," Ballard called, "smoke drifted across there, but they can't git out o' there without us seein' 'em. With that bluff beyond, they gotta go one side or the other." Ryan looked up seeing, as he focussed, a movement in the bushes.

"There," Daley shouted, "afore they shoot again." The other three levelled their muskets and fired, sending their shots into the bushes, where the movement had been, shrouding the stream area in dirty powder smoke, which cleared only slowly away. A scattering of further shots came from the men nearer the road till Bradlee's distant voice yelled again.

"Cease that damned stupid firin', ya ain't shootin' at anythin' ya kin see." But, Daniel was looking across the stream for, from the brush, there had been a cry, a high pitched scream, immediately after the shots, and now as the smoke eddied, there was sobbing from those bushes across the stream. In this lull, Peters scrambled down, pulled Hill to his feet and, yelling for the surgeon, began to lead him away towards the road. Daniel Ryan too scrambled to his feet, ignoring the surge of pain in his buttocks, knowing, as he did so, that something was wrong, something about that scream, the sound of that voice…. He started across the creek, using the rocks as stepping stones, mindful as he went of his disintegrating shoe, but still almost stumbling as the upper and sole flapped on each second step. He reached the far bank and weaved through the grass and rocks, making for the patch of bushes, aware that he was being followed by Ballard, Daley and Vallance, but it was only when he was most of the way there that the thought came to him that, but for his bayonet, he was unarmed. He reached the bushes and pushed aside the first branches, stopping as he looked into the space immediately beyond.

Kneeling on the ground among the branches was a boy, who could not have been more than twelve years old. His hands were covered in blood and he looked around at Daniel, with an expression of terror on his face. Beside him lay another boy, his face hidden by the long grass, but, if anything, smaller and younger than the first. The front of his shirt was covered in blood and he wriggled and cried as he lay. Ballard swore bitterly as he arrived and took in the scene, but Vallance pushed past him and made to swing his musket at the kneeling boy.

"Ya bushwhackin' little shit," he shouted, as the boy, squealed shrilly and raised his arms above his head. It was Daley, who was behind Vallance, who reacted first, grabbing at his tunic and breaking his momentum just enough for him to miss the boy and half stumble, as Ballard almost simultaneously turned and grabbed at his arm, dropping his own musket as he grappled with him. The two of them scrambled and got hold of an arm each as they yelled at Vallance, while Daniel Ryan pulled the kneeling boy to one side.

"Charlie!" Ballard yelled, and Daniel felt the boy, whom he held, jump. Vallance seemed to falter as his temper turned.

"He's a boy, Charlie," Daley shouted, "a stupid, bloody child." Others arrived and pushed into the bushes, Thompson appeared and immediately knelt beside the fallen boy, as Gibben lifted the two muskets from the grass. Daniel Ryan looked at them, even as he still held the other boy's arms.

"Damn game pieces," Gibben said, as those close by could already see, small calibre guns, and pretty antiquated ones at that, with flint locks and swan-neck hammers. Gibben turned to show the weapons to the group of arriving men, among whom was William Boyce. The lieutenant immediately went to where Thompson crouched over the wounded boy. The big corporal turned as Boyce arrived over him.

"Stomach likely," he said. "He's hurt pretty bad." Boyce turned to Daley,

"Surgeon," he snapped, "and tell Mr Sterling to make it now." Daley nodded and moved away past the onlookers. Now Jeffers came up and, taking a long look at the scene, immediately began to chivvy the watching group away. A few minutes passed before Daley came back to push through the branches into the patch of grass. He was followed by Jeremiah Yorke, the assistant surgeon, with an orderly behind him, carrying the medical bag. Boyce looked at him inquiringly.

"Mr Sterling is attending to Private Hill and will be here directly," the younger man said. He pushed past and knelt beside the boy. It had not looked good from the start, Daniel Ryan had thought, but now this was largely confirmed by the surgeon's reaction. He tutted and sighed his way through his tending to the boy, examining his back, where more blood stained the grass beneath where he lay.

So there was an exit wound Daniel Ryan observed to himself, though whether that made things better or worse who could tell? The examination went on until the bush branches rustled again and Sterling appeared, a flustered, flushed Sterling who beckoned his assistant away to one side with a peremptory finger and crouched beside the boy to tut and sigh in his turn as he assessed and probed his wound. Having done, he waved Yorke back to work and the latter, having fussed some more, gently removed the boy's shirt and began applying a pad from his bag to either side of his torso, to staunch the bleeding. Thompson and Daley supported the child's limp body. Having bandaged both pads into place, they laid him down again and Yorke stood up as Sterling turned and spoke to Boyce.

"Ball went straight through," he said, "and there's no bone damage that I can see, but there's a lot of tissue damage and extensive bleedin'. He may have a chance, but we need to get him out of here and into a hospital or at least back to wherever he lives." He looked at the other boy still standing, with Daniel Ryan's hand on his shoulder. "Do we know where he lives around here?"

"What's yore name boy," Ballard turned to the boy? Daniel felt him jump again in his hand. He bent down and spoke to him.

"Answer boy, ain't nobody goin' to harm you now." The frightened child looked from Ryan to Ballard to Sterling and then back again.

"Toby Hartman," he said, in what was little more than a whisper.

"Who's this you're with," Daniel continued, anxious to keep the boy talking?

"He's my brother," was the answer, "his name's Henry". Daniel persisted with his questions, as the others left him to it.

"Do you live around here?"

"Over there," came the whispered reply, with a vague movement of his arm.

"Can you show me where it is," Daniel asked him. The boy nodded dumbly. Sterling looked at him.

"Alright," he said. "Somebody get on over there, wherever it is, and bring 'em back here." He looked at Boyce, who indicated to Ryan and Thompson.

"Go with him," he said simply. "Column's movin' on anyway, so we'll all have to catch them up later. Bring them back here with a cart or some way of movin' the boy. We'll get him out of here and over to the road." He indicated to Ballard and Daley. "Here's your help," he said to Sterling. Thompson turned to the boy,

"Home," he said simply. The boy looked at his brother.

"Will Henry be alright," he asked? Sterling looked back at him.

"That, boy, is in the hands of the lord," he said.

Daniel Ryan retrieved his musket that Gibben had brought over, then he and Thompson each shouldered one of the fowling pieces and pointed the boy away, following after him as he started along the creek, heading roughly parallel with the road.

"What do we say to a family when we've just shot their child," Daniel asked his friend?

"We tell 'em what happened," Thompson replied, "there ain't nothin' else to do, besides, that boy ain't the only one that got shot."

"I suppose you're right," Daniel said, "but none of that is goin' to make them feel any better."

The farm was small, consisting of a house, which had only a ground floor with a rustic porch out in front, a chicken run, significantly empty Daniel Ryan noted, and a smokehouse, though all of the other structures were dwarfed by the barn. There was nobody working outside and they walked around to the rear of the house but still found no sign of people. Thompson stepped back, away from the building into the yard, while Daniel stood nearer to the door with the boy, Toby.

"In the house!" Thompson's voice was loud by any standards, but this was far from his full-blooded bellow, being almost polite, Daniel thought, by comparison. There was a pause and then a female voice came from inside.

"Are you rebels?" Thompson stepped closer to the door.

"Don't matter none what we are, we're lookin' fer Mrs Hartman," he answered. "We got her boy here." From inside the house the reaction was immediate, with audible movements and a shout of alarm.

"You leave that child be!" There were hurried, approaching footsteps, which carried to them clearly through the open windows at the side of the building. Daniel stepped back away from the porch, taking the boy with him. As he did so the door opened and a woman appeared, youngish, and attractive, Daniel Ryan thought, but with the lines of hard work, and likely child-bearing too, plain in her features. She ran the few steps towards where the boy stood with Daniel, followed by an older woman. Daniel released the boy forward towards them.

"Maa!" he shouted and, bursting into tears, he ran to her, lunging into her arms to bury his head in her blouse as she pulled him close to her.

"Where's your brother," she asked him, "where's Henry?" He pointed back towards Ryan and Thompson, for the two women to fix their gaze on them accusingly.

155

"Do you damned rebels make war on little children," the older woman spoke for the first time, her voice hissing and hostile? Thompson sighed.

"Yo're boy is hurt ma'am," he said, "and there ain't no easy way o' sayin' it. They both ope……." His words were drowned out in a screaming cry let out by the younger woman that made the hair on the back of Daniel Ryan's neck creep.

"Where is he," she screamed? "What have you god-forsaken heathens done to him?"

"He is with our surgeon ma'am," Ryan told them, "and he is having his wound seen to." The older woman had taken her younger companion by the arm, as her loud, wrenching sobs continued.

"Amy," she said, "come now, you must try to calm yourself, and we must go to him," but the younger woman continued to sob, clutching still at the other boy beside her. She turned to Ryan and Thompson.

"May god damn your miserable souls to hell for this," she said through gasping, sobbing breaths.

"Likely he will," Thompson answered, raising his voice for the first time. He held out the fowling piece and Ryan did likewise.

"You better have these," Daniel said. "We reckon they're yours." Both women looked at them and then at the old flintlocks. "They're the ones your boys used to fire on us," he added

"They shot from bushes," Thompson said, "and hit one of our boys in the arm. Happen he'll likely lose it." The two women made no answer as he walked across and leaned the musket against a water trough in the yard, watching while Ryan did the same. The older woman looked immediately across at the boy.

"You," she cried, "you were told. You were warned, not to take those pieces out. You were warned that goin' near that road when the soldiers were here would bring trouble." His

156

mother pulled him at last from where he had taken refuge behind her.

"How could you do this," she cried? "You're older and you should know better. What's happened to your brother now, because of all o' this?" Thompson stepped across to them and his voice this time was gentler as he spoke.

"Do ya have a cart or a buggy or some such around here ma'am," he asked her, "to go bring yore other boy home?"

The boy Henry Hartman was still alive when they got back to the side of the road where Sterling, and Yorke, together with Ballard and Daley, waited, though Boyce and the others had gone to rejoin the never ending procession on the road. They had left the other boy at the house, with an even older woman, who seemed to be crippled and confined to a chair, while the two women they had originally seen had come for their child, bringing their cart, drawn by a single mule, along the dirt track that led from the farm down onto the road. Ryan and Thompson had had to guide the cart on a tortuous line, mostly on the verge to move along the road, in the opposite direction to the long column of soiled and sweating infantry, interspersed with guns and wagons, till they reached the place where the others waited.

The injured boy lay in the shade, cast by a clump of roadside trees, wrapped in a blanket, but his face was completely white when Daniel Ryan looked at him. He shifted his gaze to the two women. Already the faces of both were streaked with dust and Daniel noticed tear stains lining both of their cheeks as they approached the half-conscious boy, crouching beside him to talk to him gently and stroke his brow. At this, his mother broke down again, sobbing and wailing in the same disturbing way that she had at the farm. The older woman took hold of her arm.

"Don't Amy," she said, "be strong, don't weaken in front of these damned rebels." Sterling chose this moment to step across to them and introduced himself.

"I am Thomas Sterling ladies, surgeon with the Confederate States Army and I have tried to help your boy today." They both looked into his face.

"Yo're a doctor," the older woman said? He nodded gravely.

"Will Henry live," she looked into his face?

"I can assure you that I have done everything I could for him," Sterling answered. "His fate is now with god." Daniel Ryan looked at him. Trust Sterling, he thought, if he could pass on the blame or the responsibility, even the almighty himself wasn't safe. Yorke gestured to Ballard who nodded to Daley and they both moved to where the boy lay, and bent to lift him gently, still in the blanket, carrying him round to the rear of the cart, to place him carefully on the straw palliasse, from the house, that Thompson and Ryan had put there before they had left the farm. His mother now walked around with them.

"Why are you here," she asked them between sniffles? "Nobody wants you up here?" The two of them said nothing. The older woman looked at her.

"Ride with him Amy," she said, "I'll take care of Ole Blossom." Amy sniffled still and looked at the cart as Yorke hurried around to her.

"If you will permit me ma'am," he said, bending down to cup his hands at about knee height for her to step up. Daniel Ryan watched her ascend, to sit in the cart beside her stricken son, getting a brief glimpse of white calf, above her boots and under her skirts, as she did so. She settled herself at the front of the cart, still sobbing loudly, while the older woman went to the mule and grasped its bridle.

"May God punish you rebels in hellfire," she said, "with your slaves, your iniquity and your shame."

"Reckon we'll all git a turn o' that," Ballard grunted in reply. Without waiting for any further response, the woman pulled on the bridle, jerking the mule rudely into motion. The cart jolted and the boy groaned as the younger woman, cradling his head, sobbed. Sterling had gone immediately across to the tree, where a horse was tethered, to mount up and pull the beast out into the road, signalling to the nearest of the passing files of infantry to halt, to the irritation of their dust-covered lieutenant. As the old lady pulled the cart out onto the road, Sterling gestured to his assistant.

"Go with them," he said, "and settle the boy in his home." He looked at Thompson, "go too," he said.

The family had already set on its way, and Sterling started off up the road himself, riding in time with the cart as the mule plodded away towards the farm track, which lay about a quarter of a mile further on. The halted infantry moved off again, as the remainder of their own detail at the roadside shouldered their muskets, blankets and canteens and walked on beside them, tramping after the cart and the surgeons. When they reached the track, Sterling reined his horse in and raised his hat to the two women as the cart rattled past and turned off the road. Thompson shrugged to the others and turned off, following Yorke and the cart into the dip that marked the farm track's junction with the road. The cart heaved and jolted away on the track, bringing more cries from the boy and still deeper sobs from his mother. Soon it was lost to sight in the woods that covered the ever widening margin of ground between the track and the road, but, even above the sound of tramping feet, jingling harness and creaking, rumbling wheels, Daniel could still hear snatches of the younger woman, Amy's, sobs coming to him through the trees.

With the cart and the patient dispatched, Sterling replaced his hat and shook his reins, shooing the horse into a faster walk, beginning at once to draw away up along the side of the dusty files of men on the road. Soon the other three were left on the verge, where, armed with the pass that Boyce had provided to Ballard, they had opted to wait for Thompson, watching the passing of the column, surrounded in its cloud of enveloping dust as they did so. They sat themselves on the grass in the tree shade, to be glanced at by various passing men. Daniel pulled his degenerating shoes from his feet and examined them to see if there was anything further to be done with them. It surely did not look like it, rather it was only a matter of when they became totally impossible to walk in and, as before, that time looked like it would soon be here. His mind turned to the boys, and this latest, crazy event of war that they had all just witnessed, as he pulled the shoes back onto his feet. Stupid it had been of those children to come near the soldiers with guns, he thought, and stupider still to discharge them at the resting men. Boys were boys and sometimes they did crazy things, but this piece of folly had cost this one dearly. The men had done what soldiers do when they were fired on. They had fixed where the gunfire came from and had fired back, and now, from the look of him, the poor, stupid child would pay with his life. Even if he was not yet dead, he had looked as though he soon would be. Daniel pondered it all. It was chance, but not even just chance, for, to a degree at least, the boy Henry Hartman had been his own executioner. Underlying it was their own army, and its arrival here in someone else's country, that had set up and prompted what had just happened, only hours into Maryland. At that his mind turned to Fitzpatrick and Kane and Jones and, for the first time, he found himself wondering about what they were doing here.

Daniel was still mulling these kind of thoughts over in his mind when they saw Thompson and Yorke returning down the track. The three of them got themselves to their feet and collected weapons to set off up the road, walking at the side of the column on the verge, while still Daniel pondered. Was there no way that it could have been avoided he asked himself? There had been something about the sound of those old flintlocks that he had noticed at the time. They had discharged with a higher pitched sound than the heavier military weapons, he had noticed that, but, being a soldier, his mind had turned to think of cavalry instead of anything more out of the ordinary. But at least, he told himself, he himself had not fired at the boys, His musket had been back near the road so he at least was not to blame. But did any of that matter, for, if it had been Daley or Ballard with the canteens, he would have done what they had done today and it likely would not have ended up any different, and in the final analysis, would who had fired the actual shot make any difference at all to Henry Hartman's fate?

The column pressed on, enduring the heat and dust, now with the river well behind them, to arrive as the sun set at the regimental camp near the hamlet of Buckeystown, on the way, the camp talk said, to the city of Frederick. Fresh water was fairly plentiful but there was no sign of the commissary wagons. Philipps and Gibben had already built their mess fire and the recently arrived detail set out what food they had in their haversacks this being mainly what they had foraged or begged along the road, mostly mixes of corn or fruit, with few messes having much of anything else. What they had was collected into the pans and, while the others grouped around the spitting mix, Daniel Ryan, worn down by the torment of his backside, sought out the surgeon.

Thomas Sterling tutted and shook his head as he gazed at the group of sick who had assembled at his tent.

"How many o' you men are here becuz a' loose bowels," he asked them? Most grunted or lifted a hand in reply.

"It is yore misfortune that my standard remedy of opium for an open bowel is not available," Sterling told them, "due to shortages in the supply." He stood there, having a good scratch at his greying beard as he looked around the group. "Calomel pills, my stand by treatment are not available either on account of there bein' so many bowel disorders in this here regiment," he went on. "You men should go and see my assistant, Mister Yorke, right over there," he pointed, "for he has prepared a supply of another remedy. It is a mite slower, but it is equally certain," he told them gravely. He waved them off to where Yorke, was setting paper twists on a blanket laid out on the ground. As the afflicted men moved that way, Sterling stalked off, heading towards the cluster of other officers who stood and lounged around a tent awning under the nearby trees. "Likely having drinks before supper," Daniel thought bitterly as he stared briefly after him.

Yorke looked up at them as they clustered around him.

"Bowels," he inquired? There was a succession of nods.

"Take a twist," he said, "and boil a pinch of it in water in a cup, drink it when it's hot," he added.

"What's in it," one of the men grunted?

"It's a herb mix," he told them. "It's made from sweet gum, slippery elm, willow and dogwood bark. Very efficacious," he added, "but finish the dose if you want the cure to be certain." Some of the men moved away, clutching their little twists of paper, but Daniel Ryan dallied as they dispersed. Noticing this, Yorke gave him a quizzical look.

"Ah," he said. "You were there with those children...."

"Do you have anything for the rash," Daniel said, interrupting him, but taking care not to raise his voice?

"I do beg your pardon," the youth replied.

"The rash," Daniel repeated, "my backside feels like its on fire," he said.

"Ah...um," said Yorke, "We don't have no salves left around here for that. Maybe you could try lard or fat or something of that kind to soothe it."

"Lard," Daniel said, "where do I get lard around here?"

"Afraid I can't help with that," was the reply, "but do persist in taking the herbs and your condition should improve."

"By that time my ass might have fallen off too," Daniel retorted.

The night had something of a chill to it, but he could not sleep anyway from the discomfort of his buttocks. He lay there, tossing around, unable to find any degree of comfort, and was additionally forced to rise four further times for trips to the bushes, and, with this further antagonising, his backside seemed worse still. No matter what way Daniel tried to lie back on his blanket, there was no easing the harsh, burning pain. He was awake when the daylight came, with a chilly period of grey light, which showed wisps of mist forming near the ground, as the drums sounded their summons to parade. The ranks assembled to hear from Rodger that the days march would take them to Monocacy Junction and there camp would be set up and the men would be assigned company duties. As they formed for the march the mist around them was steadily burning off in the growing heat of the rising sun, but Daniel Ryan was more preoccupied by the prospect of another dusty march, in disintegrating shoes, with his inflamed buttocks recording every step of the way.

Chapter 7
Mrs Emily Franklin

Monocacy Junction turned out to be only a handful of miles from the camp at Buckeystown, though Daniel Ryan had to leave the column twice in the course of the three hour march there to make for the bushes and relieve his condition and, having done so, to scuttle after his comrades as fast as his throbbing buttocks and flapping shoes would allow. Again the dust was bad, enveloping the column of men, clogging in eyes, noses and mouths and plastering the skin with a brown layer that adhered to the sweat and imparted a ghoulish look to the labouring figures. It was as well, Daniel Ryan thought, that the company had not been called upon to make a full day's march in these conditions since he for one, and likely numerous others, would not have lasted the ordeal out. They arrived at the junction in the middle morning and were dismissed in an area already well settled by other units of the assembling army. Here they would stay, so Jeffers told them with no orders for any further marches meantime.

The camp at the junction was situated to the south of the city of Frederick, though Company B, like many others, spent the remaining part of the day sending details of men patrolling around some of the nearby farms, since the town itself had been declared off limits, attempting to buy provisions of almost any kind, a forlorn idea, considering that virtually all of the army was camped in the area. With little to show for their efforts, supper consisted of still more of the fruit and corn flour stew and the boys turned in with the pangs of hunger largely unsatisfied. The following morning, with assembly done and nothing for breakfast, Rodger approved further details to continue the quest for rations. Boyce and Bradlee assembled a group, including Daniel and Otis Ballard, to forage around still more of the outlying localities around Frederick to requisition or buy anything of use, with, in addition to any sort of food, soap being highest on their list. They formed up and moved out, Daniel Ryan now almost hobbling from the effects of his affliction.

After most of the morning hours at it, their quest seemed largely fruitless. The farmers either closed up their homes, with barred shutters and locked doors, or pleaded poverty, since so many famished rebels had already been around. It seemed likely that Jackson's men, who had been here an extra day, had again gotten a head start on all the places to forage. Eventually Bradlee had had enough of this and, with a tacit nod from Boyce, he set them off in pairs towards the town itself to try their luck.

"It's against orders to forage in town," he said, "but the old man ain't hungry, and he likely don't need too much of a wash neither, so what he don't know won't hurt him none. Jest stay outa trouble and, if ya do end up under arrest, then I never heard o' ya."

They used the back lanes to make their way into Frederick in an effort to avoid the cavalry patrols and provost details, set up to prevent the very thing they were attempting. The men made forays onto the wider streets when the coast seemed clear only to find that many of these doors also were closed to them. They moved carefully on towards the commercial district to find that the shops and stores there were similarly shut and by just after noon, when some of them re-assembled, although a few pieces of varying meat and some vegetables had been accumulated, the overall haul remained disappointing.

Bradlee directed them to move out in pairs, trying some of the private homes as they made their way back out of town for anything else they could acquire and Daniel, with Otis Ballard, started off down one of the side streets. Patrols of Stuart's cavalry were still around and, when they resumed knocking on doors seeking more provisions, their luck deserted them for it was not long before they were disturbed by a call from the street behind them.

"What do you boys reckon yo're doin'?" They whirled to see that the challenge came from a grizzled cavalry sergeant sitting across the street on a mangy looking horse, with his carbine across his saddle, accompanied by three of his men.

"Why lookin' around fer vittles or soap or anythin' we kin use," Ballard answered.

"Ya ain't heard about the orders then," the sergeant persisted? They looked at him blankly, while around him the other horsemen exchanged smirks and shook their heads to each other.

"Reckoned we'd just try and get a bite to eat around here," Daniel told him.

"No ya won't," was the reply. "General's orders are nobody gets ta roam around town and annoy all the nice Yankees, however much they may have it comin', funny how you boys ain't heard o' that?" He pointed back south out of town towards the camps with his carbine and with a shrug to each other, they moved away from the door to spend a few seconds dallying on the sidewalk. But the pointing weapon was insistent, so, acknowledging that fact, they turned and started down the street, heading back towards the camps, Daniel still hobbling painfully with his affliction.

"If ya come back in," the sergeant called after them, "ya won't be goin' back out."

"Yeah sure," Ballard muttered. "Reckon the damned cavalry'd enjoy goin' to all o' that trouble to stop a man gittin' a bite to eat." He raised a hand in acknowledgement without looking back.

The heat was still strong, even though it was now well into the afternoon, and the roads out of town were busy with wagons and horsemen, some in convoys or details while others, presumably messengers or orderlies, trotted by singly, all of this traffic grinding the dust up in thick clouds around the men on foot. Daniel grimaced and fumbled for his canteen swilling a small amount of the tepid water around his mouth and spitting it out, before drinking more deeply. He turned to Ballard.

"Surely there's a way back out that gets us away from some o' this," he said? Ballard spread his hands.

"Yore guess about that is as good as anybody's," he replied. Daniel hobbled on, scanning, as they went past the intersections, for anything that looked like a route out to the south, but it was Ballard who called to him at one corner and pointed towards a lane that ran between some of the houses and seemingly onwards from there.

"If ya wanna try it," he said, "but jest remember, if it goes no place, we're stuck with cross-country or comin' all the way back here." Daniel shrugged at him.

"What else is there to spend the time on," he said. "Maybe there's a chance of findin' somethin' to eat this way, if it's a back road." At that he made for the lane, with Ballard grinning at him.

"You're the one with the sore ass," he said.

The lane led on out of town, never growing to the width of the more important roads, but it was certainly a comfortable cart, if not wagon, size and even included a few places where vehicles could pass each other while still staying on its surface. There was no traffic on it today as they made their way south, gradually leaving Frederick behind. They inspected the homes and farms as they went but found them, as in town, largely

167

shuttered and locked. Daniel shuffled painfully, vainly seeking a gait that eased his condition, while Ballard admired the local crop raising.

"Helluva size o' corn cobs around here," he observed. Ryan, nursing his infirmities, was disinterested.

"You'd know about that," he retorted.

"Whadya mean I'd know?"

"You, bein' from distinguished, Bulloch County farming stock."

"Farmin' stock? My ass, I ain't no farmer."

"I thought your family were farmers and owned half the county."

"Hell, no" was the response. "That'd be my Uncle Hedley, he's got land, but not me and not my pa neither. Joe, now he's a farmer. He's got a wife 'n' two kids t' prove he kin raise things."

"What's happenin' to his farm while he's off on this frolic?"

"His pa and his grandpa, lend a hand. His pa lost an arm in some accident, a few years back, but he's as strong as a damned bullock and as stubborn as a mule and he still works his passage."

"So what did you do Otis, if not farmin'?" Daniel found himself suddenly curious, in spite of his discomforts, now that his assumption about his comrade had proved wrong.

"Me, I was a cooper. Our family turned out the best barrels in the county."

"A cooper?"

"Yep."

"Did you like it?"

"Couldn't have, leastways not that much. Enlisted didn't I?"

"Guess so."

The conversation was disturbed by the faint rattling sound of approaching wheels on the road behind them. They looked around to see a moving cloud of dust rising above the trees and bushes back towards town. Both headed over to one side of the road as the vehicle clattered closer, looking back again, as the noise grew, to see an ancient buggy, drawn by a threadbare, old horse, approaching, trailing the cloud of dust behind it. As it rounded a bend in the road, they could make out something of the occupants. The driver was an old negro, with grey side whiskers and a straw hat on his head. He wore a white cotton coat, and had an air of staid, self-importance about him as he steered the vehicle outwards, to ride clear of Ryan and Ballard. Sitting behind him, under the shelter of the extended awning, was a little old woman, her shoulders covered by a white lace shawl and her head with a wider brimmed straw hat, which did not entirely conceal the silver hair gathered behind her neck. In her hand was an ostrich feather fan, which she flicked to and fro around her face. Daniel hobbled further in towards the side of the road, as the vehicle drew close, almost stumbling as he reached the verge and caught his flapping shoe on the grass. The old woman, apparently noticing the near trip, turned her head to look as the buggy clattered past. The vehicle pulled on ahead of them, and, as it did so, the woman seemed to speak to the driver, who immediately whoaad at the old horse and pulled on his reins, steering the buggy over to a stop, some yards ahead, on the opposite side of the road. The woman leaned out from under the awning and called something across to them, upon which they both stopped and looked, with Ballard cupping his hand to his ear to indicate that he had not heard. The old lady called again.

"Is that man hurt?"

"Yes ma'am," Ballard called across, "well he ain't shot or nothin' ma'am..." Daniel glared at him.

"Why don't you drop my damn pants and show her," he snapped at him in a loud whisper? His friend gave him an almost imperceptible wink in return.

"Let's jest see what comes outa this," he said quietly, as he removed his hat and smiled through his beard towards the old lady, "even if it is yore ass that does part o' the job," he added between his teeth. He started across the road, while Daniel leaned on a fence rail watching his companion spend the following minutes in conversation with the old woman, gesturing back towards Daniel occasionally as he spoke. Several times, in the course of her talk with Ballard, the woman looked across to him, until, in a not unkindly way, she beckoned him over. He hobbled across, feeling embarrassed as well as tormented by his condition. The old woman looked at him with a benign sort of an expression on her wrinkled face, but Daniel noticed immediately as he reached the buggy that her eyes were bright blue and, as his own eyes adjusted to the shade cast by the buggy's awning, that there was just the suggestion of a twinkle to be seen in them.

"Your friend has explained your ahhh.... condition to me," she said. "I think that I may be able to help you, but certainly not out here on the public road." She spoke to her driver.

"Marcus, we will take these two ahhh.... visitors back to the house with us."

"Yaz'mizz," was the reply from the grizzle-haired old man, in a tone that suggested that very little surprised him any more. He waited on his seat, with the brake on and the old horse held firmly in check, while Ballard helped Daniel onto the seat beside the woman, who had retreated to the opposite corner of the leather covering. He then carried both muskets around to the other side of the buggy, to balance them against the driver's seat, before clambering up onto it beside the old negro, who hastened to do as his mistress had, shuffling across to the furthest corner of the seat. Daniel grimaced, finding sitting in the buggy little of any sort of relief, and, arguably even more painful than walking.

Having shuffled along the seat as far as he could from Ballard, Marcus released the brake, shook the reins, and clucked the old horse into motion with the jerk of the carriage moving off registering considerably on Daniel's discomfort scale. The animal settled into what was clearly a familiar pace, suggesting, by its easy motion, that very little surprised it any more either. Daniel, still trying to ease his buttocks on the seat, looked across at the old lady.

"I'm most obliged to you ma'am," he said quietly, "though I am surprised, having some idea of the needs of the army, that you still have your horse."

"Oh dear no," she said. "Matilda would be of no use to your army or to any other." Daniel looked quizzically at her.

"She has joint troubles," she continued, "on account of her being not much younger than Marcus and me and this is about the extent of what she is able for these days. But don't thank me young man," she added primly, "I haven't helped you yet." She looked on as he continued to squirm on the seat, trying to find the least uncomfortable position for the buggy ride on the uneven road.

"You two are the first rebel soldiers that we have seen on this road," she said and Daniel looked across at her again.

"We came across it by accident," he replied. "I'm surprised if others haven't been on it before us. We were heading back to our camp nearer the railroad and it seemed to lead south, so we chanced it in the hope that it would be quieter." It was her turn to look quizzically at him.

"Less dust," he said, "and maybe some places to find food that haven't been bled dry by other boys."

"Ah," she nodded. "In truth, now that your army is here, the local people, in so far as they are leaving their homes much at all, are using these back ways and leaving the main roads to the soldiers. It reduces the chance of being robbed, or worse."

"Do they think we're all thieves," Daniel asked her, surprised, to an extent at least, by the comment?

"Many do," she answered. He shook his head, but said nothing more. She continued to look at him, but did not elaborate on what she had already said.

"I do not live far from here," she told him finally, "we shall be there directly."

"There," turned out to be a two storeyed, white-painted wooden house, which stood off the same back road beside a grove of evergreen trees, about half a mile from where they had been picked up. Marcus wheeled the buggy, the motion causing Daniel Ryan to squirm still further, as they entered a driveway, which was wider than the road they had just left, and drove on up to where the house sat, partly shaded by its trees. He finally brought the vehicle to a halt before a broad front porch, where two rocking chairs sat, motionless in the heat. Ballard was off the seat promptly, hurrying round to assist the old lady from her place with fine southern gallantry before, rather more brusquely, helping Daniel down from where he sat also, while Marcus opened the front door for his mistress. He then looked around to where Ballard and Daniel still stood beside the buggy.

"You gen'men round to th' back," he told them firmly, indicating the way with his hand. Ballard shrugged and went to retrieve the muskets before making to assist Daniel, but was irritably pushed away for his pains. He shrugged again and, after handing Daniel his Enfield he followed on, shaking his head as he watched him shuffle around the side of the house, along a little path, trimmed with climbing flowers on one side and with flowering bushes on the other.

"Home sweet goddam home," Daniel heard him mutter as they followed the path and reached the rear of the building to find that Marcus was waiting for them at the back door. He gestured gravely towards a stone outhouse.

"That' the place," he said and Daniel hobbled across to lift the metal latch before pushing the heavy, wooden door open and stepping inside.

His first impression was of how cool it was inside the thick-walled stone building. He looked around as he stood near the door to see that there were shelves all around the walls and these were crowded with bottles and jars of all sizes, full of coloured preserves and cordials and whatever else. A large trestle table stretched up the middle portion of the stone floor, with a stool at each end. There was a blackened stove in one corner and daylight was admitted by a window on either side of the building. Daniel stepped across the room and leaned his musket against a bench to one side of the table. Ballard followed him inside to lean his own musket there also before taking up station near the door.

"Mubbee they're aimin' to stick yore ass in one o' them jars," he said, grinning again at Daniel. "Jest lately ya'd a' bin better off leavin' it some place like that." There was a noise outside on the path and he moved aside hurriedly as the old lady appeared, carrying a metal basin full of water, which she set down on the bench near the table, looking disapprovingly at the two muskets as she did so. She was followed by Marcus who carried a large leather bag in one hand, a further bucket of water in the other and a cotton towel over his shoulder, but, though regaled in this way, he still just about managed to maintain the air of dignified aloofness that he had shown since they had first come across each other out on the road. They all stood for a few seconds and looked at each other, till the old lady broke the silence.

"And whom do I have the um... pleasure of addressing," she said? Ballard cleared his throat.

"Otis Ballard, ma'am, Bulloch County Georgia, an' this here's Daniel Ryan from Bryan County...."

"And does Mr Ryan's condition prevent him from holding a mannerly conversation," she inquired?

"No ma'am," Daniel replied sheepishly, "I beg your pardon."

"Well, I am Mrs Emily Franklin," she told them, "and Marcus here is a member of my household. You," she gestured at Ballard, "may wait outside. There is a bucket of water and a bar of soap out there for your use, should you feel the inclination."

"Why I'm much obliged to ya, ma'am," Ballard replied. He started for the door, only to be stopped by the old lady noisily clearing her throat. He turned as she pointed towards the two muskets, still leaning against the bench.

"I do not believe that we shall be requiring these," she said.

"No ma'am," he said. He stepped over to lift Daniel's musket, along with his own, and made for the door. Mrs Franklin turned to Marcus, as he passed through the doorway and out of sight.

"If you would be so kind Marcus," The grizzled old man paced over to the door and closed it firmly as his mistress turned at last to Daniel Ryan.

"You are not the home made southerner Mr Ryan are you? I am sure I detect much more of an Irish brogue than a southern drawl in your speech."

"I was born and raised in Ireland, Ma'am," Daniel answered, "but I came to Georgia.....," he did a quick addition, "....more than four years ago now."

"But you have taken up the south's rebel cause as your own, regardless of your origins," she inquired?

"Bryan County in Georgia has been my home now these past years," he said firmly. "It was threatened with invasion and coercion by Linc..., your president's order. I was not prepared to see that happen and do nothing."

"That is not how folks up here would see it," she returned.

"I am sure it's not," Daniel agreed, "but, until now at least, nobody's been invading their homes."

"I think it goes under the idea of duly executing the laws of the country," she said tartly.

"That's a pretty weak excuse when you're gettin' your things looted and bein' forced out of your place by the Yankee army," Daniel retorted. He stopped there and almost bit his tongue. It would be folly, he thought, to get into an argument and end up antagonising the old woman. He looked at her, beginning to wonder if she was, in the light of his opinions and remarks, already reconsidering helping him.

"Beg pardon," he said. "I didn't mean to be rude." She looked into his face, with a serious expression at first, but then the corners of her mouth went up a fraction and the blue eyes twinkled.

"Well alrighty," she said, unbending a little. "I didn't think you'd be apologizing for your rebellion, but anyhow, please settle yourself face down on the table," she said, "once you have removed your pants." Daniel looked at her aghast.

"Is this fittin'…..," he began?

"If you wish me to help, I will require to see what it is that I am to help with," she answered briskly. "Oh spare me your blushes please, Marcus is right here and none of us will be seeing anything we haven't seen before." She turned to the bag, which Marcus had set down on one of the stools, while he nodded towards Daniel's ragged pants. Daniel still stood, reluctant to commence on this indignity, but then he thought of that harsh, burning pain over the last days and nights and the torment of every movement. Getting some kind of relief from that would be worth anything, well, almost anything. He slowly removed the blanket roll and his equipment belts before pulling at his much-repaired belt, releasing the tongue and letting it loosen. He turned away from the old lady as he let the trousers fall to his ankles, wincing as the waistband and belt passed over the inflamed rear area. She glanced across at him.

"No underwear," she said, though Daniel could not tell from her tone whether it was a question or a reproach. He felt himself redden and did not return her look.

"Saves time in an emergency lately," he muttered. "They're rolled in the blanket," he added, feeling even more embarrassed.

"Table," she rapped, "on your front." Daniel stepped over to the table and rested his hands on the scrubbed wooden planking before putting a knee onto the surface. Shifting his hands along he levered himself onto the table till his head was at the end where Mrs Franklin stood. He gave her a long-suffering look before gingerly stretching himself out on the table top, resting his hands under his forehead at one end, while his feet dangled over the far end. His backside felt raw and the cooler air in the room almost seemed to be irritating it further He glanced furtively around again, feeling exposed and vulnerable as Mrs Franklin, stepped to the side and looked at his buttocks.

"Such modesty," she murmured, "and in a soldier."

"Comes from a good, god-fearin' upbringin'," Daniel rejoined.

"That, if so, is to others' credit rather than yours," she told him before stepping back and turning to where Marcus stood near the other end of the table.

"If you would oblige us Marcus," she said.

Marcus moved around the table and waited there till his mistress, having rinsed her hands in the basin of water, stepped away, whereupon he soaked a cloth in the same basin and rubbed some strong-smelling soap upon it. Then, holding Daniel's thigh with one hand, he washed down his whole rear area with the soapy cloth. Daniel wriggled and writhed, and tried not to call out, as his backside throbbed and stung while the, none too gentle, cleaning proceeded. It seemed interminable to him, and his whole buttocks area became a pulsing, burning mass of pain, but the washing was at last completed. Marcus rinsed the area with more water before taking a cotton towel and wiping Daniel's buttocks and legs down, while he wriggled and gritted his teeth anew. This done, Mrs Franklin stepped up to survey the "affliction," further.

"Very inflamed," she muttered, half to herself, "and blistered also." She prodded gently at his freshly laundered buttocks, with Daniel wincing sharply as she did so.

"It surely wasn't my idea or my wish, ma'am," he told her.

"But here you are anyway Mr Ryan," she said, "whether you chose it this way or not." She turned to her bag and pulled a succession of jars from inside.

"I have a salve here that should bring some relief to your condition," she said. "It will sting some at first, but then it will settle and you should find it beneficial."

"I'd truly settle for that ma'am," Daniel told her. She selected a jar and removed the lid, poking her fingers inside and taking a generous slab. Daniel squinted around at the, "salve." It was a rather disagreeable shade of brown in colour and had an unfamiliar, aromatic smell.

"Beg pardon, ma'am, but what is that stuff?"

"This "stuff," as you put it, is a soothant," she answered. "It is made from herbs and there are some bark ingredients also…"

"Tree bark," Daniel exclaimed, "what in thunderation….?"

"Come Mr Ryan," her voice was firm and emphatic, "where do you think most medicines come from but plants and trees, and, from the way you are hobbling around, I would have to try pretty hard to make your situation much worse without shooting you?" Daniel fell silent, and, looking around, he saw her standing there opposite the raised hummocks of his buttocks, her fingers, balancing the large lump of the wicked looking, brown substance, poised and waiting.

"Are we proceeding," she inquired, her voice rising, as though she was addressing a child? Daniel looked away and nodded briefly. Immediately he felt his skin cringe as she slapped the salve onto his buttocks and began to spread it around, gently smoothing it over the whole area of his posterior. It felt cold at first and it was only as she rubbed it into his skin that he began to feel it heat up. She took another portion on her fingers and spread it into the crevice between his buttocks. My god, it was getting hot, he thought, and the old lady was making sure it got right into all the damned places. Much more and she would maybe have succeeded in making him worse after all. He shifted and squirmed on the table.

"It's ho...t," he said, his voice growing louder with the words. She raised an admonishing hand.

"Have a little patience please," she said. "It will only be that way for a short time." Daniel put his forehead back on his hands and clenched his teeth, but sure enough, already, as the moments passed, he could feel the burning discomfort beginning to subside as a numbness started to spread over the area. He stayed still, trying not to wriggle or shift his buttocks and, slowly, his whole backside began to calm. He sneaked a look around at it. Both buttocks, and his upper thighs also, were stained in the dirty brown colour of the salve, with a thick layer of the stuff covering the most affected places. It surely looked, he reflected, as though he had not made it to the bushes in time, but it was helping, he thought to himself, there was no doubt that it was helping.

"Better," she said?

"It is," he told her. He sighed and looked at her as she wiped her hands on the cotton towel.

"Stay there meantime," she told him, "and let the salve start to do its work." On an impulse, he turned on his elbow and looked at her.

"Why are you helpin' me," he asked her? "I wondered at first if you were a southern sympathiser or somethin' like that?"

"Goodness me no," she answered. "I am a patriot and wish to see the union preserved. I have two nephews serving in General McClellan's army, and my own son works in the navy department in Washington."

"Well why are you helping ….. well rebels," Daniel was even more puzzled at her answer?

"I am involved with an organisation called the United States Sanitary Commission," she told him. "It was formed last year and is dedicated to improving the welfare of our soldiers, especially sick and wounded soldiers."

"On the Yankee side," Daniel said.

"Indeed," she answered.

"Well, why me," he asked again?

"You are a soldier," she said, "and an enemy soldier, but you are still a human being and you were obviously in some distress, back out there on the road." Daniel was silent, there was little doubt of that, he thought to himself.

"Are you plannin' to try to keep us here, and hand us over to the Yankees, as prisoners or something like that?" Even as he said the words, he knew that the idea was ridiculous.

"Fat chance we'd have, Marcus and Mona and me, even if that was what we wanted to do, with your army spread all over the county. No, Mr Ryan, my intention goes no further than helping to relieve your... ah.. discomfort." Daniel was silent for a second or two, until an overdue recollection of the requirements of manners prompted him to reply.

"Well I am most grateful to you for that ma'am," he told her.

"Give the salve some more time to take effect and dry," she told him. "I will go meantime and arrange for you to receive some better pants than those things on the floor, though we have no shoes here that would fit your feet. I will speak to your companion, Mr Ballard... was it? Perhaps, since our southern visitors to the state of Maryland are all so ravenously hungry, we had better provide you both with something to eat. To be truthful, it is a matter of some surprise around here that the famished hordes of your starving army have not already stolen everything we have."

"They're starving," Daniel told her, "because there's little left in most of northern Virginia now that the Yankee army's spent the last year there. As for not takin' everything up here, in payment for all o' that, well that's General Lee's orders."

"Ah yes," she said, "General Lee, we have heard a lot about him over the last few months. He is said to be a true southern gentleman, as well as a better general than most of ours, at least this is what we hear. It's such a pity he is devoting his considerable abilities to the breaking up of our union."

"Maybe you can't have a union at the point of a gun, ma'am."

"But what if you should win," she retorted, with a degree of emotion showing in her voice for the first time? "What if you should succeed with your southern Confederacy? This continent could become as divided as Europe and its ground would be soaked in blood from the same kind of never-ending wars."

"Strikes me that the Yankees have soaked plenty o' Virginian ground already ma'am," Daniel returned.

"I shall not debate further with you." Her voice had returned to its previous, controlled and even tone. "When you have cleaned yourself up further and dressed yourself, you and Mr Ballard may have a meal out here. In the meantime I will take my leave of you to prepare for that." She lifted her leather bag and nodded to Marcus who stepped over to retrieve the water basin and at that, in dignified procession, the two of them left the outhouse. Daniel Ryan lay there, basking in the luxury of his treated buttocks, listening to the silence in the room, but still hearing an occasional splash of water from outside as Ballard concluded his own washing. On the floor beside the table, he saw the other water bucket, with a cloth and a cake of soap wedged between the handle and the rim. A wash would be just a further luxury, he thought and he began to carefully ease himself over to the edge of the table to get started on it. Things had taken a turn for the better, he concluded, especially if Mrs Franklin was as good as her word about feeding them.

It was late afternoon when a further laundered Daniel Ryan, having been provided with a set of cotton underwear and a pair of brown corduroy trousers by Marcus, settled, in company with a cleaned up Otis Ballard, to large portions of fried chicken, greens, potatoes and apple- buttered wheat bread, with even a glass of cider each to wash it all down. The meal had been brought out to them by an older black woman, whom Daniel reckoned must be, "Mona," and served on the table, where the buttock treatment had lately taken place. The damp stains of water from his ablutions were still visible on the planking but he had not shared the finer details of what had transpired with his friend for fear of once more becoming the butt of his sarcastic humour. Mona had also brought a further glass of a yellowish potion which she had set in front of him with the announcement that Mrs Franklin's instructions were for him to drink it.

"What is it," he had asked her?

"Jest drink it down," she had repeated. "All of it," she had added sternly, "ev' last drop." Daniel had done so, gulping the contents down and enduring the evil after taste, as he muttered his thanks to Mona and turned to the food she had brought. They ate two portions each, savouring the luxury of good and well-cooked food. After a time, Mona came back for the plates and glasses and when she had disposed of them, she returned, along with Marcus, bringing them a cotton cloth bundle, which Ballard took, glancing inside to confirm that it contained more food. The meal completed, they donned their belts and blanket rolls and lifted their muskets from where they lay.

"I'd like to thank Mrs Franklin again," Daniel said to Marcus.

"She takin' her af'noon rest right now," the old man told him, "an' I ain't gonna be goin' wakin' her none."

"Then please pass on my thanks to her for what she has done for us," Daniel told him. Marcus nodded gravely.

"I'll do that, sah," he said, and stood by while Ryan and Ballard stepped out of the door and started away along the flower lined path to the front of the house, with the tall negro following on after them, as though to make sure they were going without raiding the smoke-house. They reached the front of the main house and Marcus fumbled in the pocket of his white coat. He withdrew a small glass jar of what looked, to Daniel like the salve that the old lady had treated him with, and handed it over.

"Mizz Franklin says to make showah you got that," he said.

"I'm obliged to your mistress," he told the old man, "and to you."

"Dat's showaly ouwah pleasha sah," Marcus said stiffly and gave a small bow of his head. Daniel nodded to him and then turned and followed on down the drive, not intending to hurry overmuch to catch up with Ballard, who was a few steps in front of him, His backside was surely better, not cured, but much improved on before, but even so he would not tempt providence by chasing around anywhere. He looked back towards the house. Marcus had gone from the step, but at the far right window of the upstairs floor, his eyes were suddenly drawn to something, a movement, a dark shape, a figure, standing back from the window itself but watching them go nevertheless. It was the old lady, he was sure of it. Without thinking further, he raised his hand, in acknowledgement and farewell.

"Are ya settin' up camp here or what," he heard Ballard call and he looked around to where his friend had stopped and turned in the middle of the sunlit drive.

"Just showin' some reasonable breedin' and manners," he called back, "nothin' you need to trouble about." Back at the house, there was no response from the upstairs room, so, after looking towards the window for a few seconds more, he turned and started to follow after Ballard once more, on down the driveway towards the road, pushing the jar into his haversack as he went. That would be worth its weight in gold, he thought, as he made his way down the hot gravel way, and he would be keeping it damned safe.

But already, especially with having just eaten his fill, he could feel that familiar motion commencing in his bowels, and, in response to that sensation, he increased his pace. It really would not do at all to be ducking into the bushes that lined the old lady's drive after all that she had just finished doing to help him. Daniel clenched the muscles of his buttocks and stepped briskly on towards the gateway. He reached the end of the drive and moved out onto the road, beginning at once to look for a place to go to toilet, even as his mind was turning over the events of the last couple of hours, knowing, as a result of those events, that he now less than ever understood the Yankees. He jogged quickly into a tall cornfield on the other side of the road, seeing Ballard shaking his head in amused and feigned exasperation as he pushed through the first of the rustling stalks and waxy dark green leaves.

He pulled down the corduroy pants and the underpants in one movement, squatting as he did so. It seemed insane that that old lady, up that dusty driveway back there, had been willing to help him, a rebel enemy, to the extent that she had. Why in a matter of days, or weeks, or who knew when, the armies could be in collision again and he could be shooting at her nephews if they were, as she had said, in the Yankee army? Yet, in spite of all of that, she had not hesitated. There was no real explaining it or understanding it either. It really all just went to prove that there were different sorts of Yankees, the same as any kind of people, and you could not label them all together any more than anybody else. He let his mind linger on those thoughts briefly, as he squatted there among the corn stalks, concluding eventually that nobody had a monopoly on kindness, any more than on vice, but it was still just about the last thing that a man expected to happen to him up here in the middle of enemy country.

Chapter 8
Loose Bowels and Bare Feet

Their return to camp enabled the best mess meal of their time at Frederick to get under way. With Mrs Franklin's chicken and potatoes as its nucleus, the six of them dined on the proceeds of all of their foraging and, for the first time since crossing the river, felt near to satisfied at the end of the meal. It was cooked in the improvised canteen half pans, each of which now sported metal handles, riveted in place by a blacksmith whom Thompson had found and had managed to convince that assisting the Confederate army was a sensible idea. Each handle had a hole near the end, for convenient fastening to a belt for ease of carrying. The meal finished, they turned in and, for the first time in days, Daniel Ryan slept soundly.

It was the Wednesday morning when their own division left the camp between the town and the railroad junction. Orders had been issued the previous evening to cook the customary three days' rations in preparation to march, but this, for much of the army, was something of a hollow sham. Although most men, over the course of their stay around Frederick, had managed to forage or beg some decent food, in Company B, as in the rest of the regiment, there were only remnants of this at best. Daniel Ryan's mess had a little bacon, together with the contents of the requisitioned cornfields and apple orchards, to prepare for the coming days. They parched their corn and chopped the bacon, baking the mix into crude flat scones. It was not even a shadow of three days supply of food, but it was all they had until something else, whether the absent commissary or some local windfall, came their way.

The sound of bugles had roused them while it was still dark and the three quarter moon was near the western horizon as they went to assembly with the first traces of a clear dawn visible on the opposite skyline. But, having paraded for a brief roll call and orders and then formed their column of march, their setting off had again been delayed by congestion on the road. Other formations, with their wagons and guns and additional artillery also, had march priority and the delays in getting all of them started held up anyone else who wanted to use the roads through Frederick, thus it was some time before they had stepped off on the main road into town.

The streets were lined with scatterings of the local people, though most of the homes and premises remained locked and shuttered, as the column tramped on through, following Market Street as it led through town. The watching onlookers were largely subdued and silent, with only an occasional waving of a stars and bars flag or a muted cheer from a few particular groups. Union flags were more in evidence at some of the windows, and in the hands of watching children, as the men of Toombs' brigade marched through, pausing at Market and Patrick Streets, while more columns of men, wagons and guns passed across, before heading out of town on the National Road, another of those macadamised turnpikes, whose hard, stony surfaces were so much more severe on the feet of the many bare-footed soldiers than the dirt roads they had been mostly accustomed to.

Both Daniel's own shoes were now deteriorating again, with a pronounced side rent in the leather of the outside of the right shoe and the beginning of the same thing on the inside of the left. As he struck out to the west on that hard surface, he grimly acknowledged that he might, before long, be joining those whose bare feet already suffered the blisters and cuts from long successive hikes on these harsh and abrasive highways. But his buttocks at least were considerably easier. He had applied the salve from the jar each night before turning in and the improvement had been steady. Daniel thought again of the little woman who had gone out of her way to help him and his mind lingered fondly on the fried chicken meal that he and Ballard had eaten at the house and shared with the other four of the mess on the Monday. But, from their own supply wagons they had gotten nothing now since Leesburg, and, for most of the men, that last ration had sufficed for one day only making for an uncertain future as far as food was concerned.

The army was heading west, on the Boonsboro road men said, with Old Jack's divisions up ahead and this went some of the way towards confirming last night's rumours of an impending attack on whatever garrison lay at Harper's Ferry, some miles to the south west of Frederick. The Ferry, lying at the lower end of the Shenandoah Valley, just across the Potomac, was still occupied by the Yankees. It seemed bad tactics for the enemy to leave troops there, to be cut off by the Confederate advance, but, since they had done so, the place would have to be taken one way or the other, the camp tacticians reckoned, for it sat squarely on the route where their own munitions would be coming to supply any continued stay north of the river. So Jackson was on his way to capture the place, taking the larger part of the army, but not all in one column, for the various march routes of today hinted that the Ferry, if it was indeed the objective, would be approached from different directions. The town was seemingly dominated by high bluffs on three of its sides, so the sensible thing would be to occupy that high ground, divided by the Potomac and Shenandoah Rivers, which was surely the key to investing the place.

Even on this stone-covered national road, the dust, without any rain for days on end to fix it, was still an ordeal, particularly here, well down the column, with so many other formations having preceded their own division along the way. Visibility was again reduced to the few files ahead or behind, with the infernal cloud gradually inflaming the men's eyes and noses and catching in their throats, as they drew their wheezing breaths of the humid, polluted air. Some of them had now contracted skin boils on their necks and arms and livid eye styes from the dust rubbing on the skin, and these stood out in angry livid blotches on their skin.

Canteens emptied quickly in the rising heat, regularly used to rinse throats, tongues and mouths of the dust, but refills were irregular, depending on the occasional farm well or creek. Progress too was disjointed, interrupted repeatedly by the halting of the units in front and, at these times, the ranks simply stood in the eddying dust and rising humid heat until the delay up ahead was resolved and the column moved on. It was only late morning, but already the first men were beginning to stumble from the ranks to collapse on the verges. They had passed no creeks or streams for the last while and, on the hips of many men, the now empty canteens bumped and clanked hollowly against other pieces of equipment.

Up ahead, emerging from the light brown cloud, was another of these country hamlets. A gathering of two or three homes and sure enough, out at the fence was the now familiar group of women and children, with the latter waving little home-made Union flags.

"Looks like we got no friends here either," Gibben grunted and sure enough as the column passed the flags were waved with renewed energy.

"You ain't wanted up here," one woman called.

"Yo're boys ain't wanted down south either," Ballard growled hoarsely, "but that ain't stopped 'em comin' on down." The replies were ignored as the men shuffled on, shrouded by their dust and wearied by it, by the heat and by their growing thirst.

The road led up over Catoctin Ridge and as they neared the summit, another few rooftops began emerging from the gloom above the heads of the men in front.

"Maybe water here," was the thought in Daniel's and surely other minds also, but, as they drew closer the familiar sight was repeated. The women and children, and this time an old man also, stood in a wide gateway, but when they looked there was activity there. Sure, a little girl held her Union flag in front of her face, but others went back and forward from the gate and they were taking buckets to and fro from the rear of the house nearest to the road. It was water, and the thought was borne out by the actions of those in front, for the column was slowing and the men were unhitching their tin cups in anticipation.

As they drew closer, the scene emerged from the dust cloud. At the side of the road three big, wooden tubs lay and these were being replenished by a succession of buckets, brought by sweating women and girls. The troops, as they passed, were dipping their tin cups into the tubs and drinking deep, before taking another cup to drink on the way. Daniel limped up, imagining the cold water on his lips, anticipating, longing. Then he was there, sinking his cup down and enjoying the cold sensation of the water on his hand. He raised the cup to his lips and drank. It was cool and sweet and delicious, washing the dust away and cascading its beautiful coldness down his dry throat and into his stomach. He drained the cup and bent again as a woman with long, pleated hair arrived with a further bucket of water, to top up the tub. She poured it in, with Daniel feeling the welcome coolness of the little spatters and splashes on his skin. He looked into her face, meeting her eyes for an instant.

"I'm truly obliged to you ma'am," he said. Her face was already red from exertion, but her words were firm as she looked back at him.

"Just remember that it was a Union lady that gave you rebels that water," she said. In the line behind Daniel, Mick Daley straightened up from the tub.

"Keep your Yankee water then," he growled, and he stepped back from the tubs.

"Don't be so gaddamned...., beg yore pardon missy," Ballard called, "don't be stupid Mick." But Daley was gone, with his shoulders set in that belligerent pose that marked his temper to his friends, while the others moved on at a more careful pace, balancing full cups of water as they reformed their files.

Boyce had arrived and having taken his own turn at the tubs, moved away with those of Daniel Ryan's mess. As the men still slurped gratefully on their carried cups of water, the lieutenant's attention came to rest on the set of Mick's shoulders and the absence of any drink.

"Not thirsty Daley," he inquired?

"Not that thirsty," Mick told him.

"If you take offence that easy then you'll get little of anythin' in these parts," Boyce told him. "If we get over east to Baltimore and that part of the state you'll see friendlier faces there, but not up here." He paused and let the files pass him, falling away down the column as the dusty men plodded by. From the rank in front, Thompson spoke.

"That's mountain folks," he said. "Hear tell it's the same in the Virginia mountains and on down in Tennessee and Carolina too. Them mountain folks don't have no time fer no southern Confederacy. They're Union to the backbone."

"If they don't want us up here then I surely ain't inclined to stay around and pester 'em," Ballard replied. "If we ain't wanted here then the sooner we're back in Virginia, the better I like it."

"I'd go along with that," Daley grunted hoarsely. Behind him Daniel, suffering blisters on his feet now in the wearing out shoes, gritted his teeth in irritation. Mick's stubbornness meant that he would stay thirsty. With no water himself now, it was likely, unless some further supply were quickly come across, that his friends would have to share whatever remained to them with him or see him drop out, another clear consequence of his quick temper. Sometimes Mick Daley was nothing but a trial to his friends' patience.

In the early evening, they crossed Catoctin Creek by a covered, wooden bridge, to descend briefly onto lower ground, before climbing again, up into the start of the higher South Mountain passes, making their camp, as it grew dark, on the lower slopes in a tree surrounded meadow. Daniel's bowel problem persisted, stubbornly refusing to settle much, in spite of Mrs Franklin's medicine, but on a diet of cooked or uncooked fruit and rough corn he was not greatly surprised. Many others had similar difficulties and some had worse. What was different however was that since the old lady Emily Franklin had anointed his backside with her "soothant," it had improved out of sight, compared to how it had been prior to her intervention. Each day since, he had rubbed more of the salve on his hindquarters, feeling it sting, prior to exerting its soothing, healing effect. There was still just over half of the contents of the jar remaining, and he guarded it closely, in case, with his continued diarrhoea, the problem re-emerged.

Their mess had little but the crude cornflour cakes from the previous day's preparation, together with some hastily foraged apples to eat in camp that Wednesday night. The mixture of apples and corn remained the bulk of what the men subsisted on and Kane and his supply of vegetables and herbs seemed far away. In his absence, Ryan, Ballard and Gibben had taken turns at preparing what food was available but the "meal," tonight, again sparse in both quality and quantity, was poor fare, eaten with little conversation, until, with the plates cleared and licked, Philipps muttered laconically to nobody in particular.

"If this is life in Maryland, ya kin goddam keep it."

Daniel examined his shoes again before he turned in. He had been suspicious of these shoes since he had procured them from the not quite dead Yankee back at Manassas. They were the best fit he could find, to be sure, and he had taken them for that reason, but they had been well worn, even back then, and, having had them less than two weeks, he was finding that the uppers of both were now cracking and detaching from their respective soles. The leather of each shoe rim had rotted and broken, so any kind of a repair was unlikely. In addition, his first blisters had emerged today, a further trial that would likely worsen tomorrow if he persevered with the shoes.

So many of the boys were now barefooted, or had their feet wrapped in scraps of canvas or carpet, and one more would make no difference this way or that. Daniel, who, even since his boyhood in Ireland, had always had shoes of a fashion, though often hand me downs stuffed with cloth or paper, knew that his own feet, when deprived finally of shoes, would suffer for the want. All around him, even in this remaining portion of Company B, were boys whose lack of shoes led them to fall behind each march, with their lacerated and blistered feet the cause, to limp on pathetically after their comrades. They came hobbling eventually into camp each night in ones and twos long after the other men had settled.

On this campaign, such men made up a large proportion of the stragglers who dropped out of the column. They were to be seen along the roads, detached from their regiments, from shortly after commencing the day's march in the mornings, with the numbers steadily increasing through the course of the day. There were other reasons for men straggling to be sure, stomach and bowel complaints crippled men, forcing them also to drop out, and there was thirst and simple exhaustion in the sultry heat and dust, which took still more from their places. But crippled feet was likely the most compelling cause and Daniel examined the near destruction of his own shoes with dismay knowing that, for him, these trials were close and coming closer. There were rumours of militia and maybe other troops up ahead, blocking their way north and maybe a run into these would solve his and some of the other boys' problems, but failing that, the trials of bare-footedness beckoned to Daniel Ryan, threatening to add still further to his list of personal woes.

Thursday dawned with a cloudy chill around them, in the lower reaches of the mountain pass, which only began to wear off after they had been on the road for some time as the heat rose. Today however, the clouds did not break, persisting instead to maybe hint of rain on its way down the Potomac valley to the west. They climbed the final stretch of forested slopes of South Mountain to Turner's Gap finding that near the top, the land flattened into a series of little plateaus, where sections of the woods had been cleared and little, hard scrabble farms hacked out of the inhospitable terrain.

Having crossed the summit, the column began to descend, back into the woods which clothed the mountain sides, staying on the National Road as it stretched away from the passes to curve steadily on towards the northwest. They reached Boonsboro while the morning was still unspent and settled into camps around the town. But hardly had they rested themselves and replenished their canteens from a local well, when they were ordered to assemble again, to push on north as the humid heat of the day grew towards its worst, and the dust cloud rose again above the column of labouring men. By staying on the turnpike it became steadily clearer that their own march was not to the Ferry, but since this road was said to lead on north and west to Hagerstown, the conclusion was quickly drawn that it instead must be their destination.

The files abounded with talk. Was the general taking them still further north, for Hagerstown was reputedly up near the Maryland – Pennsylvania line, but other rumours persisted, of Yankee militia units moving down from Pennsylvania into Maryland to threaten the northern flank of the Confederate force? What could Lee's plans be? If the camp stories were near to the mark, the army was now divided into sections, which were operating many miles apart and their own route suggested that, as far as Lee was concerned, the current invasion was much more than a move to supply and feed his troops on northern soil. The speculation coursed up and down the column, while the day again grew sultrier, though the veil of cloud persistently obscured the sun, and gradually the talk diminished as the men put their minds to their test of endurance on the road.

Parties had been detached to forage the nearby farms, offering Confederate money, or notes of requisition, in exchange for food. But what was possible was limited by these foragers having to keep some sort of pace with the rest of the column and what was obtained was insufficient for the numbers of hungry troops. The route was now through valleys and ridges, with streams of good water here keeping the canteens reasonably well supplied for coping with the ordeals of heat and dust, but now also, from among the woods and valleys to the west, there came occasional flurries of firing as the cavalry locked horns with whatever prying Yankees were indeed out there.

The column on the national road had dismissed for the third hour halt of the march when Jeffers came across to position himself among the company groups, who lounged in a roadside meadow, content enough with this, since the dust was carrying away from them on the warm snatches of breeze.

"You lucky boys," the First Sergeant shouted, "On yore feet. Git yoreselves up, git them muskets collected and come with me, lively now." There was a sluggish response to this, with some waiting to see if he would relent by taking some and leaving others, but no, it was the whole company and he, with the help of Bradlee and Bailey, cajoled and poked until they had a rough rank of sullen boys in front of them. Jeffers paced along, smiling his, "have I got bad news for you," smile.

"You lucky boys," he began, "you lucky, lucky boys…" Around him they exchanged glances while he continued.

"The major's gone and picked us all to head off into the trees over there," he gestured with his thumb at the fields and woods to the west of the road, "to help our good friends in the cavalry take care of whatever blue bellies they've tangled with, so those boys in the mounted arm kin gallop off to chase after other ga'ls up ahead o' the column." There was little reaction from the rank, though some of the boys were probably starting to think that a little prowling around in the woods for a while would at least bring a change from, and be rather less taxing than, a solid day of marching.

"Skirmish order," Jeffers bellowed and the boys moved across to the road, pairing off as they did so. Daniel paired with Ballard, seeing Thompson move towards Gibbon and Daley towards Philipps as Company B crossed the road and pushed into the stubble field on that side, making their way towards the woods that spread out ahead of them. Up ahead, near the edge of the trees, horses stood in groups, their reins held by cavalrymen. The lean animals switched their tails at the plentiful flies and searched for the tastiest morsels among the dried up growth of summer grass along the edge of the field. The arriving infantry line was pointed on into the trees by the horse tenders, but, on reaching the wood, they halted there to deploy, hearing the spasmodic crackle of muskets and carbines from the interior grow louder as they moved, in an irregular line, into the shade of the trees.

There was a cavalry officer there, a bushy-bearded lieutenant, just inside the tree line, together with a sergeant, the officer brandishing a large pistol in his hand. Boyce moved towards them and Daniel heard an indistinct mutter of conversation before the cavalryman moved away along the line, signalling as he departed to the sergeant, who moved off further into the trees. Jeffers waited with Boyce and he waved the sergeants towards them. There was a further briefing from the lieutenant before the NCOs headed away for their sections, with Bradlee making his way to Thompson's group.

"We're headin' on into the trees," he said. "Cavalry boys say thar's Yankees, but they don't think thar's many of 'em. They'll be militia most like since the Potomac boys are all still off east o' the mountains, but we don't take 'em lightly cuz they got loaded guns too, as y' kin hear." He paused briefly while the crackle of firing in the woods still continued.

"We leave our baggage here, then spread ourselves out. So let's kick their blue, Sunday-soldier asses and git on," he added, "cuz the other good news is that there ain't no rations to be had this side o' Hagerstown." With blankets and haversacks discarded in a pile near the edge of the wood, and Jack Milton left in charge of them, he gestured them on into the trees and, they moved off, opening the spaces between each pair as they went.

"Watch out fer our cavalry boys," Bradlee admonished as they advanced. There was a mutter along the line in response, though, Daniel thought, there were those who mightn't want to pass up the chance of a shot at the britches of their own horsemen.

The woods were less hot than the stubble field they had just left, but there was still humidity in there and the beads of sweat soon rolled down Daniel Ryan's face and trickled down his back. His eyes slowly adjusted to the comparative gloom, where only isolated pools of brighter light and colour, where the daylight was able to penetrate the density of the tree canopy, contrasted with the deep shadows of the interior. The boys moved on into the trees, their feet scrunching on the layer of decomposing leaves and dead branches and twigs, which carpeted much of the ground and hearing the screech and twitter of the multiplicity of birds and other creatures whose habitats had been rudely disturbed by this further episode of human foolishness. They negotiated gullies and outcroppings of rock, as well as the occasional uprooted tree, victim of some past storm, which leaned crazily against a neighbour or lay, rotting slowly, on the forest floor. Daniel felt the sharpness of an occasional twig or wood fragment push against his foot through the open seams of his shoes as he looked along the rough rank of dispersed men, visible in the comparative gloom only as vague grey or brown shapes, which flitted in and out of the trees and undergrowth in the limited light.

Up ahead the shooting continued, more a staccato sequence of shots than any kind of consistent firing, but enough to show that whoever was out there was not intending going anywhere else just yet. Eddies of smoke drifted among the trees, mixing with any remaining wisps of ground mist, where the last of the overnight moisture had evaporated in the heat of the day. The shooting was drawing closer now, with even an occasional muzzle flash visible up ahead of where Company B prowled its way forward. Out in front of Daniel a grey shape rose from a bush clump and singled out Bradlee who had positioned himself to his right. The figure turned out to be a sergeant also, with a wide brimmed hat, a thick moustache and a ragged cavalry jacket with faded black lace sewn across its front. He carried a short cavalry carbine, which he continued to reload as he spoke to Bradlee.

"Infantry late as usual," he observed caustically?

"Maybe so," Bradlee replied, "but we won't be pullin' out till the job gits done." The man showed his teeth through his moustache but otherwise ignored the riposte, indicating forward with his ramrod instead.

"They're out in front as y' kin hear," he said. "Most likely militia or local home guards o' some sort, but they ain't in no hurry to disengage. Every time we've went after 'em they've faded back, but as soon as we start to withdraw they move on up and it all starts over again, so we got ourselves a real church dance waltz out here." There were more footsteps in the leaves and twigs as Jeffers came up and the cavalryman half-turned to face him.

"If'n you deploy around here, I'll pull my section back through you boys and see if we kin draw them into your fire and maybe that'll convince 'em to let it be," he said.

"We'll jest wait for 'em then," was Jeffers' reply. He gestured to Bradlee who moved away, signalling to the men nearest him to halt and take cover. Jeffers watched him go for a few moments before turning again to the cavalryman.

"Major's got our Company A over to the right with orders to get on their flank and work around behind 'em, so holdin' here's plenty good enough till they git in position." The sergeant shrugged and turned to call one of his corporals across.

"Start pullin' the boys back through the infantry line here," he told him. "You ain't gonna go shootin' my boys," he said to Jeffers.

"There's maybe boys that might like that idea some," Jeffers told him, "but, if I tell 'em, they'll hold fire till yo're clear."

"Good huntin' then," the cavalryman said as he moved away. On Bradlee's bidding, the section was already moving into cover. Ryan, and the others of his mess, settled themselves behind an uprooted tree, save for Thompson who moved off to help set the line. The five of them selected cartridges and commenced to load and ram them, before poking their muskets through the tangle of remaining branches to bear on whatever emerged from the forest up ahead. Daniel settled himself in place, squinting through the mess of dead branches and jagged spiny twigs that festooned the rotting tree. He was aware of more sharp spines and other debris pushing against his feet through the rents in his worn out shoes as he scanned the trees in front of him. His eyes searched out in front for signs of movement up ahead, but there was nothing to be seen, so far, in the comparative gloom of the wood.

Thompson had returned and he hissed a last warning along the line.

"Hold here, under cover, fix bayonets but don't fire! Not a shot till ya git the word!" Along through the trees the boys had gone to ground, burrowing among the leaves and dead branches if no rocks or tree trunks were close enough to use for cover. There was now little sign of any of them beyond those immediately on either side. Daniel crouched there, settled behind the remains of the tree with the others. He pulled his bayonet from its scabbard at his left hip and moved it out towards the muzzle of the musket, drawing the weapon gently back towards his body to let him reach. He slotted the bayonet socket over the musket muzzle, sliding it down and moving it the quarter turn to the right to set the socket slot in place on the musket front sight, before twisting the securing ring around to fix the bayonet in its place. All around came the succession of metallic scrapes and clicks as others did likewise. This done, he pushed the musket barrel forward again through the dead branches, seeing the barrels of the others' weapons re-appearing on either side among the jagged tangle to rest on the moss covered trunk.

So far they could see nothing up ahead, but the crackle of shooting persisted and gradually drew closer, until, after a few more minutes, increasing signs came of moving grey or brown shapes among the trees, undergrowth and drifting smoke. The figures drew closer as the cavalrymen pulled back, moving from cover to cover and still taking occasional shots at the unseen enemy as they did so. But the Yankees were out there out ahead, for there was no mistaking the occasional buzz of bullets droning past.

A sudden movement out in front made Daniel's heart jump, as a ragged brown figure jogged the last few yards to their fallen tree and vaulted over the lower part of the trunk, snagging a sleeve on the jagged branch remains as he passed. He grinned through his beard at the crouching infantrymen.

"Kick their asses good," he muttered and was instantly gone, to be followed almost immediately by another smaller man, who skirted around the fallen tree rather than attempt to vault it as his companion had done.

The shooting continued and the smoke drifted around as bullets whizzed in either direction. Daniel crouched still lower, unnerved by the experience of being in the middle of such an exchange of fire. The sweat still ran down his face, forming drips on the end of his nose, which he wiped away with his sleeve. He reached forward with his right hand and grasped the slide on the rear sight of the Enfield moving it carefully along until it was set at almost minimum range, before moving his hand down to the cap pouch at his belt, flicking open the cover and feeling for a cap which he placed on the musket nipple. Ahead there was still no sign of movement though the shots still came whizzing through, one thunking into the wood of the tree trunk, causing the five of them to instinctively duck down as splinters of wood, moss and bark flew up.

Daniel Ryan's heart was pounding again as he gazed intently into the trees, straining to see some sign of the enemy emerge through the half light, wanting the whizzing bullets and the waiting to end. He looked along, past his own messmates at the tree, to now see glimpses of further men of the company out beyond them, poised there in their grey-brown line, while the exchanges of fire continued around them, though still there was no sign of any enemy. But the shots were undoubtedly getting closer, with the yellow muzzle flashes from the weapons of the advancing Yankees increasingly evident in the shadowy woods. Daniel continued to watch as more sweat rolled down his face, afraid to move his sleeve to wipe it away now lest that movement betray his position to whoever was out there, but so far, other than the shooting, there was no sign of Yankees.

There! Or was he imagining it? A dark shape, moving across, but then gone, lost in the wisping smoke and the gloom. He waited and watched and then heard Ballard murmur.

"Jest step on up boys, right on up here." Then another fleeting sign, this time a quick movement of blue caught in one of the shafts of daylight that probed through the trees. They were coming, drawing closer, because now, between the gunshots, he could hear the noise of their feet on the dead leaves and branches of the forest floor. Another figure appeared out in front, dark and shadowy in a more deeply shaded portion of the wood. Daniel moved his musket around to bear on it, but almost immediately sighted another, slightly farther back, but almost directly in front of where he lay. The man crouched as he came forward with little shafts of brighter daylight playing on his tunic and his musket barrel as he moved. Then his face was momentarily illuminated in a larger patch of light revealing clean-shaven, youthful features.

The thought of Henry Hartman flashed through Daniel Ryan's mind, as he watched this boy approach, then his eyes registered on another shape further to the left, and another, as the Yankee line took form, using the trees, undergrowth and rocks for cover as they sent a steady succession of shots after the withdrawing cavalrymen. Still Daniel waited, now drenched in his sweat and with his heart hammering against his ribs, as the Yankees drew closer. They moved across the remaining space towards where Company B lay, with muskets primed and sights set, ready to flay these blue figures, whose fate was being further sealed by every forward step that they took.

Daniel gazed at the boy he had noticed earlier as he emerged from behind a tree. God, he was young and this was close, unlike any of the fighting he had so far seen. In all of their fights till now one had simply fired into a cloud of battle smoke, or at best at a vague blue smudge, never really seeing what execution was being done in that billowing blue-white shroud. No, this was different and here they would see. This was now close up and almost face to face. The boy out in front had again veered away to the right, but immediately Daniel sighted on another Yankee and, as he did so, he heard Jeffers' voice bellow from further along in the trees.

"Fire!" Daniel squeezed the trigger as around him the wood erupted into bedlam. His own weapon lurched back into his shoulder and, just as the smoke engulfed him, he saw the blue figure out in front catapult back in a misting spray of red as several bullets took him in the space of a second. Around Daniel, there was an instant of pause and then a chorus of shouts and screams rang out as the Confederate line leapt from cover and made for the stunned Yankees. Daniel scrambled to his feet and jumped onto the tree trunk, his leading foot levering him up onto the moss covered wood. But immediately a pulse of alarm seared across his mind, as his other leg moved forward, on feeling the stub of a rotted branch push into the open rent in his shoe. He tried to free his foot, but, for that vital second when he could have retained his balance, it remained there, snagged by the jagged branch. Daniel felt his body lurch forward, totally out of control and pause crazily for a second in mid air as his shoe wrenched free. Dropping the Enfield, he vainly tried to manoeuvre his hands to cushion his fall as he crashed to the ground on the other side of the tree, feeling the breath thumped from his lungs and the rotted leaves and dirt push into his face as he landed. He tried to roll, but his trouser legs prevented him, being impossibly snagged in the branches and twigs of the tree. He managed only a half-twist and looked up through the smoke as he lay there to see a figure just feet from him. But it was a figure dressed in blue and, in the instant that this registered, Daniel Ryan found himself in eye contact with that same youthful Yankee, who now stood with his mouth open in shock, but he still held his musket and he moved it now. Daniel could see the boy draw breath and steel himself as he took those vital steps towards him and began to swing the musket butt down towards his head. He moved his hands to protect himself, but he knew it would not do. The heavy metal butt plate would bludgeon all before it and there was nothing to be done. He braced himself, knowing that this was the end, involuntarily closing his eyes. But, in that split-second, he heard a breath-stopping thud and, on focussing again, saw a brown figure crash into the Yankee from the side, pushing him off balance and careering him in a half-stumble back against a tree. Then the brown assailant thumped his own musket barrel into the boy's head and immediately reverse swung the butt into his ribs. Daniel heard the grunt as the man swung and knew immediately that it was Mick Daley. The boy went down and was finished by a sickening thump of the musket butt. Daley paused to peer at his fallen victim then turned to look at Daniel.

"I'd hate t' see ya try to climb a real tree Daniel," he panted, "seein' the trouble you jist had with one that was flat on its arse." Daniel struggled to disentangle his legs from the clump of jagged branches, feeling the material of Mrs Franklin's corduroy pants strain and tear as he pulled himself free. He scrambled to his feet, immediately feeling the pain in his foot from the branch splinters still lodged in the remains of his shoe. Daley had crouched to prowl in the dead boy's haversack and pockets as Daniel sat down again on a smoother part of the dead tree trunk, to begin picking the jagged spikes from his shoe and tossing them away.

He felt a queasy feeling in his stomach as he finally stood up and moved stiffly across, catching a sight of the disfigured mess of blood and broken bone that was the boy's face. He swallowed before reaching down for the shoes, only to see at once that they were impossibly small. Daley got to his feet, stuffing a piece of bread into his mouth. He offered a piece to Daniel who ate it greedily ignoring the sick feeling that persisted in his stomach.

"We better move on with the rest of them," Daley muttered, spitting out fragments of the bread as he spoke and continuing to chew as they both moved away, Daniel taking a final glance at the dead boy as he did so.

There were more blood-stained shapes among the trees as they moved forward, with Daniel limping on his injured foot, but not one still had shoes on his feet as he walked on, with his own footwear flapping more than ever around his feet. The right one, worse after its skirmish with the tree, had its heel now also flopping clear of the upper with every step. Both continued to shift on his feet, antagonising the blisters on either heel, but he was thinking less about that as he followed Daley through the trees. For Daniel Ryan was finding that another idea was forcing its way into his mind, as he still thought about the dead boy back there, an idea that emphasised to him that up here things were different. Here it was others who were defending their homes and communities and maybe, as he had thought the other day when Henry Hartman had been shot, this was what Kane and Jones and Fitzpatrick had really been getting at before the Ogeechee Volunteers had left Virginia.

Around him the others appeared, gathering into a group, with various items of plunder, mostly food, in their hands. The company slowly collected and, at a wave from Jeffers, began to move on back, making their way towards the edge of the woods and the road beyond. There was no sign of pursuit now as they reached the tree fringe that bordered the stubble field, to turn and start picking their way along the margin to where they had left Milton and their equipment. A few of the company were already there, scrambling into their belts and blanket rolls while the others arrived. Some of them pulled on shoes or examined the other booty they had gleaned from the Yankees, while the remainder of the company assembled. The boys stood around, many of them chewing on captured food, with a few comments exchanged about how well the bushwhacking of the Yankee militia boys had gone. But the talk then faded and they were quiet for a time. Eventually, Ballard swung his canteen into his hand to unstopper it and take a long swig of water before looking around at his companions.

"Maryland," he almost spat the word. "All southerners up here, recruits by the thousand, so who were them boys then? We kin do whatever we want," he continued, "but it seems to me like most folks up here jest ain't gonna take to us no matter what. If we was on fire," he concluded, "most of 'em wouldn't wait around to piss on us" Others around him nodded and a few grunted in agreement.

The column, leaking its sick, lame and exhausted men, steadily shambled on along the National Road on the last leg of the way to Hagerstown. Daniel, having seen his right heel detach completely, largely due to the episode with the tree, finally gave up on the shoes, tossing them onto the verge in disgust to find, that although the heel blisters and awkwardness in walking were relieved, the burning heat from the road and the sharpness of its surface stones imposed immediate further discomfort. It called now for additional concentration to try to keep one's exposed and vulnerable feet from the worst of the stones and other debris, which lay in their path, knowing that any lapse in this could mean further injury. Thankfully, as the afternoon went on, the cloud increasingly gathered, until a drizzling rain arrived to lay the dust and cool the surface of the road on which he hobbled.

They reached the village of Funkstown, several miles short of Hagerstown, to find the main column halted there and camps being set up. But feeling of relief at this was short-lived, for they quickly learned that Toombs' brigade had been pushed on the last few miles to occupy Hagerstown itself. So their own hike continued, on the less congested road, as the drizzle misted down. It was evening when they came in to Hagerstown making their way, to the town square. The public buildings were all under guard as they came in, to wait in the drizzle until nearly dusk, before being ordered to retrace their steps through the streets, finally setting up camp on open ground at the south eastern edge of town.

In gathering darkness they collected fence rails and other debris and, as Daniel laboured to get something of a smoky fire kindled, the others set off to forage. There had been no sign of the commissary and, although there was word of supplies being requisitioned in town, so far none had gotten as far as the camps. Daniel worked on the fire, while he attempted to treat the blisters and cuts and, having burst the former and washed the latter, he left them to harden in the open air, feeding steadily more wood onto the fire as he waited for the foragers to return.

The haul was sparse, being mostly corn, gleaned from fields around town and therefore needing parched. Gibben and Daley had gotten a few more apples, and this, together with a few morsels from their brush with the Yankees, was all they had. So a bitter apple stew again was supper, but it was widely regarded as an aggravation for suspect bowels, of which there were plenty in the company and regiment, never mind the brigade or the rest of the army. Having peeled, crushed and cooked the fruit with the corn flour, the boys sat in silence and ate the concoction. The camp settled in the darkness as the drizzle eased and, with the camp grounds already picketed, further details were set off into town to take their turn of guard duty in the square, on the main roads and at the railroad depot.

The morning came, and with the day came the sun and with the sun came the heat and when paraded they had been told that there was no march that day, which meant that this open ground was not the place to be camped after all. Rather than fry all day, the boys struck their camp, as the heat grew, to cram themselves along the edges of the field where there was tree and bush shelter, and where some of the others of the brigade had settled already. There at least was the benefit of the shade, although the original occupants did not take kindly to others crowding in upon what they saw as their camp space. There was no more word of the much-rumoured Yankee militia, instead, it seemed that the closer they had gotten to Hagerstown, save for their own brush with them back down beyond Funkstown, the less there was to be heard about any approaching enemy, and now, having reached the town, all mention of them had pretty well ceased.

Daniel, with the others had taken a turn at guard duty at the Cumberland Valley Railroad depot through the middle part of the morning, while more of Longstreet's brigades marched through town, heading straight on out to picket the various approach roads that radiated out of Hagerstown. Arriving also was a steady traffic of the army wagon trains, creaking and grinding in along the street, their wiry horses and mules labouring in the heat as they hauled on through. The men at the depot stayed in the shade, as far as they could, to be stared at by a variety of the citizens of the place, who, though mostly reserved, made no hostile or unfriendly move. Little boys came occasionally to hang around the soldiers, teasing or questioning their visitors.

"You a reb'?"

"My pa says yo're reb's."

"Which one is the general?"

"You lookin' for black folks?"

"You all stink."

Two girls came by also and dallied briefly to talk, in spite of the guard detail's infested and malodorous state. Daniel Ryan and his companions were only too pleased at the opportunity, however fleeting, of a little female company.

"Why this is the most exciting thing that's happened around here for ages," one, who said her name was Sally, inquired. "Are you rebels really goin' to stay on around here, like occupy the town and hold us all to ransom?"

"Up to General Lee, ma'am," Gibben told her. "His job to decide them kind o' things, but if this is how things are up here, I'd surely be happy to stay awhile."

"I'd stay if you promised us some regular meals," Daniel added.

Lucy, the other girl, was more critical in her comments.

"Don't you ever get the chance to wash," she asked? The boys grinned at each other and then at the two females.

"Ain't always possible to fit that into our day," Ballard said eventually.

"Is there really going to be a battle around here," the first girl, Sally wanted to know. Her companion was horrified.

"Don't say that Sally. Don't even think about it. That's the trouble with all of this, why there's a lot of Hagerstown boys been hurt or killed already in this war. Look at Billy Summers."

"'Fraid that's the way wars are, little lady," Ballard told them. "Plenty of our boys gone home crippled, or in the ground as well, cuz of, "all o'this." The two girls did not pursue the matter, but chattered on about other things for a few more minutes before departing.

On returning to the camp, details of them set out, in the continuing absence of the commissary, to try more of the surrounding farms for food and Daniel Ryan, together with Otis Ballard and Tom Gibben made up one such group. They succeeded in getting some peach-buttered cornbread, from a farm woman, which they gobbled immediately, though little else was forthcoming, save for the foraged cobs of corn from the fields, to return to camp with. Thompson and his group had obtained a little bacon and this provided some grease to cook the parched flour into something resembling flapjacks for the evening meal.

Saturday came and the provisions requisitioned locally were finally assembled in town, with much of it being immediately transported out to the camps and issued at last to the troops there by the lately appeared commissary. For the first time since the food from Mrs Franklin, Daniel Ryan, together with the others of his mess and the rest of Company B, got a ration of meat and wheat flour and even some vegetables. Hardly had the issue been completed however when the members of the mess were called, hurriedly portioning their ration into haversacks, before being marched back into town for their next shift of guard duty, this time assigned to the courthouse up the street from the rail depot.

The day had grown hot again when they were relieved and they returned to the camps with a fine edge on their appetites for the cooking to get under way. The rations issue was assembled to be fried up into a stew with the flour made into the now familiar dumplings and the men ate it greedily in the early afternoon, even having sufficient left over to save for a later meal.

But now, as evening drew on, the camps were beset with very different rumours. Far from the approach of militia, or any other Yankees from the north, the word was now of trouble back south, towards South Mountain and Frederick beyond. The main Yankee army had apparently not lain long around Washington licking its wounds from last month's battle at Manassas. Pope, it was said, had been relieved of command, with McClellan back in charge and a re-organised Army of the Potomac had, days ago, left the Washington defences and marched northwest into Maryland. They must have wasted little time, for they were now said to be around Frederick and had thereby moved into the area where their presence was a direct threat to the divided southern army. If the Yankees pushed on through the Catoctin and South Mountain passes, then the Army of Northern Virginia could be swallowed up a piece at a time by the advancing enemy, especially if the Yankees maintained this uncharacteristic energy and resolve.

Night fell and the off-duty men in camp settled themselves, but with no official word of what was happening or what lay in store. Around the fires while some men took to their blankets, others still sat, turning over the news and the rumours. The old man, some said, had issued orders for the army to concentrate, so they might well be heading back the way they had come by tomorrow. Somehow the campaign up here had changed and the Army of Northern Virginia had become the quarry rather than the hunter. Unless that pass through South Mountain, where Daley had refused the Yankee woman's water, could be held until the separated pieces of the army could re-assemble, then disaster might well result. The men around the fires reckoned that, with most of the army detached to Harper's Ferry, there was only Harvey Hill's solitary division close enough to defend the mountain passes. Hill had the reputation as a fighting general and of never doing anything, whether getting a night's sleep or eating his dinner, half-heartedly, but he only had one division to stop the whole Yankee army. Longstreet's units would have to get back from Hagerstown down to South Mountain, and damned quick, to reinforce him. That hinge between Boonsboro and the mountains was suddenly the key to the army's survival, for if the Yankees got there, they would be closer to the separate pieces of Lee's army than those pieces were to each other and directly threatening the rear of some of the men at Harper's Ferry. This meant that their own column had marched up here to north western Maryland just to turn around and march all the way back again, to prevent the Yankees from striking at those separated parts of the southern army before they could come to each other's aid. To make matters worse, if all of these rumoured developments, were true, the coming march was not just a matter of retracing their steps. With the hot and humid weather persisting, with all of the sweat and dust, the coming march now seemed to have all of the hallmarks of a race against time.

Chapter 9
Sharpsburg

Drums and bugle calls roused the camps while that Sunday morning was still dark. On assembling, the orders of the day gave no word of leaving, as the rumours had suggested. Instead the brigade was to continue to garrison the town and guard the wagon trains that remained here. These latter were to be started west for the Potomac to cross to the safety of Virginia at the town of Williamsport. But, while Toombs' men remained, Daniel Ryan, during another period of guard duty at the town's main square, watched as the roads through town filled with other troops, Hood's and Kemper's men, heading south back the way they had come towards Boonsboro. For their own units, there were no such orders so the men took their turn at the continuing guard details in town. Those returning from this were dismissed to a late breakfast with still no news of their own departure.

The breakfast of the remains of last night's ration was served up with the sun high over the eastern mountains. Daniel ate his portion in company with the other five without much comment, licking the plate before packing it away into the inner section of his haversack. Nobody had food to carry now, so haversacks were no burden. The brigade had subsisted largely on a hand to mouth basis here, with anything that they obtained being immediately devoured and there was little sign of this improving. The meal done, men turned to camp chores. Wood was collected and more of the now familiar guard duties were allocated, until, in the late afternoon, Daniel's next turn came, to pace around the front of the courthouse once more, escaping the hazy sun in its front entrance, feeling the hot stone steps burning at the soles of his bare feet as he did so.

Evening came, back at the camps, and still there was no word of marching, though there were fresh rumours of fighting having taken place down beyond Boonsboro in those very mountain passes they had traversed on Thursday. In the camps there was now an edge of nerves and restlessness. Belongings were gathered and blankets rolled in readiness. It was inconceivable that they would be left up here if there was a fight coming. Orders must come, but when?

It was well after nightfall when the men were called to assemble once more, doing so by torchlight, as the house lights of Hagerstown twinkled out beyond the camp grounds. The call had come at last. Wagon trains had been started off through the day, heading west, with one of "Tige" Anderson's regiments, which had not marched with the rest of its brigade, escorting them to Williamsport. Their own orders were to start the last of the trains on the Williamsport road under escort, while the rest of the brigade headed south, not for Boonsboro, but on a different road to a place further west where other units of the army would assemble also.

Escorting wagon trains was a job that nobody wanted. The dust cloud on a road travelled by wagons was proportionally worse, with the surface broken down ever further and the loose dust kicked up in even thicker clouds by the heavy iron rimmed wheels and the hooves of the horses and mules. In addition, there was the problem of droppings from the animals. The roads quickly became littered with horse and mule mess, which, as well as forcing the infantry onto the verges to avoid walking in it, attracted dense clouds of flies to torment the sweating men even further. Wagon trains were a chore and everybody knew it.

In alternating blackness and the occasional illumination of an elusive moon the men set off, heading first into town to the square before taking Potomac Street to the south, with, even at this late hour, a selection of the townspeople turning out to watch them go. Daniel Ryan even caught sight of the two girls, Sally and Lucy, from the depot, and he ignored his vulnerable feet for long enough to raise a hand as he passed, getting little smiles from them in return. A little barb of sadness coursed through him as he moved on, with the brief little episode of innocent banter with the two of them seeming far distant now.

As the column marched on out of town other thoughts began to impose on his mind. On this road out they were heading south so they could not be accompanying the westward bound, main wagon trains after all. Others must have that chore, though as the dust cloud grew around them their own ordeal seemed unpleasant enough. His feet remained a liability. He had prepared them as best he could, but already, as the road stretched out into the darkened countryside, he could sense his problems gathering again. Here, on a night march, the dangers on the road for those without shoes could not be seen, and he found himself repeatedly blundering into stones and sharper things, which inflicted progressively more injury on them. On they went, almost due south, but it was not long before the first of those barefooted or otherwise suffering men began to be glimpsed, hobbling along the edge of the road, or squatting on the grass there, looming like ghosts, out of the moonlight and dust to be smelled and passed by the men still with the column and then lost again in the gloom as the moving mass tramped on.

Daniel's feet too were deteriorating steadily on the stony surfaces. Each now sported a collection of lacerations and bruises and stones on the road felt like glass. He limped on, trying not to leave the column, but feeling, with each step, that he was nearing the point where it would be inevitable. With injuries wosening there was only the prospect of coming daylight and the brief hour halts for him, and the other sufferers who remained, to treat the injuries they had and maybe avoid more.

As first light approached, he could feel by the sticky wetness of each step that his feet were leaving blood trails on the ground. His right foot, as a lancing, agonising jab of pain had told him, had also picked up a thorn. He could feel the thing, with every further step, pushing deeper into the flesh of his instep. Mercifully an hour halt was due and, the column fell out for this brief rest, with light in the eastern sky and the grey gloom of the coming day revealing something of their surroundings and nearby there came the sound of running water. Tom Gibben took the mess canteens to seek the source, as Daniel set to doctoring his feet once again. Ballard came over looked at them, peering in particular for the thorn, but there was little that he could do, in the partial light and in the brief time that was available.

"Ya'd be best gittin' a pass," Thompson, who had watched the proceedings, told him, "leastways till ya git that out and cleaned. I'll tell the lieutenant if ya want." Daniel was reluctant to drop out and anyway, he would have trouble dealing with this problem personally, since he could neither see, nor comfortably reach, the place on the instep to try to withdraw the thorn, but Thompson soon discovered that Linus Cooper too had lacerations on his feet, and Boyce had arrived to scrawl a pass for him to leave the ranks. Seeing this, Daniel assented and Thompson moved back across. Boyce came over presently and took a look at Daniel's feet, peering closely at the thorn puncture.

"If that stays in, it'll infect," he said. Daniel said nothing in reply and Boyce produced his notepad and a pencil, scribbling down a brief note, before passing the sheet over for Daniel to stuff into a pocket.

"Follow on as soon as you're able, Ryan," he said. "The march is straight on down this road to a place near the river called Sharpsburg. The army is concentrating there." Even as he spoke, the assembly call came, and Gibben returned with the refilled water canteens while the others started to collect their equipment and move away onto the road. He thumped Daniel's full canteen down on the ground beside him and peered at his foot.

"That'll infect your foot if you don't git it outa there," he told Daniel.

"You a doctor," Daniel snapped? Gibben grinned at him.

"The creek is right over there," he said. "You'll see it from here when it's light. You should take yourself over there and wash it once you kin see what you're doin'." Daniel nodded, squinting over in the brightening dawn light to look for the place.

"Look after it," Gibben said as he moved on to pass out the other canteens.

"Be seein' ya," Ballard grunted, as he slung his canteen over his shoulder followed by his blanket roll.

"Have supper ready," Daniel told him.

"I'll have the goddam mint juleps mixed 'fore we eat," Ballard retorted. Philipps, Daley and Thompson each raised a hand as they moved off. Daniel watched them go, tramping away now alongside the first of the brigade wagons to be quickly lost in the light brown, almost white, dust cloud. A feeling of loneliness and vulnerability flooded into his mind, as he watched his friends depart, in spite of the scattering of other men who still dallied around the stream. The fracturing of their group around Leesburg had changed things and Daniel had come to feel an increased bond of kinship with those who had come north of the river into Maryland. But now they were departing and, save for the similarly lamed Cooper, he was on his own and he found the feeling unsettling. Cooper hobbled across, as the company files moved away in their pall of dust, and sat himself down on the grass.

"Soon be more settin' along here than there is in the column," he said. He gestured towards Daniel's feet. "I'll doctor yorn if you doctor mine," he added.

"Seems like a fair enough trade," Daniel replied. "Tom reckons we should head for the creek over there, so we can wash them some." Cooper grimaced through his beard.

"It'll soften' 'em," he muttered, then he seemed to reconsider.

"How far is "over there," he asked?

"Oh no more than a short step, I reckon," Daniel told him.

They sat off the road beside the little creek with several other men who had left the column for similar reasons. Daniel bathed his feet and wiped the cuts and lacerations with a washed through, but still grubby handkerchief. The thorn had then duly come out of his instep, between Cooper's blackened finger nails, but not without some pulling and manoeuvring and he still felt the throbbing pain in the foot that had resulted. Cooper's foot had been less complicated, requiring a more simple clean up and now he sat, with both of his feet in the creek water, while Daniel wiped the blood from his instep and got ready to do the same. Other men came to refill canteens in their turn, taking care to do so upstream, when they saw the extent of the doctoring going on further down. Daniel pushed his left foot into the water, enjoying the coolness and then gingerly followed with his right. The water stung the thorn wound, but not for long, as its flow steadily cooled the foot and dulled the discomfort.

The sky was now light with daylight full and the horizon hard, though cloud had again obscured the sunrise. Daniel sat there and stretched back, balancing himself on his hands. Compared to previously, this was luxury, but he knew that it could not last, that soon they would have to dress their respective injuries and get started on the painful hike to rejoin. He twisted around to look back towards the road. Out there, the continuing procession of men and wagons still made their way along, obscured in their dust cloud with the last of the infantry shuffling by on the verges and the vehicles, laboriously hauled by their bony, emaciated horses and mules, on the road itself. Scattered along the sides of the road, as far as could be seen in the dust cloud and the growing light, were more individuals and even groups of men who had dropped out of the column, mainly the shoeless, like Daniel Ryan and Linus Cooper, treating their suffering feet, but some others also, who languished in the grass at the verges, immobilised by stomach or bowel afflictions or simply too ill or exhausted to go further. Daniel looked along the way, almost incredulous at what he was seeing. From the sights along this road it almost seemed as if this part of the army was visibly disintegrating, with the exhausted, the destitute and the ill, as Cooper had said, almost comparable in numbers with those who still struggled on with their regiments.

His eyes moved on to take in a further sight. There, on the opposite side of the road, from where the two of them squatted, there was a minor commotion taking place around a wagon that had stalled. Men from nearby were being pressed into service to drag it off the road as Daniel watched the scene. It looked more like a damaged axle and if that was so, then that wagon would be going no further. The mules hauled and the troops pushed, but the movement was minimal, barely moving the wagon onto the grass which divided the road from the creek, but now at least, the following vehicles were able to resume their journey. The men gave it up and headed off down the road, while, around the wagon there was a discussion between the driver and others of the train, who had pulled their own vehicles in while the obstruction was dealt with. A mounted officer arrived, while Daniel still watched and, after some more talk, a proportion of the boxes of ammunition being carried by the broken down vehicle were redistributed to the others that had halted. Only part of the load could be moved, and a considerable number of ammunition boxes remained on the wooden tailboard. While the driver busied himself with unhitching the mules, passing soldiers were directed over to the roadside and invited to take an issue of ammunition, an invitation that most of them declined, in view of the extra weight involved. Cooper, watching it all, nudged Daniel.

"They'll be leavin' what they can't issue or put in them other wagons," he said.

"Well I surely ain't lookin' for extra things to carry," Daniel told him.

"It ain't that," Cooper said. "Look yonder, there's a tarpaulin on that wagon and if they leave that then we kin cut it up with these other boys fer our feet." Others along the creek, seeing the same opportunity, were already on their feet and starting to move across towards the stalled vehicle. Cooper now was up and making his hobbling way, followed by Daniel, over to where the serviceable wagons were being waved back onto the road by their lieutenant, with the mules from the abandoned one having been tethered instead to the departing vehicles. Ryan and Cooper pushed their way across the road, to where others of the shoeless stragglers were already gathering, while a sergeant made ready to fire the broken down wagon.

"Ya ain't burnin' that there canvas," a large barefooted corporal said.

"I'm burnin' everythin' still on this here wreck in about a minute," was the reply. The gathered men looked around at each other upon which the corporal promptly produced a knife and moved around the wagon, quickly cutting the rope ties which still fastened the tarpaulin to the front portion of the vehicle. Other men, including Ryan and Cooper, pulled at the heavy canvas, hauling it clear of the wagon and onto the grass beside the road. They gathered round to inspect their prize, with some pushing beginning, as some produced knives to cut sections for their feet.

"Hold on," the corporal raised his voice. "There's enough here fer everybody."

"You look out fer yore own," snapped another man, "I'm takin' mine now." The corporal shrugged and sheathing his knife, he strode the few steps to where the other man had begun to slash at the canvas. He hauled him to his feet with one hand, while restraining the man's knife hand with his other. The soldier began to shout, but his protests were cut short as he was pushed backwards over onto the creek bank and pitched bodily into the water. The corporal turned to the others.

"Now we cut this into proper parts," he said, "and ev'body gits a share, less'n somebody else wants a wash in that there creek." He looked around the group, with his gaze falling on Daniel Ryan who, still holding one side of the canvas, happened to be one of the closest. Daniel returned his gaze.

"That's just fine with me," he told the man as a couple of other men began to throw the remaining ammunition onto the road verge, while still more of the barefooted from along the road, seeing the chance of some measure of relief for their suffering feet, moved to join the waiting group. Tarpaulin canvas, while certainly not shoe leather, was much better than nothing.

The cover was quickly cut into sections by the corporal, helped by Linus Cooper, while others, including Daniel Ryan, man-hauled the heavy canvas around to help as the waiting crowd grew larger. Early in the cutting and issuing, Daniel had stuffed two pieces into his tunic for Cooper and himself, as some further pushing and jostling began. Having gotten canvas sections, some of the men salvaged lengths of rope from the wagon, which they began teasing out into strands to make crude ties for the canvas which would now protect their feet. The work went on until the busy troops were disturbed by a shout from the road. Men turned to see a mounted captain at the head of a small detachment of horsemen.

"You men better move on unless you're stayin' to welcome some Yankees," he called. "Thar's militia at the least back there and they'll be followin' along here lookin' to bushwhack anybody they can, once the last of our boys are by." He turned his horse's head and moved away, as the group started to disperse. Cooper and Daniel Ryan headed back to the creek to wash the dirt and dust from their injuries once more. They then set to cutting their canvas into shape, piercing a series of holes in each piece before threading rope fragments through for holding this makeshift footwear in place, and finally donning and fastening them. Having gotten themselves as ready as they were going to get, they scrambled to their feet. Cooper went over and foraged for a handful of cartridges from the mess on the grass bringing back a bundle for Daniel also, which he stuffed into his pouch.

"Best have some in case he's right," he grunted. "How're ya fer caps," he added.

"I got some," Daniel replied, "but I wasn't intendin' waitin' around to start a fight."

"Reckon the sooner we're outa' here the better," his companion said. Across the way the canvas was by now virtually gone. A few men still dallied, picking through what scraps remained, as the two of them moved out onto the road. A few others still lay or squatted at the roadside or along the creek, unable or unwilling to go further, but most were now in motion, or in the process of wrapping their feet to do so. In ones, twos and in small groups the lame procession started down the road, following after the final wagons and their screen of weary infantry who had just passed along in the last of the dust cloud. Behind them, in the distance there was a succession of scattered shots, indicating that some militia at least were down there and not too far away. Men looked around and some attempted to increase their pace.

The day was becoming hotter and the dust was up as they continued their hike, but having footwear of a sort, a refilled canteen and a washed face and arms from the creek, Daniel Ryan felt as prepared as he was going to be for the renewed effort. Walking was still pretty much a painful hobble and there would still be a need to watch where he put his feet among the sharper stones, and other mess on the road, but having some kind of protection on them was endlessly better than having none.

On through the hours of the morning, in company with other groups of lamed and infirm boys, Daniel Ryan and his companion hobbled on, heading southwards, hearing, as they went, continuing gunshots back up the road to the rear, not close by, but certainly not far enough back to communicate any great sense of security to those who made their painful way down that Maryland road. The day was bright but it remained sunless, with hazy cloud, and the air once more stickily warm while the dust maintained its discomforts. Walking, though now easier, still had its trials, as blisters and abrasions, already on Daniel's feet, seeped or bled making the canvas stick to the skin until some different movement of the foot wrenched them painfully apart, upon which the whole process began again.

It must have been some time near to noon when they began to see signs up ahead that the army had indeed halted. As they crested a rise to a substantial farm, they could make out something of a defensive position, up ahead, with artillery positioned to the west of the road facing away towards the east. As they drew closer, groups of men came into view, settled, mostly in the shade of the clumps of woods which were dotted around, but with some in the fields also, contriving to escape the heat, under blanket awnings. Fires had been kindled along the line, but so far, the smell was mainly of their wood smoke, rather than of anything much being cooked on them. Around here the land was rolling with a succession of low ridges, which boasted well-cultivated fields around prosperous looking farms. These, dominated by their colossal barns, nestled amidst a mixture of pastures, ploughed fields, stubble fields, where the crop had already been gathered, and some fields of tall, still standing corn which had not yet seen the harvest. Stone outcroppings rose in parts of those pastures or cleared fields and glimpses of these could be seen in the stretches of woods also.

The road led on to the south, where, this time to the left, further batteries of artillery had halted and set up, across from a little whitewashed meeting house at the edge of the woods, where more groups of their crews could be seen settled and resting. There were many troops here. Would this be the place, Daniel Ryan thought, where the whole army was again gathering, with the men who had fought in the mountains yesterday coming west to this place and those who had gone to Harper's Ferry heading back north across the river to get here? Farther down the road, the procession of wagons, that had all morning preceded the invalids, still rumbled on over the next rise, where the church towers and rooftops of a small town to the west of the ridge line were coming into view. This must be the place Daniel thought, as Boyce had told him. What had he called the town here, it was set on that western slope of the ridge that flanked the road, and it had a white plastered church, with a curious square tower, which dominated the place from its position nearer to the top of the ridge. Here the traffic was heavier still, with lines of wagons and caissons parked along the road obstructing the passage for everyone else.

Still following the wagons they hobbled on over the crest of the ridge and now most of the little town was in view, with successions of white clap-boarded houses and streets and lots that teemed with men, animals and vehicles. Ryan and Cooper gazed at it all, gradually taking in the sight as they pondered on where to begin looking for their comrades. Daniel let his eyes run along the streets that faced him. Did Marse Robert really mean to fight here? Maybe he would not give battle, waiting instead to simply cover this part of the army's withdrawal to the river, which Boyce had said was near, maybe over those rises to the south or west. There they could rejoin the others units from Harper's Ferry. Daniel found his mind disbelieving that thought even as it came to him, for nobody was moving out, whether towards the river or anywhere else much. This part of the Army of Northern Virginia was settled and deploying over the ground and it was this that convinced Daniel Ryan that there would indeed be a fight here. His stomach began to tense involuntarily at the prospect while, as though to echo his thoughts, Cooper turned and spoke.

"Looks like Marse Bob means to fight," he said quietly. Daniel nodded, feeling the muscles of his stomach clench still further.

The wagons ahead of them had halted, blocked by the congestion in the town, but the two of them shuffled on, making their way past the traffic, to a dusty road junction where a provost detail was trying to get some of the stalled vehicles moving again. They moved towards the men who stood by the roadside, while a sergeant argued with teamsters out in the road itself.

"Toombs' brigade," Cooper inquired? The nearest man shook his head.

"They ain't up here," he said. "Reckon they're with the rest of 'Ol' Neighbour's,' boys down south o' town." He pointed a grubby finger. "Follow this here road on south through town and, when ya git t' the edge o' town, bear left."

"Obliged," Cooper told him.

"What is this place," Daniel asked the man on an impulse?

"This here's Sharpsburg," came the answer, Daniel Ryan nodded, recalling Boyce's words back up the road. The two of them turned to limp away through the jumble of the army's rear echelons, heading south to seek out what remained of the Ogeechee Volunteer Rifles.

They made their way on through the little town, stepping around the vehicles and guns that congested the streets, passing across several intersections as they converged on where the buildings ended and the fields resumed. At the bottom of the street lay a final junction and there they came up to a corporal and several infantrymen engaged in guiding men and traffic.

"Toombs' brigade," Cooper asked again?

"Some o' Toombs' brigade got detailed to guard the wagons," he was told by one of the enlisted men, "so they're off at the river with the trains. The rest o' them are down at the bridge, down there," he gestured to where the road stretched away to the left from where they now stood. "There's a creek crossing down there. That's where yore boys'll be. Follow the road," he said, "on down to the creek. Ya'll see it when ya git thar." Cooper raised his hand in acknowledgement and the two of them moved away once more. As they did so there came an outbreak of cannon fire from over beyond the town. All around them, faces turned towards the sound, though there was nothing to be seen from where they stood. Ryan and Cooper exchanged glances. It was surely best to get themselves rejoined if this fight was starting already.

"Let's get on down there," Daniel said, turning to see that Cooper was already on his way.

There were more guns pulled over to side of the road, as they left the town and started to descend the hill with almost all of the artillerymen gazing up across the creek, looking for some sign of what the cannon fire meant. But, although there were now traces of rising smoke to the northeast, there was nothing else to be seen. Further down however, the way was quieter, with fewer troops to be seen, and those mainly stragglers, like themselves, seeking their regiments. The road stretched on through a dip in the undulating ground south of town, following a dried up stream course between two sizeable farms as it wound down towards where the creek, marked by trees along much of its length, was now visible. Upstream, the cannon fire had ceased as they came upon a picket, giving them their company and regiment to then be waved on.

"How far," Daniel asked a man.

"Ya'll see a stone bridge further down," he said. Our positions are on the bluff on this side o' the bridge." They nodded and passed on, seeing almost immediately, along the road, a group of horsemen sitting in discussion, while their horses cropped what remained of the roadside grass. Among them Daniel saw Robert Toombs and several of his staff, together with the powerful figure of William Benning. The group sat their horses, watching the thin straggle of rejoining men pass on down towards the creek as they continued their talk.

As Ryan and Cooper came up to where the officers dallied, there came, from back up on the road behind them, the dull rhythmic thud of more horses' hooves. They looked up the road towards the town, to see a further group of riders approach, with the burly figure of Longstreet, out ahead on that big brown horse of his, easily recognisable in spite of the dust. The ground shook as the party drew close and cantered by, smothering the men who stood at the roadsides in their light brown cloud. The horsemen passed to rein in around Toombs and Benning and their smaller staffs, while the dust drifted off into the trees beyond. Daniel watched as "Old Pete," and his retinue brought their horses to a stop just a few yards away. Salutes were exchanged between the officers as enlisted men lingered and listened around them. Daniel watched the general remove his wide-brimmed hat and flap it several times in front of his face, as though to cool himself.

"So we have the Ferry," They heard Toombs say. Around them men exchanged glances.

"This mornin'," Longstreet replied, "so at least we can start re-assemblin' the army now. How are your deployments down here general?"

"Colonel Benning has command of our men here," Toombs answered, "what's left of them. Our Fifteenth and Seventeenth Regiments are off guardin' wagon trains." Longstreet's gaze turned to Benning.

"I'll see if I can get them back," the general said, "as I take it, from that answer, that you are short-handed, colonel, like everybody else," he added. Benning nodded grimly.

"Without the wagon train guards," he said, "we have just three regiments down here, but half of their men are still scattered all over these damned Maryland roads," he said. "They are starved, and lame and sick, and the good lord alone knows how many of them will still come up, or what'll become of the ones that can't. But you mark my words general, these boys down here, the ones who've stuck with us through all o' this, they are the finest we got. They're gittin' themselves set down here now, and they'll be ready when the Yankees come on, but when you see them get killed off, later, or in the mornin', or whenever the fight comes, ya won't ever git any more like 'em." There was a pause, as though Benning's words were being digested, before Longstreet turned his fidgeting horse to move on.

"I know it, Rock," he answered. "I know it," and at that he put spurs to the big horse and cantered back up the road, followed by his staff, to send still more dust billowing around the watching men along the road verges.

The spectacle over, Ryan and Cooper resumed their hike, past where the remaining officers still sat, following the road, which now turned more sharply to the right, to descend the remaining distance to the creek. A rail fence stretched along the roadside to their right, and, coming into view through the trees that lined the water were the spans of a large stone bridge. It was an imposing structure, with three substantial arches stretching out across the brown sluggish creek with a parapet on either side. On the bank to this side, the ground rose sharply, revealing pockets of troops along that fence line, that continued on towards the bridge and they waved them into cover as they came up.

"Thar's patrols an' pickets o' Yankees bin arrivin' over there a'ready," an older corporal told them as they arrived at their position. "They ain't started no trouble yet, but we ain't givin' 'em no invitations neither."

"Who are you boys," Cooper asked the man?

"Twentieth Georgia," was the reply, "who're you boys?"

"Ogeechee Volunteers," Daniel Ryan told him.

"Other side o' the bridge," the man said, "on this side o' the creek." They nodded in acknowledgement and turned to go, hearing him call after them as they moved away, "and don't go walkin' on across, or some Yank with a loaded musket might jest save ya the trouble o' comin' back over."

The creek valley slowly opened to them as the road continued to curve. This western bank further down was steeper still, becoming more of a bluff than a slope and it was sparsely wooded down to the water's edge. Up to their right on the steep bank, near the top of the ridge ran a stone wall, manned by groups of soldiers while, farther away along the bank, there was a cleft in the hillside with soldiers up there also. Across the bridge, the eastern bank, while fringed in places with trees and bushes, rose more gradually across a stubble field to a further belt of woods which covered the crest of the higher ground opposite.

Ryan and Cooper left the road and scrambled across the fence to hobble some way up the steep bank before turning to move on parallel with the creek once more. They passed the bridge approach to arrive then at a smaller farm track, which angled up the bluff on this side of the bridge, coming immediately upon more soldiers, deployed along the slope, guarding this particular approach to the creek.

Above them, visible through the trees, was the cleft they had previously seen, now revealed as a quarry, where men could be seen stacking rocks into a stone barrier at its mouth. The heat here, though still considerable, was less oppressive than out in the open with the air slightly cooler and damper among the trees and vegetation. They came upon more men, and were beginning to pick out familiar faces, when they heard an even more familiar voice.

"You two had a nice day's furlough?" They turned to see Adam Bailey, making his way along, nearer the bank of the creek, where a picket line was in place. The sergeant picked his way up towards them.

"At least we got here," Cooper told him. "There'll be plenty up on that road that ain't got back yet, and some that maybe won't neither," he added.

"Some of 'em's our own boys," Bailey told them. "The company had twelve men, and the regiment less than a hundred, when we got in this mornin'. There's bin others comin' stragglin' in ever since. You two ain't the first and ya surely won't be the last today. The others are on over there." He gestured with his hand as he turned away.

They moved on as Bailey had directed them, back up the slope, towards where the track climbed the bluff from the bridge, reaching where the remains of Company B of the Ogeechee Volunteers were now stationed. It was not much of a position since few men were available to hold it. Ballard and Thompson were there, together with Gibben and Philipps, but Daley was not. He had dropped out that morning north of the town, Ballard said, and there had been no sign of him since. The rest of the company here seemed to amount to not much more than the dozen men that Bailey had spoken of though Daniel noted that the three black men were still there, crouched in a shallower dip a little further on. Surely more would come in, he thought, so long as this sudden recent surge of Yankee energy didn't bring them across here in an all-fired hurry to start the fight before the many southern stragglers could rejoin.

Everywhere seemed, to be the same, Thompson told them, with too few men on all these ridges around the town. It all made a crazy kind of sense. The army had been campaigning since June, with inadequate supplies of clothing, equipment and, most of all food.The men had had few rests lasting more than a day or so, and it had all just gotten too much for too many of the boys. Maybe what happened at Leesburg had been a warning, for they were broken down now, spread out along those roadsides of western Maryland, as Benning had said, with still more hobbling on their way back to Virginia or riding in ambulances, unless the Yankees had picked them up in the course of their advance. This army which had begun to re-assemble along this creek was little more than a fraction now of the numbers it had brought to the Potomac just two weeks ago. Many of its units were still absent and now all the signs were there that its enemies were closing in, and, far from being an offensive to grasp final victory, this campaign now looked like a struggle for survival.

For the Yankees were out there now, across the creek there, not in any numbers down here just yet, but behind the sparse line of pickets and skirmishers across there, who knew how many of them were gathering in the woods along the line of the stream all the way up past the town and on to the north? But what had happened, Daniel asked the others, since everyone knew that McClellan was the slowest mover on God's green earth? He had proved that all through the spring and summer, so how come he had suddenly become forceful and aggressive in pushing his divisions forward to maul at the southern rearguards in the mountain passes?

"It sure ain't like McClellan to git a shift on hisself at all," Tom Gibben said, "but this is different. If he's really gotten over his slows, he could have most o' his men down at Harper's Ferry by now, givin' ole Jack' trouble, so we don't even know that the boys from down there are gonna make it back over the river to join up with us here." He gestured to the east. "Jeffers says the Yankees are arrivin' up on the road into town by the thousand and we only got three divisions in line here. They could overrun this whole place any time they want to get started, but them that have arrived, apart from shootin' a few cannon off, have jest sat themselves down to boil coffee and ain't made no move to come on over the creek."

"But we're diggin' in down here, so we likely ain't goin' no place either," Philipps put in. "River's only a few miles back from here, but it looks like the old Man's ready to fight, however many there are of 'em."

But fight them with what, Daniel Ryan thought as he looked around him? If Gibben was right, General Lee had woefully few troops to prevent the enemy columns rolling straight across the creek, up over these ridges, through the town and on to the Potomac River beyond. Since the Yankees over there outnumbered these men by thousands, they could be crossing over and attacking - well, right now. Just about the only good thing seemed to be that they were back to showing no kind of hurry and, save for the cannon fire they had heard earlier, all remained quiet along the creek.

But how soon could help arrive for the men here? At best, if Jackson's forces were returning from Harper's Ferry, as Longstreet had told Toombs and Benning, right now they would be strung out on the roads across the river, between there and here. All being well, some could start arriving back tonight, or, failing that, tomorrow, but in the meantime, the general had only this fragment of his army to hold the Yankees at bay till those others got here. What was worse, with most of the supply trains sent to the far side of the river, there were still no rations, so it was nothing but corn and apples, as before, to keep a man's body and soul together and his bowels tight.

True to Bailey's words, more men had come straggling in. The crippled and the exhausted kept arriving as the hours passed. They had gone through the sparse camps looking for their companies, picking their way among the men there, disturbing any who were trying to rest, as the afternoon turned to evening and the evening moved towards night. Among them was a pale and sick looking Mick Daley, who had said little but had taken to his blanket in the bivouac on top of the bluffs almost as soon as he had arrived. As night fell, those relieved from duty down on the hillside above the creek, returned and any who had kept corn or apples or berries prepared and ate what they had. Still the stragglers shambled in, most looking spent and ill, but conversely giving some measure of re-assurance that, having wasted their chance today, if the Yankees tried to cross over the creek in the morning, there would at least be some additional muskets to oppose them.

But the attack did not come. The men were summoned from rest in the darkness and took their positions, reinforcing the duty line along the hillside. When daylight came, the creek valley was obscured by a bank of mist, which only cleared as the morning advanced and the sultry heat grew again. But, even as the visibility improved, there was little to be seen across the sluggish brown water of this Antietam Creek, save for the line of advanced pickets, who had been stationed along the fence on the far bank to give early warning of any enemy movement. There were Yankees over there beyond those wooded hillsides, but day was now full and the mist was almost gone and still there was no threatening move. Daniel Ryan let his eye wander along the creek valley, ignoring briefly the armed men who waited along its banks. The place was an image of pastoral tranquillity. Up beyond the bridge, the trees stretched their branches out over the meandering brown waters, creating dark pools of shadow, which looked cool and inviting to the men on the hillside. The creek was certainly not deep. Around the bridge, it was around twenty yards wide and its waters, while tinged brown by the silt and soil it carried down, were clear enough for the boys on the bluffs above to make out the rocks and plant growths on the stream bed all along from the triple-arched crossing. As the morning slowly advanced, the illusion of peace and tranquillity persisted, with only the digging and fortifying now under way on the western bluff giving any tangible hint of approaching conflict.

The sun was near to overhead, though no more than an indistinct yellow smudge in the lightly clouded sky, when the the creek valley was finally disturbed by signs of still more of the enemy arriving. Dust rose above the wooded hilltops on the far side of the creek, and that tinkling clink of metal equipment, that heralded marching infantry, came to the ears of the southern soldiers. Men stopped working and looked across, watching the moving dust cloud and finally collecting their weapons as a line of enemy skirmishers began to emerge from the trees opposite. A spatter of musketry began and persisted as these men engaged the southern pickets around the bridge approach, moving out to deploy in the stubble field firing and reloading as they went. This desultory fight dragged on, with the shooting rising into clusters of shots one minute only to fade into near silence the next. All the while, beyond those hills and trees on the far side, the Yankee build up of force went on, with more and more men arriving, the tell tale noises of their coming still audible during the periods when the picket shooting faded. There were guns too, batteries of artillery were coming up, with their harness jingling and the thunder of their teams' hooves and their iron shod wheels seeming to shake the earth, allowing no mistake as to their arrival, even though there was nothing of them to be seen.

The picket fight had been going on for a while when a couple of companies of Confederates jogged across the bridge, to push out past the line of pickets already on the far side. They deployed across the stubble field, engaging the Yankees farther up there, seemingly intent on testing the resolve of the enemy. All of a sudden those Yankees were on the defensive, moving back up the hill towards the trees in the face of the southern push. Daniel Ryan's company, in common with the other men working on the western bank, paused again in their preparations to watch the spectacle as the firing across the way rose into an angry rippling crackle and the Yankees gave ground in response to this new Confederate foray.

For a while the southerners seemed to have the initiative, as the withdrawing Yankee pickets steadily disappeared into the screen of trees and brush, but hardly had this taken place, when the tide changed again. This further turn was announced by another increase in the gun fire, which sent denser clouds of off-white smoke into the air around the tree line opposite. In due course, still more of the enemy began to emerge from cover and, at this, back the Confederate line came, pausing to return fire, trading shots with what looked like a substantially reinforced enemy, before moving back again, drawing gradually closer to the pickets around the bridge, who had opened up a spirited fire in their support. Having passed through the line at the rail fence, most of the withdrawing men re-crossed the creek, some of them helping injured comrades as they gathered to negotiate the bridge. None of them, Daniel Ryan noticed, waded the creek and he wondered if this might be to conceal the shallowness of the water from the Yankees on the far side.

The withdrawal completed, the firing receded to a more languid exchange between the Yankees in the field and along the tree line and the Confederate line along the fence at the bridge approach, with neither, for a time, seeming to want to make any more of it than that.

But then, from up there beyond the trees, artillery opened up in support of their infantry advance and these guns maintained a persistent fire. It soon settled into something that was certainly no full scale bombardment, but rather a slow and steady succession of shells, some bursting around the creek area, where the pickets ducked and squirmed to avoid the descending fragments. Further shells sailed across the water to explode around the wooded hillside, causing the still working soldiers there to seek cover also on hearing the tell-tale, tearing-paper like, sound of their approach.

The humid Tuesday edged through its afternoon towards evening, and although there were more and more signs of the Yankees building up their numbers, beyond that higher ground on the eastern bank of the creek, there was no sign of a real advance or attack. While shells continued to come tearing in, to explode over the ridge to the west of the creek, their infantry had pulled back to the tree line. But now word was filtering along the southern line that, unit by unit, the army's absent divisions were arriving back from Harpers Ferry. Jackson himself, it was being said, had gotten back near the middle of the day, and his arriving troops were being fed into the line, strengthening and extending the southern position. Now there was word of a cavalry screen extending their own line downstream from the bridge positions, preventing it from being outflanked by any Yankees who might take it upon themselves to wade the creek waters further down.

But, although there were plenty of Yankees over there now, they were showing no signs of wading across, or of advancing on the bridge itself. Their skirmishers maintained their tit for tat exchanges with the forward southern pickets and, as the evening finally came, it seemed that, for all of his men and guns, General McClellan had allowed this day also to waste away, reverting to his previously habitual "slows," hesitating to attack just like he had down on the peninsula all through the early summer. With the southern troops arriving back from Harpers Ferry, perhaps the crisis of being overwhelmed had passed and now, if they finally came on, the Yankees would find an army with enough strength to halt and repulse them.

With no sign of anything but further desultory shelling and picket firing along the creek, Ballard and Gibben had gone foraging. Thompson was on picket duty and Daniel Ryan spent his off-duty time bathing and doctoring his feet. Thompson, before he left, had given him a pair of thick woollen socks that he had gotten from somewhere and, with these inside the canvas moccasins, there was a degree more protection for his lacerated soles, and still painful instep, that they had not known for some days. Daniel tied the canvas back in place, feeling that things were improving somewhat for him as well as for the army. Upstream, in the waning afternoon, there was a further outbreak of artillery fire, which caused men to once more leave what they were doing and look. But it did not last and as the day ended the desultory shelling, all up and down the line of the creek, died away at last restoring peace to the valley. Work details of men were relieved and made their way to the camp behind the crest of the bluff to make what they could of whatever food they had been able to acquire.

Ballard and Gibben had returned, though with nothing but corn and apples which were prepared and mixed into the familiar hash and warmed in the improvised pans from Manassas. Mick Daley roused himself, still looking pale and ill, as the food hissed and spat in the pans, to be greeted with some harsh words about his timing. They ate the bitter mixture up greedily, being barely finished when the sergeants came around calling their men for an ammunition issue. The boys moved to the rear to form a line and move along past where the wagons had parked. Many stuffed pockets as well as pouches with cartridge bundles and caps, willing to chance the additional weight of an extra bundle or two on the basis that they weren't expecting to carry them anywhere further than down to the positions nearer the creek. As the evening closed in, a drizzly rain commenced, pattering down onto the leaves and branches around them, soaking the dead grass and gradually turning the earth to mud. Men began to wrap their musket locks with cloths, and stopper the barrels, knowing that their reliability might well be important when tomorrow came.

At dusk the duty details were changed with the off duty men sent forward again, spending what remained of the light in improving still further the defensive position on the bluffs overlooking the bridge. Daniel Ryan's mess was formed into a detail set to improving the trenches they had dug, collecting stones from the quarry and rails from the farm fences, building them into little parapets along the length of the earthworks. They laboured in the descending gloom, with some measure of shelter from the rain given by the trees, but still the earth grew steadily muddier and the men slipped and slithered increasingly on their errands. With the rain still pattering down they stuck to their work, until much of the hillside had been transformed into a pattern of trenches and firing positions. If the Yankees came across down here, the boys muttered, they would certainly pay a price for their passage.

In the darkness there came a final exchange of artillery fire, up the line to the north, but, before long, it too faded into silence, although scattered outbreaks of musketry continued. With full darkness, the work on the bluffs above the bridge finally ceased. Still the Yankees on the far side sat, out of sight in those woods or beyond the ridge and hills, with even the Confederate picket, which had been left in place across the creek, able to settle undisturbed along the fence line on the eastern bank. What was visible however, now that night had come, was the glow of many campfires beyond those hills and woods on the far side, giving some idea of the size of the force that had been gathered there.

Some time in the night, relief arrived for Ryan and his comrades and they made their way back up the hillside, slipping and stumbling on the wet ground in the darkness, till they arrived at the bivouac, where the off-duty men sheltered around their smoky fires. For near to two days now the enemy had sat over there, gathering their numbers, but making no real move. Surely tomorrow, or some time pretty soon, they must steel themselves and launch a real attack across the creek. With the armies manoeuvred this close to each other it was almost inconceivable that there would not be a fight, so now it was much more a question of when it would be rather than if it would happen. The tensions, always seen before a battle, were there again as a result, with a growing wish among many of the boys, born in some measure of exasperation, to get it done and get it finished. The shifting and deploying of men and guns had gone on for so long now, and here they still were, facing each other across the sluggish creek anticipating a battle, but still awaiting it.

"What in the hell's keepin' 'em?"

"Why don't they come on?" Such comments had been heard again and again as the preparations to receive an attack had continued. Tomorrow, the men told each other, surely tomorrow would bring the real fight. In the meantime, the newly arrived off-duty men, in their wet clothing, settled into wet remains of blankets and tried to sleep.

Daniel Ryan was among them, but, as that night on the hillside stretched towards the first light of a new day, real rest did not come. That feeling was in him, as always before a fight, the tightness in his stomach, marking the apprehension of waiting that would not go and let him fully relax into rest. The continuing scatterings of picket firing up and down the line showed no sign of stopping. His attempts to sleep therefore alternated between bouts of fitful dozing, when weird dreams of death and worse coursed through his tired mind, and periods of wakefulness when he lay and listened to the popping of muskets, hearing also, in the moments of quiet between the firing, the rain drops drip from the trees. This particular fight had taken so long to come, but now, by all the signs to be seen and recognised, it was surely just about here.

Chapter 10
The Stand at the Creek

The dawn over Antietam Creek was not really that much of a dawn at all, for, as on the previous day, a blanket of mist had collected in the creek valley, thickening up as first light came on and restricting the coming of day to a simple lightening of its grey-white cloak. The off-duty men had again been called in the darkness, to go scrambling down the muddy hillside to their positions in the humid gloom, with those occasional musket shots, from the pickets the only sign of the continuing presence of the enemy. Now they stood to arms, manning the rifle pits and other positions that they had prepared the previous day and evening, lining the rebuilt stone wall, which ran along the hillside, and the barrier of stones that marked the entrance to the quarry. They peered down into the mist towards where they knew the bridge was, but could see only vague, ghostly shapes of the trees on the nearer bank as they looked towards the water.

Far up to the north, even before the daylight had fully come, the sound of artillery fire erupted. No desultory exchange this, but heavy concentrated fire. Around Daniel Ryan, the faces turned in the gloom to look that way, as if some kind of sign might be seen of whatever had begun, though there was only the mist, damp and white, engulfing everything. But the heavy thud of those distant cannon served notice that today, as predicted by many, would be the time to fight and kill or maybe worse. The artillery from up the line was soon joined by quickly growing volleys of even more distant musketry, likely up beyond the town, Thompson reckoned, and these soon swelled into a furious, crashing chorus of fire, audible between the artillery salvoes, with the noises of both guns and small arms assuming a peculiar, flat, almost toneless quality in the mist.

The din continued to grow until they knew it could be nothing less than full scale battle. There was a murmur of anticipation, along the line above the creek, as the crouching men acknowledged to each other that the Yankees had finally gotten themselves ready and the real fight had started at last. Up and down the line too came the nervous comments that Daniel Ryan had heard before. These men wanted to appear more confident and at ease with the prospect of imminent battle than they really were, desiring to give an impression of calm, or even of unconcern, to those around them when, in reality, Daniel knew that most of the boys' heartbeats could barely be contained in their thumping chests.

"Looks like Old Jack's gotten the first dance."

"Yankees finally got up early huh?"

And then there was that other saying that men had increasingly started to use. Daniel's mind lingered on this thought, even as the gunfire further north along the creek still grew. It was supposed to have come from a Yankee passenger, who had been travelling on one of the trains that Stonewall Jackson's men had wrecked down at Manassas last month, on the evening when they had captured the railroad line and cut Johnny Pope's supply route. The man, when he heard that the rebels, who had wrecked his train and captured him, were commanded by the famous "Stonewall Jackson," had begged to be stood up, in spite of an injured leg, to look upon the great man. But when he saw Jackson, in his worn and faded uniform, dingy forage cap and oversized cavalry boots, he had refused to believe it and, even when assured that it was so, he had shaken his head.

"Oh Lord, lay me down then," he had said to those captors who had supported his weight while he stood to see the general. His words had spread through the army, being used in almost any aggravated or unusual situation and so, even along here this morning, with full battle joined upstream, the words still came along the line.

"Oh Lord, lay me down then."

Preston had reinforced the skirmish line down at the waterside, though these men had been posted along the creek's edge rather than crossing over as the most advanced line of the Twentieth Georgia's men had done. Those dispatched forward had simply vanished into the gloom, with no word of any kind coming back. So the others on the hillside waited in their wet and muddy places, while the whole valley showed no signs of movement, save for the drifting and eddying of that white, mysterious mist. After a while, with daylight here, the cloud began to thin. Trees and bushes along the near bank of the creek became dimly visible, but over to the east across the water, there was still nothing to be seen through the persisting whiteness. Around Daniel Ryan, there now commenced a succession of cracks, as men fired off percussion caps, to test or dry the locks of their muskets after the overnight rain, illuminating themselves in brief yellow flashes of light as they did so. Daniel did likewise, removing his wrapping cloth and firing off three caps to dry and warm the firing mechanism of his own Enfield.

Suddenly, there came more cannon fire from across the creek, but this time much closer, their discharges masking the battle sounds to the north. The shells, unseen in the mist, and with the gunners firing blind, tore overhead, with their distinctive sound, to burst, somewhere on top of the bluff behind their own positions. This fire continued and the crouching men on the wooded slope followed those tearing sounds of the passing shells, looking up into the whiteness as successive missiles swept over, all of them, so far, bursting up over the crest of the hillside to the rear. From up on the ridge, Confederates guns began to reply, sending their own projectiles arcing across the creek to burst, equally invisibly, on the hillside beyond, and so this unseen artillery exchange down on this stretch of the creek took shape, with more guns joining in as the light grew.

So far the Yankees had not gotten the range in the misty valley and the infantrymen, crouching in their cover, could feel a degree of security in their concealment. But it would not last and they knew it was only a matter of time till the grey-white obscuring cloak dispersed, and the artillery spotters of both sides would start correcting their gunners' aim. Indeed, it was happening already, Daniel, looking down towards the creek, was suddenly aware that the light brown limestone of the near side of the bridge, invisible only minutes before, was now in view through the thinning off-white shroud. It was maybe something around a hundred yards away, to his left front, down the slope of the hill, with its pale stones, and the slatted wooden facing boards that topped its parapets, gleaming and glistening wetly in the damp morning air.

As the crouching men watched from the hillside, vague movements were to be seen beyond the bridge, which must be some of the picket of southern infantry moving into place on the far side. But there was no sign of the enemy, even as the mist continued to thin, and the opposite bank of the creek slowly emerged from the grey gloom until they could begin to make out the detail on the far side. That road, that led down from Sharpsburg, over the bridge and on towards Rohrersville, ran parallel with the water for a stretch. It was flanked on its other side, beyond the rail fence, where the hunched southern pickets still crouched, by that belt of harvested land, on which the cut stubble still lay, which sloped up to those further screens of woods and brush. Now, in the improving visibility, the men on this side could see further downstream along that road to a farm lane, beyond which a freshly ploughed field led on to a further one of standing corn. As these features across the creek emerged, Daniel strained his eyes for a sight of activity, but there was nothing. On that east bank, the southern picket waited, spread out along the fence, which separated the stubble field from the dirt road and the creek, covering the far approach to the bridge undisturbed.

There was only the continuing artillery exchange, crashing out above the storm of battle up to the north, to betray the presence and any aggressive intent of the Yankees in this part of the field. Judging by the discharges of the Yankee guns, some of the artillery shells were coming from downstream, tearing over still unseen, save for the occasional hint of a smoke trail, mingling with the remaining mist, as the projectiles soared across to burst above or even in the margin of trees behind them, sending their showers of metal fragments, mixed with blasted pieces of branches and leaves, cascading down onto the hillside, but still largely beyond most of the waiting infantry.

Upstream, that fighting, both musketry and artillery, still audible between the closer artillery salvoes in the creek valley, now raged with an intensity that they had seldom before heard. Down here, in contrast, as the growing light and warmth steadily burned off the mist, the men maintained their watch towards the creek, on whose brown sluggish waters the palest gleams of morning light now played. Save for the cannon, there was still not a sign of movement. That full hell of noise from upstream, now interspersed by the distant yells and cries of the embroiled men, had not yet come to this place where Daniel Ryan and his comrades crouched, hunched in nervous expectation. But it could not be long, it surely could not be long, before down here too would see the full horror of what these armies of men had devised for their appointed tasks of assailing and killing each other.

The light was full along the creek, and the last remains of the mist were dispersing, when the artillery fire began to grow in intensity. Daniel let his gaze range along the hillsides opposite to come to rest near that ridge crest up to the north east, where they could now see some of the Yankee cannon, with the tiny figures of their crews clustered around them working their guns. They were beyond effective musket range, but some of the boys on the hillside began taking shots at them anyhow, and a few eddies of musket smoke from these shots began to drift across the slope, merging into the remains of the mist.

"Look at those shits," a somewhat recovered Mick Daley said, pointing across towards the distant artillerymen. Daniel squinted his eyes and watched as the gunners crouched behind their pieces, and, with their quarry now in view, they were turning their elevating screws, he could see their distant bodies moving with the motion, shortening the range, while, behind at the limbers, others, their number six and seven men, would be cutting the shell fuses that little measure shorter and now the ordeal over here would begin in earnest.

"Yeah," Daley went on bitterly. "Look at 'em over there, settin' their goddam guns to send their goddam shells straight down our goddam throats."

Daniel swore, and, pulling his musket back, he flicked open his ammunition pouch, selected a cartridge with his groping fingers and began to load, biting, pouring, spitting the bullet and pushing the paper into the barrel, before drawing his ramrod. He rammed the bullet and charge home and replaced the ramrod in its channel, set a further cap in place and then eased the slide on the rear sight of the musket along to near maximum range, before pulling the weapon up to his shoulder to aim carefully at a crouching figure beside one of the cannon. He squeezed the trigger, hearing the report of his own weapon blast in his ears and immediately feeling its recoil lunge back into his shoulder. The cloud of smoke cleared slowly, to be quickly replaced by more, as various men on the hillside opened fire, seeking to disrupt and delay this visible and deliberate preparation of the enemy gunners. Daniel reloaded his weapon but did not fire again, having blunted the edge of his irritation at having those gunners in view as they tried to kill him. He felt in the pocket of his tunic, closing his fingers around those four blue, cleaner cartridges that he had scavenged after Manassas. It was shaping up to be a long day, and he did not want to waste them.

At length those distant cannon were ready and the white billows of smoke exploded from their muzzles, engulfing that whole portion of the far bank. A second or two later, the sound of the salvo reached them even as the shells, black dots trailing their smoky wisps, that mingled with the last of the mist, curved across to burst above the trees and cascade their deadly hail downwards. They could hear tree branches snapping, as they were showered by the metal fragments, and now the first men on the hillside were slumping from their place, among the grass and vegetation on the slope, or grabbing and clutching at wounds. Those in the muddy trenches crouched lower, while some renewed their fire on the artillerymen that they could still see, as the battle down here was at last fully joined. Daniel aimed again and sent another shot towards the cannon, just as he heard a shout from close by and men began to turn to face directly across the creek.

At last there was movement over there. On the hillside opposite, a long rank of dark figures had emerged from the woods that covered the crest of the more gradually rising ground on that far bank. The last wisps of mist swirled around them as they quickly formed, and, at a signal, began to advance, down into the stubble field, aligning their march to make for the bridge, where the southern pickets had already opened fire on them. Further along that far tree line sparkling orange flashes, and spurts of off-white smoke, showed where other Yankee infantry had opened fire, supporting their advancing comrades with their musketry. Daniel Ryan gazed at them for a few fleeting seconds, hearing the minie bullets begin to buzz past, as he bit and poured a further cartridge, feeling the pounding in his chest grow and hearing as he did so, Jeffers' voice shouting the order to load to the ready. Around him men began to sight on the advancing Yankee line as Daniel completed his ramming and fumbled for a further cap, hurriedly fixing it in place as he heard the shouted order to aim and he pulled the Enfield up to sight along the barrel. The order came to fire and the creek bank exploded in a deafening blast of noise and smoke. The muskets were immediately lowered for reloading to begin as the blue-white cloud began to thin and clear.

Below, on the far bank, the Confederate pickets were pulling back, making for the bridge approach to sprint across to the safety of the western side. Beyond them, in the stubble field, there were now gaps in the advancing Yankee line, visible for just long enough for the men around Daniel to take a hurried aim before the next volley blasted out, wreathing the waterside with smoke once more. Then another, and another, until numbers of inert or wriggling, fallen shapes among the stubble and the dirt, marked the enemy progress from the trees. Another volley blasted out and over there, as the smoke drifted away, the Yankees had begun to falter in their advance, even as the first of them had almost reached the fence line. The formation began to leak men to the rear, until, group by group, they turned to fall back.

The advance finally stalled just short of the fence and as a further volley tore through them, they were all pulling away, with a few of them diverting their line of retreat to assist injured comrades as they went. Up the hill they went, many of them double-timing to gain cover and the firing slowly subsided as their dark figures reached the tree line and vanished among the leafy branches and shadows. The order to cease firing came, relayed along the near bank by successive shouts and the cloud of gun smoke slowly dispersed from the creek valley. The artillery fire however continued, not a heavy bombardment, but more like that of yesterday with a continuing sequence of dutiful shots whizzing their shells over to burst anew among the trees and resume their slow attrition among the huddling southern infantry below.

Time passed, with the artillery and further desultory small arms fire across the creek occupying the men and slowly increasing the number of limp, ragged, grey-brown shapes among the grass, while a thin but steady straggle of wounded men picked their way falteringly up the bluff to the rear. Eventually, in what must have been mid-morning, with the sky filled with the same high cloud as the previous few days and the artillery fire continuing without pause, there came a further shout. The men came to the alert, peering across to catch sight of any further enemy move. There were dark figures moving again, visible up there on the far side between those two small summits, their drab blue tunics and polished musket barrels and bayonets visible as they emerged from the trees onto the stubble field, with many more men than previously, forming for a purpose and that could only be the forced crossing of the creek. Overhead, the next salvo of shells burst, sending their whizzing fragments, mixed with their shower of leaves and branch debris, down through the trees, while across on the far side of the stubble, the blue column still prepared. Then the musketry too began to swell as other Yankees along the tree line again stepped up their fire on the southern positions.

Almost immediately word was passed along for the main line to hold fire and leave this part of the fight to their own skirmish line along the creek bank, saving the fire of the main body till the forming enemy column advanced. The men on the hillside now got themselves hunkered down, with their muskets prepared, among the wet, smelly earth of their rifle pits, and let the spirited musketry below follow its course, while the shells continued to tear overhead and the steady hail of musket shots now buzzed up through the trees where they crouched. Seconds more passed, until, at last there came a series of shouted commands, fragments of which could be heard across the creek. Bugles sounded, but hardly had this registered, when, with those deep-throated Yankee cheers, the formation on the hillside surged into motion, making straight for the eastern approach to the bridge. In response, the men in the rifle pits opposite, slid their long musket barrels onto their makeshift parapets, adjusted sights and took aim at the approaching enemy. There was a pause, seemingly endless to Daniel Ryan but likely only seconds, as his heart thundered and the minie balls buzzed past or ricocheted from the wood and stones of their positions. Then came the shouts of command and, as he squeezed the trigger and his musket butt lunged into his shoulder, the hillside all around him erupted in smoke and noise as the regiments there opened fire.

The first fusillade had the character of a volley, but after that, the men fired at will, biting and pouring cartridges and ramming rounds home with frantic urgency, as the onrushing Yankees closed towards the bridge approach. But as they came, successions of men were knocked from their places in the ranks to sprawl or writhe in the stubble. They were nearing the rail fence now, but, on closing towards the approach, they did not attempt to cross the bridge. Instead most took cover at the fence, previously occupied by the Confederate picket line and opened their own fire on the bluffs opposite.

A number of them, having negotiated a wall, north of the bridge, scrambled down onto the bank and began to wade out into the creek just upstream from the bridge, where the tree branches overhung the water, but these men, moving more ponderously in the water, were promptly shot down. The survivors, seeing their companions' fate, faltered and pulled back to the far bank to join the remainder of their comrades. These had contented themselves with taking cover, some behind that wall, extending north from the bridge parapet, while the others clung to what shelter they had found along the rail fence. From such cover as they had gained, they tried to return fire on the hillside opposite, but a mere glance could recognise the considerable disadvantage they were under in doing so. Already the field behind them was littered with the blue shapes of their fallen while, along the creek side, especially at the rail fence, where their shelter was sparse, still thicker clumps of their casualties lay. From these places they were attempting to engage an enemy with prepared positions and the advantage of higher ground, from where a withering hail of bullets was being directed down upon them.

Those Yankees were in a hole, Daniel Ryan thought, and the longer they stayed there the more they would suffer for it. On the hillside, the men kept up their loading and firing, as the clouds of gun smoke drifted around through the trees, able to see only glimpses of the tell tale litter of fallen men steadily growing beyond the wall and the fence opposite them. From up on the crest of the bluff behind them, artillery added their fire to the battle, dropping shells into the area around the bridge which scattered their killing fragments also on the embattled infantry there. The fire on the Confederate positions was heavier, but, although occasional men slumped down into their trenches, these were few compared to those who kept up the storm of fire at the far bank. As the small arms fight across the creek went on, the enemy artillery still rained their plunging cascades of shell fragments, or shotgun blasts of canister through the trees, severing still more branches and leaves, to join the shower of metal fragments whirring down onto the ground below.

The fire fight went on, but it was clear that the Yankee rush on the bridge had faltered. Some had begun to withdraw from their exposed position, with those along the fence line moving first, in ones and twos to begin with, but soon larger numbers were starting back, to run a gauntlet of Confederate fire as they pulled away, up across the stubble field to the cover of the woods. Soon all of those remaining were following, jogging up the hillside to the tree line beyond. The men at the wall on the other side of the bridge gradually followed suit, pursued by further musketry until all, of those still able to, had vanished into the distant trees. The shooting on both sides of the creek, now subsided, but it did not altogether stop. The Yankees, in the woods on the far hillside kept up their fire of musketry on the western bluffs, being answered in kind by the dug in Confederates.

Down along the road, stretching on around the far side of the bridge approach and all across the field, the fallen lay. Some of them squirmed and cried, or tried to crawl away, up the stubble covered slope to safety. Others lay where they had fallen, twitching or trembling while still more were inert and quiet, lying like untidy, blue bundles sprawled in the almost dried mud of the road or field. In the brown waters of the creek also, lay the sodden dark shapes of those who had tried to wade across. Some languished in the shallowest water near the bank, but several more floated down on the slow current, drifting under the bridge arches, tracked by spreading reddish brown stains, which, being darker than the muddy waters of the creek, marked the path of their slow passage downstream.

Ballard was in the same rifle pit as Tom Gibben and Daniel Ryan, and, as the firing diminished, he paused and gazed down at the enemy dead and wounded and, while the others around him lowered muskets and wiped the sweat from their faces, he spoke.

"Look at it down there," he growled. "This place is a trap fer the bluebellies. I tell ya, if they jest keep the cartridges supplied, we kin kill them off jest as fast as they keep comin' along over thar." From beyond him in the next hole Thompson answered.

"They better keep the cartridges comin'," he muttered. "I already shot off more'n half o' what I started with this mornin'." Daniel Ryan slumped against the lower rear wall of the trench. He could feel the cold dampness of the earth seeping through his clothing, but he was already wet with sweat from the growing humidity of the day as well as from the nervous tension of the battle. Sure they had good position and good cover up here, but it was far from safe with the Yankee artillery keeping up their uninterrupted bombardment of shells, coupled with the musketry from over there on the far side. Both were taking a toll from the defenders on the hillside. Here their own dead lay still and quiet, and the wounded cursed or cried, while a few orderlies, braving the fire of all the guns, came to drag and carry a succession of them up the hill to some kind of safety.

Daniel lounged there against his trench wall, as his heart rate gradually slowed again, but feeling tired and listless. There was, he thought, a fury, a frantic energy surge in the course of a fight. He had felt it at the Garnett Farm and at Malvern Hill down near Richmond, in the summer, and again at Manassas last month. Battle was a brutal intimidating experience, but he knew that as he experienced it again and again he was becoming almost accustomed to it. If you could get past the cold fear of being killed or maimed, which always weighed on the mind before a fight, then the fight itself changed things. There would always be skulkers, men like Hendricks or Cole or Hazel, who found other places to be when the shooting started, but most would battle through, braced by this surge of energy. Some minority even seemed to find battle exhilarating, though, to Daniel's mind, they were fools.

But however one coped with the fight itself, there was always this feeling of utter, listless tiredness afterwards, as the blood cooled and the tension passed. He pushed himself up to squint across the creek at the multitude of dark-uniformed shapes that littered the far bank. Maybe Ballard was right about this fight. It was less like the previous ones and more of a trap. He lounged back down to sit again. With this position they could hold the Yankees at bay, through the live long day, as long as the ammunition kept coming and as long as the Yankees didn't find another way across. Daniel stretched his hand and hauled his ammunition pouch round to inspect it, having to shift from where he slouched to do so. They had taken extra bundles of cartridges at the issue last night, but he must have already fired off nearly thirty shots this morning as there were only two sealed packs of ten cartridges each, plus another four from a broken open package, remaining in his pouch. Sure he had one more pack in one of his jacket pockets, and, as he finished counting those at his side, he fumbled the additional bundle from the pocket to pack them also into the pouch, breaking open the wrappings of greased paper around them, to allow quick access to the cylindrical paper cartridges inside, before closing over the flap of the pouch and returning it to his hip. He went on to check the cap pouch at his belt, before replenishing it also from a further handful that he had placed in his other pocket. Around him, the boys kept the talk going, as Daniel next tried to clean his musket lock, spitting on it and wiping furiously at it with the same grubby handkerchief that got pressed into all sorts of roles.

He borrowed a pricker from Ballard and pushed the fine, needle point into the musket nipple hole, moving it around several times before pausing to wipe or blow away the black deposit that emerged, repeating the process several times before he tossed the instrument back to its owner. That finished, there was little else to be done now, other than reload and wait for the next move from across the creek. He selected a blue-wrapped cleaner from his pocket and reloaded, settling back against the trench wall when he was done. The Yankee shells continued to come in, tearing across to burst above them, as, on an impulse, he pushed himself back up to risk another long look across the bridge and the creek below. There was nothing to be seen, save for the litter of dead and wounded, and he slumped back down to sit in the remains of the mud, reflecting that, with all those cannon and all those men across there, the

Yankees seemed set on crossing this creek and, that being so, they surely wouldn't leave it long before trying again.

Perhaps something approaching half an hour had passed since the repulse of the previous attack. The valley had remained active, with the cannon sending their steady sequence of shells across the creek. A few Confederate guns had maintained their bombardment also, and the exchange of musketry had never quite died down, but now the gunfire grew again. This time its focus was seemingly upstream from the bridge, with artillery and musketry both contributing to the growing racket. Daniel heaved himself up once more, but, from where he crouched, he could make out little through the trees and smoke that shrouded the creek beyond the bridge and the ground around it. But the noise swelled quickly into something like a full scale fight, with the men of the Twentieth Georgia, on that far side of the bridge, fully engaged with whatever enemy move was taking place up there. On the battle went, under its thick shroud of gun smoke, with firing also continuing around the bridge, but no sign here, as yet of a further advance by the enemy.

But now, as the day grew towards its middle, there was infantry activity on the far bank once again, only now it was downstream from the bridge. Down there following the sound of more bugles, the signs came from that far cornfield, beyond the ploughed ground south of the corpse-strewn stubble. Men were assembling down there, the shining bayonets and musket barrels above the dark ranks were again clear evidence. The Georgians on the hillside, called to alertness by officers and sergeants readied themselves. Bailey came along their own line calling to his men.

"They're a comin'."

"We got eyes," Ballard retorted.

"Well use 'em to sight on them there Yankees," Bailey told him, as the Yankee artillery fire again intensified, another likely sign of a coming attack. Daniel hauled his ammunition pouch around to his front again, as other men were doing, while the musketry from the far bank rose once more in its intensity. He gazed through the trees, downstream across the creek, and at the cornfield beyond the road, seeing the signs of the enemy as he primed his weapon with a cap. The muskets and bayonets were still there, visible above the swell of the ground, in a solid formed rank, clearly a column awaiting their orders. But, even as he watched they moved, up onto the ploughed field, staying in their files as they broke into double time, heading for the road not in a line of battle but in a column. Files of four men, as though on a march, were shuffling forward on the run with others sprinted ahead of their main formation to pull and haul at the rails of the fence and so allow the column to pass through unchecked onto the road beyond. The order came relaying along the southern positions to open fire with the Confederate infantry, on the hill and in the quarry and redoubt, opening up a fraction before the men on the hillside, but with the whole adding up to a blistering volley of fire, which struck the closely packed front of the blue formation like a fist. The volley of musketry hit the leading files of the enemy column, just as they reached the fence where those front ranks had begun to veer through the narrow gap made for them and head for the bridge.

That scathing first volley was what did the damage. Daniel saw the head of the Yankee column, buckle as it reached the gap in the fence, with virtually all the men of its leading files crumpled or slumped to the ground. Those behind stumbled and faltered, confined by the fence, unable to easily go around the jumble of fallen men who now blocked their way. They picked through the bodies, as still more of them were hit, and, waved and shouted on by their officers, went pushing forward. But their real momentum was gone, checked and broken by that first deadly volley. On reaching the road, the survivors inclined to the right, to start along the road, ignoring the searing fire from across the creek where the southern troops flayed them from their left flank, while renewed salvoes of artillery shells burst repeatedly overhead.

Up on the hillside opposite, the trees were hung with smoke as the men loaded and fired, keeping up a savage intensity of musketry on the Yankees who pushed on across their front, making for the bridge approach, though with ever diminishing resolve as more and more of their number collapsed from their places in the column. Some still tried to go on, but many of those still unhurt were faltering, attempting to recross the fence for cover, or dropping down behind any bush or hummock in the ground along the creek side of the road. Their advance ranks now stumbled to a halt and tried to level their own muskets to answer the fire which tore at them. But they were out in the open, the focus of every Confederate weapon and they could not stay. Daniel caught glimpses of them while he loaded and fired, as quickly as he could, pumping shot after shot at the Yankee ranks that emerged and vanished repeatedly through the drifting, acrid smoke. His ears rang with the deafening discharges of the muskets around him, which added their sound to the overwhelming thunder of battle noise all across the creek valley. His eyes smarted and watered from the smoke and he occasionally wiped a sleeve across them, while still biting, and pouring, and spitting, and ramming, and aiming, as fast as he could. The smoke swirled and he could see the Yankees again, stalled there on the road now, a jumble of struggling and fallen blue figures. It was starting to bleed men away, back along the road and across the fence and through the fields, towards the trees. Daniel saw them go. Men, who were not cowards, but had seen that what they had been asked to do was impossible, being tantamount to a sentence of death if they stayed out there in the open on that road.

Seeing the attack stalled, the Confederates redoubled their efforts and, watching this killing of almost helpless men continue, a dart of compassion crossed Daniel Ryan's mind.

Those trapped, dying, blue-clad figures down there, were men, not just Yankees. He had talked to men like these and traded with them down on the peninsula. They were flesh and blood, with families and homes and feelings, and when you shot them, they bled and died; each one of them, with all of his virtues and talents, lost forever. Although this whole bloodbath had been begun by their invasion of the south, up here it was not quite the same. This was their country. It was Union not Confederate flags that most of the children in Frederick and Hagerstown and the farms all along the dusty roads had waved. Even as they had put out their buckets of water for the parched southern columns, they had made their preference quietly clear.

"We are up here killing them in their own land," the thought went through Daniel Ryan's head, even as he loaded and fired the now searingly hot musket. Was this what Fitzpatrick and Kane and Jones had refused to do? Had they seen a basic truth that Daniel and the others had ignored, or not realised, in their quest to simply win? It did not do to think this way. It was harder to kill when you began to think of the enemy as someone to be pitied or understood. Daniel gritted his teeth and stuck to his loading and firing, burning his hands, wet and slippery with sweat, on the hot barrel of the Enfield.

But the Yankees were going. Their whole column, what was left of it, was now broken and heading back the way they had come, with a scattering of them running across the field for the cover of the trees up the slope. They went, pursued by the bullets of their enemies, leaving another litter of dead and wounded all along that road by the creek, and, from the Confederate side, a high-pitched rebel yell, which must have raised the hackles of the neck, whatever side of the water you were on, rose to blend with the gunfire. Daniel Ryan yelled with the rest for it was a shout of triumph. The enemy was stopped again. We are still here. The Yankees are broken and running, and, if they want this bridge and this creek crossing they will have to do better than this. No, it did not do to see the enemy as real people, Daniel thought, as he lowered his burning hot musket and let it rest against the crude parapet of the rifle pit. Better if they just stayed damn Yankees, while you had to go on shooting them. But, looking down at the trail of fallen along that road and the jumble of slain at the gap in the fence, where they lay in clumps and clusters, those dead and dying boys, whose leaders had failed them, by putting them out there to be slaughtered and, even as he yelled, Daniel Ryan still could not help but pity them.

It was noon, or very close to it. The sun had appeared to bathe the valley in its glaring light, as it had several times during the morning and now it shone on the clusters of fallen men who lay along the road parallel to the creek, around the rail fence and littered the fields beyond. Many of them lay still, but from those still conscious rose a succession of cries, for someone to come and help them. Most of all they cried for water, in a welter of wails and sobs that competed vainly in its pathetic volume and intensity, with the persisting gunfire all around. For still the enemy artillery kept up its barrage of shells, less intense for sure than during the infantry attacks, but exasperating in its continuity, for there seemed to be no hint of a halt in it. The shelling forced the surviving men on the hillside to continually crouch down in their cover, as cascade after cascade of branch splinters and metal fragments whipped and shivered down among the trees And the Yankees were coming closer, manoeuvring some their guns steadily forward to bring the hillside into almost point blank range, as though closing in for some kind of kill.

For, although the dead and wounded lay thickest on that far side of the water, on the hill above the creek's western bank, the Georgians had suffered also. Men lay slumped at the bottoms of many of these rifle pits now, while their comrades rummaged through their ammunition pouches for their remaining cartridges. Orderlies still moved among the positions in the trees, taking their own chances with the enemy fire. But there were not enough of them, and for every wounded man who was helped or carried up the farm lane to safety, more lay unattended, save for what their comrades around them could do in their rudimentary attempts at care. For the orders had been clear, there was to be no leaving positions to help the wounded, so those injured largely remained at or near where they had fallen. The tired men around them, begrimed with black powder stains, which had adhered to the sweat on their faces and hands, organised what ammunition remained, tried to clear their fouled muskets, drank the remains from their canteens and waited for whatever the Yankees would do next as the sunshine faded again.

Above all they counted that ammunition. Those paper cylinders were scarcer than ever now and no supplies of fresh ones had been obtained from the rear, in spite, so they were told, of repeated requests. It was all a mess up there, according to those who had gone, or had talked to someone who had. The town was choked with stragglers and god knew where the ammunition wagons were. The army had been locked in combat since dawn and was just about holding its own, yet, the enemy attacks had been pressed furiously and they were likely not finished yet. So, while the shells still crashed around them, the men foraged for what cartridges remained among the wounded and the dead, and nursed the hurts they had gotten from those cascades of wood and iron. They looked also across the brown waters of the creek, now stained darkly red in a number of places, and on past the huddles of dead and wounded clogging the road, and the others who lay on up across the stubble fields, and on to where the enemy in the brush and trees beyond still kept up their fire. So far, they were holding them, but ammunition was getting critically short and the Yankees were giving no indication of quitting.

Straight across on the other side of the creek, among the trees beyond the stubble field, there was a renewed activity and it soon became clear that many more of the enemy were milling and massing there. The battle down here was clearly far from over, but on the Confederate side, with their numbers reduced and ammunition nearly exhausted, there was little left to continue it with. Daniel Ryan counted his cartridges, passing them through his fingers in the almost empty pouch. He had had nine left, plus one cleaner, but the six of them had decided to pool and divide what still remained and this reduced Daniel's supply to seven. He left them and closed the pouch to spit again onto the musket nipple, moistening and softening still more of the black powder residue that had collected and now lay congealed there, clogging the musket, affecting its discharge and intensifying its recoil. He scrubbed at the goo of saliva and powder residue with his handkerchief and then nudged Ballard to use the pricker again. Having done what he could, he reloaded, with one of his precious seven shots and was replacing the ramrod when, above them, a Yankee shell burst. They hunched down into the trench hearing the shower of fragments and foliage cascade down around them and Daniel Ryan winced as he felt a sudden, hot needle of pain from his right sleeve and he looked to see blood there. He cursed and stared at the red stain for a few more seconds before leaning his musket against the trench wall and, reaching with his left hand, he carefully started to manoeuvre the cloth away, feeling the hot pain below as he did so. He tensed himself against the pain and fumbled with his fingers, made slippery with the blood, to eventually remove a reddened splinter of wood. Painful enough, he thought, as the discomfort pulsed through his arm, but at least it was not hot metal from the shell itself, and it was as these thoughts went through his mind that, even above the renewed tumult of guns, from the trees across the creek, there came a deep-throated cheering as that gathered formation of Yankees broke from the tree shelter opposite and charged at the double quick straight down from the trees and brush, down the slope through the stubble, making straight for the bridge.

They were not using the road, this time, Daniel thought, as his fingers hurried for a cap. The road was too much of a gauntlet to run and anyway it was clogged and obstructed by dead and wounded from their previous efforts. No, this was going back to the original tactic, and the sensible one, straight down the hill, towards the bridge, but with much bigger numbers this time. Shortest distance, simplest route, least time for getting shot down by the men opposite on the hillside and at the wall or the quarry. Daniel pushed his musket across the stone parapet, cocking it as he brought it up to his, now tender, shoulder. He sighted quickly and fired, seeing through the smoke that the first Yankees had almost reached the fence around the bridge. As the leading men got there they began pulling sections of the rails away to allow easiest passage. Daniel grabbed for another of his remaining cartridges, feeling his forearm throb as the blood slowly wet his shirt sleeve and ran down in a little rivulet onto his hand. Still the musketry and a few artillery shells from the Confederate side, punished the approaching enemy, but now all around, there was a perceptible falling away in the volume of fire as, having used their remaining rounds in the furious first response to the Yankee advance, more and more men on the hillside were running out of ammunition. The enemy were at the road now, but rather than rush the bridge entrance, they were taking cover along the fence line below the bridge and the wall above it, where those of the earlier attack had sheltered. But these were so many more in numbers, and as more and more of them collected on either side of the parapet, the volume of their fire on the hillside grew quickly in its intensity, supported by a rain of shells and canister from their cannon.

Through the drifting smoke on the far side, even as he went furiously on loading and firing, Daniel Ryan glimpsed a flurry of movement, of horses, reversing a squat howitzer like cannon into place on that flat ground just up from the bridge. The team were halted and the gun unhitched and positioned by its crew. All of this was done with comparative impunity for there was now insufficient fire from the Confederate side to seriously hinder them. The gun placed, the team of horses were galloped away up the gradient of the field and then this weapon too was adding its weight to the onslaught across the creek. As the enemy attack gathered and grew, there were shouts all around on the bluffs, where the musketry was slackening further, fading away like the flow from an emptying barrel. Daniel looked around as he began loading one of his final cartridges, to see men leaving their rifle pits and moving away up towards the ridge. He looked back to see the Yankees suddenly move again, surging round, from the fence and wall on either side, onto the bridge, waved on by their officers, while the fire on them steadily drained away.

"Goddam it," he heard Ballard curse and he looked across at him.

"If they'd only given us more ammunition we'd 'a' stopped 'em," Tom Gibben shouted at Bailey who now crouched behind the next rifle pit.

"Don't look at me," the sergeant shouted, "I got one shot left."

Down at the creek, the Yankees were on the bridge now with two of their flags almost beside each other as the leading files forced their way across through the renewed clutter of dead and wounded. But up here on the hill more men were leaving their trenches, shouted away by their officers, acknowledging that the whole position was now in danger of being overrun.

The blue vanguards were across now, pausing at the western approach in ranks or groups, to fire volleys of musketry up the hill, much of it just to their right towards where the stone wall lay. Those on this side fired in the downstream direction and it was one of these shots that took Adam Bailey full in the neck. He had begun to straighten up from where he had been crouching at his favoured place, beside the tree next to the trench along from where Daniel Ryan was finishing his reloading and the shot sprayed blood from the sergeant's wound and sent him sprawling onto his back among the undergrowth. Daniel turned to see, catching an expression of utter surprise on the sergant's thin face and the mess of blood in that side of his beard as he lay collapsed in the grass. Thompson was already heaving himself from his own trench and he made his way over to the stricken man's side, kneeling to examine the wound, but, even from where he was, Daniel knew that, though the eyelids continued to flutter, it was hopeless. Thompson looked at them and shook his head before moving away again.

All around them now, the hillside was alive with scrambling dirty, grey-brown figures pushing away up the steep slope, some following the track while others, mainly those from the trenches nearer the creek, struggled up through the trees and brush.

"This ain't the place fer us no more," Thompson shouted, waving the others from the trenches nearby. They scrambled from their rifle pits, Daniel feeling, as he moved, the now familiar trembling weakness in his legs as he began to climb. He felt pain from his shoulder, bruised by the musket recoil, and a painful throbbing from his injured right arm. As they started up the slope, he caught sight of Boyce, up above, standing nearer to the track, waving them away from the creek and on up the hill with his sword. Some men were making their way across, towards where the track ran diagonally up the hill, to join those from nearer the bridge who were already on it, while others simply headed straight for the top from where they were. Daniel Ryan's group, seeing that the shortest route to the track would take them within dangerous range of those Yankees, who had now fanned out in a semi-circle from the bridge, did the latter, opting for the climb through the undergrowth rather than risk the greater danger of a bullet out on the track.

Daniel scrambled on up, feeling the branches and the thorns pull and tear at his clothing and occasionally whip across his face. He could feel the cuts and wounds on his feet, tormented by the mess of broken branches and other debris on the hillside, as sharp twigs and fragments pushed through the canvas moccasins and socks, making him wince. He gritted his teeth as he climbed, with the thought flitting across his mind that the last thing he needed right now was another thorn in his foot. The ragged group of survivors around him struggled on, gasping and panting increasingly, uphill through the underbrush to reach where Boyce still stood, heading from there to join the crowd on the track beyond. Daniel's breathing was laboured and hoarse and his legs felt as though they would imminently give way beneath him. The sweat was running down his face and body, soaking into his already damp clothes, while the blood continued dripping from his right hand, staining the stock of the Enfield and making it slippery to keep hold of.

At last they reached the track and pushed their way among the other retreating troops, moving up through the last of the trees to the top, as the pale sunshine faded again.

"Move on boys," Boyce shouted after them. "They've gotten across downstream, so they'll have us in a bag if we stay on here." They pushed on, still gasping for breath, with men's faces glistening as rivulets of sweat ran down them, streaking the powder stains on their features into lurid patterns. Daniel looked back, down through the trees and the drifting smoke, towards the creek. More and more enemy troops were pushing across the bridge and they were now over in substantial numbers. Groups of them were starting to advance up the hillside in pursuit. They were moving up the slope on either side of the bridge approach, still firing on their retreating enemies, while the unending sequence of shells from their batteries continued to arch over the trees to explode around the top of the ridge.

Above Daniel's head, at the top of the slope, the pale sun emerged once more to shine down through the branches, spotting the grass and brush with its light, while this chaos of blood and noise went on all around. He shifted his gaze back to the front as they passed the crest of the bluff to see the smoke-stained figure of William Benning, pushing a line of men out to either side as skirmishers, then waving his sword away towards the open field to the left, indicating by that, and his hoarsely bawled shouts, where they were to head.

"Due west," boys he shouted, "head for that cornfield and look to yore left, cuz there's more Yankees across downstream." The retreating men moved on, entering a field of stubble, which stretched away across undulating ripples in the ground, dry enough now to raise dust as they crossed. Up to their right front was the ridge which concealed the town. Closer, on the crest of the intervening slope beyond the northern end of the stubble field, there were lines of southern infantry, facing towards the creek, while lower down the slope, the defenders from the bridge retreated across the front of these formations.

Daniel's heart was still thudding like a piston in his chest and the cut stubble stalks were hard on his injured feet as, with the other survivors, he skirted the left section of the field. At last he reached and began to scramble across a swaying rail fence, struggling on legs that felt devoid of strength and energy, before starting across a further field of ploughed ground. The day was hotter and more humid out here in the open and the sweat continued to drip down from his nose and chin onto his already wet jacket, but at least the turned earth was easier for a man with no proper shoes and he hurried on with the others. He looked around to see Thompson, Gibben and then Daley close behind him. Ballard, who always ran in a way that suggested that such exertion was unwelcome and unfamiliar to him, was a little way to the left, with Philips just beyond him.

Daniel returned his gaze to the front, in time to see that they were approaching another rail fence, beyond which stood a wall of tall green corn stalks. Men were gathering there, taking turns to climb this barrier, and, as their group reached it, panting and perspiring, they too paused, giving them time to look around them. Daniel wiped his sleeve across his face for the umpteenth time, casting his eyes ahead at the field of still standing corn that lay beyond the fence. The stalks swayed, and shivered as the men already across pushed through them and now a gap had appeared at the fence in front of him and he gripped the top rail and clambered over the shaking structure. Daley followed him, with Phillips pushing behind him, as Daniel looked again to see that Thompson, Gibben and Ballard had crossed a little further along. Thompson pointed ahead and they lunged into the field where the crop stood higher than their heads.

Daniel moved quickly, making his way between rows of swaying green stalks and waxy leaves, which waved and slapped into his face. He held his musket out ahead of him with both hands, to afford himself some protection, feeling his right shoulder ache as he did so, thankful, in any event, for this cover from the pursuing Yankees who, from the continuing sounds of musket fire behind them, must be close to the top of the creek bluff. Ahead of them the ground now stretched down into a gully, where still more corn stalks stood and the men around him descended to start across this dip. On through a flatter section of the field they stumbled, gasping for breath, before beginning to pant their way up the far side and on through the remaining corn to catch sight of a jumble of men, similar to the one back at the fence, milling around out in front of them.

They pushed through the last of the corn to cross the field margin joining the crowd who waited their turn to scramble across a limestone wall. Beyond the wall was another ploughed field, and, as Daniel Ryan looked across this expanse of scrambling brown figures he heard, through his wheezing intakes of breath, the shouts of an almost equally breathless Adam Rodger, just then catching sight of him where he stood, beyond the wall, with his sword in his right hand.

"Form men, form," he gasped. "This side o' the wall and reform." Daniel Ryan halted, leaning against the man in front as he awaited a turn at the wall. He glanced over to the side again at the captain. Rodger was moving away now, stretching his sword one way and his left hand the other along the line of the stones of the wall, directing, the scrambling men to where they were to deploy as he stepped away up the slope to the right. Daniel took in the chaos of arriving, clambering and deploying figures as he waited, leaning his musket against the wall as those in front cleared away, and resting his hands on two of the top limestone boulders before starting across. There were men on the other side already, begrimed and wheezing men, but they had begun forming a line, a sparse line thus far, pushed and pulled into place by a dishevelled Sam Bradlee, but that line was gradually gathering substance, as still more of them reached the wall and clambered over to join it.

Daniel made it across the stones in an ungainly stumble, feeling the top ones move and falter as he grasped at and trod on them. He hurriedly retrieved the musket, as another man began to follow and stopped there on the other side, finding himself on a rough farm track, which ran along this side of the wall. His clothes were heavy with sweat, his face and hands dirty and begrimed, his shoulder and feet hurt like fury, his arm throbbed and his legs felt ready to buckle. His heart still pounded in his throat and chest, but he was alive and here.

Around him other voices had now taken up Rodger's call.

"Reform at the wall!"

"Stand firm at the wall!" The shouts rang out among the NCOs who had reached the line and as more men scrambled across the stones, with some of these rocking dangerously as men balanced their weight on them, a gradually strengthening formation assembled on the track. Jeffers was there now and his loud voice, sounding above the shouts of other NCOs, seemed, after their feverish retreat from the bluffs at the creek, to have an almost calming effect on the men as though now, it was back to some kind of business as usual.

"Git yoreselves sorted," the First Sergeant yelled. "Git lookin' fer yore officers and form on them. This ain't no mob and it ain't gonna be no mob." Gradually his shouts were heeded and the men at the wall began to move, interchanging with each other, to gather into their company groups, though these seemed pathetically small. Daniel and his comrades formed on Boyce, who had placed himself slightly downhill from where they had crossed the wall.

Now, for the first time since the start of the last Yankee attack at the bridge, Daniel Ryan had the chance to attend to his throbbing arm. He looked down at his sleeve, where the blood had run from his cuff onto his hand, drying now and congealing underneath, beginning to stick the sleeve of his shirt to the skin of his wrist. He turned and leaned his musket against the wall again, before reaching for his canteen to moisten and then remove the sleeve from the wound, but there was not a trace of water inside. Tom Gibben, who was nearest to him, looked across. Daniel gestured towards his arm and his friend shook his own canteen, with both of them hearing a faint swish of water. Gibben unstoppered it and swirled it, before taking a small mouthful and passing the canteen to Daniel, who moistened his own mouth before pouring most of the trickle that remained onto his bloodstained sleeve, wincing involuntarily as the water sloshed onto the wound. He handed the canteen back to Gibben, who drained it, before slinging it back over his shoulder, while Daniel tugged gingerly at his jacket sleeve, pulling it up from the cuff with his right hand, wincing again as the pain increased. Ballard came over and peered at the sleeve.

"Don't look much," he grunted.

"That's fine when it ain't your arm," Daniel told him.

"I got troubles o' my own," was Ballard's answer and he pointed to his leg where a sizeable bloodstain marked his pants.

"If it hadn't a' bin in the leg, I'd a beat you up that hill and over that field anytime," he growled, and then grinned into Daniel's face. Daniel looked away from his own wound again to shake his head disparagingly in return.

"You!" He retorted. "On your best day, you'd need a damned horse to catch me." He heard Ballard snort as he returned his attention to his arm, while the other two looked idly on. He gently manoeuvred the jacket sleeve above the throbbing area and now began to roll up his blood-soaked shirt sleeve. There! It was an ugly incision into the muscle of his arm, pulsing as the blood welled out again. He touched it, and jumped as he felt a jagged remaining fragment of the splinter. Damn, so he hadn't gotten it all out. He paused, gathering a deep breath and rested his hand on the top stone of the wall, feeling the pain from the damaged muscles extend up his arm as he braced himself for what he knew he must do.

"It's got to go," he thought to himself and then felt for it, ignoring the pain as he grasped at it with his finger nails and pulled. The darts of pain shot up his arm and he grunted, releasing his breath slowly as he peered at the splinter of bloodstained wood, before tossing it away. He ran his fingers gently across the surface of the wound. There was no further agonising pull of any remaining part of the splinter and he inwardly sighed with relief. He pulled at his pants pocket with his right hand to find that the handkerchief that should be there was gone. Gibben looked at his face and laughed.

"Ya look like somebody jest stole your drawers," he said.

"My handkerchief's gone," Daniel retorted, "that's bad enough for me right now."

"Use yore shirt sleeve," Tom Gibben grunted. Daniel looked at him.

"It's the only shirt I've got," he retorted. Gibben produced a clasp knife.

"You got anythin' else," he inquired? Daniel shook his head and his friend pulled at the already loosened and folded back sleeve. He cut most of the fabric away with his knife and then cut it into strips, tying them together to make an extended length, before stretching the remaining cuff section over the wound. He wrapped the longer strip around it several times and knotted the ends.

"Now you got most of one shirt," he said as he returned the knife to his pocket. Beside them, they heard Thompson's voice.

"Now who might these fellers be," he muttered? Around him, other men at the wall turned and looked. A column of troops had negotiated a rail fence some distance to the rear of the men at the wall and were starting across the ploughed field towards them in a rough line, sending dust into the air as they came. The boys watched them approach, seeing their ragged red flag emerge from the dust and smoke and at that several voices spoke up from along the wall.

"That there's the Fifteenth's colour."

"It's the goddam wagon minders," Daley shouted, "too late fur the fightin'."

"Sure 'nough."

A jumble of shouts and calls greeted the arriving men as they approached. Closer the formation came and still more of the boys at the wall recognised their comrades. At this critical moment, the remainder of their own brigade had returned, from the escort duty they had been saddled with at Hagerstown, to join at last with the survivors from the bridge. More shouted comments, and a few sarcastic insults, were exchanged, as they came up, but Daniel knew from the tones and expressions on faces how relieved the boys were to see these men. The arriving regiments were deployed along the wall by their own officers, and the newly arrived Benning, to push in among the exhausted men already there. On the colonel's orders a skirmish line of them was sent into the cornfield as far as the edge of the gully, but out in front, the noises of battle had subsided into a languid artillery exchange. Gradually, the tension along the wall eased. The reinforced line settled there and some of the waiting men began to work on their fouled muskets, readying them, as far as they were able, for further use. It was quiet out in front, but that didn't mean it would stay that way.

To the rear however, things were moving. Toombs was there, in a huddle with the other more senior officers, who had seemingly gathered to confer, and the result, as they dispersed, was Preston calling his company officers to issue instructions, which duly came along the line, shouted on by the sergeants.

"Company will move to the rear and form!" That was Jeffers, relaying the order as he moved along. The boys shuffled back from the wall, beginning to collect into a group, as they looked around in some puzzlement. Bradlee arrived, striding along the line, and seeing the inquiring looks, he growled at them.

"We got hardly a cartridge between us, and, by the looks o' this, we've lost near half our men." he nodded along the sparse rank. "What the hell use are we to anybody like that? With the Fifteenth and Seventeenth boys and them others takin' over here, fer now at least, we're relieved."

"Relieved," the word washed through Daniel Ryan and his gratitude was like a wave of warm pleasure. Relieved, and, with the afternoon wearing on, the occasional spells of pale sun now showed the beginning of its progress from its zenith towards the smoke shrouded horizon. The Yankees were making no attempt to advance from the top of the bluff above the bridge.

The cornfield was silent, with their own pickets reporting no movement. Maybe, just maybe this meant that there would be no more fighting for today. "Relieved," so there would be a chance to recuperate and treat hurts, to look for water, for something to eat, above all to rest and maybe even sleep. More commands rang along their line, bringing the thin ranks to order and, shouldering their weapons they formed into files and shuffled off. They moved away across the field, following the Second and Twentieth regiments' survivors. Away from those newly arrived at the wall across the ploughed ground, breaking ranks to cross a fence, before wheeling to the left across a clover field to reach still another fence, which ran along beside a dirt road, uphill towards the crest of the ridge towards the town. Daniel looked up at the ridge as he waited his turn to cross the fence. Up there beyond the crest a heavy pall of smoke drifted, most likely over Sharpsburg itself, a pretty sure sign that the weight of this battle had been felt there also, but maybe, he thought, just maybe the Yankees had done their worst.

Chapter 11
Edge of Disaster

They clambered across the fence to the road and formed their files again, before starting up the hill. Back over their right shoulders, along the distant wooded curve of the creek valley, the smoke rose into the air as cannon still fired across the now trampled and disputed fields. Across, on the higher ground to the south of the village, more smoke billowed as southern guns maintained their fire on those creek bluffs, to dissuade the enemy, who had crossed over the bridge, from coming further. But no sign of an advance was to be seen, so this was no longer full battle. All around the fields, though the thud of artillery was unceasing, the musketry had faded so that now it was little more than a spatter of picket line fire. The blue columns of the enemy had halted. They had been held, and bled, and stopped, and showed no sign of renewing their attacks. The thought found its way into Daniel Ryan's tired mind that this battle might well have spent the worst of its force and he found himself profoundly hoping that this was so.

The surviving men from the bridge trooped steadily up onto a flatter part of the road, and on again to a further stretch where it dipped slightly as it led towards the edge of the smoke engulfed town of Sharpsburg. The men moved wearily, plodding through the now dried mud, passing fragments of formations and smaller groups of men in the meadows beside the road. Some simply lounged or lay, finished with fighting for the day by their lethargic appearance, while others sluggishly reformed, responding to the shouts of officers, who encouraged or berated them in turn to return to the fight. It was a scene of perplexing confusion. What kind of a struggle, shook this many men away from their units to the rear of the army's fighting line? What did their absence from their units portend for the battle's outcome, if they could not be prevailed upon to rejoin their comrades? These thoughts were in other minds too as the comments up and down their own files showed.

"Helluva lot o' skulkers around here."

"Lot o' boys takin' a day's furlough right now."

"Anybody in this here army still fightin' Yankees?"

Presently the men ahead began wheeling away off the road to the left, with the column following on into a field of scorched yellowed grass, where still more groups of idle men sat or lounged. Their own files were directed past most of these and on to the far end of the meadow where a substantial grove of oak trees stood. On reaching the tree shelter, the men were halted. Details were called by the sergeants and dispatched to seek rations and water, while those spared duty on them were stood down, to move away under the trees where other groups of men already lay, flopping in their turn onto the shaded grass there. Some of them, in spite of the continuing artillery duels beyond the town, were asleep within seconds.

Daniel Ryan was not aware of how long he had dozed. In truth he could not have done so for more than minutes when he was disturbed by the empty clunk of his canteen on the ground next to his head. He opened his eyes immediately to see the container sitting there among the strands of grass and clover. Looking up he saw Daley's face and heard his voice.

"Not much of a damn drop to be had any place." Daniel pushed himself up to sit and look around before lifting the canteen and shaking it, hearing the faint swish of something inside. It sounded and felt like precious little to him.

"Is that all," he grunted looking up at Daley.

"Ye're lucky with that," was the reply. "There ain't no creeks or streams up here, so that's worked out well water." Even as the words registered, Daniel heard Jeffers' voice, as the First Sergeant came along under the trees. The sun had emerged again and his eyes registered on the light that moved on the sergeant's tunic as he approached. He was summoning men to form in the middle of the tree grove, where a small group was already beginning to gather, as he caught sight of Daniel and the others of his group.

"Ya'll have ta do," he growled, gesturing to them. "On yore feet! You lucky boys, yo're off to find the ammunition wagons to git some bullets fer all the other tired boys down here who ain't hardly got so much as a goddam cartridge between them."

"Does he think we ain't tired too," Gibben growled under his breath? Jeffers stood there and beckoned again, with a sarcastic smile crossing his face. Daniel Ryan further inspected the contents of his canteen before moving across, consuming much of the foul tasting liquid in a deep mouthful, screwing up his features at the taste as he went.

"Tired," the First Sergeant mused? "You boys can't be tired. You bin sittin' on yore butts down on that shady creek bluff all mornin'. This here is jest the start o' yore day's work. Move yore lazy hides!"

The tramp along the road into Sharpsburg in the heat and humidity was weary and laboured for the jaded men of the detail. The sun had disappeared again behind the clouds, but the sultry heat was still tedious as they headed north on the dirt road into town. Otis Ballard limped on his injured leg and Daniel Ryan took a brief look at his arm, lifting the edge of the makeshift dressing, where the blood had come through the binding of shirt fragments in a slowly spreading further stain, to peer underneath. Along the way, still more groups and clusters of detached men and stalled vehicles congested the road and, to the east, the cannon fire thundered on unceasingly. As they drew close to Sharpsburg itself, the pall of smoke thickened and drifted while the traffic of men, wagons and guns grew steadily. At the edge of town, Jeffers halted his detail and briefed them, gesturing towards the tumult of smoke, noise and activity up ahead as he spoke.

"We're headin' in to find the ammunition wagons," he growled, "a straight ahead sort o' job till ya try and do it. Like other things in this here army, they bin moved around some since they left Hagerstown on Sunday. First they got sent back across the river, for reasons that I can't even figure out a guess about, but then yesterday they got ordered back. Some bright boy at headquarters noticed that there were a few thousand Yankees linin' up over the creek there and it might be a good idea to have some bullets here to shoot at 'em. So since the issue last night, they wuz supposed to be set up on this side o' town where boys that were fightin' Yankees might expect to find 'em. But then some bunch o' sloppy no-goods down at the creek there let the Yankees git across and so the train's bin moved again, inta town fer safety I hear, but who in the hell knows where, since, as ya kin maybe see, things are a mite stretched up here. If we kin find our own then that'll be fine and dandy, but we gotta find some that'll give us bullets, else we're as useless as a sow with no damn teats. So, when we git t' each block in town one o' ya'll be sent off either way, go straight up or down the street yo're put on, till ya find the wagons or ya run outa any more town fer lookin' in. Whichever happens, ya come back to the church, see the spire there," he pointed, "and ya rejoin the rest of us there. Be damn quick once yo're sent," he added as he waved them on ahead. The detail shuffled off again, to make their way steadily into the smoke-shrouded chaos of noise and confusion of the town, and as they went the boys began to stare in increasing disbelief at the sights that confronted them in the crowded streets.

Sharpsburg remained under persisting artillery fire, with salvoes of shells screaming in every half minute or so to burst in streets, gardens, backlots and buildings, sending columns of flame, metal fragments and other debris showering around among the shifting smoke. Clogging every street and lane, was an utter bedlam of traffic. Some vehicles had halted or stalled, obstructing the passage of others around them, many with some or all of their teams killed or disabled by the shelling. Other vehicles still attempted to force a way through along the almost choked streets. Artillery caissons careered along, returning for more ammunition, their drivers lashing their lathered teams as they cursed and bellowed at others to make way. Picking their way in also came an almost continuous procession of military ambulances and commandeered civilian wagons, carts, buggies and carriages, all of them carrying ever more relays of wounded men. These vehicles lumbered past, marked by their nauseating smells and by the blood that trickled through their floorboards and dripped onto the ground below. Still more vehicles laboured in every direction through town, lumbering or pushing their way past those which lay parked or abandoned or those snarled at the intersections. All around the streets and lanes were dead animals, cut loose from their vehicles, their harness still around their bloodied forms. Still more displaced men thronged the town, singly, or in groups, some coming or going, under the command of officers, while others simply wandered in the cluttered streets. Many more sat slumped in doorways or on porches, sprawled beneath trees or bushes, detached, stunned, skulking or simply exhausted, and, in spite of the shelling, making no move to go anywhere. Their battle was obviously over.

It was clear that the larger buildings, in the centre of town, had all been pressed into use as hospitals, and around these places, where hosts of ambulances clustered, were the worst scenes of all. Wretched, blood-soaked remnants of men were being bundled out of the vehicles by harassed orderlies to be laid among the many others who already languished there on the congested and blood-soaked ground. Desperately wounded boys lay in their scores on any scrap of space that remained around the buildings, or even along the sides of the streets themselves, waiting under swarms of flies, for some of the harassed, blood-spattered surgeons and orderlies, who laboured in the midst of this carnage, to come and help them. All around these makeshift infirmaries, there hung an even stronger stink of the dismal, stomach-churning, mix of ambulance smells: blood and urine, ether and faesces, all overpoweringly strong in the nostrils of everyone whose business brought them near these places.

Inside those buildings, only god, apart from the sufferers themselves and those who vainly tried to treat them, could know what was taking place. The screams and cries were unceasing and harrowing, even outside on the street, while below some of the windows piles of disfigured, amputated limbs lay in discarded, blood-soaked jumbles. As Daniel Ryan gaped at these, recalling in it all his experiences in the summer, his eyes caught a further flicker of movement as rats scavenged among the gruesome collections, scattering for cover, when a shell exploded nearby or when still more crimson fragments from the surgery tables inside were dumped out of the windows to add to the dismal piles outside.

Even as the passing detail of men looked on all of this, the unceasing procession of ambulances continued. More vehicles rumbled up, almost jostling with those already there, bringing still more broken, crippled and dying men to join the overflowing mass of those already disembarked and, as the traffic lurched past, the harrowing cries of their occupants assailed the ears of all those nearby.

"Oh God, oh God, God, God….!"

"Jesus, kill me, just kill me…"

"The pain, oh mother of God, gimme somethin' for the pain!"

"My leg, oh lord, my leg!"

"Momma, Oh Momma."

"Let me die God, please...." The whole of Sharpsburg seemed a picture of blood, confusion, destruction and chaos and those of the passing detail looked around as each successive sight came to their eyes, appalled and disbelieving of what was taking place before them and mistrustful of what it all might mean.

Through it all, the enemy shells tore endlessly overhead, their approach marked by that familiar rasping sound, to crash into the streets and buildings of the little town sending ever more showers of earth, stones, wood, plaster and glass showering into the air and across the streets. The "Blues" detail moved on through this chaos, with men dispatched away at each intersection, to head off in search of the ammunition wagons, while the rest of the group moved on to the next corner.

Daniel Ryan was one of the pair sent off by Jeffers from the middle of town, and he crossed the road to head down the hill to the west, picking his way among the congestion of men, animals and vehicles. He moved from intersection to intersection, seeking in vain for the wagons, passing the wreckage and debris of buildings and vehicles as he went, until he reached the edge of town. But, other than artillery vehicles, there were none of Jones' divisional wagons here, and Daniel turned at the last building, looking on out along the slightly rising road that led out of Sharpsburg to the west and the jams of semi-stalled vehicles that stretched into the distance until they were lost in the smoke and dust. Their own wagons might be out there, he thought, but Jeffers was right. It could take a man the rest of the day to find them and that would do little good for a regiment that needed ammunition now.

He turned slowly and started to retrace his steps back along the street and up the hill towards the centre of town. Ahead of him, still more shells crashed in. One of them burst over towards the side of the street, bringing down two mules from the team of a stalled wagon and showering dirt, blood and other debris into the air. Daniel ducked and looked away from the remains of the men who had been working there as he moved on up the hill, guided by the taller outline of the church as it emerged through the drifting smoke. Large sections of the external plaster had been gouged from its walls and the chaos of ambulances, wounded, blood and stink continued all around it as he came up, looking around through the milling crowds for his own comrades. In the tumult of sounds around him, he heard a shout of his name and he turned to see Jeffers and four of the others of the detail on the other side of the intersection. He moved across, dodging through the traffic, to rejoin the group, indicating to Jeffers the fruitlessness of his own search as he reached him.

Others of the detail arrived back successively and they stood, grimly observing the scenes across at the church, exchanging looks but few words, as they waited, seeing, to Daniel's mind, too much here of what their own fate might easily have been today, or might still be. Presently, above the bedlam of noise, they heard another shout, and turning they made out the approaching figure of Abe White, stepping around the vehicles as he made his way across the street. He had news of wagons and Jeffers started the detail off to find them, leaving Phillips to guide those still to return. Down the next lane they headed, following White, to see, near the bottom of the hill, yet another collection of vehicles lying halted, against a clap board fence. The wagon drivers were hard at work, lifting down the squat ammunition boxes by their wooden end handles to successive details of men. The lieutenant in charge shrugged when Jeffers told him their identity and of their needs.

"This ain't Toombs' train, it's Drayton's," he shouted above the noise of the shells and the traffic, "but the captain says nobody from the division gits turned away as long as they're goin' to shoot the damned stuff at the Yankees.

If you got boys here that kin git the stuff back, then bring them on up and take what ya kin carry." Jeffers nodded grimly and moved towards the nearest wagon.

"You got Enfield rounds," he shouted to the corporal on the wagon? The man waved in return.

"We got every damn sort under the sun," he returned. "Ya could likely git Fourth o' July firecrackers some place up here." Jeffers gestured his men forward, to first replenish their own supply from a hurriedly levered open box. Bundling the packages into pouches and pockets, they moved on to get their ration of percussion caps, while those finished supplying their own needs moved over to where Jeffers and Thompson had begun lugging further boxes of cartridges and caps from one of the wagons down onto the road.

"Don't reckon they know where the commissary wagons are," Thompson called as he looked across.

"Maybe we'll be headin' off to look fer them next," Gibben shouted back.

"Not a chance," Ballard told him, as he grasped the other box handle. "Ordnance boys kin always git to the places where the commissary don't. That's the way this army works 'n' always has. Vittles don't have no importance in this here army." They lifted the box away, allowing Ryan and the newly arrived Philipps to step up for the next one.

Their mission completed the men moved away, making for the south side of Sharpsburg once more. Perspiration trickled down Daniel Ryan's face and body as well as his arms and legs making him feel still more drained and sluggish, as he grasped the handle of the heavy box in his left hand, to spare his injured arm, carrying his musket slung on his shoulder by its strap. Jeffers waved them on and they made their way out through the chaos on the streets, struggling past the shifting jumbles of vehicles and men who thronged them, as still more shells tore in, to add further destruction to the scene. Eventually, they were away from the buildings, heading on through the slight dip in the road towards where the remainder of the regiment rested.

On their arrival, they set the ammunition boxes down in the oak tree grove and, as the resting men were called in relays to replenish their ammunition, those of the detail settled for at least a brief rest. Daniel Ryan, with the others of his group, sank down under the trees, fitting themselves into what space was there. Daniel drank a further mouthful of the stale contents of his canteen and looked again at his injured arm, seeing with some degree of relief that, under the improvised bandage, the blood had clotted, drying and hardening into a crimson-brown crust.

The ammunition issue was still going on, and the afternoon was now advancing, when the horseman found them. Gibben saw him first and signalled to the others.

"That there captain's on Toombs' staff ain't he?" Ballard sat up and squinted at the rider.

"I recall that feller has a habit of bringin' bad news," Thompson muttered as the others looked, seeing the officer trot his horse over to where Preston stood to dismount and speak to the major. The substance of the message quickly found its way among the trees, muttered from group to group and man to man. It was bad news, the worst, as it spread around the grove and along the line of men round the ammunition boxes, for down there, on the fields above the creek, the Yankees were advancing.

Already Rodger, Boyce, Jeffers and Bradlee were coming along through the trees calling those, who had filled their cartridge pouches, to assemble. The boys dragged themselves to their feet and moved into their ranks, seeing others doing the same thing farther along the meadow. Preston stepped out in front of them, even before the last men had taken their place and the ranks still moved as he spoke.

"Men," he called. "There's no time to be lost for the news is bad. The Yankees are moving out from the bridge and heading across towards the town and the road here." He looked along the sparse ranks of dirty, ragged men who remained. "I know that this day has been hard on us. You have already done all that men should be asked to do in one day, but there are no other troops to support those boys back at the wall and if the Yankees take either this road or the town over there then the whole army is cut off from the river ford at Shepherdstown yonder and the day is lost. We must go back and lend our help in drivin' the enemy off." There was no response from the ranks and, though Daniel Ryan felt his spirits sink at the thought of still more fighting, he knew in his heart that there was little else for it. Without further pause, Preston nodded to the company officers in their places around the formation. Orders were shouted and the remnant of the Ogeechee Volunteer Rifles moved into files and wheeled off again, in the wake of what was left of the other two regiments, out of the tree shade, over through the yellowed meadow onto the same road they had tramped up little more than an hour before to seek relief and rest. Though the men around Daniel seemed largely resigned if not resolved, the comment and complaint among some in the ranks began to grow, much of it foul and profound.

"We got bullets, but no water worth a damn and no goddam vittles."

"Some relief!"

"Ain't no relief in this damned army."

"Work an' fight a man to death around here," that was Daley's voice, as officers began to take note.

"Sergeant Jeffers, start taking those men's names," Rodger called.

Hearing the shouts behind him, Preston pulled his horse to the side of the road. Reining in, he dissuaded the name taking with a wave, calling out, so that the passing men, as well as the officers, could hear.

"Goin' back down ain't good news for nobody round here," he shouted, "and, at a time like this, boys have gotten good reason to cuss some, jest as long as they keep movin' their feet t'ards the enemy while they're doin' it," he added, as a ragged cheer broke from the men around him. The major spurred his horse into motion again, steering the animal to the left, off the road through a gap that had been opened in the fence, while, across there to the east, where Yankee guns had increased their fire, the smoke rose in thicker clouds as regular salvoes of shells tore overhead to explode beyond the road.

The files wheeled to the left to follow the major onto the field, making their way across the pasture to the rail fence they had negotiated earlier. As they re-formed beyond the fence, more horsemen emerged from the smoke. The mounted figure of Toombs could again be made out, in company with two of his staff, riding towards the road. The brigadier was red-faced and sweating profusely but, when he saw the approaching men, he wheeled his horse and trotted towards the column, riding up to walk the animal along beside the files, while he spoke, initially to Preston, but then aiming his words at all of them.

"Good men," he called. "Good Georgians. I never doubted you, but we must stop them. We must stand fast here and push them back. Let's throw them back in the damned creek." Again a cheer of sorts greeted the Brigadier's fighting talk. The men looked up at him, and then at each other, as they tramped on past, making for the wall, still hidden in the drifting smoke.

"Press them back boys," Toombs called after them as they moved on across the field, "throw them back in the creek."

The marching men were silent as they closed on the wall and were halted there on the farm track to wait. The other regiments were moving, called on and pushed by their officers and NCOs, to move along, thickening their line along the left or upper section of the wall and leaving these lower stretches to the newly returned men. By the end of this to and fro shuffling, a double line of muskets pointed across the wall, along its whole length, into the cornfield.

Out in front stretched that same field, though many of its corn stalks were now trampled down, carpeting the ground away from the wall towards the rim of the gully. Through these trampled gaps, a few stretches of the gully's far rim were visible when the smoke drifted and thinned. Out there beyond the farthest section of the corn, dust now rose into the sky, stretching along their front and drifting lazily in the languid airs of the later afternoon, before vanishing again in the smoke from another salvo of shells. The enemy vanguard, Daniel Ryan thought, as he watched the smoke disperse and the dust re-appear and seeing it confirmed as he caught a glimpse of distant flags waving as they moved. Then a succession of bright, rippling glints were visible, from what must be bayonets and musket barrels, though there was still no sign of the men themselves. Daniel glanced over to their right, down the gentle slope, along the row of gun barrels that lay across the wall and on across the fields but, beyond the men at the wall, there was nothing. No troops or guns, or support of any kind were in view, but, down over those trees, beyond their flank, further ominous swirls of dust heralded the approach of more formations of men.

There had been word of cavalry out there but he could see nothing of them and he looked back to the front with misgivings in his heart. Somebody, he thought, be it general or colonel, or "Marse Bob," himself had better be doing something about that flank, or the whole line along this part of the field might not be staying here for long. He looked out to the front again, where the approaching rank of shining musket barrels and bayonets was entering the cornfield. It must, by the number of flags, be a full brigade of several regiments approaching this makeshift position at the wall. With those kinds of numbers they were fully capable of wrapping around the open right flank and dislodging the whole line.

Daniel Ryan had been with the main army something under six months, since their arrival in Virginia in the spring, but he, like others, had quickly learned and now well knew the cardinal rule for soldiers, that trouble came from letting the enemy get at your flanks. Being flanked was the worst kind of news, for an enemy that got on your flank could fire down the whole length of your battle line. Well, here, today, out there to their right, was just such an open flank, inviting the advancing Yankees to help themselves. Deep misgivings about being stuck out here worked steadily through Daniel's mind, for if ever things had looked bad in previous fights it seemed nothing compared to this. Over to the south of the town full battle had been joined and the air was filled with more dense clouds of smoke, blotting out the ridge line that concealed Sharpsburg. Volleys of musketry now mingled with the cannon fire as the fighting intensified and the smoke drifted slowly across into the valley. Indeed this battle was not done. It had acquired a new force, a lease of life that was seeing yet more Yankees push forward out of their bridgehead above the creek, heading for that vital Harper's Ferry road and the Shepherdstown road beyond, where lay that equally vital ford, the southern army's only line of retreat across the Potomac River.

The enemy must be stopped, it was obvious to everyone that they must be stopped, but, looking around at the spent and wearied men around him, who had retraced their steps back to the battle to do what they could, it seemed to Daniel Ryan that if this was the best the army could do for reinforcements in such a vital part of the field, then the army was as near to outright disaster as it had ever been. He found himself inwardly cursing Maryland and Yankees and generals and this whole damned bloody war, that had put him here with his friends and comrades, stuck in a trap, unable to move as it would open the army's only line of retreat to the enemy. But, though they could not go, it was impossible to stay without letting the Yankees outmanoeuvre and overwhelm them. They would be outflanked and blasted into the same bloody remains of men as those who languished in that half-destroyed town over the ridge up there.

Out in front, through the drifting smoke, one could now make out the advancing Yankee units, marked by their flags and gleaming bayonets. They had reached the middle of the cornfield, and were beginning to descend into the gully, with part of their line of approach diverted by a clump of trees and an outcropping of limestone rocks. The units were spreading out into the field, moving irregularly, with those to the left of the enemy formation seeming to pull away from the others in both the direction and the pace of their advance. But it was clear enough, on looking along what could be seen of the approaching enemy line, that their left could, as feared, overreach and flank the southern troops at the wall, crumpling them and rolling them away from their position.

Along the wall there were more shouts and heads turned to look. Farther out still, downhill on that flank, were those other dust clouds, further around towards the road in their rear. Were these still more Yankees, maybe the ones who had earlier forded the creek downstream from the bridge? There was a murmur of talk along the line at the wall, a ripple of unrest, because everyone along there could see that dust. Perhaps they could see too much, the whole extent of the approaching threat, both out in front and this new menace off beyond their right.

Behind the ranks, Benning paced, coming along to the regimental officers in turn to offer words of encouragement that the men would hear.

"They won't wait around if we hit 'em hard. Aim low boys, give it to them low." The boys heard his words, but still they looked around at the threatening clouds of dust beyond their right and the mutters of discontent continued to move along the wall, even as the colonel walked his horse on down the line towards that threatened flank.

Out in front, the Yankees were out of sight now, down in the gully, with not even their flags and bayonets visible. But they would not be long in re-appearing and when they reached this side, the crisis would be imminent. Still the men exchanged looks and then cast their eyes further as that other dust cloud came closer, drifting almost behind them. In the cornfield, the men of their own brigade skirmish line were coming back through the stalks, the approach of some of them marked by shaking strands of corn. Suddenly out on the road over their right shoulder, a column of dark clad soldiers emerged from the dust cloud and over the rim of pasture land, to begin a diagonal approach that would bring them squarely into the right rear of Benning's men at the wall. Along the waiting line there were shouts of alarm.

"Yankees!"

"It's the bluebellies that got across downstream!"

A number of the boys moved back, away from the wall, as the shout coursed up and down, as though to face this new danger, while along the line, their sergeants tried to yell and push them back to their places.

"Stand where y'are there!" It was Jeffers voice, bellowing the words. From a little further along, they heard Rodger's voice shouting at the men around him. Daniel looked around towards the captain, seeing his sweat-lined face was twitching as he stood, looking at the approaching troops with an expression of disbelief on his features. Further along still, Benning stood up in his stirrups with an expression of grim concern on his face as those dark, distant ranks came closer, gathering form as the dust cloud thinned and eddied away around them. Above the head of their deploying column were their flags, limp in the sultry air, and, as more men at the wall began to turn, to gape and step back in uncertainty from their places, a breath of breeze struck the flags and half-spread them.

Daniel got a glimpse of a ragged, blood-red banner, with its stars set in the familiar blue saltire, as the roaring, screaming yell welled up around him and his own heart rose in his chest. These were Confederate troops, and the deafening yell of triumph and relief rose and swelled from the chests of the men along the wall. At this moment, of all moments, at this place, as disaster threatened the whole army, help, from God knew where, was arriving and in the very nick of time. Off behind them, on the distant road, were further clouds of dust with more men and guns too, dim obscure shapes but now unmistakable as reinforcements for their makeshift line. And now, all along that line, a second shrill and sustained scream rose, as, to their right, more dark-uniformed Confederates, moved across the stubble field and into the meadow beyond to extend their line beyond the wall. Above their ranks flew more southern battle flags and with them, men could make out the blue palmetto banners of South Carolina.

"It's Gregg!"

"It's the boys from the Ferry."

"Thar's more! Lookee there, over at the road, that's more of 'em on the way!"

Daniel looked at the dust as the South Carolinians moved into line with their muskets at the shoulder. There was a lump in his throat as he turned again to the approaching enemy. The scream around him faded and the mutter moved along the line as up ahead, the tops of the Yankee flags and the tips of their bayonets began to crest the gully in the cornfield. Now they would see, he thought. More men still were arriving, coming up in the rear of their own position to intermingle with their own men and lay their muskets across the wall. Daniel turned to a fair-haired boy, who had suddenly appeared beside him, whose fuzz of a beard barely merited the name, and whose face and blue tunic were stained with sweat and dust.

"You Gregg's boys," he asked him? The boy nodded.

"Thirteenth South Carolina, Gregg's brigade," was the croaked reply. "Helluva day fer a march like we jest had," he added, his voice little more than a hoarse whisper. "You boys got any water?" Daniel reached for his canteen and shook it with whatever remains were inside, as other men along the wall did the same. The boy's eyes lit up as he took the canteen, draining it instantly of its remnant of water. There were more shouts and Bradlee came along the line. At the wall, the heads turned at the sound of his voice.

"Pull back boys," he shouted, "move back from the wall and form there." He gestured to the other side of the track and then on up the uneven ground to the left where, emerging from the smoke that drifted over the field from the batteries of guns on the high ground south of Sharpsburg, the leading elements of the Yankee force had emerged from the gully and was heading straight ahead, about a quarter of a mile beyond their own left.

"We got more troubles now," Bradlee muttered, somewhat needlessly, as the men formed around him.

"Give 'em hell," Daniel muttered to the blue-uniformed youth as he moved away. The boy nodded again as he placed a cap on the nipple of his musket.

Already, artillery pieces uphill to their left, their fire marked by great plumes of smoke, were launching canister towards the approaching enemy. Benning's men struggled into a column, while still more men came up towards the wall, and, on the order, their own formation moved away. The South Carolinians were left behind them there as they followed the track to the left, and on reaching the end of the wall struck away uphill across a clover field. Daniel squinted over towards the road to their left, seeing, farther down the hill, still more columns of dust heralding the approach of yet more troops. They too might be just in time if they hurried themselves, he thought, as he returned his gaze to the fighting going on under its own cloud of smoke and dust towards the top of the rise and the town beyond.

The head of their own column had veered to the left, still moving uphill, but now heading directly towards the road, which was obscured from view by yet another of these Maryland cornfields. Their front files had reached the fence and were scrambling across it while those behind slowed and faltered as they waited their turn. A few men were set to hauling the rails from a section of the fence which speeded things up for those behind. But as the column reformed on the road, the agitated figure of Toombs emerged again from the dust and smoke, galloping down towards them from the direction of the town with the same two of his staff trailing behind him. There was a brief but feverish talk between the general and Benning, upon which the order came along the column sending their weapons to right shoulder shift and the double time was called, to groans of renewed complaint from some of the weary men.

"Goddam all fired rush agin!"

"Can't quite go any place and git to stay there kin we?" The shuffling column headed up the hill, the grumbling soon silenced by breathlessness as the men pushed on through the dust and smoke, with their heavy muskets bouncing rhythmically on already bruised shoulders. Up ahead, fringing the right of the road, was that cornfield, its tall stalks completely obscuring whatever lay beyond on the fields that led up to the ridge line and the town beyond.. As the rearmost files reached it the order came down to halt and deploy and the sweating, panting men formed along the fence line facing into the tall green corn.

Another order came to move forward by the left and the grumbling boys were set to scrambling across the shaking, shifting fence rails again, wheeling to begin pushing through into the rows of standing stalks, which stretched above their heads, blocking completely their view of what lay beyond and quickly swallowing up the advancing files. But hardly had they entered the field and begun to push their way through the leathery slapping stalks, when they came upon their officers who stretched their arms and weapons out to either side, calling to the men as they came up.

"Form boys, form!"

"Left wheel boys, Let's get deployed!"

"Into line now, come on boys move yourselves!"

They pushed through the corn, lengthening the line across the field, now facing roughly north up the hill towards the town, at right angles to the road, able to see almost nothing through the forest of tall, leafy stems, but hearing the thunder of battle continue without pause. Muskets were primed, then, with a succession of relayed shouts, the line started forward again, moving up through the waving, waxy leaves and stalks, with a few men even pulling at the nearest cobs of corn and stuffing them into haversacks as they went. Then ahead there were bright gaps in the leaves and they suddenly emerged into the smoke-wreathed meadow beyond.

A picture of confusion quickly emerged from the drifting smoke. Ahead, a section of artillery stood, pointing across their brigade front, but these cannon were silent, the grass around them marked with the gunners who had been shot down at their pieces. A little closer to the road, lay a chaos of abandoned caissons and fallen horses, still trapped in their traces, the wounded beasts struggling and screaming as they pulled and kicked against the inert mass of dead animals still harnessed to them. Of the surviving gunners there was no sign, but even as this thought flashed through Daniel Ryan's mind, he became aware of that deep-throated cheering that the Yankees were known for as, emerging from the smoke to their right, was a blue-uniformed formation, covering the last of the distance towards the abandoned cannon. As Daniel took this in, a group of those Yankees broke from their ranks and sprinted forward to caper around the guns, one of them clambered up to stand on the carriage with one foot on the barrel, as he waved his musket and his cap in the air to his comrades around him.

Beyond, drifting in and out of the smoke, more of the enemy formation had veered away on a diagonal towards that vital road and now stood halted there less than a hundred yards from it. The army's escape route was all but cut. But now it was the Yankee flank that was open and threatened by the wheeling advance through the cornfield and even as their own section of Benning's line moved out of the corn and prepared their muskets, the front portion rose up from the grass bank at the roadside, quickly resting their muskets on the rails of the fence to align on the enemy front. The Yankees at the abandoned guns had begun to move, waved away by their officers, to rejoin the others still halted on the pasture beyond. In the southern ranks at the edge of the cornfield the men were called to the ready, quickly followed by the command to aim, even as the crashing volley from the men along the road roared out and the whole area was swathed in dirty off-white smoke. A second later their own first volley crashed out adding its own cloud of stinging smoke. Daniel winced as the Enfield recoiled into his shoulder, bruised and sore already from the hours of firing at the bridge. Down the weapons thumped and the reloading began, as men glanced into the smoke to see the first traces of confusion in the enemy lines.

Up in the clearing smoke the Yankees struggled among those cut down by the volley, to turn their left files and meet this new threat, but even as they moved to re-align, the second southern volley thundered out from the fence. Daniel saw that hail of bullets sweep through the blue ranks, knocking men from their places in a fine reddish mist, as he brought his own reloaded weapon up for the second time. Their own second volley roared out as the smoke cloud swallowed up everything in front. Again the men struggled to reload, and were levelling their weapons for a third volley when the first reply came whizzing back from the beleaguered formation up ahead. The minie bullets whizzed through, bringing men down with the dull wet "thunks" of impact, but the others around Daniel, levelled their muskets again and their next volley thundered further smoke and death towards the stalled enemy. As they furiously fumbled further cartridges from pouches and pockets, there came more musketry. A heavy volley crashed out from away to their right, farther around the flank of the enemy, but nothing was to be seen of this in the dense smoke. Ahead artillery discharges were smashing in, the sweeping blasts just visible in the smoke cloud. The volleys continued to crash out with nothing at all to be seen now in the stinging, eye-watering gloom, until more orders came, lost at first in the crash of battle, but relayed on by NCOs.

"Cease firing! Reload to shoulder!" More cartridges were bitten, poured and rammed and the ranks were straightened, until, with the smoke beginning to drift away, they moved forward on a further order, reloaded and ready, advancing into the shifting smoke cloud, wheeling to the right as they went until the road was behind them. They now marched obliquely away from it, passing near the abandoned guns and the fallen men and horses, as still more shells tore in to explode up ahead. Then they were among the Yankee casualties, many of them wriggling and shuffling on the ground and crying out with shock as well as pain.

"Jesus, oh Jesus!"

"Oh my God, my back!" Then the smoke ahead thinned enough to reveal the Yankee line beyond, its standing men interspersed with the fallen.

More shouts were relaying along the line, a halt and prime order, as the next Yankee volley discharged, but this was more ragged and irregular than the previous one and now the southern muskets were up to the ready again and the next thunder of smoke, flame and heavy lead bullets belched towards the enemy. The smoke thinned quicker this time, on an eddy of hot breeze and, as the officers ordered the "fire at will," the men could see glimpses of the Yankee formation beginning to falter. Individual men at first, then twos and threes were leaving the line to move away, back across the field the way they had come. Then another volley from out beyond their right lashed the enemy, smothering the ground in still more smoke and Daniel strained his eyes to see another rank of southern troops, their colours flapping idly above their line, emerging from the cloud, having added their fire to that of Benning's line.

Out in front more men were drifting away from the Yankee ranks, making for the rear, away from the punishing musketry and the exploding shells, while those who remained, pushed into gaps by their bellowing officers, now looked dazed and reluctant. It was, Daniel thought, a body language that they knew, for they had seen it at Savage's Station, and Manassas as well as earlier that same day at the bridge. Men moved in a certain way, sluggishly reluctantly, when their resolve and will to prevail left them, and, as Daniel furiously loaded and fired his musket, he recognised these signs and mentally grasped the signals he was seeing. They would go, they would run with just another push, and, when you saw these signs, of faltering and hesitating, there was only one thing to do, apply the pressure even more to give that final push and end it…..

They were all going now. Their colours, which been shot down and retrieved several times, started moving rearwards as the surviving men gave up their blood-soaked place, just short of that all important road, and moved back the way they had come as still more shells came in to explode above and among them. They were making their way across the pasture, heading for a further ploughed field, which was divided, like the big cornfield to the south of it, by the gully. They were not exactly running, but going pretty emphatically to the rear, away from that scathing fire that had poured into them in a great arc from their flank as well as their front. Daniel and those around him kept the pressure up, loading and firing, until the Yankees were gone, across the fence and on over the rim of the gully, moving steadily out of view. Up here the men paused, resting the butts of their fiercely hot muskets on the ground, breathing heavily as though they had just run in some sort of race. Daniel's throat was dry and harsh, and he was overcome by a bout of coughing as the orders were shouted for their column to advance. From the left came the mounted figure of Brigadier General Toombs, with several other officers behind him. Toombs reined in his horse and raised his sword high.

"Georgians," he shouted, his voice barely audible in the continued din of gunfire. "They are running before us. Let's push on and drive them back over the creek."

His answer was a shrill yell as the boys, those who were still amenable to this kind of exhortation, or those in whom the madness of battle had a firm hold, waved their muskets while he passed on. Around them the scavengers, clutching their trophies, hustled back to their places in the ranks as the sergeants took firm control again. Their weapons were shouldered and with that, Toombs pointed his sword forward towards the field and the gully rim where the last of the Yankees had now disappeared.

"Guiding right, forwaaa..rd march," he yelled and, with other voices relaying the order, the ranks jerked into motion back into the smoke, completing the last of their realigning till they faced towards the gully. Now as the smoke finally drifted away it was possible to see a little. As they advanced, they could see that as well as having supporting troops to their right, still more men, marked by waving flags had emerged from the gloom to their left, prolonging the line further up the ridge slope towards the town. Benning had appeared also, yelling at William Best who carried the "Blues" colour.

"Wave that damned flag as high as you kin boy, so those damned gunners up on the ridge kin see it."

Still the cannon thundered in their unceasing barrage of flame and noise and death. It seemed that the shells and solid shot came from almost every direction. Confederate artillery fired from the southern outskirts of the town. Their shot curved and whizzed towards whatever Yankee infantry still stood between the creek and the rise and further, engaging the Union batteries located on the ridge above the creek and others still deployed on the far side.

Around Daniel Ryan the air was baking hot and humid and the noise intense, as the smoky trails from shell fuses criss-crossed the sky, tracing their path from guns to targets. To the left was yet another cornfield, with an orchard beyond, while, down the hill away to the front right of where the men of Toombs and Benning now pushed their advance, the large cornfield crackled and roared beneath a further cloud of off-white gun smoke as the Carolinians grappled with the remainder of the enemy force that had advanced through the corn. But, up ahead, across the ploughed field, there were more vague images of drab blue tunics and gleaming weapons, this time emerging from the gully through the wreathing smoke. Those images quickly gathered substance to reveal a fresh Yankee line, advancing through the turned earth to halt and gather along the fence line that separated the pasture, through which the southerners now pushed, from the ploughed expanse beyond. The response in the southern formations was immediate, orders came relaying along, halting the line and the muskets were primed and readied. The thought crossed Daniel Ryan's mind that, in spite of Toombs' rousing words, there seemed to be plenty of Yankees, like these assembling men up ahead, who did not seem to be consenting to being driven into the creek, at least not without a struggle.

But, looking ahead, even before their own order came to fire, there were signs that the Yankee line at the fence was already in some difficulty. Those Confederate guns, on the high ground near the town, had these men under fire and by now they had gotten the range just about dead right. Shells were exploding over and among the enemy and blasts of canister were scything across the field, flailing fragments of wood out of the fence posts and rails, along which they had deployed, and doing their execution beyond with relentless persistence. Taking in all of this through the drifting smoke, the southern line readied their weapons and, on the order, presented their muskets to send their first thundering hail of minie bullets towards the enemy line, starting their reloading with a measure of hope in their hearts that maybe these men would not stand long. The smoke drifted and cleared slowly and the ragged return fire gave further indication of the disorganisation of the enemy. Reloaded, the southern line fired again, with the musket lurching painfully into Daniel Ryan's shoulder on its recoil with each discharge. Then another frantic process of tearing and pouring, inserting and ramming, with the spent caps being flicked away and replaced as the muskets were swung up again. But this time there was no further volley, instead the muskets were returned to the ready and the line heaved into motion again, leaving behind their scattering of inert dead and writhing wounded, making for that faltering formation up ahead at the fence.

Into the smoke they went, with Daniel's heart thudding again in his chest and his throat, waiting for the searing, blasting hail of lead which, by normal reloading time, was already overdue. The smoke drifted and eddied, revealing the ground in front of them and then fence sections swam into view and below them the human wreckage of battle lay, with here and there an arm raised in some kind of plea for help. But, other than those casualties, the fence was deserted. The Yankees had pulled back, making off from the fence to seek the respite of the gully beyond it, away from the hail of fire that had sheared these crying and groaning men, who now littered the ground, from their ranks.

The southern infantry headed on, to reach the fence and scramble over and past the remaining posts and rails and, as the smoke cleared, Preston shouted to the colour carrier, as Benning had already done, to swing the flag as a sign, to the cannoneers up near the town, as to who now held this position at the fence. Other men began to break ranks, as they drew close to the squirming, writhing mess of fallen men on the ground, and, on an impulse, Daniel went also. They may have food or full or part-full canteens, was the thought that crossed his mind, but, more importantly, on their feet they had shoes.

The officers bellowed, but there was something less than full intensity in their shouts and the jumble of needy men struggled through the Yankee fallen, seeking out the dead primarily, to take shoes, canteens, haversacks and anything else which could be quickly grabbed, Daniel crossed the fence and scanned feverishly ahead at the feet of the dead, looking for an impression of suitable size, before....... there. They were bloodstained, but he cared nothing for that, grasping and fumbling at the laces and hauling them from the feet of the still twitching boy to stuff them into his jacket, before turning with a hint of sheepishness in his manner, as though he still harboured some trace of embarrassment about plundering for essential needs from the enemy dead and dying. He moved back towards the line of approaching troops and halted in front of a surviving section of the fence to take a canteen which was being passed along by Phillips for each of them to take a mouthful as far as it went. Daniel gulped the tepid liquid gratefully and passed the canteen on to Thompson, it tasted stale, but right then he would have emptied it had his comrades' needs not been equal to his own. He swilled the liquid around his mouth several times before swallowing it, while around him the rank of sweat-soaked, smoke-blackened men waited as the scavenging went on among the fallen Yankees out ahead of them, on the other side of the splintered fence. Seeing this Daniel Ryan pulled the newly acquired shoes from the waistband of his pants and scrutinised them. They were certainly not new, but they were a damned sight better than what he presently had on his feet.

It was as he made to loosen those now ragged and holed canvas covers on his feet that the first volley thundered through their ranks, bringing down a jumble of men, who stumbled and lurched into their comrades as they fell. Among them was Sam Bradlee, still pacing his line, who went down with a neat hole in his temple which was instantaneously followed by a dark red spray from the other side of his head. Daniel stared, as the wiry sergeant spreadeagled his body on the grass beyond the fence, appalled at this latest random death of yet another comrade. Bradlee lay there like a rag doll, with his face upwards. The shout came along the line immediately, to those on the other side to re-cross the fence and return fire, but still Daniel stood, looking at Bradlee, as the blood welled into a pool on the grass around his head. He tore his gaze from the fallen sergeant and looked. Around him, men scrambled back across, jostling with the others who had remained on that side, most of them moving much quicker, Daniel reckoned, than they had when they had gone the other way. He began to stuff the shoes back into his haversack again as he heard Jeffers bellow his name. Resting the musket against a damaged fence rail, he clumsily vaulted the fence by leaning his uninjured arm on a post. He recovered the musket and crouched, grasping at the stock of the Enfield, beside the same post, seeking its scant protection even as his mind acknowledged how frail a barrier it was to the volleys of lead and iron that continued to sweep around this field.

Daniel struggled to make himself concentrate after Bradlee's abrupt end. He swallowed the foul tasting bile that had come up from his throat and checked that a fresh cap was in place. He levelled his weapon on the remains of the rail and peered into the smoke for a target, struggling to control the trembling in his legs and the thundering of his heartbeat in his chest. Others around him fired speculatively into the drifting cloud as more bullets whizzed past, with some splintering the already damaged posts and rails of the fence. Swimming through the smoke came the sight of distant flags, two colours, flapping gently in the hot air out there on the far side of the gully. That would do for a target, Daniel squinted along the sights and fired, aiming just below the colour, feeling this latest painful jump of the weapon into his tender shoulder. He fumbled in his ammunition pouch for another cartridge, just as another salvo of shells from those Yankee guns above the creek burst overhead.

Beside him, the others of his mess crouched, seeking their share of shelter from the posts and rails of the fence, while all along the line the fire fight went on across the width of the ploughed field and its gully. The opposing lines stood maybe three hundred yards apart. That was near to maximum effective range for many men, he found the thought drifting across his mind, except maybe for the marksmen who had an instinct for killing with these weapons. But there was scant opportunity for precisely aimed shots now, in these drifting clouds of gun smoke from their own musketry, and from the multitude of other weapons across those fields, which repeatedly obscured the enemy line or hid them completely for long periods of the time.

Up in the sky, in the brief moments when it could be seen, the sun had emerged once more as it sank, with agonising slowness towards the smoky ridge line, while still the musketry and artillery thundered, savaging the ranks of vulnerable flesh and blood that faced each other across that gully. All along the fence line, men fell, some swept from their place in the line as though by some great force which bowled them over, pitching their bodies away, as if by the swipe of a giant hand, to lie or squirm yards from where they had stood or crouched. Others simply sank down, as though weariness rather than injury or death had claimed them, until one looked and saw the blood, that spattered the ground around them and still, as afternoon became evening, the fire fight went on.

But Tom Gibben's death was neither of these things. It was a shell fragment, and it must have been a large one, for it took away most of his head, even as he knelt only feet from Daniel Ryan. It was the splashing of dark red gore across his clothing that told Daniel of the event and he looked immediately to where Gibben still knelt, with his hands still moving, even with only the lower portion of his head still in place. His body stayed there for several seconds before toppling over, to lie still amidst the other fallen men. Daniel felt the vile taste rise again in his throat, as his eyes rested on what had become of his friend, for Gibben was more than just a comrade. He was another of their Eden Station group, going back to those chairs around the window table in Ed's tavern. He was Constance Warner's cousin also and now he was dead. Daniel felt the tears squeeze from his eyes and trickle onto his cheeks as he continued to look. He began to move, making to examine his friend's body, but knew instantaneously that, with the injury he had just seen, it was a hopeless waste of time and effort. Philipps, seeing him start to move, nudged him back into his place.

"Don't go," he grunted. "There ain't nothin' anybody kin do fer him." Daniel lowered his head and felt more salty tears fill his eyes. He let his glance run along the portion of the fence line near them, where that almost equal mix of northern and southern fallen now lay. There was nothing that could be done for most of them, for, with this unending fire fight continuing, many of them had been hit again and again after the first wound that had brought them down. There was nothing any of them could do for they were all trapped now in this charnel house of a field, where these dead and mutilated boys lay so thickly while still more fell as the bullets whirred through and the shells soared unendingly above. Until the sun went down and night came there was nothing to be done about any of it save to anchor this right flank, keeping the Yankees penned back away from that vital road behind them.

They must play out this obscene ordeal of loading and aiming and killing as long as they survived, but, even when darkness stopped this latest and largest episode of the death struggle that these armies had gotten themselves into, it would not end there. No, it would not end. It would be just an interlude until the next time. Daniel gritted his teeth and pulled at his ramrod to continue his loading. The whole region, between north and south, was just a killing ground now, and every collision between the armies brought more hours and days like today. Today was less than three weeks since the previous major blood-letting at Manassas, and now it was all happening again with more smoke and hellish noise, more death and stink of blood and gore and once it ended here there would be still more after that. Men like Tom Gibben, and Sam Bradlee and Ossie Rice and Adam Bailey and John Gower, the new corporal since Manassas, he had seen them all fall today. They were just a part of this latest episode, and there would undoubtedly be more. Since the springtime, the months had been marked by these successive, savage footprints of the war, Seven Pines and Mechanicsville, and Garnett's farm, and Savage's Station and Malvern Hill and then on to Manassas and now this, and the cost to their own company and regiment was becoming overwhelming and the next time would soon be looming. As he went on with the drill of loading and firing with his heart still pounding like a hammer in his chest, he caught a glimpse Boyce too falling to lie among the tangle of dead and wounded at the fence and the thought swam into his head, would any of them survive all of this?

But they must win. As Daniel Ryan loaded and fired his searingly hot musket, ignoring the pain of his shoulder and arm, he grimly fixed that thought in his mind above all others. They must win, because it was unthinkable that all this sacrifice of blood and loss of comrades and friends would be wasted. They must stay strong and hold these marauding Yankees back. They must somehow strike the blow that would finish the whole thing and they must stay together, and stick the whole thing out, until it was finally done.

As the weak distant circle of the sun, blood red in the drifting smoke, at last dipped onto the horizon of the ridge where the chaotic town lay, and then slowly slipped from sight, the dusk began to gather while still the searing gunfire thundered. It was only as the actual darkness approached that the shooting along the fence line at last began to wane and, all over the field, the cannon stilled, the battle noises faded and the burning hot weapons, stained and fouled with their black coating of powder residue, were at last lowered and put aside.

All around the wearied and stupefied men who remained, the dead and dying lay, and now that the guns were still, after this hellish fight, which had lasted from dawn till dusk, the sights and sounds of what it had all cost became clearer. As the smoke thinned and drifted away on the finally cooling air of the coming night, the calls of those wretched men began, as they always did, and these were in so many ways more harrowing than the noise of battle itself. From everywhere the cries wailed out, some simply yells or screams of agony, while others were forming what must be words, garbled words that were impossible to understand. But so many more of the fallen called for help, from friends or brothers, from distant mothers or from a still more distant god, who, despite his endless mercy for men, had still allowed all of this to happen. The shouts and screams made the flesh of the living creep and, even as exhaustion stole over them. As they heard this litany of the agony of thousands of their fellow men, the thought came that they too, but for sheer chance, or the grace of that distant god, could lie there also, adding their own voices to that dreadful chorus.

"Help me, please, help me!"

"Oh my god, my shoulder!"

"Finish me, finish me, I can't stand this!"

"Oh Mother, Oh god!"

"Water, please, water!"

"Somebody help!"

As the full darkness came and the scenes slowly faded from sight, Daniel still looked around him. Up above the ridge top to the north, the sky glowed lurid red, casting a subdued hint of illumination across the stricken fields, as the fires in Sharpsburg still burned and flickered and the crackling of flames could now be faintly heard above all of the other sounds from those fields where that carpet of dead and dying lay. Up there near the town itself, and stretching away down over the ridges towards the creek, the first lanterns had begun to appear as some, maybe surgeons or orderlies, gradually encroached onto the parts of the battlefield that lay within their lines, to pursue their grisly work, seeking those who could be helped. Their progress was marked out by those pinpoints of yellow light that they carried with them, moving and twinkling like fireflies in the gloom. Occasional shots still rang out, whether at those who tried to help the fallen or because in some places the antagonists were so near to each other that the least movement on either side might prompt further firing.

A few men from the fence line now left their places and began to pick their way among the trail of dead and dying, looking for a friend or relative perhaps? He heard Jeffers' voice and turned to see him assisting in lifting Boyce's limp form into a blanket to be carried away, while, along the shattered fence line, a few others tried to minister to the injured nearest to them. Others still, engrossed with the needs of the living, pulled morsels of saved or foraged food from their haversacks and chewed them cold. Still more headed out among the dead, to rifle through the haversacks of the fallen Yankees for rations or water or, better still, for real coffee. Others pulled and hauled at the clothing or shoes of the still warm corpses, laying early claim to the things, which they needed and those dead men had no further use for.

But there were those who did none of these things, finding that, even in this expanse of destruction and continuing suffering for so many of their comrades and their erstwhile enemies, their own physical tiredness and torpidity brought a more urgent need than even hunger, destitution or compassion. These men simply sank down where they had fought, onto whatever patch of blood-stained grass, torn up earth or trampled crop was available, content to let such sleep of utter exhaustion that they might be able to get sweep over them. Among these latter were Daniel Ryan and his remaining companions. Pausing only to pull the rude canvas moccasins from his feet and take the plundered shoes, which had protruded from beneath his haversack since Bradlee had fallen, he pushed his feet into them. A moment to lace them, and then a last look around the darkened field with its twinkling lights, strands of drifting smoke and its chorus of cries, moans and entreaties for help, before his head too rested on his good arm. He was dimly aware of Daley already snoring nearby, and then, amid yet another hell on earth, of the dead and the crippled all around him, in spite of his numb aching shoulder and the throbbing of his crudely bandaged arm, Daniel Ryan also fell into an exhausted sleep.

Chapter 12
An Utter, Empty Weariness

For the second successive night there was little real rest to be had through those surreal hours of darkness. The smells of smoke and blood, and other unspeakable things, intruded persistently into the consciousness, while the noises from the field went on without pause, disturbing the exhausted sleepers and leading, at best, to a succession of fleeting dozes rather than anything more substantial. It was still dark when Daniel awoke for the umpteenth time, but now there was a hint of light over in the eastern sky, beyond the trees that lined the creek, and the dim distant line of the mountains way beyond. He felt dirty and stiff and his injured right arm and his shoulder in particular, ached. Around him others slept, but in different parts of the field, the lanterns still moved, marking the places where those invisible orderlies went on with their work of seeking out those whom they could find and help. Across the meadows and the trampled corn fields, the cries and screams had not gone, but many had subsided into a chorus of mutters and groans, a less strident reminder than previously of the agony of those who lay scattered around the fields, but still an unavoidable trial on the nerves of the living.

In places the blasted crops still smouldered, casting wavering lines of smoke across the fields as that smudge of light hardened over the distant shoulder of South Mountain.

Dawn, with its lingering hint of greyness across the landscape, now steadily revealed the expanse of destruction and death, all around, which would no longer be hidden and closed out by darkness or exhausted sleep. Daniel Ryan let his mind dwell on the scale of this destruction for a moment, as his eyes swept around the adjacent fields, but just a glance told him that help would, for many of these boys, be a long time coming, and for more would be too late when it did.

The morning was again cloudy and mist was gathering with the dawn, collecting in the gullies and folds of the ground, but thinner and sparser than that of yesterday. Daniel painfully heaved himself to his feet, feeling his limbs only slowly come to some sort of life and start to discard the ache of cramped tiredness. His mouth felt dry and gritty and his shoulder and arm throbbed anew as he began to make his way along the line of dead, stooping to grasp at any canteens that remained, shaking them and listening for any sounds of water inside. As he picked his way through the debris of the field, inwardly celebrating the luxury of again having shoes on his feet, more men were to be seen along the line of the road up ahead, stirring and moving as the light grew stronger, passing slowly from that dull half-light towards full day. He looked up to the higher ground, that ridge line towards the town, emerging last from the receding darkness, revealing the smoke from Sharpsburg's fires still curling into the air.

There was movement up there and Daniel narrowed his eyes as he made out a little cluster of horsemen picking their way through the guns and debris near the crest. The leading rider rode a grey horse and he knew instantly who it was, for he rode awkwardly, with his hands higher than normal for a horseman. It was Lee, with his splinted, bandaged arms still raised at that peculiar angle in their slings, making riding difficult. But he was out inspecting his lines nevertheless, seeing for himself where these, the best and bravest of his men, if Benning's words were to be believed, had fought and endured, and where so many of them had fallen. As the light strengthened, Daniel could make out the orderly, who, as a consequence of the general's injured arms, walked ahead of him, leading his horse by its bridle. It was a make do, awkward way of getting about, but the general was there regardless of it all.

As the group picked its way along, Lee was pausing to speak to the men whom he came upon and Daniel could hear a few muttered snatches of the voices, even at that distance, over the continuing moans of the many wounded. Three of the general's staff followed where he went, keeping a slight distance from him as they walked their horses behind him and pausing when he did. Daniel watched them pass along the crest of the ridge and go slowly on till they were moving out of sight, obscured by the curve of the slope, but the muttering fragments of the distant voices still came to him, even though the sights no longer did, until, with the group now gone from view, he moved on again.

He had to go all the way back to the road to find water and it was not from dead men that it came, but from the soldiers of the artillery battery whose guns they had retaken yesterday. They were Mackintosh's men, of Powell Hill's Pee Dee artillery, they told him. He had asked them if they had water, having already noted that their buckets were full.

"We ain't here to supply water fer the whole damn infantry," one man growled in reply? Daniel looked wearily into his face.

"It was us infantry that got your damned cannon back," he rasped in return. The man made to retort but then looked around as a sergeant approached.

"If ya fought fer these here guns then ya deserve a goddam drink," he drawled and he waved Daniel towards one of the buckets. They watched him replenish his canteen from it and he looked back at their faces, blackened by powder stains and creased with weariness. They were boys, the thought crossed his mind, mere boys, but they looked more like old men. They were here, among the dead horses of their battery that still lay, mixed among the dead men of both sides, having only begun the task of clearing the ground. Here, near the road at least, the job of moving those wounded had begun, with groaning, crying sufferers being carried by a small procession of shuffling men over to where ambulances were arriving in relays on the road. The tired mules harnessed to their vehicles, stood with their heads bowed low towards the ground, getting such respite as they could, while they awaited whatever further insanity their masters might see fit to subject them to.

Daniel took in the picture of men and beasts, spent by their efforts of the previous day, but going through the motions of beginning this new morning without anything like sufficient time to recover, whether physically or spiritually, from the hell that had been yesterday. He thanked the artillerymen once more before turning to retrace his steps across the pasture field, pausing to drink again before heading on through the grass, the debris and the fallen towards the fence where some of his comrades had now begun to stir. Ballard was on his feet, and he grasped greedily at the near full canteen that Daniel offered to him.

"Answer to a prayer," he grunted.

"Didn't know you prayed that much Otis," Daniel said.

"Nobody said it was my prayer," Ballard replied, lifting the canteen to his mouth once again, "but if I was prayin' today, I'd pray to be the hell out of this place."

"Leave some for the others," Daniel told him just as Thompson stirred, to be passed the already half empty canteen. He too drank deeply and then nudged at Daley, who grunted but did not stir so the canteen was passed on to Phillips.

"Leave him be," Ballard grunted, gesturing towards Daley. "He'd sleep through his own goddam funeral."

"I'll be at yours first," Daley growled, opening one eye and twisting half upright to take the offered canteen from Phillips' hand.

"Likely ya will Mick," Ballard said, before commencing a huge yawn, stretching his arms, out and up in a huge arc, "and it could be today if the Yankees are game fer another push this way." He turned away to pace around the immediate vicinity of the fence, scrutinising the field.

"Worst yet, I reckon" he grunted, half to himself. Nobody replied. Some things, Daniel Ryan thought, were sufficiently obvious not to have to be stated.

It was bright daylight now, but a sunless, cloudy day, whose mist dispersed only slowly. Jeffers arrived, sporting a bloodstained cloth around his head, as he stalked along the line of dirty, powder-blackened men at the fence, summoning them together for a brief roll call. Rodger was behind him as he began and Daniel wondered if that meant that Fenwick, as well as Boyce, was dead or wounded. The men stood in a rough line, easy enough, Daniel thought, for thirteen of them. He glanced around, noticing that Josh was among those present, but of Eli and Matthew there was no sign as, with the roll called, Rodger stepped forward.

"We will attend to our dead and wounded," he said. "No truce has been arranged on the field, so you must not move onto ground held or commanded by the enemy. If you encounter them, and they fire on you, or show hostile intent, take cover and return fire. If they are collectin' their own over there, then leave them be. You will be formed into three details in the charge of Sergeant Jeffers, Sergeant Sangster and...... Corporal Thompson, you are acting sergeant, as of now, and will take charge of the third group. We are seeing to our own dead and injured first." He looked at Jeffers. "Carry on First Sergeant," he added wearily, before turning and pacing away. Jeffers barked some more instructions before dismissing them.

The five of their own mess moved out and set to work. Orderlies had begun to move among some of the wounded on this part of the field and, as the morning began to pass, the company details mingled with them, working in their groups of four or five, to move the injured of their own regiment, initially from around the fence, but thereafter moving gradually back towards the road. They used blankets, with a man at each corner, to carry the casualty over to where several ambulances had pulled part of the way across the pasture field, grimly closing out the sight of many of the wounds and the shrieks and cries as they manhandled and moved the sufferers.

Their own wounded took the balance of the morning hours and once it was done, they were set, after a brief rest, to commencing the task of burying their dead, whose bodies were already beginning to swell and discolour in the heat. They made first for where Tom Gibben lay, hunched on his side, at the wrecked remains of the rail fence. Nobody looked much at the mess that was Tom's head, as, with no spades, they used bayonets to break up the earth, and plates for clearing it away, to make enough of a hole to keep the scavengers away from his remains. They laid out the blanket they had brought and lifted his corpse onto it, smelling the strong, horrid odour of putrefaction as the remains were disturbed. The blanket was folded around him and they lifted him into the hole, to begin pushing the piled earth over him, firming it down with their feet. Then the four of them stood up, as though not knowing what else to do.

"Do we try and mark it," Daniel said? The others looked at him.

"What do we want to do that for," Daley asked.

"Suppose his folks want to get him back, at least if we mark the place they'll be able to find him," Philipps replied. Ballard was sceptical.

"Mark it if ya want," he said, "but the Yankees, or the farmers are just as likely to move the boys that get buried here. Ya've seen the size o' that damned corn? This is prime growin' land so the damned farmers'll want it back fer sure." Daniel pondered for a few moments more, looking at his companions in turn.

"We can't do anythin' about the farmers or the Yankees," he told them, "but, if we leave a marker then we've done the best we could for a friend." Philipps turned away and scouted around briefly before returning with a broken fragment of a wooden box section.

"It could be a waste o' time," he said, "but it jest might help if his folks want to come find him." Daniel drew his bayonet, as the others moved away to go on with the grim day's work. He turned to the board and started to laboriously scrape letters onto the wood, finding it difficult to shape the curves or cross grain strokes on the hard unhelpful surface, seeing in his mind as he worked, the face of his friend and finding the memories of the things they had shared coursing through his thoughts. A shudder went through him as those recollections came.

"No," he thought as the sentiments threatened to overcome him. It was the same as the summer, when other friends had been taken. He must not do this. He must not let it wash over him this way. He must put it all from his mind or it would be too much. Another time he could think of it, another time, when there was less to do and less hurt at the losses that this life and this war were forcing him, and so many other people, to bear.

Eventually the board was done and he was pushing it into the soft freshly turned ground, just as Jeffers came by.

"That's a damn waste o' yore time," he growled.

"I'd maybe do it for you too," Daniel Ryan told him.

"It'd still be a damn waste o' yore time," was the answer as the First Sergeant moved on. Daniel paused for a few moments more, looking down at Tom Gibben's crude grave, before heading across to where the others had gone, joining them there in lifting more of the bodies around them into another freshly dug hole, before moving on again to repeat the process as the day stretched into afternoon.

The hours passed with all three company groups moving gradually along the line of the shattered fence. Where blankets were available, they wrapped the bodies in them before burying them. Some of the sights were stomach turning, and sometimes worse, and where men had been mutilated or dismembered, they dug the hole as close by as possible and simply levered what remained into it, using their feet or pieces from the remaining fence rails. Saul Phillips took the water canteens away some time after noon to seek more water and returned with them partly filled. The others of the group paused to drink greedily from them, before stoppering them and slinging them on their straps.

"Ain't no creeks up around here," Phillips said, "but some o' the farm wells ain't dry yet."

"I'm dry enough to take it from a farm puddle," was Daley's response.

As the time wore on, and the grisly work dragged forward, they gradually cleared the ground on their own side of the fence, but so far had not gone beyond it to recover the men who had been felled there by those first enemy volleys. They stopped and discussed it briefly, the prospect of being fired on was still present and they had heard some desultory musketry along the line at different times through the morning. But, as Thompson said, those Yankees across the way had had all morning to fire across the gully but had pointedly not done so. As a result, in the middle afternoon, their own details had crossed the fence and begun to collect the men who still lay beyond it. They had descended the first few feet into the gully when Phillips called to Thompson and pointed towards the enemy line. The others, still apprehensive as to the enemy intentions, stopped and looked also. Over on the far slope of the gully a ragged white cloth was being waved back and forth on a musket ramrod. The five of them looked around at each other.

"Wave somethin' white," Daley said. They fumbled in pockets, but nothing suitable was found. Thompson dispensed with the formalities however and simply waved the Yankees forward. It took a couple of minutes before the first of them appeared. There were no officers, but a ragged line of men was led forward by a sergeant and these began to retrieve their wounded from the eastern slope of the gully, moving progressively across towards the western side in the course of their work. Inevitably, Thompson's group found themselves working close to some of these men and, regardless of Rodger's order, conversations started up. One such began between their own group and a few of the enemy detail.

"Busy damn day in hell," one Yankee muttered, to nobody in particular. Philipps looked over at him.

"Many's a good boy afore his time," he answered. Another Yankee, just beyond the one who had spoken, straightened up and looked at him.

"Why're you rebs up here," he said? "There ain't no southern Confederacy up here." Ballard straightened also and returned the man's gaze.

"Reckon we needed the vittles," he retorted, from where he stood beside Daley. "There ain't nothin' to be had in the whole o' northern Virginia since a whole mess o' Yankees come down last year and took all that them folks had." The Yankee reddened at the words.

"Plenty o' us reckon that ain't no more than rebels deserve," he said.

"Well don't go hollerin' when ya get some of it back," Daley retorted. Another Yankee, had joined the first one and he seemed less inclined to turn talk into argument.

"Reckoned we'd all a' had enough o' fightin' fer a spell," he growled, casting his eyes around over the field? The Yankee private moved away, while the southern group looked after him.

"His brother's out here some place," the other man added, "and he ain't found yet." There were nods of acknowledgement about that and Daniel Ryan looked after the man, feeling a tinge of compassion even for him, a Yankee, as he too looked for an answer that he did not want to find.

They continued their work as the bodies swelled and blackened in the full heat and humidity of the day, though it remained cloudy. The Yankees stayed also, pulling their own wounded from where they had fallen on this side of the gully. Daniel found his eyes straying towards them during any kind of a pause and coming back to his mind repeatedly was what he had thought down on the peninsula. They were so much like themselves. If you took away their silly little kepi caps and their curious nasal accents, there seemed precious little to distinguish them from the southerners, but his musings, and the men of both groups, were interrupted by the arrival of a blue clad officer. They had seen him coming, picking his way down the slope into the gully and striding across towards where the men worked.

"What in the blue blazes are you men doing down here," he called at his own men. All stopped their work as he covered the remaining distance and, on his arrival, the sergeant gave a salute that Daniel Ryan noticed was not returned.

"We agreed not to fire in order to recover our wounded, sir," he answered.

"You had no damned right to do anything of the sort," the officer, a lieutenant, told them in the same disapproving tone. "There's no official truce anywhere along here, so get back to the lines and you rebels get back to your own. If you're still out here in five minutes our men will be ordered to open fire."

"Reckon a lot o' these boys layin' out here are gonna die if they don't git help, truce or not," Thompson growled in reply. The captain flushed.

314

"That's no concern of yours or mine," he returned. "Arrangement of a truce is up to ranking officers and, until they agree to it, there's nobody authorised to recover casualties out here between the lines." Ballard took a step away from the corpse he had been moving and shrugged.

"If ya count around," he growled, "ya'll find near all a' them still lyin' down here are wearin' blue. If you want to watch 'em die from up there at yore fence then we ain't gonna lose no sleep over that." The lieutenant made no reply, but signalled the enlisted men away with a wave. Thompson did the same and the five of them turned to go. Thompson raised his hand to the union sergeant, who did the same.

"See ya in hell, reb'," he called as he gestured his men to the rear with his thumb.

The work went on through the afternoon as the clouds now thickened and lowered, and, although Daniel Ryan felt his stomach repeatedly heave at the sights he came across, another part of him was reassured by the task. For as long as this pause to collect dead and wounded lasted, even if both sides only worked within their own positions, the fighting would not resume. The presence of those busy Yankees out on the field was, in some way, a guarantee against further attack, and the afternoon was well advanced before the blue figures on the far side of the gully had moved away. They headed east, bearing a last cluster of their casualties away towards the tree line, which marked the higher ground above the creek. Daniel and the others paused at the fence to watch them go as distant thunder came to their ears.

"Reckon that there ole George McClellan ain't in too much o' a hurry to come at us agin," Ballard said.

"Too late now," Philipps said, "even if he wants to, be dark afore too long."

Large droplets of rain had begun to fall as they collected their equipment, shortly after the enemy details had departed from the far side. Each of them carried what they had gleaned from the fallen, mainly some salted beef and a few hardtacks, but it was food, and all along that destroyed fence line, men were hauling sections from the splintered rails and posts and carrying them a little to the rear, into any cleared spaces, to build cooking fires, while others set up crude shelters to protect these from the increasing rain. With a fire burning and shelter for it being seen to by Daley and Phillips, Daniel Ryan cut the beef into chunks on a board. Ballard still carried one of the canteen half-pans and they had earlier retrieved the other from where it had hung from the dead Tom Gibben's haversack strap, as the thunder peals drew closer. Daniel poured some of the water that remained in his canteen into the pans and dropped in the beef to soak a little, cutting the process short to empty the pans before returning them, with the meat, to the fire for frying, as the rain now poured down. As soon as the beef began to spit and sizzle, there was a change in the mood around the fire as the others finished rigging a further gum blanket for shelter and gathered to watch while Daniel's cooking continued. It was always the same, he thought. Somehow the prospect of food could spur a kind of revival in the most jaded and wearied men even in a damned downpour of rain with thunder and lightning along to keep it company. Thompson reckoned it was because a man had to be alive to smell food and the whole thing led from smelling it on to eating it. Plates were quickly produced and wiped while talk turned to meals, and this, Daniel Ryan mused, in a field, lashed by the elements and still littered with many of their own and the enemy dead. Having set the beef to fry in its own grease, Daniel poured the liquid off into the other pan, dropping in fragments of hardtack, that Ballard had finished breaking on the board with his musket butt, to spit and sizzle in their turn. The others fidgeted around until finally the contents of both pans were dished onto the five plates and they set to eating with an energy that belied their previous fatigue and listlessness. The food disappeared quickly and the plates were licked and stored in haversacks as the rain and the thunder began to ease.

"Wasn't much of a dinner," Daley muttered.

"You should've shot the Yankees with the best rations then," Daniel told him. Ballard shoved Mick with his hand.

"No sech thing as a good day on the farm with you is there," he said?

The rain, although slackened to a drizzle now, did not go off, so the men stayed under whatever shelters they had been able to improvise, and, as evening came, word began to circulate of a rations issue. Jeffers appeared, directing them to send mess members over to the road where the issue would be made. Phillips and Daley got the job, while Daniel took the canteens along since water butts and tubs were said to have been set up to supply the men.

There were already lines forming and these grew further as the three of them approached while the rain continued to fall. Ambulance wagons rumbled by with still more wounded men, now having to compete with the commissary vehicles for road space. Looking back over the ground, Daniel Ryan could see that some areas were clearer now, with what had been almost a carpet of fallen men now broken up and more dispersed, with, in many places, only the remaining dead still on the fields. Clearing them all, he thought to himself, would surely take days more of work?

The wagons were parked on the margin, which adjoined the road, and they split up, with Daley and Phillips making for whatever food was available, while Daniel awaited a turn at the water tubs with the five canteens. Further wagons came and went as a murmur of talk rose among the waiting men.

"Reckon they'll come on agin in the mornin'."

"Think the old man'll fight 'em agin?"

"We better be out' o' here afore that."

"Thar's bin wagons headin' down to Shepherdstown yonder all afternoon and the cap'n reckons we've gotten most o' the wounded boys that we kin move to the rear by now."

"Won't regret seein' the back o' this damned place."

"Won't be sorry to see the back o' this damned state."

Daniel listened to the talk, but said nothing. He felt wearied beyond measure and a sense of guilt sat upon him that he could not disregard, for his mind kept returning to the burying of Tom Gibben and the feelings of loss that were so sharpened by friendship. What would become of him? His remains would lie here in the north, and the Yankees might even move him to some forgotten hole of a mass grave, unless his family could do something about recovering him. They ran a mill near Eden Station, where he had a younger brother and three sisters as well as his parents. Would they try to claim Tom's body, the way that others had after the fighting around Richmond? Would they be allowed to come and claim their son, up here on Yankee territory and take him home? Who would tell them of Tom's death? Gibben was the third of their own close group of friends that the war had taken and, like the others, it left a feeling of great emptiness in the heart.

He looked across at the rations wagon where Daley had started to wrangle with Luke Petersen about some damn meaningless thing, while Jeffrey issued the food. He could smell the odours from the men around him as he waited, strong and pungent, but then they all smelled, not only of the sweat, powder smoke and the pretty routine body smells of long unwashed men, but the stink of the dead, among whom they had laboured all day, was upon them also. At last, his turn came at a water tub and Daniel stepped forward where a grey-bearded sergeant stood to submerge the canteens he carried in turn, absent-mindedly watching the bubbles as they filled. When they stopped, he lifted them out in turn and stoppered them, before swinging them successively across his left shoulder and moving away, feeling the cold wetness of the water from the canteens and their straps soaking through his already wet jacket and shirt. At the roadside, Daley and Philips waited, with meat wrapped in a cloth and a bag, presumably of flour.

As they began to head back across the field, Phillips was the one to speak.

"Word up thar's that we're gittin' out o' here," he said. Daniel looked at him.

"When," he asked?

"Tonight," was the reply.

"Back over the river," Daley muttered and Phillips nodded, as on they walked with their full canteens and their bundles of precious rations. Little more was said, but in Daniel's mind the feeling was one of relief. This whole Maryland adventure had long since lost any appeal for him, and, from the talk at the water tubs, this was so for many others in the army also. The campaign had been little more than a two week ordeal of rags and destitution, of blistered and lacerated feet and shortages of food, with much of what it had been possible to obtain being over or unripe, resulting in the epidemic of stomach and bowel sickness that had afflicted so many of the army.

As if that were not enough, the people up here, save for very few, had not welcomed them. From old Mrs Franklin, back at Frederick, to near everyone else they had met on the roads, they had tolerated them and sometimes helped them, but that help had been out of sheer humanity, rather than from any sympathy towards their cause. No, Daniel thought, he for one would hold no regrets about leaving. He let his feelings wander as the image of Tom Gibben again swam across his mind, followed by the boy, Henry Hartman, with his poor little chalk-white face. What morsel of good had it all done? There was nothing that he could think of, for he felt exhausted and defeated by this whole damned Maryland business, not so much by the Yankees, but just by being here with all that it had cost. The apparent pointlessness of it all, coupled with his profound tiredness seemed to engulf him in an utter, empty weariness that was spiritual as well as physical. It was time to be gone, to be away from this place and everything that had befallen them here. He sighed deeply, letting the air slowly out through his mouth and with it, his feeling of frustration and resentment faded a little, supplanted by the more immediate matters of life and living. Cooking and likely some more eating would be next, unless orders to move came too soon to allow it, and although Daniel Ryan felt an overriding desire to wash, he knew that there was little prospect of that.

The rain continued, drizzling steadily down as the evening passed, making the building up of their fire a smoky and tedious job, but they persisted and got sufficient of a blaze revived, to get on with the tasks of further cooking and eating. Ryan and Ballard got busy again, preparing and cooking the familiar hash of chopped bacon and corn flour dough and when the food was ready they all sat under their improvised shelters to eat once more. By the time they had finished their meal and begun to pack the remainder away into haversacks, the rain had eased to almost nothing, but around them a mist was beginning to gather.

The field was now muddy, and the sodden grass and ground brought a pervading smell of wet grass and soaked ashes, to mingle in their nostrils with the smells of the dead, as they gathered for evening assembly. A roll call revealed that five further members of Company B had rejoined, including Eli, who sported a large bandage around his arm. Rodger confirmed the news of the withdrawal across the river and briefed them as to how this would be done. The wagon trains would be first to go, followed by the infantry and guns, with cavalry remaining to cover the movement. Fires in the camps were to be left burning, to mislead the enemy as to their intentions, though nobody much believed that it did. The line would contract, like a deflating balloon, the captain told them and the pull back would begin as soon as full darkness fell. The departure was, of course, to be with minimum noise, he added, and the men of the brigade would withdraw onto that Harpers Ferry Road, to avoid the town, branching off onto a further road, named for a nearby sawmill, which would take them to the ford.

The men were dispatched to their dusk positions along the fence line and once darkness fell, Ryan's section was retained for the final outpost duty, spending the next two hours out at the edge of the ravine. Daniel was paired with Daley and, as they crouched among the wet brush, they could see the glow of their own camp fires to the rear and that of the Yankee fires out in front, with occasional sounds of movement among the enemy pickets also coming to their ears. Eventually the detail was recalled and, as they withdrew, they passed through a further picket line, Tennessee men from Archer's brigade, moving out to replace them.

The night was dark and the mist had grown thicker as Ryan and Ballard collected their belongings and joined the sparse column which now constituted the Ogeechee Volunteer Rifles. They waited in their files and went on with re-arranging their equipment to avoid the noises of belt buckles, tin cups or canteens on bayonet sockets or scabbards. Some stuffed their cups into haversacks, while others left them in their usual place, fastened in the securing strap of the haversack but moved it around to the front of their hip away from the things it might clink against. Jeffers, Sangster and Thompson, the latter looking a mite embarrassed at his new status, paced around the few files until, on the order, they were moved off, over towards the road once more, leaving behind the blasted, and still littered, fields and the ruined town, shrouded in darkness now, up over the ridge to their right. Feet swished in the wet grass of the meadow, but there was little other noise from the moving men. Even so, the sergeants shooshed and indulged themselves in angry whispers as the files made their way towards the road, from which, as though to mock all of their own efforts at keeping noises down, the wet rumble of traffic in the mud was clearly audible.

Their column snaked across the field, moving around the dim forms of bodies and horse carcasses, still strewn on the grass, till the files ahead halted, presumably at the fence, bringing everyone else to a stumbling standstill in their turn. Corpses still lay around where they stood, vague shapes in the darkness, but the smell was unmistakable. Whispered comments ranged up and down, some ghoulish, while other men, Mick Daley among them, dwelt on how Yankee and Confederate dead smelled different, Daniel heard but did not respond to the talk. Up ahead the continuing creak of wagons and harness and the slop of mud told their own story of the traffic, clogging the roads to the rear as the army withdrawal went inexorably on.

Presently the march was resumed and they crossed the fence through a gap, wheeling to the left onto the road, breaking files to space themselves along the margin, while the endless procession of wagons laboured along the road itself, heading southwards, downhill, away from the town. The surface was now liquid mud, which splashed up from the animals' hooves and the wagon wheels over the men's clothing with every step. Down the hill only a short way the moving procession of men and vehicles was wheeled away to the right, by the signals and muted commands of a provost officer, onto another road, heading west now with passing fields and trees visible only as dim surreal shapes in the overcast gloom.

Progress from the start was punctuated by delays, during which the infantry stood in the mud and waited for the column up in front to move on again, continually hushed from comment or conversation by officers and sergeants. Eventually the vehicles and men alongside them would jerk into movement as the withdrawal resumed with only the splashing tramp of feet and hooves and the swishing, spattering rumble of wagon wheels as the mud-plastered procession of men, animals and vehicles moved steadily away from the town and the battlefield, making their way towards the river. More delays were encountered, most notably at the junction of the Sawmill and Shepherdstown Roads, where the traffic was both heavy and slow. On the river road at last a further seeming eternity of starting and stopping ensued on the liquid surface, but now, ahead through the mist, they could make out a dim glow in the sky above the trees and, as they drew slowly closer, lights could be made out. After still more halts and delays they came in sight of the river, able at last to see the congested ford.

The river banks and the fording place itself were lit by a row of flickering torches, held by a succession of cavalrymen along the last approach to the Potomac and out onto the river itself, to guide and speed the column. These were supplemented by a substantial bonfire on the bank itself onto which a detail of men tossed more wood. Long lines of infantry, guns, caissons and wagons could be seen, stretching down the muddy approach and on out into the water. Along the slippery and now narrowing road they picked their way, seeing the illuminated waters of the river, with rocky ledges, over which the current surged in a continuing splashing cascade, upstream from the ford, looking eerie and unreal in the guttering flames of the torches.

Even as they came closer to the waterway, and the river beyond, the column stumbled to yet another halt, to wait for a further time, while the wagons continued their lurching slither down through the mud, their teams slipping and struggling with the treacherous footing. Ahead the men could now see the line of the canal, with its tow path still following the route of the river, spanned here by a makeshift bridge of wooden planks. There was maybe enough space on it for the wagons and guns and maybe a single file of infantry to edge across on one side, but, with the timbers now wet and mud-plastered, the footing would be slippery and dangerous. While a growing cluster of men waited to use the precarious passage, others, did not pause, clambering instead down the bank to wade the almost empty canal itself.

The lines of waiting men ahead gradually thinned, as successive units waded or took their turn, on the muddy planks, until the Ogeechee Volunteers were summoned forward to resume their approach. They gingerly negotiated the span over the canal to find that beyond, on the approach down to the river ford, the mud was deeper still, for here, as at White's Ford that eternity ago, the bank had been dug down into a sloping approach to allow the wagons and guns of the army to negotiate their way to the water's edge. Men kept their balance with difficulty as they slithered down its slope to the river to halt again awaiting their turn to start across. Spaced across the river towards the far bank, the cavalrymen waited, holding those torches, which cast their guttering light out across the water only dully in the mist and overcast, but marking the way for the labouring infantry.

Out onto river, and on along the road on the far side, the unceasing procession of men and vehicles stretched, their progress guided and illuminated by the mounted men. No time was allowed on the muddy approach to remove pants or shoes, a pointless exercise in all of the rain and mud. Rather it was straight ahead, splashing through the shallows, with the shock of the cold water, eliciting shouts and curses from the men, as they stuffed hats into jackets and pulled at canteens with free hands in readiness to fill them. Out into the river they pushed, and Daniel pulled his canteen stopper with his teeth, using his free hand to submerge the container and, having done so, and feeling it reassuringly heavy with river water, he slung it over his shoulder again on its strap. With the same hand he splashed more water into his face, rubbing it across his skin and through his beard growth and his hair. Next he changed hands and did the same with the other, to continue this parody of a wash, until the faster-flowing water in midstream demanded his full concentration.

The horsemen waited, standing in the tide with their hissing, flickering lights, marking the line of the ford to prevent the men straying off into the deeper water on either side, but providing only islands of illumination on the river. All along the column, men called out the names of their units, keeping their groups together in the strange misty gloom. Near the middle of the river a mounted officer sat, calling to the struggling infantry as, they laboured across, straining against the river current.

"Keep it movin' boys. Stay together and keep it movin'."

Up and down the files there was a steady sequence of comments and curses about Maryland, confirming that nobody much, in what remained of the Ogeechee Volunteers, had any regrets about leaving the place behind them.

They pushed steadily on, the marching men flanking the wagons whose teamsters laboured, with shouted oaths and whips, to prevent their teams stopping to drink and thereby bringing the whole train to a halt, or worse. Wagons tilted and jolted and men repeatedly stumbled on the stones and boulders of the river bed, Then, as the water shallowed, the dripping men and vehicles closed up, the infantry shaking the water from their clothes as they emerged onto the muddy western approach, feeling their feet sink and slip in the slime, which pushed up around their shoes and made the going still more treacherous. On the bank, men dallied off the road, reforming files disordered by the fording and this done, moved off again, bickered at by sergeants as the road rounded a curve away from the riverside. Up past a house they tramped, seeing wide-eyed, white faces, that must be children, at one of the windows as they passed, a momentary image, immediately lost in the misty darkness. A short way along the road the column was guided off into a field to join a growing rank facing the river. Batteries of artillery were already deployed there, presumably to defend the crossing against any move by the enemy to molest the withdrawal. The men shivered as they waited in ranks, stamping feet and rubbing or slapping hands to stimulate circulation and warm themselves as the last of the drizzle kept their clothing stubbornly saturated.

The rain finally ceased and they were relieved from their positions overlooking the river, as the first hint of coming daylight crowned the distant mountains. The column of march was reformed in the field and headed for the road. Out on the road the exhausted troops resumed their struggle in the mud, with the liquid slopping of their feet and the animal hooves mingling with the creak of wheels and harness and the perennial clink of metal equipment as the new day came, clear and bright. Conversation and comment began to spread up and down the files, but it was sullen, dissatisfied talk, with none of the wisecracking, jokes or snatches of songs, which often marked their time on the road and made the tedium of the march more bearable. Among these men who shuffled along these muddy Virginia roads the mood was stubbornly sombre, for what they had suffered during their time in Maryland was vividly fresh in their minds. Some good boys were not making the return crossing and many of those who were, reckoned that the fording of that river back there had brought to a close the worst episode of their soldiering so far.

A few miles down the way they were halted and dismissed to bivouac as the sun poked above the eastern horizon. Pickets were posted, and those spared the immediate inconvenience of this duty quickly stacked their muskets. A few then produced some cold remains of rations to chew on, but most men made straight for their sodden blankets and, in spite of the squalor and the discomfort, within minutes, the bivouac was quiet.

Chapter 13
The Valley

The progress of the army back into Virginia was not free of alarms and detours, with the main one being the retracing of their steps, during the Friday night back towards the river, when word came of a Yankee force crossing over. The division had been roused and formed into column to move back down the drying roads to form a defensive line astride the Charlestown Road, a couple of miles back from the ford, waiting there until word came that the Yankee attempt at pursuit had been met and hustled back across to the Maryland bank by those same brigades of A. P. Hill's division, beside whom they had fought last Wednesday, outside Sharpsburg.

But still the campaign did not seem to be ended, for while the cavalry were set to watching the fords along the river, the rest of the army, with Longstreet's men leading, turned westward and began a laborious tramp, parallel to the river, towards Martinsburg. The roads were firming, though not yet returning to dust, but still the march was an ordeal for the bone-weary men. They set off late on the Saturday and marched well into the night, with the mood of pessimism turning increasingly to bitterness among many. There seemed to be no end to this campaign even on this side of the river. Straggling increased again with the route marked by the limping hobbling procession of ill or lamed men who had failed to keep up with their units. In addition, a rumour had circulated that the general was planning to recross the Potomac into Maryland further upriver. This news honed the sullen discontent simmering in many of the men into outright criticism of the whole campaign, with the general getting a full share of the hard words that went up and down the column.

"We'll still be marchin' when our feet are wore down to the ankles."

"Generals don't have t' march, if'n they did they'd make us march less."

"At the rate we're droppin' men outa this column, there won't be nobody left to cross back over no river."

Well towards first light the brigade had stumbled to a halt to drop into exhausted rest somewhere off the road, still short of Martinsburg.

But there was no resumption of the march on the Sunday. Instead the army remained where it had halted. Camps were set up and, late in the day, to the great relief of the men, their commissary wagons came creaking around. It was old Cal Jeffrey in charge as usual, with his brand of sarcasm to match Ballard's, but the men cared not, for enduring Cal's abrasive wit meant food of some kind. It was bacon and flour again, but grateful for anything, the men set up their fires and pans, in an improved frame of mind compared to that of the previous night. Fed and with no march orders for the following day, they rested around their fires before turning in, with even some banter and wisecracking going around, a sure barometer of a turn in rank and file morale.

After several more days, the columns moved again, but this time the route was to the south west, making for Winchester, the camp rumours said, with further stories that a large portion of the men who had straggled, and those who had refused to cross the river, were camped there and would be rejoining their units. On arriving around Winchester, they made more formal camps around the town between Mill Creek and Lick River, this time with sinks dug and camp streets laid out. Changes were immediately noticeable, the most welcome one being that regular and more varied rations began to arrive in the camps. Fresh meat and vegetables now supplanted the bacon and flour army staples and even some molasses came, along with more of the makeshift coffee substitutes also to further help morale. As days passed, the supplies arrived regularly on the wagons of a seemingly rejuvenated commissary and in addition to fresh beef, pork and vegetables even chicken appeared. Above all there was rest, for, when routine duties and drills were done in the camps, the men were given free time. Health and strength began to return as men sought to wash and mend or replace the equipment and clothing that the campaigns just ended had reduced to near fragments.

It was on the sixth day after the regiment arrived around Winchester, with the weather still settled, though less oppressively hot, that the column of their returning men marched back into camp, complete with a provost detail. Stragglers, who had made it back across from Maryland, had been rejoining in small groups since the camps had been set up, but today's group were the men who had not crossed the river, through sickness or lameness, or for refusing to go. Those in the camps turned out to watch this return and there were some shouts of greeting at the recognition of comrades, though many men said nothing, watching the arrival in a silence that almost had a hint of sullenness about it.

Among these returning files were the men of Company B. Daniel Ryan quickly picked them out as they came. Matt Weald was there, with Cartwright, Kane, Morris and Jones, and after a few seconds more he saw John Fitzpatrick also, but his feelings were mixed at the sight of the three of their own. On the one hand there was certainly a sense of pleasure at seeing familiar faces once again, but Daniel knew that, in his own mind, it was not as simple as that. He could, in one way, especially with how he himself now felt about the time spent campaigning across the river, understand, and even sympathise more with those who had refused to go. It was not their own country, and most of the people up there had, time after time, made that plain, but in turning their backs on their comrades, these men who had remained behind, had broken a cardinal rule of soldiering, namely that of group loyalty.

Since joining the regiment, the essence of their comradeship had been loyalty, to the army and the regiment, and now too a loyalty to the old man. But loyalty and trust existed above all among the men of messes, who shared duties, rations, danger and friendship through a bond that was extended to nobody else. Daniel Ryan's group had existed since before the war. They had volunteered together back in Eden Station, had opted to leave Savannah and come to Virginia together, but up here, the bond had been broken, not by impoverished farm boys, who needed plough furloughs to go home and provide for starving families, but by men who had chosen to stay behind when the army and their comrades and friends had gone on. These men had been missed, especially on that desperate day last week at Sharpsburg, where their share had had to be borne by others and Daniel knew that he did not feel kindly about that at all. As a result of the losses at Sharpsburg, there were now almost as many men returning as there were in camp. The company and regiment would be substantially strengthened by their arrival, but the cool reception given by some of the men to those returning confirmed that something important had been lost in this episode and it remained to be seen if it could be gotten back. If Fitzpatrick, Kane and Jones had been friends, going back well beyond their enlistment, since the crossing into Maryland, Daniel knew that things had changed. He had grown closer, in friendship and trust, with Ballard, Thompson and Philipps, and even the ever-troublesome, but steadfastly ever-there, Mick Daley. His friendships had shifted, largely out of necessity, and it was far from certain that those previous bonds of comradeship could be fully rebuilt.

In the assembly ground in the middle of the camp, Preston stood, watching the returning men arrive and parade, waiting with the other Sharpsburg officers. They also were a depleted group, with a few still sporting bandages and dressings, but they were there, and Daniel wondered if this was the major's way of emphasising to these returning men how the regiment had bled and suffered without them. Several officers were among the returning ranks including Lieutenant Parker of Company F, but he had had dysentery after Manassas and had been incapable of going on into Maryland. Was his face now flushed by the march or by something more like being counted among those who had refused to go? It was impossible to say.

Preston waited until the files had turned into line before stepping forward, while the balance of the men already in camp edged closer to watch and listen.

"You are welcome back, all of you," the major called. "We are glad to see you, very glad, and, by the living God, we would have been even gladder to see you on Wednesday of last week for that was when we were reduced to the numbers that you can see here in camp today." There was shifting of feet and a downcasting of eyes as he went on. He was certainly offering something of a veiled, but public, rebuke to these men, who had left their places in the regiment. There was a certain subtlety about how it was being done, but Preston's object was clear. Thompson, stood close by, as they listened to his words and he muttered quietly to Daniel.

"He surely ain't breakin' out no best drinkin' whiskey for 'em is he?"

"Would you," Daniel asked him?

"Reckon not," was the reply.

The major duly finished saying his piece, whereupon company officers and first sergeants were summoned to take charge of their returning men, while the watchers dispersed

331

to their fires. In due time, the newly arrived showed up in their company camps. Thompson had just departed to be duty sergeant and Daniel had resumed his seat at their fire with Daley, Philipps and Ballard, repairing equipment, as Jones, Kane and Fitzpatrick approached. Daniel saw them come out of the corner of his eye and he gently elbowed Ballard, who sat beside him.

"I see 'em," was the murmured reply, as the returning three came up towards the fire and stopped a few feet from where they sat. Philipps lifted his hand in greeting as Kane stepped forward and spoke.

"How're you boys?" He extended his hand and shook hands with each of them in turn, followed by the other two. Phillips looked at them.

"Mubbee still a mite wearied," he answered. A silence followed, with nothing said at all for several minutes, till John Fitzpatrick spoke.

"If you've somethin' on your minds boys," he said, "you might as well say it."

"Trust him to speak up." The thought flashed through Daniel Ryan's mind, as the four of them looked around at each other, but it was Daley who answered.

"You boys were my friends," he said, "before this and after all this still, but I never felt kindly about you leavin' us to it all across the river." Daniel looked at Mick, reflecting that although his words had not been pleasant they pretty well expressed what they felt about it all, but the thought was interrupted by John Fitzpatrick's response.

"We did what we thought was right," he said evenly. Daniel looked around at them, feeling that he must support what Mick had said, rather than leave it unsaid..

"I ain't lookin' for lastin' trouble," he said, "but we came up here to Virginia all together in a group, we all talked it over back in Savannah and we decided together and we came. It went ill with me at Leesburg, when you boys decided that the rest of us didn't matter to you so much as your own high fair-mindedness did." He caught sight of Jones' brows lowering as he finished speaking.

"I ain't back here fer no lectures from you boys," he retorted. "If all we're goin' to get back here is you tellin' us how wrong we all were then I ain't stayin' around to hear it." Daniel caught a movement out of the corner of his eye and glanced sideways to see Daley start to rise, but Philipps got a hand on one of his sleeves from his other side, while Daniel hurriedly grabbed the other. Daley pushed against them for a few seconds and then seemed to calm.

"That's fine with me," he growled at Jones. "We got on well enough while you were skulkin' back here." Now it was Jones' turn to stiffen and start forward, till Fitzpatrick and Ballard pushed him away also.

Daniel looked around them all, with a feeling of angry exasperation rising in his chest. If they didn't already have a war, they could surely rely on Daley and Jones to start one. The seven of them were divided further now and having looked around the angry faces, Kane shrugged.

"Have it your way," he intoned and turned away, followed by Fitzpatrick, who led Jones with him. The others stood and watched them go. Ballard shook his head.

"That sure went well," he said. Daniel turned and looked at him.

"You did nothin' to make it go any better," he snapped. Ballard shrugged.

"Weren't nothin' fer me to say about it," he said. "It was you boys that enlisted together. Joe 'n' me came later to all o' that. If all o' you can't let it pass, there's nothin' I kin say'll fix that." Daniel glared at him, but he found himself already thinking that he was most likely right.

As the days passed, the camps around Winchester resumed regular drills and inspections as the army slowly recovered.

Some of the not so seriously wounded began to return, among them Matthew Hale, favouring his left leg which was still not returned to full use, and seeming genuinely embarrassed at the reception he got on his return. A variety of the boys went out of their way to speak to him, confirming that most of Company B had settled to the view that a man who would volunteer, fight and bleed for it was welcome no matter what else was different about him.

But not all the detached men had returned to the ranks. A scattering of them, including Jack Elliott and Rufus Fenton from their own Company B, had stayed away, deserters now, numbered among the confirmed skulkers from various units of the army. Bands of them were said to be straggling south, through the Shenandoah Valley, resisting every effort to get them to return by fading away off the roads onto the lesser used paths and trails. They were, by all accounts, subsisting themselves through unofficial foraging and theft from the local farms and there were even stories of some of them bushwhacking commissary parties and engaging in mean little skirmishes with the local militia details who tried to police those areas, creating a further burden for the local people.

Kane, Fitzpatrick and Jones stayed away, messing in their own group and saying little more than what they had to say to the others. This rankled with Daniel Ryan, but he knew that especially with Jones and Daley bearing their respective grudges, there was little to be done about it in the meantime. Philipps was a little more philosophical.

"Give it time," he said. "They'll come around, 'specially when Mick smells Isaac's cookin' a few more times."

"Are you sayin' there's somethin' wrong with our cookin', around here," Daniel returned.?

"Hell no," Saul answered with a grin.

In the camps, a smattering of clothing began to arrive, some of the light brown tunics like the ones that had first been issued to Ogeechee Volunteers in the spring, when they were leaving Savannah, but, with thousands of men in need of replacements for worn out uniforms, these first consignments were nowhere near sufficient. Settled and established in their camps now, many men immediately resumed writing their letters home, to assure families, first and foremost, that they had survived, but, in most cases, looking to those families to help supply some at least of their needs, long before the quartermasters would likely get around to it. Sure enough, as a result of the letter writing, from around the end of the month, a steadier stream of replacement clothing began to arrive, having been sent or brought in response, with most men receiving replacement garments this way rather than through the army. But fewer were able to obtain shoes, so the barefooted largely remained so.

The quartermasters too were able to procure little in the way of footwear and, as a result, the army began to organise itself to make up the shortages, using the hides of livestock, that had been butchered by the commissary for meat. Attempts were made to tan these and the results were used for making footwear, but the quality varied from unit to unit. In some regiments, men with cobbling or shoemaking skills were detailed to work on this, and shoes were the result, while, in other units, the attempts were more rudimentary or crude, such as shaping the leather into soles and piercing it for stitching, before drying it, by burying it in the earth and setting up the camp fire above it, with the result, when it was dug up, being as hard as a board. This was fashioned into sandals by stitching on straps or rawhide thongs which could be fastened across the foot or even around the ankle. They were not shoes, but they sufficed for some of the barefooted men, though even with this kind of expedient, barefooted soldiers by no means disappeared completely from the ranks. Some of the men who already had shoes equipped themselves, in this way, with a pair of replacement soles, copied from their current ones, and stored them in haversacks for future use.

"Good place for 'em," Thompson reckoned, "cuz, if we head back over the river, some of them boys'll likely finish up eatin 'em."

At the start of October Boyce returned, declaring fimself fit for duty even though the wound in his gut had not fully healed. The story spread through the camp that he would be dead, but for the notebook in his pocket which had absorbed some of the force of the bullet he had taken, but he himself said nothing on the subject, simply resuming his duties around the camp without fuss. Most of Company B were glad to see him back, as the view that he brought a measure of common sense, that Rodger was maybe perceived to lack, to the company's affairs was common among the men.

As time passed, even soap arrived. Men were able at last to wash properly, both themselves and their remaining uniforms, but simple washing, unless it included disinfecting, did not reliably remove the lice from infested garments. As a remedy, the boys took to holding sessions in camp, when they went lice hunting through their clothing and also in the bodily recesses where they gathered. The favourite refuge for those almost invisible, pests was along the seams of the garment, especially those with skin contact, and a favourite way of dealing with them was by heating garments over a fire and listening for the crack as the lice burst with the heat. These events were initially accompanied by shouts of pleasure or triumph from the assembled men. But repetition soon took away the novelty and though the remedy was continued, for its function rather than its entertainment, it never quite seemed to solve the problem. Hardly anybody got completely rid of the affliction and even when the initial results, after persistent and painstaking lice hunts, had been encouraging, it was not long before the men were scratching again. Ballard, as was customary, had a verdict on the subject.

"Killin' lice is fine," he pronounced, "if it weren't fer every damn relation they got comin' to the funeral and stayin' on after."

Captain Rodger produced his own answer to the problems of infestation among the men. Having heard that some of A. P. Hill's division had been ordered into the Opequon Creek to kill off their crops of the "greybacks," he declared his intention of doing the same with Company B, especially since Captain Harmon of Company E was said to be similarly enthusiastic about the idea. The men heard the rumours that Powell Hill's remedy might be coming their way and many sent all possible signals of disapproval and reluctance that they could think of back up the line through the NCOs to try to discourage the idea, but without success. Rodger was determined that it would be done and in early October it happened. The men were paraded in the afternoon, but, instead of the customary drills, they were ordered to stack arms and equipment belts. Having done this, they were formed into column of files and marched off to Lick River to be deployed into ranks on the riverside. Rodger stood there on the bank for a moment or two, perhaps considering in his own mind if the whole enterprise was worth the attendant inconvenience and resentment, but not for long.

"We will bathe the men," he rapped out to Boyce and Jeffers.

"Yessah," Jeffers answered, his face inscrutable, as always, when dealing with officers.

"They will immerse themselves completely sergeant," the captain added. Jeffers nodded and turned towards the waiting ranks.

"The company will move forward," he called with something of a smirk forming on his face.

"Goddam best officers always lead by example," Ballard said to those around him, though without troubling overmuch to keep his voice down.

"Company.….., forward march!" Jeffers gave the order in his customary bellow, glaring along in Ballard's direction as he did so. There was a falter, a second of hesitation, when it all might have become insubordination or even mutiny, but it did not last. The men shuffled forward, splashing into the placid waters of the river, to wade out into midstream. When they reached the point where the water came up to their middle, Rodger nodded to Jeffers.

"Company.……., halt!" again the familiar shout came and the ranks shuffled to a standstill, with the splashing ceasing while ripples spread their circles steadily outwards, from the now stationary men, across the surface of the river. Jeffers looked over to where the officers stood.

"Carry on First Sergeant," Rodger said and Jeffers nodded again.

"The company will duck on down under the water," he yelled, "heads under and stay there awhile."

Out in the water, Mick Daley, among others, was becoming more irritated by the minute.

"What's it all for," he called out, "does it kill the damn lice or do anybody good? Not a bloody bit of it."

"It may give yore fleas a miserable, wet day," Ballard observed, "but it, sure as hell, don't kill 'em all and it jest annoys the goddam lice." All along the river the comments rose.

"Talk about it all ya want," Jeffers bawled, casting his eyes along the spectacle of waiting men, "but do it under the damn water." Ballard swore and ducked underneath, staying there for several seconds, blowing gurgles and bubbles to the surface. He came up with a scowl on his face.

"Don't know what the damn greybacks thought o' that," he said. "Mubbee it ain't the lice at all. Mubbee what Rodger is really tryin' to do is save our damn, sinful souls by dunkin' us out here." Daniel Ryan had closed his eyes and ducked under the water, just as Ballard spoke, but he burst into laughter at

338

the thought. He immediately surfaced, spluttering out water from his mouth and nose, to see Ballard, still standing there, and now grinning at him, stretching out his arms, as the water streamed from his hair and beard.

"Brother!" Ballard shouted, "brother Ryan, are ya saved in the purifyin' waters o' the lord?" Daniel started laughing again and then shouted back at him.

"Glory be! Glory be, for I reckon I am saved, even if I had to swallow half the damned river to do it."

"But did ya truly see the light and are ya truly saved," Ballard intoned in his best preacher's voice? Daniel nodded furiously.

"I saw, I truly saw and I truly am, cuz my soul is filled with the good lord's river water," he bellowed back.

"Amen to all o' that," Thompson said laconically. "Yore souls may be saved, but yore minds have gone."

"You didn't see any bloody light down in all o' that weed and muck," Daley growled, while the others around them just stood and gaped at them as though they had gone mad, but Ballard was beginning to enjoy himself.

"Hallelujah, brother," he shouted, trying not to laugh. He stretched his hands in the air and called to those around him.

"Ya ornery passel o' misbegotten sinners," he berated them. "The lord is stretchin' out his hands to ya out here. He is offerin' y'all salvation, out on this here river. Git yoreselves down, go on, git down on yore knees there. Wash yoreself under the cleansin' waters there and embrace the lord's goodness." Around him some of the saturated men began to guffaw and chortle, while others, most likely the more religious, looked on in silence, or called out in disapproval at this apparent blasphemy, but Ballard was undaunted.

"Cleanse yore blackened souls and wash away yore sins," he shouted, "leave them behind here in the purifyin' waters of the lord."

"Yeah, then you got a clear conscience, before you get back to sinnin' some more," Philipps said. Daniel nodded gravely to him and then raised his hands and addressed Ballard.

"It's true brother! Oh lord it's true. I'm cleansed, I'm reborn, I feel...... better already."

"Oh Hallelujah," Ballard replied, shouting the words above the splashing, "it's a blessed miracle." Around them, other men now began to join in the parody, ducking underneath to emerge with any, "suitable," comments they could think of, while Jeffers and the officers watched from the bank, seemingly unsure of how to react to all of this. Out on the river, the men went on with their bodily and their spiritual cleansing and the whole episode steadily deteriorated into a shambles of splashing, shouting and laughter. Along the way a little, someone started on "Rock of Ages." Others joined in, while still the shouts went on.

"I am saved! Praise the lord, I am saved!"

"My sins are gone, I kin see 'em floatin' downriver a piece."

"Hallelujah brothers, I'm cleansed."

"My greybacks is cleansed too."

On the river bank, Rodger's face was turning from flushed to crimson and from crimson to purple. Beside him Boyce was trying to suppress a smile. Jeffers simply stood, watching as the spectacle of mass salvation proceeded before his eyes, but, aware of the disapproval evident in the manner of the captain beside him, he kept his face diplomatically inscrutable. Eventually, since it all showed little sign of stopping, Rodger turned to him and rapped out an instruction.

"Get them out of there if you please sergeant!"

"Yessuh," Jeffers rapped. He turned towards the river, to the continuing orgy of splashing and religion, and drew in a deep breath.

"Company............!" The tumult in the water gradually subsided and the bedraggled assemblage of the "born again," Company B turned towards him.

"The company will move to the bank and reform ranks!"

"Praise the lord," came back the shouts from some of the boys, and the crowd of cleansed, and mostly highly amused, ex-sinners began to splash their way over to the side, to emerge from the river, and form on the bank, as the water streamed from their clothing and hair forming puddles and pools around where they stood. Rodger by this time had paced away, as though unwilling to involve himself in any way with his command's blasphemous embracing of the lord's mercy.

Patching and mending became almost standard uses of much of the men's free time and gradually the soiled and worn out rags that had characterised the army in Maryland, began, after much attention, to resemble something wearable again, though the washing never again consisted of taking the company back wholesale to the river. Holes were patched in uniform jackets, and tears were darned or stitched. Thread and needles were again in demand as those skills were renewed and refined and, among some of the men, taken up for the first time in their lives. All of the repairing, and improvising did improve morale. Washing themselves and their clothing and replacing or repairing their tatters rekindled the boys' sense of themselves as soldiers and, as the weeks passed, the combination of better food, regular rest, restored clothing, and the programme of drills, inspections, reviews and activity, changed the brigades from assemblies of weary and despondent tramps into formations of disciplined and purposeful soldiers again. The army also grew considerably more powerful, with more of the recuperating men returning to their places as well as the previously returned stragglers and refusals swelling the numbers in companies and regiments to respectable totals once more.

As a result of all of this, by the second week of October, the Ogeechee Volunteers strength was back over two hundred and seventy officers and men, though the regiment had been reduced to eight companies, as a result of its losses since the springtime. Preston was promoted to Lieutenant Colonel and confirmed in command, with Captain Henry Randolph, of Company A, getting the second in command post and a promotion to major. Rodger remained as captain of Company B, with Boyce as senior lieutenant, and a new officer named Benjamin Carson arrived to replace the wounded Fenwick. Carson was a red-haired boy, with a wispy moustache, which conversely made him look more boyish than manly. He was the second son of a Savannah preacher, it was said, and this was his first experience of military affairs. The men eyed him over and watched carefully for signs of what he was made of. Thompson was confirmed as a sergeant, as was Henry Bayfield. Linus Cooper and Wesley Corse became corporals as their own company roll, in common with the rest of the army, crept steadily back upwards from their low points after Sharpsburg to edge steadily higher as the weeks in camp around Winchester passed.

With the regiment strengthened and re-organised, rumours began to travel around the camps about pending re-organisation in the higher command of the army. Other officers, at brigade and divisional level also got a step up. John Hood and George Pickett were made Major Generals to command two reorganised divisions. "Neighbour," Jones, their own divisional commander departed from the army on sick leave. The men knew that he suffered from a heart ailment anyway, but there were additional stories in the camps that he had been sorely affected by the death of his brother in law, a colonel, in the Yankee army, and, ironically, the very man who had been shot down during the first attack on the bridge, that their own brigade had met and repulsed, last month up at

Antietam Creek. The brigade, along with "Tige" Anderson's, was transferred to John Hood's strengthened division joining his Texans and Alabamians, but hardly was all of this news digested when more was being talked about. The most recent rumours began to suggest that Toombs also might soon be departing from the army. "The Congressman," was frequently away, supposedly disillusioned with the high command, it being full of West Point trained officers, who, he reckoned, stifled the initiative of others. Ballard snorted when he heard the news.

"Reckon Marse Robert jest ain't gave ole Bob Toombs an important enough job in this here army," he said. In Toombs absence, Benning was back in charge, and, if the stories were true, the arrangement could soon be permanent, but that was up to Toombs. In most cases the men liked him. He had a thing for speech-making, but he always managed to treat the men well enough, like they were voters, some said, but they respected "Old Rock" as well. He was solidly dependable, utterly fearless and, what was more, he had shown that he could keep a cool head when the shooting got started.

The autumn progressed and the settled weather stretched on, though the sun, lower now in the blue skies, spoke of the shortening days of the advancing seasons. It was no longer hot to be sure, but there was still a mildness about the weather, once the chill of the autumn mornings had been warmed away. With the miserable heat of summer gone, the days were a mellow blend of colder mornings and evenings and warm afternoons. The men now lived in tents where these were available, or in improvised shelters made of wood, brush, clay and canvas. They would have been quite content to set up quarters for the winter here, but, across the river, they knew, from traded newspapers, that the Yankee Army of the Potomac had also been restoring its strength and its commander was being urged, by thundering headlines and editorials, to recross the river and renew the campaign against Richmond.

But the changes were not yet done, for, as that cooler, fresher October weather drew on, they began to hear more whispers about their own future. It was now being said that the regiment was to leave Toombs' brigade, the formation in which it had served since arriving in Virginia in the spring, to join another outfit, commanded by Brigadier General Howell Cobb, in Lafayette McLaws' division. Everybody knew that Cobb, like Robert Toombs, was a politician, a former governor of Georgia no less, but he also was rumoured to be leaving the army to go back to his politicking in the Confederate congress. His brigade of Georgians and North Carolinians was known to have suffered heavily in the fighting in Maryland, both at Sharpsburg, and in the mountain passes days previous to it, with over half of their men being lost. It was now being rebuilt, as a Georgia only brigade, in keeping with Marse Robert's emerging practice of brigading troops with other regiments from the same state. Thus, Cobb's North Carolina regiment was going to Robert Ransom's command, and their own rumoured transfer, together with that of the Eighteenth Georgia from Evander Law's mostly Texan brigade and the Philips Legion from Thomas Drayton's brigade, was a simple strengthening of a depleted unit with fresh blood.

In their new brigade were the Sixteenth and Twenty Fourth Georgia regiments, both, especially the latter, distinctly, "Irish," in character.

The Ogeechee Volunteers, since it had recruited in Savannah, as well as the counties and towns all around, had a healthy, or unhealthy, depending how men looked at it, proportion of Irish immigrants in its ranks. The men in the regiment wrangled about this, with some of them hostile to the idea of being, "landed in with still more Micks," while others, including most of their own Irish, were much more favourably disposed towards it. Still more settled for a wait and see attitude, but when Tom Cobb, Howell's younger brother, and colonel of

Cobb's Legion came around, escorted by Preston, to see their camp and inspect the regiment, curiosity was widespread. Could he be the man earmarked for command of the brigade, "another of that family of damned politicians," as some of the boys put it? The colonel was wide-faced and clean shaven, in an army where most men, from General Lee on down, were bearded. He had an air of business and energy about him as he moved around the camp, as though he could hardly wait to get done doing one thing so he could get on to starting something else. Like him or not, Daniel Ryan thought, he seemed marked for command, at least for meantime and complaining would not be changing it any.

Sure enough, the following day they were ordered to break up camp and were marched the short way to set up again, nearer the creek, in the area occupied by McLaws' command. More inspections followed, with the men paraded in their repaired and replaced clothing, for Cobb to prowl along the ranks again. McLaws also came around the new camp, a couple of days later, for his own look. The general was yet another Georgian, thickset of build or maybe even getting towards portly, an achievement of note, so Thompson said, in this army. He had a dark curly beard and whiskers enclosing his round face and looked imposing enough as he rode through the camp at the head of his staff, before dismounting to inspect the men. He was smiling as he strode up and down the companies, but his eyes, as Cobb's had previously been, were endlessly at work, scanning back and forth, taking in everything and seeming to miss nothing around the camp or along the files of soldiers. The men eyed him in return, with a mixture of curiosity and suspicion. "Make Laws," was the nickname his own men had given him, for an apparent habit of issuing successions of divisional regulations and special orders, and, hearing all of this, the Ogeechee Volunteers regarded it as a warning of sorts.

It was the second Saturday in October and the men had just finished morning drill when a shambling group of brown-uniformed newcomers was brought into camp by Barnard Jeffers. There was a flurry of interest, since rumours had been going around about replacements, and these might well be Company B's, and the regiment's, first sample of conscripts. Men left what they were doing and gathered around in silence, as Jeffers made himself scarce. The newcomers were soon enclosed by a sullen and hostile, if not yet quite openly aggressive, circle of older hands, who scrutinised them from head to toe, noting the new government issue uniform jackets and pants, the polished, black leather equipment belts, the new blankets, freshly waxed haversacks and the canteens, which hung in place on their owners' shoulders and hips. There were eight of these "replacements" and they stood there, some of the younger ones fidgeting nervously, as a succession of their patched and darned new comrades stepped up to poke and prod at this or that piece of their belongings.

Daley was one of the first to move in among them. He pushed his face up into that of a nervous, fair-haired boy and eyed him. Mick was an accomplished bully, Daniel knew, who surely had a pretty reliable instinct for selecting a victim and this trembling youth should present him with little difficulty. Daley glared at the boy.

"Are you damn faggots conscripts," he snarled? The boy swallowed and said nothing. Daley grabbed him by the collar and pulled him forward, at which the boy dropped his musket which clattered onto the ground as he stumbled to his knees.

"I asked you a goddam question," he shouted into the boy's face, with some specks of saliva making the trip as well as the hostile words. The boy stammered out something indecipherable in reply, at which Daley shoved him violently away, watching as he half-tumbled backwards. Daley sneered around the group.

"The goddam skulkers they're draftin' in these days, can't even talk," he shouted to a few grunts from others round about, until the performance was interrupted by another voice.

"So we got drafted, what's that to you?" Mick whirled to face the speaker, to find himself looking into the eyes of a well-built, if slightly older man. Daniel looked at Mick for his response, sure that as he did so that there was a fleeting moment of uncertainty in his face, but, having made his pitch, Daley was not for backing off, nor could he afford to without losing large-scale face. He strode across to where this newcomer stood and planted himself in front of him.

"I'll tell ya, what it is to us ya big-mouthed shit," he shouted. "This here ain't no hidin' place fer skulkers.

This here outfit is the Ogeechee Blues Volunteer Rifles. Volunteers!" he bellowed the word into the man's face. But the newcomer did not flinch, instead he stood his ground and gazed evenly back at him.

"We ain't here because we wanted to come," he said, "and we surely didn't come here to serve with no niggers," he added, looking towards where Josh, Matthew and Eli sat, but his words would only serve as a burr to a fidgety horse, Daniel Ryan, thought as he watched the spectacle. He shook his head. The poor bastard had a bit of backbone to be sure, but it would do him no good. In truth, he had now made himself a target and that would only serve to make things worse. Daley let his shoulders drop, pretending to relax, but instead moving suddenly forward to push the man backwards, the stranger stumbled initially, but, recovering his balance, he made to retaliate, only to find that he was immediately accosted by Powell, who came up on him from one side while Daley advanced on him from in front.

"Yo're a smart talkin' bastard, aintcha," Powell shouted, with a snarl on his face. "You got a name?" The man, confronted by two assailants, was now silent.

"Speak up shit," Daley shouted, "either you got a name or we'll goddam give ya one ya won't want." The man looked into his face again.

"My name is Wade Garrett," he said. Powell moved up beside Daley and pushed into Garrett's face.

"Well Wade goddam Garrett, you better l'arn somethin' here today. These boys stood around here," he gestured at the watching circle of men, "they're all volunteers. That means we formed this regiment, we made it what it is, and we've fought in it, under our own flag and there weren't nobody had to draft us. Y'see them "niggers" you jest mentioned, well they're volunteers too and that makes 'em worth a helluva lot more'n you." Ryan almost choked at these words as he heard Ballard murmur beside him.

"The good lord surely loves a convert."

"This here's a volunteer regiment," Powell went on, "so you skulkers don't belong nowhere here. We don't want ya here cuz ya are shit on the good name of any decent volunteer outfit. You been landed on us and, if ya are set to stay here, it'll cost ya, startin' with that there gear." He grabbed at Garrett's haversack and as the man made to resist, Daley kicked him hard in the groin. The newcomer doubled up and sank to his knees, upon which Daley and Powell pulled the belts from his shoulders, being joined by several others, who relieved him unceremoniously of his jacket and pants. All around now, others moved in upon the remaining conscripts, grabbing at various pieces of their clothing or equipment. The melee continued for several minutes, with the newcomers collecting a succession of knocks as well as losing their uniforms and possessions, but neither officers nor sergeants were anywhere to be seen.

By the end of it, the draftees were in a dirt-stained group, reduced to whatever undergarments remained to them, with most of them nursing bruises or weals, and with not a single item of equipment to their name. Even their muskets had been taken and those who had appropriated their things now moved away. Garrett, the man who had tried to resist, was near naked, and half-senseless and he lay on the ground covered in dirt and blood smears. Powell, clutching his trophies, waved them towards the chastened group.

"Learn it well," he shouted. "In a volunteer outfit, damn skulkers don't count fer nothin' and don't git nothin' lessen they git given it by their betters. What ya git is what we give ya, nothin' more and nothin' less."

"You think yo're worth more'n that, you prove it," Daley shouted, as he too turned away, brandishing his own spoils. As Powell moved past Ryan and Ballard on his way to his own fire, he looked each of them briefly in the eye.

"Don't mean I like blacks no better," he growled, "but I like conscripts a damn sight less'n volunteers, even black volunteers." He stalked away, leaving them to make what they wished of this complex thinking.

A number of worn, soiled and shoddy pieces of clothing, sandals and equipment were thrown into the chastened group of conscripts, over which, after some hesitation, they began to pick. Daniel, dismissed Powell from his mind and looked back towards them. It was ugly, but it was the way things were and you could hardly blame the men in the camps for that. He had, in the course of the melee, helped himself to a new belt and had exchanged his Sharpsburg shoes for an almost new pair, feeling no compunction at having done so. These draftees, who would never be with the army at all if they hadn't been made to come, were marched in here, clad in new uniforms, and with new equipment, parading their finery under the noses of men who had marched and fought for months and never gotten a sniff of anything to replace their own worn out things. It was a damned scandal, issuing new everything to damned skulkers, who might well desert at the earliest opportunity, when the long-serving volunteers were left to repeatedly patch up and repair their worn out or threadbare garments and belongings.

He glanced across to where the three black men sat. They had not moved, to join in the looting, but at least this episode had made some kind of a point about them also. They were not at the bottom of this company any more, not even in Powell's eyes.

Daniel tossed his old shoes and his repaired belt into the group and headed away, back to his own fire, where the others of the mess were examining their own spoils. Dinner was about to be rustled up, though, regrettably the conscripts had carried no rations. Daniel looked back at them as Philipps spoke.

"If any of them boys are worth a damn they kin get started on provin' it," he growled. The others nodded as they turned back to their food preparations.

The evening roll call revealed that Company B now consisted of three officers and forty two recovered and rested men, six of whom still had no shoes. But there was now a division in the ranks as to how those, on the face of it, healthy totals had been achieved, for many of the remaining old hands had no wish to serve with draftees whose presence they resented and whose motives they distrusted.

Epilogue

The Yankees were still up there on the other side of the Potomac, and their remaining across the river gave a clear hint that they too had been seriously hurt by the costly summer and autumn campaigns. Once their initial probe to the south bank, in the wake of the Confederate withdrawal, had been bundled back across by Powell Hill's men, they had, save for a few cavalry forays, stayed on the Maryland side of the river for a further month. This at least gave the farmers of Northern Virginia almost the whole autumn season to get in their crops and recover something of their livelihoods, free from enemy presence and the wholesale plundering of the spring and summer.

A trickle of Yankee papers were still being traded over the river to find their way into the Confederate camps, and, according to these, General McClellan was spending the time drilling his new Yankee recruits, re-equipping his formations and assembling the largest army yet seen in this war. According to those same papers that army now had well over a hundred thousand men in its ranks, preparing for their next invasion of Virginia, while the politicians in Washington, and the northern press, kept up their badgering for the general to get moving across the Potomac and make for Richmond once again. But, for all of their numbers, the Yankees sat passively on their own side of the river, with their generals resisting all of the press and political pressure to cross over and renew the fight.

Earlier in the month, as though to demonstrate how it was done, Jeb Stuart and his Confederate cavalry had forded the river from the Virginia side to ride through Maryland and on into Pennsylvania. They had stolen horses and supplies, taken and paroled prisoners and marked down the positions and outposts of McClellan's army before returning, by way of White's Ford with hardly a casualty. The army allowed itself a good chortle at this exploit, for it re-affirmed the superiority of the Confederate horsemen and seemed also to mark a break with the brutal endurance and attrition of the last few months, maybe hinting at a return to the good old cavalier days of the previous year. It was good to be able to poke fun at an enemy that still seemed to make poorer soldiers than southern boys did. There was army news also in the main camps. Longstreet and Jackson were promoted to Lieutenant General and confirmed as official corps commanders, an arrangement that Lee was believed to have wanted for some time. McLaws' division, including their own brigade, was formally assigned to Longstreet's First Corps.

But, if the men had begun to think that McClellan would never move this side of next year, they were soon disabused of this idea. The happy autumn period of rest and recovery came to an end, and it did so on the last Monday of the month. Word was already circulating around the camps that morning that, on the previous day, the Yankees had begun crossing over the river down near Berlin, and the southern army would soon be set in motion in response to this move. Sure enough, by evening muster the news was official. Rations were issued, and the fires burned late cooking them. The departure of the whole division had been set for the following day. They would be heading south for Strasburg and Front Royal and likely on to Culpeper, to forestall the enemy movement on the very same ground where they had commenced their thrust at Pope's army back in August,.

The morning was bright, but with a biting wind also, as the men gathered their belongings for carrying, and discarded or burned all that they would not take. A scattering of Second Corps men were hanging around the camps that morning, foraging for anything of use that would not be carried away by the departing owners, giving substance to the rumour that Jackson's men would be staying around Winchester. The columns were formed as the sun rose and stepped off on their way towards the Valley Turnpike. Even now, in spite of all of the re-equipping and repairing in Company B, four men remained barefooted and five more joined the files shod with makeshift moccasins or sandals made in the autumn camps. Their initial march was steady, but by no means forced, with hour halts observed. There was no hurry, the men told each other, since ole George McClellan never went anywhere in a hurry. They joined the valley turnpike near Kernstown, which suited the barefooted men not at all, but the column stayed on its made up surface only as far south as Newtown, turning off there to head south, camping for the night between Stony Point and Front Royal.

In the mist of a cold and wet morning, after assembly and a breakfast of their carried rations, they reformed. The march was resumed and the long columns of men and vehicles forded both forks of the Shenandoah River just north of Front Royal, before passing through the town. From there, the road led up into the Blue Ridge, making for Chester Gap through which they passed in the afternoon, to camp near the eastern entrance. The latest news of the Yankee army coursed through the column. They were still near Harper's Ferry, with ever more men and vehicles crossing over the river. The enemy host now gathering in the north western corner of Virginia, was, as reported, the largest yet seen, but, in typical McClellan style, it was seemingly not going anywhere in a hurry.

Their own march continued, across the north western part of the Virginia piedmont, closing in on Culpeper as the new month began. It seemed, from all of this, that campaigning, in spite of the lateness of the season, had still a way to run this year as, on arriving, Longstreet's units spread themselves out in a great arc of camps stretching from the Robertson River across to Madison Courthouse, while the weather turned still colder. The Yankees, they heard, were now pushing their advance ponderously south, east of the Blue Ridge towards Warrenton as predicted, plugging the gaps in the Blue Ridge with cavalry as they went. Lee had apparently read the situation correctly again and the men grinned and assured each other that he had the measure of the Yankee commanders with his eyes shut.

November came and the gangly Tom Cobb was confirmed as brigade commander. The comments continued, but he was emerging as less of a politician and more of a soldier than his brother. Men cited his command of the Cobb Legion through the campaigning and fighting of the spring on the peninsula, and on various fields since, as evidence of his suitability for command. With his appointment confirmed the drills and inspections increased and the men quickly came to understand that, whatever else the new commander was, he was a stickler for discipline.

The end of the first week of November saw two more things happen, which changed the mood of optimism in the army. On the seventh day of the month the first snows came, no light dusting of the landscape, but a heavy fall, of several inches. It blanketed the country and added grievously to the trials of the many men in the ranks, who still had no shoes, and the majority who had little in the way of warm clothing. Duties were now carried out by freezing, shivering men and sickness, largely banished from the camps through the restful and better supplied autumn, struck anew, with chills, agues and rheumatic fevers, as well as the more familiar stomach and bowel complaints, afflicting the men. With the snows still thick on the ground, further news came, bringing still more pause to the army. Abe Lincoln had relieved General

McClellan of his command. He was a democrat and it seemed that the black republican administration in Washington would keep him no longer.

There was a feeling of something resembling mild dismay among some in the Confederate ranks at this news, for "Little Mac," had always been a chivalrous opponent, not at all in the mould of men like Pope. He had been considerate of the civilians of Virginia, as far as an enemy commander could be, and there was a degree of acknowledgement of this among the southern officers and men. But now he was gone and General Burnside, the same general whose troops had attacked across that stone bridge up at Sharpsburg, was in command. So what would this mean for the armies facing each other across the bleak winter countryside of northern Virginia? Would the new general settle for winter quarters and leave the next bout of active campaigning till the spring, or would he too be driven by the nagging of politicians and newspaper editors in Washington to move at once, even with winter virtually here?

On the seventeenth of the month, with the snows gone and the browned, muddy fields revealed, orders came for the men of McLaws' division to break camp and march again. They were off once more, still farther to the south east with their destination rumoured to be the old town of Fredericksburg on the lower Rappahannock River. The Yankees, it was reported, had begun moving troops that way, so the game of move and countermove was back on and this march was to forestall whatever advance their new general was planning.

The harsh cold of arriving winter had initially frozen the previously thawed roads again, but now as the march began, the weather had broken. The troops marched in driving wind and rain, with their columns of men, guns and wagons crowding the worn muddy surfaces, which inflicted their own brand of merciless intolerance on bare or sandaled feet. Fredericksburg was down in the tidewater region, set on the Rappahannock

River at its uppermost navigable reach and it was shaping up as the place where the next coming together of the armies might well take place. The men marched on, floundering through the mud, which plastered their uniforms and skin while this latest huge game of manoeuvre proceeded and privations increased as full winter steadily closed in. The Yankee vanguard might already be at Fredericksburg, the camp talk said, so there was an urgency in reaching the place before the enemy could force a wholesale crossing of the river. It was "On to Richmond," yet again, in the worst season of the year. The campaigning was not over and those guns that had thundered all summer and on into the autumn had not, it seemed, fallen silent for long.

LaVergne, TN USA
22 February 2011
217525LV00001B/26/P